THE DOUBLE CROSS

THE DOUBLE CROSS

THE SPANISH BRAND SERIES

CARLA KELLY

Seattle, WA

Camel Press
PO Box 70515
Seattle, WA 98127

For more information go to: www.camelpress.com
www.carlakellyauthor.com

Cover design by Sabrina Sun
Brand and map by Nina Grover

THE DOUBLE CROSS

ISBN: 978-1-60381-945-9 (Trade Paper)
ISBN: 978-1-60381-946-6 (eBook)

Library of Congress Control Number: 2013933172

10 9 8 7 6 5 4 3 2 1

Printed in the United States of America

To Jennifer Fielding and Jennifer McCord,
two editors whose opinions I value.
And thanks also to Catherine Treadgold,
Camel Press editor-in-chief and publisher.
It's a pleasure to work with all of you.

Juez de campo

AN OFFICIAL OF the Spanish crown who inspects and registers all brands of cattle and sheep in his district, settles disputes, and keeps a watchful eye for livestock rustlers. In the absence of sufficient law enforcement on the frontier of 18th century New Mexico, a royal colony, he also investigates petty crimes.

Contents

Chapter One

In Which Don Marco Mondragón Decides He Needs a Dog

DON MARCO MONDRAGÓN, rancher and brand inspector for el Valle del Sol, had seldom done a rash thing in his life. True, he was only thirty-one years old, but thirty-one in 1780 in New Mexico was a better than average time on earth. His father—gone these ten years, God rest his soul—joked once that his dear son had been late in leaving the womb, "Probably debating the merits of a cold entry on a rainy night or a better arrival in two or three days when the sun was shining."

Don Marco knew his relatives and others joked about the deliberate way he approached life in his valley, edged on three sides by mountains, with sun-filled plains to the east, toward Texas. The fact bothered him not at all, because he also knew who they turned to when there was a brand dispute, when rustlers made off with the widow Señora Baca's best milk cow, or when some godless *fulano* snatched the Holy Infant from His outdoor manger during Advent in the highly fortified village of Santa María.

Not for nothing had Don Marco, brand inspector, memorized the district brand books. The slightest deviation was as obvious to him as if a child had drawn it on the kitchen wall in charcoal. Able to identify a fake brand at sight, Don Marco could locate the missing cattle almost before they had time to be missed. The Widow Baca's cow? That was no challenge. Don Marco could recognize everyone's boot and shoe prints for miles around. His simple announcement of that fact before early Mass had been enough to alarm the rustler into returning the cow in time for the next morning's milking, along with the stolen milk from the day before.

Everyone in the valley knew Señora Chavez still mourned the death of her only son. On a hunch, Don Marco paid her a visit and suggested that it would be a kind thing—if she knew of the Holy Baby's whereabouts—to clothe the Christ Child in something warmer, for his outdoor stay. The grieving mother took Marco's quiet words to heart. Her own dear boy might be cold in his coffin, but not the Son of Maria, not if Señora Chavez could help it. Don Marco's whispered words to Father Francisco had led to Señora Chavez's duty each year to make that manger comfortable. She knitted the Baby a mohair blanket from yarn she spun from the wool of Angora goats, provided by Marco Mondragón.

Slow and steady had kept Don Marco Mondragón alive during periodic raids by Comanches, when more volatile men fired too early and too often from the roofs of their fortified haciendas. Better to wait, wait, wait until a warrior was almost close enough to smell. Fire then, and waste not one ball. Word got around. Not many Comanche risked the Mondragón hacienda, and now the valley was peaceful—well, as peaceful as a New Mexican valley could be.

It had not always been so. In 1680, Pueblo Indians had driven out their Spanish masters from the colony of New Mexico, forcing them to make the March of Death from Santa Fe to El Paso del Norte. After twelve years of nursing grievances, the Spanish had returned, Don Marco's ancestors among them. Marco always reckoned that *they* were the hardy souls.

Since hardy souls seem to beget hardy souls, the Mondragóns had moved farther and farther east. Lured by a generous land grant to settle on the edge of danger, the Mondragóns finally stopped in del Sol. The valley—with its always flowing Rio Santa Maria, bitter, snowy winters, and grass so high that the cattle grew fat and lazy—became their mountain fortress. To the east was grazing land for cattle and sheep, and sad to say, Comanches. Such is life.

Don Marco worked hard on his own land and with his own cattle, and never begrudged anyone his time. He had been chosen as *juez* after his father quit the same title, due to his death, and he never flinched from fulfilling his civic duties.

Sadly, obedience to duty had led to the great sorrow of his life, but what mortal understands the workings of Deity? Not Don Marco Mandragón. He would never so presume, even when his heart broke. He had returned from a two-week brand inspection to find his dearly beloved wife and their twin boys dead of cholera. La cólera had raced through his corner of New Mexico as swiftly as a reaper, swathing a foul path that left others as broken as he was. His dear ones were already clay and deep in the earth when he returned to cry over their graves, and then mourn more silently by himself. The Lord giveth, the Lord taketh away, but why from him? Marco eventually took his anger to Father Damiano, who listened, cried with him, and gave him no more penance than a single Ave Maria for being so angry at God. "He has heard worse, my son," was all the priest would say.

That had been eight years ago, and Don Marco had never found anyone to replace his wife. One didn't replace such a woman easily. A lengthy visit to Father Damiano, now serving as assistant to the abbot of San Pedro monastery, had left him feeling less bruised, but still not inclined to seek a new wife. There was a reason even greater than his body's longing for a woman's comfort.

"Father, suppose I should ride away on another brand inspection and come home to death? God help me, I cannot," he had said, full of that same hollow feeling from years earlier.

"Patience, my son," was all the padre could offer and it was sound advice. Don Marco Mondragón was a patient man.

Now there was this matter of a dog, all because of Marco's cold feet. Felicia had brought to their marriage Muñeca, a small dog, the worthless kind of dog that did nothing more than entertain ladies. Once the scorching heat of their nocturnal merrymaking had subsided into the comfortable routine of married love, Marco hadn't minded the little dog's presence, now and then, in the bed he shared with Felicia.

Even now, as he rode south with his neighbor Don Alonso Castellano, Marco smiled to remember the way Felicia would roll her marvelous dark eyes when he set the little dog outside their bedroom and closed the door. She knew what was coming, and had generally removed her nightgown before he came back to bed. Muñeca objected, but Felicia never did.

After Felicia's shocking death, Marco still left Muñeca outside his bedroom door, at least until winter reminded him how cold his feet were, without his wife's legs to rest them on. He had allowed Muñeca to return to his barren bed. She knew her duty and curled up at his feet.

But the problem with pets—his larger canines were not playthings, but work animals—is that they grow old and die. Her muzzle white, her eyes dim, Muñeca had gone the way of all the earth during summer. Now that autumn had tinged the quaking aspens and cottonwoods of the valley the color of new gold, winter was coming. In his careful way, Marco knew it would be simpler to find a new dog for his bed than a wife, and easier on his heart.

Early October was the best time to travel to Santa Fe. When winter set in, there would be no leaving the valley, because the passes to Santa Fe filled with snow. True, his servants could supply a hot rock for his feet, but another house dog would be nice. He was going to Santa Fe anyway. He always went in autumn to take his annual report to the governor, to find out if there were new laws—invariably there were—and to buy what few supplies his well-run hacienda did not furnish.

Marco had cattle to take to market, too, as well as the massive wool clip, packed tight into bundles and destined for the Indian weavers, who especially prized what he brought from his far off valley. The journey might last a month, or even five weeks, if the cattle were contrary.

Marco enjoyed the annual journey. He never spoke much to his servants and guards, who knew his routine. He could ride in silence, alone with his thoughts. The prospect beguiled him, until he began to fear he was turning into one of those hermit-martyrs of the early church who for years sat silently on poles, until their flesh grew to the pole and they could no longer come down even if they wanted to.

Because of that fear, he offered no objections when his neighbor Don Alonso Castellano suggested they ride together to Santa Fe. Strength in numbers always trumped any quibbles about the quality of the company. Alonso was a prosy fellow, but he always brought along his own small army to keep him safe. There were few secrets in the valley; Marco knew Don Alonso was on his way to marry Maria Teresa Moreno, the daughter of one of the governor's accountants, or *fiscales*. In high summer, Don Alonso had gone to Santa Fe to make the match and secure a betrothal. The value of the marriage settlement had been discussed up and down the valley. Don Alonso was marrying into wealth, and he didn't mind who knew it.

He had shown Don Marco a miniature of his betrothed, which led the brand inspector to suspect that lack of beauty could be compensated by a trunk of *reales*. Marco sat up a long time that night, recalling with a smile the more modest dowry Felicia had brought to their marriage, along with a lovely face, striking shape and kind nature.

As he prayed in his chapel before his departure, Marco had considered for one small moment that maybe *he* should find a wife in Santa Fe. The urge passed. A dog was cheaper, would keep his feet warm, and could be located with little exertion.

Face it, you are lazy, Marco told himself as he prayed for the king, for the viceroy in Mexico City, for the governor of their colony, for the general welfare of his servants, for the cattle, sheep and goats of del Sol in his official stewardship. Not one to ask out of turn, he did suggest to the Almighty that He look with favor on his efforts in Santa Fe, which would include registering his documents with the governor, selling his wool clip and cattle, and finding a suitable dog. That was enough for any man to ask.

THE TRIP WEST through high mountain passes had offered no surprises, beyond one attempt by Navajos to frighten away some of his cattle. He and his men had rounded up his livestock again, retrieving other beeves that the Navajo raiders had stolen. Don Alonso swore with impatience, but, knowing other district's brands as well as his own, Don Marco could not rest until those cattle were returned to their rightful owners.

"We have wasted two days in returning cattle!" Alonso exclaimed. "Let the ranchers find their own livestock."

"I am a *juez de campo*," Marco reminded his companion, ending the argument. "I must do this."

In point of fact, any diversion proved more entertaining than listening to Don Alonso carry on about his almost-wife. *Am I jealous?* Marco asked himself in the third week, when his companion started over with the same tales. *Am I bored? Would I be happier if Alonso Castellano dropped into a deep hole? Patience, Marco. Just remember that he will not be returning with you; he will have a bride to coax east to Comanchería.* This thought nourished him through the final week of their journey, keeping him civil and sober, and ultimately grateful when the cattle were sold, the wool clip was in the experienced hands of the Jews, and Don Alonso was safely deposited on the doorstep of his future in-laws.

Marco would have ridden away with relief and a pure heart, if a yellow dog, all fluff and short legs, hadn't come out of the Moreno house just then, followed by a young woman with lustrous brown hair, blue eyes, and—if he was still any judge of what went on under skirts—shapely legs. He sat there, gloved hands crossed on the saddle horn, watching them.

"Can you stop him, Señor?" she asked.

He was out of the saddle just as the yellow dog dodged around Don Alonso. It was an easy matter to scoop up the yellow dog and deposit him in the arms of the young woman with blue eyes.

"*A su servicio*," he said politely.

He knew he was a blockhead to just stand there, but she had wonderful eyes. A quick glance at her shabby dress and bare feet told him all he needed to know about her status in the Moreno household, but still he admired her. *A su servicio*, indeed! From the top of her head to her bare feet, she looked like a servant, but something about her demeanor left him less than certain.

She favored him with another smile, then curtsied, and dog in arms, went back through the portal. Out of the corner of his eye, Marco noted that she remained within hearing distance, even though the dog struggled in her arms.

"You have your own dog trainer, Señor?" he commented to Alonso's almost-father-in-law.

Señor Felix Moreno shrugged. "She is the daughter of my sister. Her parents died at El Paso and we have to feed her. She has her uses."

Marco wondered if his friend Alonso was listening. If so, was he as chilled by the man's words? This was no way to treat a close relative, especially when she stood nearby, listening. He glanced at Alonso, who gave no indication of hearing a word either of them had said. Marco smiled inwardly, remembering his own terror before and during his nuptials. Not after, though; he and Felicia at least knew each other, and were both pleased with what they knew and saw. Marco doubted Alonso had even seen his future wife before, despite having made his first visit that summer. That was how the business of matrimony was conducted in New Mexico.

I leave you to it, he thought. A bow was in order to Señor Moreno, which he performed. He put his foot in the stirrup and started to mount, when Señor Moreno stopped him.

"Señor, would you honor us with your presence and stay the night?"

Two minutes earlier, Marco would have offered an elaborate protest, which would have been equally protested. Soon everyone would be protesting politely, even though they all knew the eventual outcome. That was how the business of manners was conducted in New Mexico. Everyone knew the ritual. All Marco had to do was protest one more time. Don Felix would make one more offer of hospitality and Marco would be free to go his way, the potential host justified and assuaged.

Marco changed the script, perhaps surprising himself even more than Señor Moreno.

"I believe I will, Señor. Thank you for your hospitality. You are far too kind."

He told himself it was because of the yellow dog.

Chapter Two

In Which Paloma Vega Looks Twice

YES, YOU HAVE to feed me, uncle, Paloma Vega thought, *and I am more than just occasionally useful.* She withdrew farther into the background. Her uncle always glowered when she reached for an extra apple or a mere tortilla, and she had a sudden urge to announce that bald fact to the man in the street. His quick glance in her direction when her uncle made his unkind jab—one of many she endured on a typical day in the Moreno household—was nourishment of a different sort. The stranger from Valle del Sol seemed almost chagrined that she should overhear such rudeness.

It hardly mattered, because she was suddenly diverted. In a lifetime of listening to polite refusal, equally polite insistence and that final refusal, Paloma Vega had never heard someone actually accept the ritual invitation. She looked more closely at the rider who had returned the dog to her. His cloak was of good material, his boots excellent, and he carried himself with a certain air. She didn't think he had accepted the invitation because he had no money to pay for lodging.

Paloma let her breath out slowly. Perhaps she had misunderstood. Could this be the man her cousin Maria was to marry in two days? She could barely hide her disappointment, not for any reason larger than the certainty that a man so handsome deserved someone better. Who, she had no idea, but someone better.

Maybe I am a wicked, wicked girl, Paloma thought. *Tia Luisa says I am.* But when had she ever believed a word from her aunt's mouth? Still, this matrimonial business was making Paloma peevish, especially since she would be eighteen in four days and headed for the rusty side of womanhood, old and unwanted.

Her aunt and uncle had assured her from the day she entered their household—an orphan from El Paso del Norte downriver—that she could expect no dowry, no advantage and no future that would lead anywhere but to a convent or a menial position in their household. At the age of eleven, Paloma Vega learned that the milk of human kindness soured quickly in the Moreno jug.

But there are dogs here that need me, she reminded herself, drifting quietly into the background. She carried the yellow dog into the courtyard, where its mother and brethren waited. Their tongues lolled, and their eyes were bright and expectant in that way of dogs, the most optimistic creature Our Father had created, probably right after He fashioned Adam and before Eve.

"Behave yourself, Número Trece," she admonished, setting him near his mother.

She would have sat there herself, enjoying the puppies Uno through Trece, but there was her cousin Maria, hissing at her through a darkened doorway. With a sigh, Paloma squared her shoulders. *Soon you will be married and gone*, she thought. *Would that it were me.*

Paloma saw her afternoon's work in Maria's hands: dresses to hem, seams to sew, and—horrors—probably ruffles to iron. She held out her arms.

"Could I do this work in the courtyard?" she asked. "Who knows how many more warm days we will have before—"

"Of course you may not!" Maria declared. "Papa is only just now inviting my future husband into the *sala*. Do you think I want him to glance through the window and see you sitting there with dogs and my mending?"

"Silly of me," Paloma murmured. She started for the kitchen.

Maria reached out her hand to stop her. She leaned closer, and Paloma wanted to pull away. Maria's rotten back molar, testimonial to too many sweets, was making itself known.

"Perhaps Papa will summon me into the *sala* to meet my betrothed. Or he might not, if the dowry business is still being decided." She gave Paloma a little shake for emphasis. "Tell me, what does Don Alonso Castellano really look like? I have to know."

Paloma thought about the matter. "There are two men in the street, cousin. One is tall with a paunch, and the other is tall without a paunch. They could both use a close shave. The one with the flat stomach has a dignified nose, high cheekbones and deep-set eyes of a curious, light shade of brown. The other one has a nose with a bump and eyes that poke out rather than in. Which one would you prefer?"

Paloma did not mention Señor Flat Stomach's capable air and the little smile that played around his mouth when he rescued the yellow dog from the street. That may have been her imagination, anyway. She was certain about the eyes.

Maria gave her a push. "You are aggravating and I cannot wait to be relieved of your presence!"

From your lips to Blessed Isabella of Portugal, the saint of brides, Paloma thought. *Two more days and you will be on your way to Valle del Sol.*

"That is all I noticed, Maria," she said with some dignity. She gathered up her cousin's clothes and hurried to the sewing room, where the needles were stored. She sat down beside Tia Luisa's seamstress, who was stitching the flounce on the wedding dress, her eyes red from too many late nights working under the insufficient light of poor quality candles.

Without a word, Paloma took the dress from the seamstress's lap. "Go wash your eyes," she whispered. "You'll ruin them if you don't, and my fingers are more nimble."

If only for a few minutes, she would have the small room to herself, away from Maria's tears and nerves. Paloma sat in silence as she hemmed, the thick walls insulating her from Tia Luisa's rages against the butcher, who had nothing to offer but fly-blown meat; the milliner, who refused to finish her hat until the last-quarter bill was paid; and the iceman, who insisted there was not a sliver of ice left in all of the royal colony—not for the governor, not for the bishop, and certainly not for the wife of a *fiscal*, no matter how influential she thought herself.

Paloma hemmed quickly, expertly, happy to hand the finished dress over to the seamstress when she returned, her eyes still red, but her lips smelling of fortification stronger than water. Ah, yes, the woman had brought Paloma a reward for her consideration—a handful of grapes, her first food since breakfast.

The seamstress nodded her approval as Paloma ate. "There now. Hand me that dress with the ripped hem. Your cousin is a clumsy pig."

They shared a chuckle before returning to their sewing. Once or twice, Paloma heard laughter from the *sala*, pleasant, assured masculine laughter that reminded her for a brief moment of her father, dead these seven years.

I hope that laughter comes from the man with the flat stomach, she thought. *And I hope the one with the paunch will be Maria's husband. He will weigh a lot on her wedding night.* She put a hand to her lips to stifle her laughter. *Perhaps Tia Luisa is right; I am wicked.*

She sobered quickly. If it was the other man, he deserved better.

Paloma finished and hurried the clothing into the great trunks that her cousin's personal maid was packing. The servant was in tears, which told Paloma that Maria must have just stormed through; she had been leaving human wreckage in her wake all week. Paloma touched the maid's cheek and kissed the top of her head before leaving the room, hoping to avoid her own encounter with the bride from purgatory.

Shadows began to lengthen across the courtyard. Paloma knew she would be called any minute to help finish the evening meal, but she sank down in the grass by the fountain and whistled.

Trece must have been in the shade of the portal, behind the grape vines, because he responded instantly to the summons meant solely for him. Paloma whistled again, and he bounded through the grass. Right behind him came the man with the flat stomach, which made Paloma's heart lift. If he were Maria's intended, he would not be roaming free in the courtyard.

I am relieved for you, Señor, she thought. *You have avoided a terrible fate.*

She went to stand up, but the man gestured for her to remain where she was. He came toward her, seating himself on the lip of the fountain and laughing when Trece nearly bowled her over with all the enthusiasm of dogs who adore their humans.

"Señorita, I have often wished that I could truly be the person my dogs think I am," he said, which made Paloma smile. "I am Don Marco Mondragón, from Valle del Sol, to the east."

"Thank God!" she exclaimed.

He merely raised his eyebrows, which made her pink up.

Think before you speak, think before you speak, Paloma warned herself, then blurted, "Señor, I am merely relieved you are not Maria's …" She stopped, embarrassed.

He surprised her then, maybe as much as he had surprised her uncle earlier. Don Marco leaned toward her and whispered. "I am relieved, too."

It was easy then to hide behind Trece's fluff and smother her laughter. "I should remember my manners," she said, suddenly aware that she had never addressed a gentleman who was not a relative. Servants and priests didn't count. "I … I am Paloma Vega."

"Pleased to meet you."

"Are you part of the wedding party?" she asked, still hiding behind Trece because she had no business asking questions. Señor Mondragón must be thinking she wouldn't know good manners if they slapped her on the rump.

He didn't seem bothered. He held out his hand to Trece, who bounded from Paloma to him. She watched, pleased that the gentleman knew where to scratch dogs.

"No. I merely journeyed with my friend—it is always safer to ride in a large company. He was bringing bridal gifts in his pack train, and I was bringing wool in mine and herding cattle." He looked at her and seemed to read the question in her eyes that she was finally too polite to ask. “Señorita Vega, I am here about a yellow dog. This one, perhaps?”

Chapter Three

In Which Marco Mondragón Makes a Deal for the Yellow Dog

MARCO KNEW HE had said the wrong thing when the light went out of Paloma Vega's lovely blue eyes. The yellow dog must be her favorite. He had made a mistake. Even worse was the knowledge that he could not make it better. He glanced at her expressive eyes and saw the damage was done, so he avoided looking in them again, concentrating instead on the dog. It was eager as most pups, ever hopeful but unaware that a change was coming.

You will like me, too, he silently promised the dog, *even if I disappoint your mistress.*

"W-why did you name him Trece?" he stammered, wanting to erase that look of disappointment.

It disturbed him that Paloma Vega couldn't look him in the eye, either. He knew his eyes were nothing spectacular, just brown like those of nearly everyone else he knew. He watched her, as she bowed her head over Trece, as if to smooth his puppy fur. When she raised her face to his again, her eyes glittered with unshed tears. When Felicia had done that, he'd been mush in her hands. But this was different. Paloma Vega was not Felicia and he wanted the dog.

"I named him Trece because he was the runt of the litter and his mama has only twelve teats, Señor," she said. "When you are number thirteen, life can be hard."

He could hardly bear to listen to her words. They were spoken so calmly, yet her eyes shone with her anguish. He realized this was a woman used to schooling her feelings. To show them must invite ridicule. His own brief glimpse of life in the Moreno household had already convinced him how necessary that skill must be to a powerless woman.

"You raised him by hand?"

"Sí, Señor, a little milk on a rag every few hours, then my finger, and then a small bowl."

Despite her efforts, her struggle revealed itself in the way her teeth pulled in her lower lip—such lovely lips—and in her ragged breathing. He laid his hand on Trece, smoothing his fur, too. "And he follows you everywhere?"

Marco should never have asked that. Paloma Vega bowed her head over her dog and just nodded. He wasn't sure how to redeem himself, but he wanted to try. *O, Dios*, how he wanted to try, but the words failed him, he who was accustomed to commanding. Felicia had been gone so long that he must have forgotten how to cajole a woman to his advantage. She cleared her throat, so he waited.

"Señor, there are other dogs in the litter, looking for homes."

If she had struck him, her words could not have bit harder. What stung even more was that nothing in her voice pleaded. She was simply stating a fact, not demanding to know why, in the entire colony of New Mexico, he could not find another dog.

"I wanted a smaller dog because my feet are cold," he said simply. There wasn't any point in dissembling. "My wife Felicia has been dead these eight years. She had a lap dog, a silly ball of fur that she named Muñeca."

He looked at her, but she was still concentrating on Trece's fur, smoothing it with gentle hands. Felicia had touched their twins that same way. He plunged on, hoping for sympathy. "Muñeca went the way of all dogs last summer, and my feet are even colder."

"Muñeca," she repeated. Her voice was still that neutral tone that was beginning to distress him. "Do you have other dogs, Señor?"

Again, no recrimination. "*Sí*, but they are big dogs. They guard my sheep and cattle and patrol the top of my hacienda. If I had ever put Muñeca outside, they would have eaten her for a mid-morning snack."

Startled, she looked up, her eyes still swimming, but not spilling onto her cheeks, thank the Lord. "*Dios mio*, do you think my cousin Maria knows about guards patrolling on rooftops?"

"I sincerely doubt it." He had to grin then. "It is *not* something that a man from the east with marriage on his mind would ever discuss with a future wife from as soft a place as Santa Fe." Suddenly he wanted to know. "Would, uh … would that deter you?"

He could have died with relief to hear her low laugh. "Of course not! I mean, Señor, look at you. You are alive and obviously have been so for many, many years."

"Don't pile on so many manys," he said in protest, hoping he might hear that little laugh again. "I am only thirty-one."

"My point precisely," she said.

He knew it was a joke. Thank God he had not stepped on her heart so firmly that she could not tease a bit. And that laugh. She was skinny and her dress was dirty, but she had those fine eyes and a low laugh, one meant for him alone.

She sighed. "I suppose if you want Trece ..." She stopped, and then her voice took on a hard-edged realism he never cared to hear coming from a woman. "Not that I have anything to say about the matter. He's a good dog, Señor. Excuse me, please."

Without another word, she thrust Trece into his hands and left the courtyard with considerable dignity. He tightened his grip when the pup started to whine, itching to follow.

Sin duda, it was a hollow victory. Marco looked at Trece, who was still trembling in his grip and staring after his mistress. *I should be ashamed of myself*, Marco thought, then justified himself with the cold comfort that sooner or later, she would have had to part with a charming dog like Trece to another owner.

The deed was done. He released Trece, who went immediately in search of Paloma Vega. Marco went to find Señor Moreno to finalize his deal before dinner called them away.

Señor Moreno was where Marco had left him, in the small room off the *sala* that constituted his office. Standing with him were his daughter, Maria Teresa, and Alonso. Marco waited in the doorway, watching with interest as the shy couple looked at each other, looked away, and then looked again. It amused him to see his friend visibly shaking, but the amusement vanished quickly because he knew, just *knew*, that foolish, unsuspecting Alonso had bought a pig in a poke. Anyone closely related to a family that would treat a niece as a servant was going to be disappointed. Marco also knew that Alonso might not believe him now, but would believe him soon enough.

The couple left the office after Maria knelt at her father's feet and kissed his hand. When she rose, she held out her hand for Alonso in a sharp gesture. Marco watched his friend's eyes, seeing the surprise there and the hesitation.

Don't put your hand in hers, Marco thought. *If you do, you're committed.* He let out a small sigh when Alonso did precisely that.

When she had him in her grasp, Maria towed Alonso to the courtyard, empty of dogs and Paloma Vega. Kitchen smells grew stronger and Marco know Paloma must be working there now. He probably had no more than a few minutes with Señor Felix Moreno, but how long would it take to make a deal for a yellow runt?

Señor Moreno ushered him into the office in the manner of a fellow who has just dropped a huge rock from his shoulder. This only confirmed Marco's suspicion that the Moreno family had cast a wide net to del Sol because potential families in Santa Fe were much too wise to seek an alliance with the Morenos.

The kitchen smells intensified. A look at Señor Moreno's majestic paunch told Marco he had very few minutes, so he did not waste time on preliminaries. It was only a dog, after all.

"Señor Moreno, in addition to your excellent hospitality"—he bowed and received a nod in reply—"I would like to take a little dog off your hands. I'm quite captured by your"—*O Dios*, he almost said niece—"little dog that Paloma Vega calls Trece. Could you part with this creature?"

Señor Moreno sniffed the kitchen fragrance and wiped his hand across his mouth. "Of course. Take him. He is the runt."

"I will pay you."

"For a runt?"

The kitchen smells grew fainter. Someone must have closed a door, or perhaps Señor Moreno's natural greed had a foul odor that overpowered food. The *fiscal* held up his hand as he reconsidered. "Of course, Trece comes from a long line of noble canines. Perhaps he is descended from dogs that Hernán Cortes brought to Mexico in 1519. Yes, I believe he is."

"Señor, I believe those dogs were mastiffs. They wore armor. Trece is too fluffy to have conquered the Aztecs."

Perhaps after ridding himself of a burdensome daughter, Señor Moreno was in no mood to haggle. He cut right to the issue, eliminating the bargaining dear to every man of Spain, even those in the New World. "Perhaps so, but you want him, don't you? My price is two *pesos*."

Dios mio, Trece had gone from a worthless runt to an animal worth more than two good cows. No wonder Paloma Vega had to hide her feelings. Marco was not so successful, not if the greedy gleam in Señor Moreno's eyes was any indicator.

The *fiscal* held up two pudgy fingers. "*Dos pesos*."

"That's a lot for a runt," Don Marco replied, trying to pull his tattered dignity around his shoulders, he who could usually bargain with the best of men.

He had no idea what possessed him then, a cautious man. Was it kitchen smells, Paloma Vega, the yellow dog? "Throw in Paloma Vega and you have a deal," he said.

When he realized what had just come out of his mouth, he nearly gasped at his monumental stupidity. *Did I just ask that?*

He must have. Señor Moreno stared at him for a long moment, then, to

Marco's relief, burst into loud, prolonged laughter.

Marco forced himself to laugh along, all the while wondering where his wits had gone wandering. "Well, you know, she *is* the trainer, and she appears to be a mere appendage to your household." And then he hated himself. "Oh, Señor, you know we like a good joke in Valle del Sol."

Señor Moreno nodded, stopped laughing and wiped his eyes. "Merciful saints, Señor Mondragón, you had me going for a moment!" He sighed the sigh of a man much put upon. "Such a burden on my household. Paloma was my late sister's only surviving child, from El Paso del Norte."

"Both her parents are dead?"

"A Comanche raid on their hacienda." Señor Moreno made a distasteful face, almost as if he blamed his late sister and brother-in-law for blundering in front of lances and scalping knives. "Paloma was eleven and small enough to hide under a bed, even though they burned the hacienda around her." He shrugged the shrug of the truly put-upon. "What could I do but take her into my household? She came with a little money, but we have used that to raise her, so there is no dowry."

Marco nearly said it, but stopped himself in time: *If I was given the care of a niece who had survived such an ordeal, I would love her and treat her kindly and not touch a penny of her bride money.* He hated himself again for merely nodding and trying to look sufficiently sorry for an orphan saddling her uncle with such a heavy load.

It must have worked, because Señor Moreno thought a moment longer, then slapped the table. "For you, Señor, and your good humor, one *peso* for the runt," he laughed, "and no Paloma."

"One *peso* is monstrous high, but I will pay it," Marco said quietly, possessed now of the deepest longing to get far away from Señor Moreno. He reached in the leather money bag at his belt, the pouch destined to grow much larger, once he settled with the Jews for his wool clip and his broker for the cattle. He would spend the night, leave Trece for a few more days, then return for the wedding. He would take the dog and never return to the house of such a man. Marco pulled out the *peso* and set it on the desk.

Señor Moreno reached for it immediately, the pleasure on his face so evident that it caused Marco's gorge to rise. He stood up, desperate now to put distance between himself and this poor excuse for an uncle.

Marco bowed. "Señor, if it is agreeable with you, I will stay the night and then be off, because I should be closer to my business dealings than your excellent house." He swallowed hard at that lie. "I'll leave Trece here and pick him up in a few days when I leave Santa Fe."

Señor Moreno waved a playful, fat finger at him. "Very well. Perhaps I will charge you room and board for Trece, since he now belongs to you!"

God help him, Marco could not decide if he was serious. Without a word, he took out two *cuartillos*, placed them on the desk, bowed again and left the office to the sound of laughter from the horrible uncle of Paloma Vega.

He stood in the street for a long moment, breathing deep until his nausea passed. His horse still waited patiently for him. Obviously the household staff had not been informed that Don Marco Mondragón was to spend the night. Perhaps hosts in Valle del Sol were more polite. When guests came to *his* hacienda, horses were tended promptly.

He was standing by his horse, wondering what to do to get rid of the monumental stink of Señor Moreno, when the source of his indignation came into the street.

"Hasn't my stable boy taken your horse?" the uncle of Paloma Vega asked. "I will have him whipped."

It was perfectly obvious to Marco that his erstwhile host had never given the matter a thought until he saw *him* standing there, a country yokel who would pay one *peso* for a runt. "Pray do not chastise him, Señor," Marco said, in what he hoped was his most firm *juez de campo* voice, the one that always got attention from ranchers whose brands he was inspecting.

"For you, then, I will not, since you have not taken offense at the stable boy's great neglect," Señor Moreno said. Marco's ruse must have been effective. The man went on, "I want to invite you to the wedding in two days. Dinner is ready now, Señor. Do join us."

I would rather eat the still warm carcass of a vulture, Marco thought. He managed a smile. "You are kind, Señor, but I do have another engagement right now. I will return later this evening, partake of your hospitality and then find other lodgings near the business district."

"You will come to the wedding?"

"I wouldn't miss it."

With a small salute, he mounted his horse and rode away, grateful down to his spurs that beyond one small yellow dog, he would never have another connection with the household of Don Felix Moreno.

HE RETURNED HOURS later after dark, drunk and amazed that he could even find the Moreno house. He had almost—almost but not quite, thank God—found the services of a compliant female behind the tavern. The idea was appealing, and he wasn't so drunk that the matter would not have been successful. What stopped him was what always stopped him: the thought of how disappointed Felicia would be. To his befuddlement—he knew he had drunk more than usual—what really stopped him this time was the memory of Paloma Vega stroking Trece's fur. If he had bedded a *puta*—not that the matter would show on his face—somehow he would only be confirming what

Paloma already knew about the cruelty of men. He discovered he couldn't do that.

At the Moreno stable and after dipping his head in the water trough to bring back some semblance of sobriety, Marco summoned the stable boy. He sighed to see the child had a black eye and tossed him a handful of *cuartillos* when he led away his horse.

He stood a long time in the doorway to the courtyard, with no idea where he was to sleep. He sat down heavily on the edge of the fountain.

"Señor Mondragón?"

He looked around too quickly and couldn't help his groan. As his eyes accustomed themselves, he saw two Paloma Vegas standing silent and watchful. He blinked. Only one Paloma Vega stood there now.

"I am a fool," he said simply. "I am drunk and I have no idea where I am to sleep."

She came closer. "I told my uncle I would wait up for you."

He put his hand to his head. "You are far too kind. I have bought Trece, and you are far too kind."

"He'll make you a fine foot-warmer, Señor. Let me help you."

He didn't object when she pulled him to his feet, put her arm around his waist and walked him to the door of his room. She opened it with her other hand, released him, and gave him a firm push forward in the small of his back.

"I trust you can remove your own boots. Good night, Señor." The door closed.

He wanted to tell her no, that she should help him, but he knew better. Felicia would have been so disappointed in him. He did get off one boot before he collapsed on the bed.

In the morning, to his chagrin and then his gratitude, his boots were off, his doublet unhooked and his pants unbuttoned. Someone far too kind had covered him with a blanket, and Trece was curled at his feet.

Chapter Four

In Which Paloma Confesses and Argues about Penance

THE WEDDING OF Don Alonso Castellano to Señorita Maria Teresa Garcia Moreno was noisy, expensive and soon enough over, to Paloma Vega's relief, and also her chagrin, because it meant Trece was leaving and so was Don Marco Mondragón.

He had been kind enough to return a squirming Trece, tucked under his arm, to her in the kitchen the next morning. He seemed to know she would be there, even though she was the niece of the householder. It pained her to think that her uncle must have mentioned her circumstances to Señor Mondragón. Without the cook's permission, she asked him to follow her into the patio.

Señor Mondragón didn't want to look her in the eyes, and she understood. He set down Trece, who immediately began to run around her in small circles, his tongue out, eyes bright.

That was more than she could say for the rancher from del Sol, whose eyes were not bright. She could only imagine the state of *his* tongue, after what must have been a night of serious drinking.

"I do apologize," he said finally. "You were kind."

"Señor, one boot on and one boot off is no way to sleep," she said, as she felt the rush of heat to her face. "I won't have you think that *all* of us in the Moreno household are dead to duty."

To her amusement, he tried to give her a little bow, which only made him groan and push his hand against his forehead. Paloma held her lips tight together to keep from laughing out loud, since she knew he was in pain. She decided that one pleasant use of poverty meant she would never know that sort of pain, induced by too much of the grape, grain or cactus. Besides that, she was still a lady, and her mother—God bless her memory—had raised her right until the Comanches came.

"Señor, follow me," she said, knowing he was in no shape to do much else.

Trece at her heels, Paloma led him through the kitchen again and into the stables, where Trece's mother and his siblings lolled about in a loose box by the horses. She idled there a moment, rendering herself deaf as Señor Mondragón was as quietly sick as he could be, leaning over a low barrier and liberally dousing a highly indignant setting hen.

When he finished, and obviously could not bring himself to look at her, she remembered the dishcloth she had tucked into her apron. She wetted it then calmly reached up to wipe his mouth, fold it, and press the cool dampness against the back of his neck. He took the cloth from her and pressed it next to his forehead with a small sigh.

"Thank you," he said in a voice meeker than she could have credited from a man. "You are still far too kind."

Since he didn't seem to mind her management, Paloma reached up again to press on his shoulder until he sat on a closed feedbox. "Stay here," she commanded, and returned to the kitchen for a cup of steaming, bitter chocolate generally reserved for Señor and Señora Moreno, and a hard roll, the stale kind generally reserved for her. She stared down the cook, saying merely, "He is a guest in this house."

She returned to the stable, where Señor Mondragón still sat, a frown on his face that turned into a look of acute embarrassment when she handed him the cup and roll. She could tell she was troubling him because she had seen him at his worst this evening and morning, so she inclined her head again and told him she would leave him to his breakfast.

To her surprise, he set down the cup with a half-stifled groan and took her hand.

"I don't usually get drunk," he told her. "I come to Santa Fe once a year, conduct my business and return to del Sol."

Thinking about the matter later, Paloma wasn't sure why she then told him what she did. "Señor, you needn't apologize to me," she said. She gathered her courage and looked into his eyes because she liked their shade of lighter brown. She knew she would never see him again, because he only came to Santa Fe once a year. Maybe that fact made her bold. "You'll feel better soon, and rejoice that you never have to trouble yourself with my uncle. *I* am the one who should be embarrassed for all of us. I hear he charged you an entire *peso* for Trece." She couldn't help that her voice faltered, because she loved the yellow dog. "*I* would have given him to you, because no one likes cold feet. Good day, Señor."

He watched Paloma, trailing behind the others, like Claudio not at home in either world. She should have been a cherished niece of the Morenos who had survived an Indian ordeal.

I have much to confess, he thought. *I would like to flay Señor Moreno within an inch of his life. I'll be on my knees for hours when well-deserved penance lands on me.*

The servants stepped politely aside as he approached them on the dirt path, except for Paloma. Hands clasped in front of her, eyes down, she had clearly come from confession. He wanted to say something to her, but he didn't know what it would be. As she passed him silently with a shy smile, he touched her arm briefly then continued.

He hadn't long to wait in San Miguel. Most of the mission's humble sinners had gone their way, back to tend those cooking fires, froth the chocolate into earthenware cups, stir down the lava of cornmeal porridge and coax eggs and *chorizo* to cooperate, preparing for another day of serving Spaniards.

He watched as a mother knelt on the confession bench with her small son. He overheard her gently reminding him of the apples he had thrown at the nesting chicken and the bread headed for her master's table that had somehow ended up on the floor and was barely dusted off as the child carried it into the dining room. Her hand on his back, she kissed the top of his head when he cried. She was a mother of New Mexico teaching her child.

Marco swallowed, remembering Felicia doing that very thing with one of the twins and he with the other as they confessed childish sins that surely weren't sins. They had been teaching them the ways of Holy Church. The last time he had shared those duties with her had been the last time he confessed with his dear ones. It was eight years since they had confessed as a family, guiding their children. The next morning he had saddled up for a typical brand inspection trip and kissed them all goodbye. He had never seen them alive again.

He had confessed many times since then, of course, but it brought so little comfort, because he ached for his lovely wife and children in a way he knew no priest could possibly understand. He might have been wrong there, he suspected now, as he knelt in San Miguel for confession. Perhaps his own priest had understood his hot tears of anger against God the Almighty in the confessional as well as his eventual resignation as a callus built up around his heart until nothing could hurt him anymore.

He crossed himself and leaned close to the grill. "It has been five weeks since my last confession, father," he began, then covered the usual sins of cursing livestock, especially the cow that stepped on his foot; his own use of himself because he was lonely; his unkindness when he struck a teamster who slept on watch and allowed the herd to wander as they came west. He paused, wondering how to phrase this, then blundered ahead. After all, he only came to San Miguel once a year.

"And forgive me for my anger at Señor Felix Moreno, who does not take proper care of his niece Paloma Vega," he whispered, his forehead pressed against the grill. "And my anger at my own stupidity for paying a whole *peso* for a yellow dog and breaking Paloma's heart. *Why* did I insist I needed that runt?"

He cried, something he seldom did, so great was his shame at his sins large and small. He must have been wrong, but some of the callus around his heart seemed to be sloughing away. To his chagrin, it left greater pain than before, because now he felt vulnerable again, and he did not care for that feeling. All this and more he told the priest, reliving again the afternoon when he returned to his hacienda to the sorrowing faces of his servants and the shock of death from *la cólera,* that cruel visitor.

Marco sat back on his heels then, appalled at his recitation, almost wishing for the callus again because he understood with perfect clarity now that it had kept agony at bay. Through his tears, he looked at the bleeding Cristo over the altar at the front of the church, the hanging body primitive because it was probably carved by a parish Indian who had attended no school of European Jesus-carving. The man—who knew who he was?—had only carved what he knew of harsh living and suffering in colonial New Mexico. His Cristo, bleeding from every pore, understood his congregation of humble penitents, and even Don Marco Mondragón, who suffered still.

My sufferings are still not as great as thine, Lord, he thought finally, and felt a measure of comfort he had not expected. "I don't know what to do," he said into the grill. "I am thirty-one years old, and I do not know what to do."

"About what, my thon?" came the gentle voice.

"I am lonely," he said, after a long pause, "but I see no way out of this loneliness."

It was the turn of the shadowy priest to be silent for a long moment. "Perhapth you thould lithen to your heart, now and then."

"I can try," Marco whispered back. "My penance, father?"

"One Hail Mary."

Marco gasped. "Father, that is not enough."

He heard an enormous sigh from behind the grill. "Do not argue about penanth. That ith two of you today. One Hail Mary," the priest said firmly, "and don't cheat and do two, ath thomone did earlier."

Marco crossed himself, listened to the rest of the priest's advice and left the church after two Hail Marys. The priest didn't have to know.

Thoughtful now, he walked back to San Francisco. He had spent so much time on his knees at confession that he knew the wedding must have begun.

He would just slip into the back of the church and witness the marriage of a childhood friend to a woman that friend was having second thoughts about. He would also try hard not to remember his own marriage, when he could not keep from smiling as he glanced at the equally ecstatic treasure kneeling beside him.

He glanced at the row of servants standing in the back, and saw Paloma Vega, her own face thoughtful, hands clasped together at her waist in that charming way of Spanish ladies. She wore a different dress, no less shabby than her workaday dress, but with a small bit of lace around the neckline. She was too thin. For a moment, he allowed his traitor mind the luxury of imagining her with a bosom fully fleshed and soft, because someone had taken the expense and trouble to feed her. It was as simple as that.

He returned his attention to the wedding taking place, where the Spaniards knelt on the bare floor, not dirt as in San Miguel, but polished wood. Someday there might be a stone floor here, but San Miguel would always have packed earth.

O Dios, one of Señor Moreno's other unlovely daughters was gesturing to him to move forward. He shook his head, but she continued to gesture, each flick of her hand more imperious. To spare the rest of the congregation from such an unseemly spectacle, he finally moved closer to the Spanish side, but still stubbornly not within the Moreno sphere. He belonged there no more than Paloma Vega.

When the wedding ended and the bell began to toll, Marco looked around. The servants were already gone, hurrying home to put the final touches on the wedding feast to follow. He suffocated in the smell of hair pomade and scented talcum as the Morenos engulfed him in their unwholesome claustrophobia and forced him to walk with them.

He had not a moment to spend with Alonso, beyond wishing him all success in marriage, quietly grateful that it was his friend and not he who had married into a reprehensible family. At the dinner table, he heard himself deliver a monumentally insincere toast to Alonso and his "lovely" young wife, wishing them long life and many children in Valle del Sol, when he wanted to shout at the new husband to run.

He did not think matters could get worse, but they did, when the dinner was over and the drinking began. After an hour or two of this, Alonso and Maria would be escorted to a quiet chamber and left to fumble. At the exit, on the verge of his escape, he found Paloma, face pale, tugging along the yellow dog on a rope.

"Keep him," he said, as she tried to hand him the rope.

"You have bought him, Señor," she reminded him as he writhed inside. "He … he never was mine anyway. Take the rope please."

"I can't."

He saw the anger rise in her beautiful blue eyes then as she stepped so close that he could breathe in her fragrance of kitchen odors and *piñon*. "You must. My uncle will blame me if you do not."

Wordless, he took the rope. Delicious goose bumps marching down his spine as he touched her hand at the transfer.

She stepped back. "I know you will treat him well." Her eyes welled with tears. "Your feet will not be cold. Go with God."

Before he could say anything, she turned and hurried from the dining room. Trece began to whine and tug at the leash. Marco knelt and ran his hand along the trembling dog's back. Trece looked at him, his eyes reproachful.

Marco understood dogs. He had dogs at home and they worked for him, loyal animals he enjoyed petting and feeding, when their day's labor in herd and flock were done. He knew that Trece would eventually come to love him, because that was the forgiving nature of dogs. Trece would finally forget the mistress who had patiently kept him alive when there was no thirteenth teat for a runt. His only duty in the hacienda of Mondragón would be to keep his master's feet warm, as he had probably warmed Paloma Vega's feet.

He knew Trece would forget. Marco Mondragón also knew that, grateful as he was never to have any association with the Morenos again, he would not forget that patient trainer who was too kind and too thin and who deserved better.

That's how the world works, he reminded himself as he picked up the struggling dog and left the household of Felix Moreno forever.

Chapter Six

In Which the Yellow Dog Does an Impetuous Thing

DON MARCO MONDRAGÓN spent a final night in Santa Fe, close to the stockyards, his yellow dog tied up so he could not escape. With great singleness of purpose, Marco rounded up his drunken teamsters and left them in a sodden pile by the *corrales*. He counted heads, sighed, and searched through Santa Fe's brothels and back alleys for the rest. He pried them off *putas* and sobered them all with buckets of water. By morning, most were aware enough to stay in their saddles. The rest he put in the wagon with the supplies, tents and bedrolls for the return journey to del Sol. Winter was coming and he anticipated snow before arrival at his own familiar gates.

He took time for Mass at San Miguel, kneeling silent and frowning as the little priest with the lisp performed his duties. He wondered why the priest looked on him with such sympathy; surely none of his tearful memories yesterday could have been out of the ordinary to a holy father in a harsh society. Still, there was no denying the kindness in his eyes. It touched Marco, but not enough to erase the lines of worry between his eyes. Felicia used to smooth those marks of responsibility away with her fingertips and kiss him there. Just remembering that bit of long-ago tenderness brought a groan to his lips, which caused the old lady kneeling next to him to put more distance between them.

Trece was too small to trot along beside his horse, so he carried the yellow dog in front of him as he shook off the dust of Santa Fe for another year. Gradually the pup relaxed and settled against his new master, looking with some interest at the passing scene as Santa Fe's narrow streets gave way to the open countryside and higher mountains in the purple distance.

Tightlipped and grim, Don Marco drove his teamsters forward with only the briefest of stops. Andrés, his major domo and a cheerful fellow, had by now stopped trying to annoy him with the kind of chatter that on any other journey would have amused Marco Mondragón. An older servant of his father, Andrés knew him well enough to keep his own counsel when his master was so silent. Andrés also had the perception to keep others from airing any grievances to their master, who was in no mood for petty dealings. When a chorus of moans and other sounds of ill usage started up from the wagon, it was Andrés who silenced the sufferers with a pithy remark or two.

When they reached the pueblo of Pojoaque in late afternoon, Marco resisted the urge to keep riding. The more miles put between him and those beautiful, uncomplaining blue eyes, the better for his own peace of mind. He had taken the only source of pleasure she possessed, a yellow dog. Someone with more confidence and power would have stormed, raged and lashed him with her tongue. Powerless, Paloma Vega had only thanked him for providing a good home for a beloved pet she only would have lost to another, anyway.

Miserable, he sat before the campfire in the inn yard, listening to his now-revived teamsters josh with each other and snicker and laugh over their narrow escape from Santa Fe.

I had a narrow escape, too, he told himself. I never have to see Señor Moreno again.

There had been no room in the inn for him. His teamsters had not expected the luxury of a bed. It chafed him to be turned away, until he started to protest and realized he would probably sound like that abominable Felix Moreno if he complained to a busy innkeeper.

"You are full of travelers?" he asked instead.

"Travelers are as good as donkeys, to sniff the coming of snow," the keep said. "What, I ask you, Señor, is the attraction of the north?"

From tall trees to deep canyons, Marco thought of many. Then he thought of the close streets, eye-watering open ditches and offal in Santa Fe. "The air smells good there."

An evening's wallow in self-pity left him sour and pinched in his heart and soul. He tied Trece to a wagon-spoke in the inn yard where his teamsters slept, wrapped himself in a blanket and lay down beside the yellow dog, making no effort to brush aside small pebbles and branches, because he, like a flagellant in a hair shirt, deserved to be uncomfortable. If he could not flog himself with a whip with tin barbs, he could toss and turn all night as pebbles became boulders and branches turned into tree trunks.

During the next day's travel, Marco passed from menacing silence to embarrassed discomfort, knowing he had behaved like a spoiled youth before his servants, who deserved his usual capability and good humor. He spoke cautiously to Andrés, who was relieved to see that his foul mood had lifted. It hadn't; Marco just knew when enough was enough. He turned his anger and disappointment inward, tucking it beside Felicia and the twins.

The next afternoon brought Española, and his first measure of peace. As always, he felt a certain relief to know that the confluence of the Chama with the Rio Bravo was not far. A few leagues farther and they would veer east toward mountain passes. The trip down had been necessarily slow, with mules laden with wool, and cattle lagging because they missed the open range in del Sol. What had taken five weeks would probably take no more than two, provided snow did not come too early.

They passed through Española, came to the confluence, and saw the monastery of San Pedro before them—squat, homely and welcome. His heart lifted to see Father Damiano wave to him from the open gates. He had been chatting with other pilgrims, from the look of their travel-worn clothes. Maybe the good father would have a few minutes tonight to share more of his tales of early days in Valle del Sol, when he was a new priest from Spain, still possessing the odor of sanctity that had not entirely left him. Father Damiano would talk, relieving Marco of the need to say much in return. If those other travelers had sought lodging at San Pedro, Marco might get away with saying nothing at all.

The sight of the open gate alone was enough to brighten his mood. There had been trips when the gate was closed tight against Apache and Navajo, who still roamed, still threatened, although generally farther away now. And the Comanche? They could strike anywhere.

His teamsters were equally happy to stop in San Pedro's sheltering bulk, probably even happier not to face their master's glum visage for a few hours. The more penitent among them might seek out the confessional and atone for Santa Fe.

After Vespers came supper, a simple bowl of hominy and beans and San Pedro's good bread, with honey from the monastery's industrious bees. Marco had tried to ignore Father Damiano's searching eyes, but the man knew him too well. The old man had baptized him, had seen him red and naked and squalling. There probably wasn't much he could hide, so Marco abandoned the effort as they sat together later in the monastery's *sala*. Father Damiano has closed the door against the autumn chill so Trece could roam at will, sniffing in the corners, and still going to the door to paw at it and whine for his mistress.

As Father Damiano toasted cheese, Marco told his story about the yellow dog and the girl with the bright blue eyes, and how it was Don Alonso's manifest misfortune to now be allied with reprehensible relatives. He repented of buying the little dog sitting by his feet now, resigned to another evening with no Paloma Vega. "But if I had not bought this little fellow, someone else would have," he concluded, running his fingers through the pup's thick fur. "That's what Paloma said, but I think she was just trying to convince herself. *Ay de mi*, father, what do you do about a woman who wants you to feel better, when *you* have been the cause of her misery?"

Father Damiano surprised him then. The priest sat a long time, his fingers in Trece's fur, too. "I do not have an answer for you, my son," he said at last.

That was unsatisfactory and not what he expected from a wise man who knew everything. "Man to man now, what would *you* do, father?" he asked, after a long silence of his own. "You know I am not an impetuous fellow. I look at the problem, weigh everything and then make a decision."

"Decisions for others' well-being," the father answered quickly. "When have you suited yourself recently?"

"I bought a dog because my feet were cold."

Father Damiano smiled at that. "So you did. What would *I* do? If I were a *juez de campo* who was honest and trustworthy almost to a fault, I would probably return to Santa Fe and the household of Felix Moreno, that poor excuse for an uncle. I would offer to marry the blue-eyed, barefoot girl with no prospects, no dowry and minus one dog."

Marco stared at him, his mouth open.

Father Damiano shrugged, a half smile playing around his lips. "You asked me; I told you." He became a priest then, his face serious. "Señor Mondragón, at the risk of causing you embarrassment, you are an exemplary, brave man, much like your father before you. Before you grow old, alone, there is one thing more you need to do. It will require special courage that you lack right now. You will have to function solely on faith."

Marco sighed and bowed his head over Trece. "I think I know what you are going to say," he whispered, his heart almost breaking as it had not broken in years.

Father Damiano's hand went to Marco's shoulder. "You need to learn that if you ride away from your hacienda in the execution of your duties, when you return, a blue-eyed wife and her yellow dog will be alive and waiting for you. Probably children, too, eventually. The only way to learn that is to do it."

Dios help him, he cried again, the second time in two days. So much for bravery. Father Damiano did nothing more than increase the pressure of his hand on his shoulder.

"All I want right now is a good night's sleep," Marco said finally, when he could speak again without sobbing. "Trece whines and I toss and turn." He sighed. "And now I am whining. Forgive me, Father Damiano."

The good father gave him a pat on the back and became very much a priest then. "Kneel, my son, and let me pray for you."

A loyal son of Holy Church, Marco immediately fell to his knees. Wretched, his eyes closed, he listened as Father Damiano did nothing more than ask the Lord God Almighty to clear his mind and grant him a good night's sleep, as he had to travel far tomorrow through dangerous country. He made no mention of Paloma Vega. He only petitioned the Lord for sleep.

Marco felt his mind ease as Father Damiano made a small sign of the cross on his forehead.

"All right then, let us help the Lord with this petition," he said briskly, after Marco rose to his feet. "You say Trece whines all night, keeps you awake and you toss and turn? The bed in your room is soft enough for general purposes. A *piñon* fire is burning in there right now, so your feet should be warm. Let me take Trece and tie him by Andrés. I would feel remiss if I let you leave here on the morrow with a groggy mind. That's no way to travel safely into mountain passes."

"Very well, Father," Marco replied, grateful he made no more mention of the sorest dread of his life and the reason he knew he would never take another wife. How did the priest *know*? But Father Damiano was not through.

"As for the other matter, patience, my son. Come, Trece. You can keep those wretched, sinful teamsters company tonight."

Father Damiano was right; the bed was soft enough for general purposes. The *piñon* fire had burned to coals and the chill was gone from the cold stones. He stripped and crawled between the sheets, pleased to find a warm rock wrapped in a towel at the foot of the bed. All he craved was sleep, and the Lord was merciful.

When he woke finally, he knew the hour was late, even though the room had no windows. He let the knowledge come gently, lying there warm in his bed, disinclined to move. Like a tongue rubbing a sore tooth, he allowed the memory of other mornings like this with Felicia to wash over him, mornings when he lay naked in bed with his wife, her head cradled on his arm. Sometimes she was alone with him, her hand starting to move across his body in that practiced way of a wife who knew what pleased her man.

Other times, and these equally sweet, there would be one twin or the other suckling at her ample breast. He savored again in his mind the milky smell and the soft sounds of one of his sons taking nourishment from his wonderful mother. Marco smiled in the dark now, the memory no longer a tongue on a sore tooth, but something to be treasured and recalled from time to time. He sat up, suddenly purposeful. If they pushed on immediately, they would make San Juan Pueblo before nightfall, where the beds were not so soft. Or they might push on and camp under the stars. It was safe enough in the autumn, with Indians seeking warmth and shelter, too, and less inclined to fight.

Still, there was no hurry to return home, not really. His fields were burned and the ditches cleaned. His diligent servants had been drying vegetables and curing meat until the aroma of the storerooms could bring saliva to the mouth of a man who wasn't particularly hungry. His remaining cattle and sheep were safely penned against the coming snows that might make them drift. He had a few more brand inspection trips, but they were close enough not to dread. Everything was in order in the hacienda of Marco Mondragón.

But there was no urgency to return quickly—no wife eager to refresh him and be refreshed herself before listening to his adventures in the big city, curled in his arms, her bare legs tangled with his. No children waiting impatiently to show him what they had done during his absence and looking expectantly at his saddlebags, wondering what he had brought them. His hacienda would be tidy, clean, swept and smelling of cooking odors, but there would be only a modest welcome from his servants. They liked him, to be sure, but they did not adore him, like Felicia and the twins. No rush at all to be home.

Still, a man of responsibility could not lie naked in bed forever. Marco washed, dressed and walked the familiar halls of San Pedro to the *corrales*, where he found a glum lot of teamsters and the abbot himself, Father Bartolomeo. Marco could understand the serious looks. He always felt a little less brave when stared down by the abbot.

"God's good morning to you, Father," he said politely.

"And to you, my son," came the answer, but the words held a little edge.

"Is there something the matter?" he asked. "I hope my teamsters have behaved themselves," Marco said.

That was all the opening that the abbot required. "Don Marco, upon occasion, I take the opportunity to listen to confession. While I would never repeat what was told to me by your teamsters yesterday evening, I have to tell you that I have seldom heard from a more debauched group of miserable sinners."

"Oh," Marco said, at a loss. His face flushed, mainly because he had confessed his own night of steady drinking to another, far more lenient priest with a lisp. "I trust you supplied sufficient penance to make their repentance significant."

"That is the matter about which we need to talk, my son. I have sentenced them to four days of burning the monastery's fields and clearing out the ditches. Miserable sinners."

Marco blinked. "But, Abbot, we are traveling toward mountain passes ..."

The abbot merely held up his hand to stop Marco's words. "You will, in four days' time, and not one hour sooner." He gestured to his field master. "Take away these wretched specimens and put them to work!"

When his teamsters had hurried after the monk, rakes and shovels in hand, Father Bartolomeo indicated Father Damiano, his second in command. When he spoke, his voice was kinder. "Don Marco, Father Damiano has something to tell you." The abbot made a slight bow and left the *corral.*

Marco watched him go with a rueful smile. It would not hurt his teamsters, especially those with wives and children waiting in del Sol, to work off their debaucheries. Still, four days to cool his heels in San Pedro? "What is it, Father?"

"My dear Marco, I regret to tell you that your yellow dog has run away. Andrés and I thought he was tied securely, but we were mistaken. That little rascal has fled the monastery. He's—"

"Going back to Santa Fe," Marco finished.

Chapter Seven

In Which Father Damiano Makes Confession and Does Not Argue about Penance

FATHER BARTOLOMEO, THE abbot of San Pedro, slid back the little door and exposed the grill in the confession booth. "Father Damiano, I must wonder what requires confession at this unusual time."

Father Damiano smiled, feeling not at all repentant. He knew his abbot well, but sins need to be confessed, even this one—or these two, to put a finer point on the matter. "Forgive me, Father, for I have sinned. It has been twenty-four hours since my last confession." He cleared his throat. "Actually, it was two sins—one of omission and one of commission."

He heard a stomach rumble behind the screen, and then his abbot spoke. "Well, my son? Mass and breakfast are before us, and you know we have a busy day, preparing for winter. Don Marco is pacing up and down in the courtyard and talking to himself. What two sins have you committed that require confession? You are too old to shock me. Get about it quickly."

"Last night I tied up a yellow dog next to Andrés, Don Marco's *mayordomo.* Before I even left the corral, that wicked Andrés had untied the dog and opened the gate so he could run away."

It *was* early. Perhaps Father Bartolomeo needed a moment more than usual to comprehend the gravity of the situation. The abbot's comment came after deliberation. "You are telling me that you watched another man release his *master's* property, and you did nothing to stop him?"

"Precisely."

Father Damiano listened for it, a chuckle deep from somewhere in the abbot's considerable paunch. Or it could have been another rumbling from the gut.

"Don Marco Mondragón paid an entire *peso* for a little runt of a yellow dog."

"*Un peso*? For a runt? Imbecile."

Father Damiano waited for the pause, then the thoughtful words from his abbot.

"Señor Mondragón, a shrewd man, would never pay that ridiculous sum for a runt."

"He did, though, Father Bartolomeo." Father Damiano sighed heavily, knowing his abbot must see right through his false repentance. "And I have allowed another man—someone Don Marco trusts—to rob him of his expensive runt. It was a shocking omission on my part."

"Shame on you, Damiano," the abbot said, with no sting behind the words. "Where will this runt go?"

"Right back to his first love, a blue-eyed girl in Santa Fe."

"And what will Señor Mondragón do?"

"Find the dog, I hope."

Again the long silence, and now the unmistakable rumble of a chuckle. "This is a heavy wrongdoing—to be complicit in separating a good man from his expensive chattel, on the mere hope that this dog will find Santa Fe through darkness and distance, coyotes and *Indios*." He paused. "*That* is your sin of omission? Now tell me about your sin of commission. I hope it is a better story."

"It might be. I stopped the yellow dog before he could actually bolt."

"Say on."

"It just so happened that the post rider was riding south to Santa Fe. He stops at our monastery, as you know, where we allow him to change horses and have a hot meal."

"Ah, yes. And?"

"And I gave him Trece to carry to Santa Fe," Father Damiano confessed. "After all, Trece is only a small yellow runt and very expensive. Suppose he should not reach Santa Fe, and his blue-eyed mistress? I wanted to speed an earnest dog about his business. Did not San Francisco himself adjure us to be kind to animals?"

"He did, but I cannot think Francisco wanted us to press our noses into other's personal affairs."

Another long pause, but Father Damiano was patient.

"Your penance, Father Damiano, will be to kneel in the chapel and think about some kindness we can do Don Marco, when he returns, with or without his … dog. Don't argue with me. I know you prefer to be with your books, but this is serious."

"I would never argue over penance, abbot."

Father Damiano waited for his superior to slide the window back across the grill. It was time to robe for Mass, but still he sat there.

"Abbot?"

"I should perhaps make a confession to you, Father Damiano, since you are my chief assistant in this monastery. You know that I heard confession last night from those wretched sinners that Don Marco calls teamsters."

"And very bad they were, since you sentenced them to four days' penance burning the fields."

"Ah, yes, but you know, dear friend, I have heard worse stories of drinking, whoring and general debauchery in Santa Fe."

"I would imagine you have. You have been a long time in this colony, as have I."

"Indeed. I confess it: I watched you give Trece to the post rider. I am keeping those sinners here for four days, which should allow Don Marco time to return to Santa Fe and find his, uh, expensive yellow dog."

"If he will go, Abbot. We cannot force the human heart."

"Damiano, we can try."

The abbot still sat there. Finally, "Should we light a candle or two for Señor Mondragón? Perhaps make him our special intention at Mass?"

"My very thought, too."

"Damiano, you are a scoundrel."

"I know, Father Bartolomeo. If I may, so are you."

The window slid shut and the abbot came out of the little booth. It was only a few steps to the door, which he opened and stood there listening.

"I don't hear anyone talking to himself," Father Bartolomeo said. He crossed himself, folded his hands across his comfortable girth and closed his eyes. In a few minutes, they heard a horse galloping south on the road to Santa Fe.

The abbot opened his eyes with an expression close to triumph, but not quite, because he was still a humble man. "Father Damiano, one *peso* is a lot to pay for a runt. I would have been disappointed if a man as smart as Marco Mondragón did not try to find it."

The two priests smiled at each other. Suddenly, Father Damiano felt his eyes well with tears. "There is much at stake here, my friend."

"I know," the abbot said quietly. "A good man's heart."

Chapter Eight

In Which a Runaway Returns to Santa Fe and Suffers Consequences

AFTER TWO DAYS of listening to Maria Teresa Moreno de Castellano's tears, Paloma Vega was heartily weary of her cousin and tired of all the Morenos.

Her face swollen with crying, Maria had waylaid her the very next morning after the wedding as Paloma hurried to froth her uncle's chocolate in the kitchen. Maria whined like the spoiled child she was and plucked at Paloma's sleeve for attention.

"Before God, no one told me it would be like this!" her cousin had sobbed. "He's heavy and ugly and oh, his breath!"

Paloma turned her head as politely as she could, wondering to herself if poor Alonso Castellano had enjoyed his first whiff of his new wife's molar. "I suppose you must give it time," she said, pouring the frothed chocolate into her uncle's silver cup. "People seem to keep getting married, and some of them even smile about it."

Maria's only reply was a shudder as she left the kitchen, probably in search of someone else to pour out her troubles to. Cook returned, shaking her head. With a satisfied smile of her own, she leaned close to Paloma. "That one is destined to never know how much fun a husband can be."

Neither am I, Paloma thought. She carried her uncle's breakfast to him in his small office off the *sala*, where he sat with a blanket around his shoulders because he was too cheap to light a fire in the charcoal brazier. He was already cursing the bills from the wedding. She arranged his breakfast, listening to his angry commentary about the cost of weddings in general and stupid sons-in-law in particular, and when oh when would the man take Maria to del Sol?

I think it must be a lovely valley, Paloma thought as she nodded in places where needed, and commented when her uncle probably required a *si* or *no*. She escaped the room as soon as she politely could, dropping the simple curtsy that her dear mother had taught her years ago, when they lived on a ranch near El Paso. She still remembered her mama saying, "When you are fourteen or fifteen, there will be suitors."

Two days after the curtsy lessons, the Comanches came, even more ferocious than the Apaches. Now she was nearly eighteen and too old for suitors. Paloma rested her back against the cool adobe wall, wishing for a moment to sit in the courtyard with grass underfoot and Trece ... no, not Trece ever again. A trip down the hall to Tia Luisa's bedroom to inquire what she wished for breakfast would mean listening to more complaints; that could wait. A trip back to the kitchen meant nodding and shaking her head to Cook's commentary on the family she served, New Mexico in general, and her ugly husband in particular.

When did I become the sounding board in this household? Paloma asked herself, supremely dissatisfied with a man who would buy her dog for so much money and then actually take him away, even as she knew she was more dissatisfied with herself. She was spooling out her days with an aunt and uncle who never suspected she had dreams of her own.

They weren't extravagant dreams; a mere handful of years in the Moreno household had cured her of that. She looked at her bare toes. Lately all she wanted was a pair of shoes. She closed her eyes, trying to think of a wonderful dream. It was a small one, but it made her smile: *I want to see Marco Mondragón and his light brown eyes one more time.*

She whispered those very words, looking around to make sure no one had overheard her. She closed her eyes again, wishing for good people to serve, more food, and warm clothes. Even in her mind's eye, her modest wishes were objects seen through a window of wavy glass, indistinct outlines. As she sat there in rare distress, practical reason triumphed and she bowed her head. Nothing was going to change, not ever, not for her. She could expect things, but that would be folly. It was time to pack away childish things and send them on a journey so they would not mock her.

"If you have no expectations, you will not be disappointed, Paloma Vega," she whispered again. "Say it until you believe it."

She missed Trece most at night in her narrow bed, missed his warmth on her feet. The room was tiny, but at least it was her own. Her other dress hung on a peg and there was a crucifix over her bed; that was all. Her cloak had finally worn out last spring and ended up lining the basket where Trece's mama had given birth to her litter of thirteen. Tia Luisa had promised a new cloak, but all the tentative reminders in the past few weeks had only earned Paloma a slap. Maybe when Maria and her new husband finally left, Tia might remember her promises. Paloma didn't think that she had sunk quite low enough to go to San Miguel and ask Father Eusebio if there might be a cloak someone had left for the poor.

Not for the first time, Paloma Vega wished she were a man. She could stride out of the Moreno house and try her fortunes in the army, or maybe as a sheepherder. No one would demand this or that from her and no one would ever snatch her beloved yellow dog, even a kind man with light brown eyes.

Finally she was too weary for profitless wishes. She drew her knees up close to her chest and wrapped her arms around them. She hadn't bothered brushing and braiding her hair tight that night. She had figured out two winters ago that when she left her hair long and loose, she was warmer at night.

Since the room was chilly, she had decided against kneeling on the floor to pray. She could pray in her bed and confess that next week to Father Eusebio. Paloma edged toward slumber, thinking of food always, and how much a bowl of pork and hominy would warm her. Her last thought was of Father Eusebio. If he was still sniffing in his confessional booth when she paid her next visit, she would have to steal ingredients from the kitchen for a concoction to relieve him. Of course, that would mean more confession, and she was weary of apologizing to the Lord God Almighty.

At least she was not having lustful thoughts about Señor Mondragón that required confession. All she wanted to do now was throttle him for taking her yellow dog.

EVERYTHING CHANGED THE next morning. Trece returned and broke a dozen eggs.

Tongue lolling out of his mouth and looking surprisingly hearty after what must have been an exhausting journey, the yellow dog was waiting patiently by the back door to the kitchen, the tradesmen's entrance.

Still carrying the eggs she had just bought from the blind egg lady in the street, Paloma stared at her pet. With a yelp, Trece leaped about her, knocking her off balance. She watched in horror as twelve eggs flew into the air and smashed on the hard-packed earth.

"Fulana!"

Paloma looked around, terrified, as her uncle came toward her and Trece, who licked eagerly at the mess of egg yolks and slimy whites. Before the little dog could dodge, Tio Felix struck him with the cane he used when his gout was bad. Again and again the cane flashed down on the dog, who was yelping now and trying to cower behind Paloma.

With a cry of her own, she threw herself on top of Trece, which meant the blows fell on her. She turned to look at her uncle, begging him to stop, as he struck her face. The cane narrowly missed her eye and landed right beside it. She felt warmth on her face as blood flowed.

Breathing hard, her uncle stared at her as though he had no idea who she was. Her hand to her face, Paloma stared back, then averted her gaze against the anger she saw, chilled to her very soul.

"Uncle, this is the dog that Señor Mondragón paid one *peso* for. It is not one of his brothers. You have done a bad thing."

Without a word, Tio Felix grabbed Paloma by the arm, pinching the flesh until she cried out. He yanked her into the kitchen where he shoved her toward the cook.

"Do something with her," he shouted and stalked to the door. He turned to glare at Paloma. "I should shoot that mongrel and give that hick from del Sol his money back."

"Oh, Uncle, no," she whispered.

"And as for you," he ran back to her and shook her until she cried out, "let me not see you for a few hours."

Looking the fool, he struggled to slam the heavy door, then gave it up for a bad business. He kicked the scullery maid then stormed from the room.

White-faced, the cook handed her a damp rag. Paloma pressed it to her wounded cheek, holding it there, unsure what to do when the bleeding continued. After a few minutes in the silent kitchen, the bleeding slowed enough for Cook to pack some flour in the wound.

"That will dry it out." She turned back to the fireplace and stirred the hominy. "Sit down and tip your head back," Cook ordered, her voice kind. "It's not the end of the world."

But it was. As she sat there, wishing for the blood to stop, wondering where Trece was now, Paloma knew she had reached the end of her life in the Moreno household. Her fear gave way to enormous calm. She felt her apron pocket. The few cuartillos left over from her visit to the egg lady were still there, to be returned to Tio Felix. Not this time. She stood up carefully, leaning against the table until the little sparkles around her eyes disappeared.

"Do you have a dry cloth?" she asked, surprised at her self-possession. "I am going to San Miguel, where the fathers help people with wounds."

"Your uncle will be displeased if you tell the fathers what he has done," the cook warned, even as she handed Paloma a soft cloth, one of the linen napkins the family used.

"I don't care," Paloma replied. She put the napkin to her face, pressing hard. She held out her other hand to the cook. "I fear *you* will get in trouble if this linen napkin is missing. Can you find something else?"

"No," the cook said, her eyes defiant now. "Go with God."

Paloma went quietly to her room, keeping the cloth to her face. With one hand, she peeled back her coarse sheet, too small for the bed, and put her other dress in the middle of it. She felt under the mattress for the one treasure remaining to her from her mother—a magnificent tortoise shell comb, the kind that great ladies used to anchor their masses of hair. Mama's hair had been peeled from her scalp by the Comanches while she still lived. They had overlooked the comb somehow, possibly in their eagerness to drag her outside to share with the others. Paloma put it in her apron pocket next to the cuartillos.

Wishing for shoes one more time, she slung the small bundle over her back. The hall was still deserted. Paloma Vega let herself quietly into the street, where the people of Santa Fe were going about their business, totally unaware of her turmoil and sudden resolve. She looked around and smiled with relief to see Trece by the corner of the house, his tail wagging, none the worse for wear, other than a welt next to his snout and a scarlet stain on the fur near his front leg. She knelt down, wincing at the increased throbbing in her face, and ran her fingers gently down his leg. All he did was lick at the bloody flour on her face, so she knew he felt better than she did.

"Trece, we are going to Valle del Sol, wherever that is. I must return you."

Her first stop was San Miguel, where she asked the gatekeeper for Father Eusebio. The gatekeeper must have frightened the priest sufficiently, because he came running, his habit pulled up to reveal skinny legs. He stared at the ruin of her face. She watched in humiliation as his eyes widened then narrowed in a way that made her fearful for Tio Felix.

"Please Father, can you stitch it to stop the bleeding?"

He nodded and took her hand, hesitating when he noticed Señor Mondragón's expensive yellow dog. "He returned to you, eh?"

She nodded, wincing at the sudden pain. "I am going to give him back."

She waited for Father Eusebio to remind her of her duty to her family, to warn her of the folly of such an undertaking, but he did nothing of the sort. "I think you thould," he said. "Come now, let me thee what I can do."

With warm water, Father Eusebio washed the blood and flour away, while Trece looked on with interest. "Not tho bad," the priest said as he concentrated on the damage done by an angry man over a mere dozen eggs.

The wound required three stitches and all of Paloma's resolve to keep from crying out. There were children in the next room, waiting their turn for medical ministration, and she did not wish to frighten them. Trece pressed close to her, aware of her distress.

"There now," the priest said as he pressed a tidy plaster over the wound. "Change that tomorrow, if you can. Do you have money?"

She nodded. "A little, the rest of the egg money I should have returned to my uncle." She patted her small bundle. "I have a tortoise shell comb that belonged to my mother, God rest her. I will take it to the Jew Street and sell it." She looked at him shyly then, gathering together her pride one last time and then letting it go. "Do you have any shoes in the poor box?"

Paloma looked away as the priest seemed to struggle within himself. Well, she would miss him, too.

There weren't any shoes, but there was a pair of sandals, the sort servants might wear in households kinder than the Moreno household, where bare feet was the rule. She accepted them gratefully. She didn't ask for a cloak, but he found one anyway—a child's garment that would serve well enough.

"Bless me, Father," she said, kneeling as Trece whined and tried to lick her face.

He did as she asked. "When you find Theñor Mondragón, do what he thays."

"All I am doing is returning his dog," she said quietly. "I will find some way to live."

SHE FELT HER first real fear as she left San Miguel. She stood still until it passed, then made her way to the Jew Street, where men with long beards and skullcaps bought and sold. Her mother's comb commanded a smaller price than she would have imagined. She could have wished for more, but there would have been no point.

She stopped at the door of his shop. "How long does it take to walk to Valle del Sol?"

The Jew rubbed his chin, his eyes kind. "It is a long way. Perhaps you can find a supply wagon going north, where you might pay a small coin for a seat." He hesitated. "It's dangerous, there on the edge of Comanchería."

All I have are small coins, she thought ruefully, as she nodded and left his shop. She stood outside the Jew's shop, waiting for her heart to stop its triphammer. *Comanchería. O dios, am I brave enough?*

A small roll for her and some chicken scraps for Trece constituted breakfast. Keeping to the side of the road, she looked straight ahead and followed others, mostly *Indios*, heading north. She had no worry that her uncle would follow her. The cruelty in his eyes as the cane came down assured her that he would not follow.

She walked until her feet were sore. She stopped by a wayside food stand, buying two tortillas for herself and more meat scraps for Trece, mourning every coin that left her apron pocket. No one said anything to her as she sat on the bench by the food stand. She tried to keep her face tipped down so no one could see her bandage, but she soon discovered that no one wanted to ask questions of someone with a yellow dog who was obviously running away.

As she sat wondering what to do, two noisy carts rolled into view, pulled by donkeys. She looked at the first teamster, watching how he whipped the donkeys and swore great oaths that suggested he hadn't been near a confessional in many years.

The other man was older, and so were his two donkeys, but he didn't shout at them. He led them to the water trough before he went inside for his own food. After he came out, Paloma dug deep inside for courage and approached him.

"Sir, are you going east to Valle del Sol?"

She said it quietly. In her mind, that simple question slid her from lady to peasant, because she had spoken to a man she did not know.

The old man laughed, but it wasn't a cruel laugh. "You're jesting! No one goes to Valle del Sol alone. *No one*, and you should not try. I am going north to Española. If you insist on such foolishness, you will come to a spot, a short way beyond that, where the Chama flows into the Bravo. Then you will turn east through the mountains."

"Could I ride with you as far as Española? I … I have a few coins."

"You had better keep them. It is a long way to del Sol. I hope you will change your mind about such a journey. Yes, you and your dog may ride with me. Hop in the back with the cabbages." He looked at her closely, probably taking in her bandage, her shabby dress, and the too small cloak. "If you happen to eat a cabbage, I'll never know." He rubbed his chin. "If you should eat the side of beef in there intended for the King of Spain, I might be a little upset."

It was the sort of jest poor people make. No man as impoverished as the cabbage man had a side of beef. "I will leave the king's beef alone," she teased back.

She lifted Trece into the wagon, climbing in after him and making herself comfortable among the produce. As she sat there, the rain began. "Trece, we are going to get wet," she said. "This is what is known as an adventure."

Gathering her dog close, Paloma waited for the teamster to speak to his old donkeys and start the great wheels turning. Instead, she sighed with relief as the man pulled a canvas cover over his cabbages, tying it securely. "To protect that beef," he told her.

She put the bundle holding her other dress underneath her and pulled Trece close for warmth. She was dry, not too hungry yet, and tired. Closing her eyes, she felt weary but not as discouraged as that morning, which seemed so long ago.

She slept, oblivious to the rain and the sound of a horseman pounding toward Santa Fe.

Chapter Nine

In Which Señor Mondragón Uses His Skills as a Juez de Campo

MARCO MONDRAGÓN HAD ridden in worse weather, but he felt some compassion for the old *paisano* hunched over his reins, high atop a wagonload of produce, whom he passed in his hurry to reach Santa Fe. "Go with God, old man," he called out, sorry that his horse sprayed mud on the cart.

There was room this time in the inn at Pojoaque so he stopped, mainly for his horse's sake. A good *ranchero* would never tire his favorite beast, although he was sorely tempted. As it was, Marco tossed about for a long while, hoping that Paloma Vega would not find herself in trouble if Trece returned to her.

He stared at the low ceiling, wondering how *he* would treat a niece suddenly thrust upon him after a Comanche raid. "I would pray for such a niece and treat her as my own," he said to the ceiling. "What is the matter with some people?"

The rain had stopped by morning. When the clouds lifted, he saw new snow on not-so-distant mountains. He hoped his sinful teamsters were hard at work for the good fathers of San Pedro. They hadn't a moment to spare to get on the road again, bound for higher altitudes where the line of snow would already be lower.

He arrived in Santa Fe in early afternoon, stabling his tired horse at the inn and seeking a room for himself. He walked to Felix Moreno's house and knocked, half thinking—and maybe hoping, if he was honest—that the girl with the bright blue eyes would open the big door.

Instead, it was a servant he had not seen before. Or perhaps he had.

Servants all tended to look the same, a thought that made him wonder how good a master *he* really was.

"Is your master at home?" he asked, speaking softly because she was young and looked so cowed already.

He stood in the *sala*, his misgivings mounting, as precious time passed.

"Señor Mondragón, you have come for your naughty yellow dog."

Marco knew the sound of falsehood. He had heard that cajoling tone from many a *ranchero* who harbored someone else's cattle in his own corral, and sought to distract the *juez de campo* with blandishments, if only for a few minutes.

"I thought he might return here," Marco said, turning around, pleased that he towered over the well-fed *fiscal*. "Better bring him to me. I promise to chain him to my wagon when we stop for the night."

Señor Moreno's face fell. Or rather, his pudgy chins appeared to sag together in some approximation of distress that his harder eyes did not exhibit.

"Señor, I cannot. That troublesome niece of mine has run away with him. Before she sneaked away in the night, dragging your howling dog with her, she robbed me of all the *pesos* in my strong chest!"

Unlikely, Marco thought. *I think you put your strong chest in bed with you, you miser. You probably hump your wife with one eye on that box*. "Then why are you not heading a posse to find her? Señor Moreno, I don't believe you. Paloma would not steal."

"You don't know her," the man said quickly, his company face gone. His eyes narrowed into slits and he stepped back. Marco could nearly hear the gears clanking and turning in the man's mind. "Unless you *do* know her in carnal ways, when I thought you were trustworthy guest in my home. Deceiver! Maybe she has run away from *you*, afraid for herself more than your dog."

"You are evil," Marco said, making no attempt to hide his own menace, which was genuine and growing greater each second he looked at the *fiscal*. He moved toward the little man, who backed up against a low table and sat on it. The table creaked.

"May … maybe it was not *pesos*," the man admitted, avoiding Marco's glare. "Maybe it was *reales*, Señor, but it *was* my money. And my wretched niece is gone!"

"I would flog you if I had a whip," Marco said. He turned on his heel and left the *sala*.

The householder shouted after him, brave now that the imminent threat was gone. "We know nothing in this house. Return here and *you* will be flogged, you hick from Valle del Sol!"

Marco Mondragón, respected in his own valley, stood in the street until his breathing returned to normal. *I have found cattle and the Christ Child missing from a crèche, and lost children and wandering chickens*, he thought. *Surely I can find a yellow dog and a girl with blue eyes who perhaps, just perhaps, is looking for me.*

As it turned out, Felix Moreno's staff was far from loyal. Marco heard a "Psst!" from the corner of the house. Looking behind him to make sure Felix Moreno was not in sight, he strolled casually toward the sound.

He was disappointed not to see Paloma, but there was an older woman with a long apron, the Moreno's cook. Brazen, or maybe desperate not to be seen, she took his arm and yanked him around the corner, surprisingly strong for one so old.

"Whatever he told you, don't believe it," the woman hissed.

"I don't."

She gave his arm another tug, which made him think she had sons his own age. She took a deep breath. "When your foolish dog returned he startled Paloma and she dropped a dozen eggs. The master saw this and started beating Trece."

"I thought as much."

"Don't interrupt me." She glared at him, obviously lumping all men in the same kettle. "Paloma tried to stop him and got the cane for her troubles."

His own niece, Marco thought, appalled.

When he didn't speak, the cook scowled at him again. "Don't you have anything to say?"

"Cook, whether I speak or don't speak, you have me condemned," he pointed out.

She had the good grace to loosen her grip on his arm, which, truth to tell, was starting to ache.

"I did what I could but it wasn't enough. She told me she was going to San Miguel, where the priests have some skill at doctoring." She shook her head. "Blood everywhere."

It was Marco's turn to grasp her arm. "*O dios*, please tell me she—"

The cook must have seen the sudden fright in his eyes because she patted his arm now. "She is wounded but well enough. She had such a fire in her eyes! The master will be lucky if she never returns to this miserable household."

"San Miguel?"

"Go, and hurry."

He did hurry, arriving out of breath at the mission church, where he demanded to speak to the priest with a lisp. He could have beat his head against the door frame when the priest who came told him that Father Eusebio had left the mission, carrying the vessel for Extreme Unction.

"Not for Paloma Vega?" he asked in sudden fear, thinking of his wife and children. It struck him forcefully that he was now adding the quiet Paloma Vega to that particular pantheon of loved ones. He thought that door had slammed shut years ago. Perhaps the Lord and His tender mercies were not through with him yet.

"Not for Paloma. I was tending others, but I saw him stitch her pretty face and get her a pair of sandals from the poor box, as though she was going on a journey."

"Did … did she say where?" he stammered, thinking of Felicia's boots and shoes and dresses he had packed in camphor and put away. She had loved beautiful clothes and he had indulged her without a qualm. By God, he would do it again, if he could.

"If she did say, Father Eusebio did not tell me," the priest replied with a shrug. His expression turned thoughtful. "He did mention one thing more—a beautiful tortoise shell comb, the kind ladies wear."

"She had such a possession?"

"Apparently. She may have stolen it, but I doubt Paloma Vega would steal anything." The priest smiled. "And that yellow runt was trailing at her heels. That much I did see." The priest looked at him with kindly eyes. "I wish I could tell you more. Oh. Father Eusebio also gave her a child's cloak. It was all we had in the poor box, what with winter coming."

Marco nodded, thanked the priest for his information and left San Miguel, but not before handing him two *pesos* for the poor box. He could have purchased the best milk cow in Valle del Sol with two *pesos*, but the poor needed it more.

Outside the church, Marco looked to the right and the left, wondering what to do. He sat down on a bench in front of the church, slowing down his racing brain with the logic of a *juez de campo*, he who inspected brands and occasionally investigated petty crimes.

So you are going on a journey, probably to return my dog—your dog—to me, he reasoned to himself. *I know you have no money, other than a cuartillo or two. The comb belonged to your mother, dead these seven or eight years. You're a practical woman, for only a practical woman could have survived all these years with such a bad man.*

He stood up slowly and walked to the stockyard, where he had bargained with the Jews over his wool clip and cattle. He found Señor Abrán Boulafia, who was patiently dickering with another *ranchero* over a small herd. Marco sat down to wait, but soon leaped to his feet to walk back and forth. *Hurry, hurry,* he wanted to shout, but negotiations took time.

He could have kissed the Jew's feet when Boulafia finally nodded at the cattleman and motioned for him to follow his equally bearded clerk to the office to draw up agreements.

"Don Marco, you are wearing a path from one tree to another. What do you need?"

"Señor Boulafia, where would a person go to sell a comb for a lady's hair? I have never dealt with any Jew dealers in Santa Fe except you."

Señor Boulafia did not even blink at such a strange request. "Try the little alley behind Paseo de Peralta. You know, close to the old Pecos trail." He seemed to feel familiar enough to tug on his beard and grin. "Are things at such a pass that you must pawn a comb? Don Marco, I know I paid you well for that wool clip."

Marco returned his smile. "You paid me well," he said. "You have done so ever since I came here after my father's death—twenty-one and frightened."

"It appears that the son has turned out as worthy as the father," the Jew said.

"Thank you, Señor Boulafia. I am looking for someone who might need to sell a lady's comb."

"Then I pray to the God of Abrán, Isaac and Jacobo that you find her," the old man told him, and it felt like a blessing as potent as the one Father Damiano had left on his forehead two days past.

"See you in a year, Abrán," he said, calling him by his first name, something he had never done before. Perhaps it was time.

He did not know Santa Fe well, but he found the alley. To his dismay, there were a number of shops—narrow and dark because the sun did not shine in the alley—where such a transaction might have taken place. Some were open, some closed now for the noon meal. Four shops yielded nothing. The fifth shop was closed.

The sixth gave him what he wanted.

All Jews looked alike to him; he wondered if Señor Boulafia had a brother. "Did a young woman with bright blue eyes come in here recently to sell a tortoise shell comb?" Marco asked, with no preliminaries. He knew this was no way to do business or ask for information, but time was his enemy.

Again, he could have fallen to the earth in gratitude when the man, his eyes wary, nodded slowly. "I bought such a comb from such a lady." His eyes seemed to own the memory again. "She had a bandage next to her eye and a yellow dog at her heels."

"The very one," Marco said quietly.

"She didn't dress like a lady, but she *was* a lady." The older man's eyes seemed to darken. "She was a lady fallen on hard times." The eyes darkened further. "I hope you have come to relieve her burden and not add to it."

Marco looked at him, surprised at the Jew's impertinence with a Christian. He thought of Paloma with sudden hope. She did have a way of bringing out a man's protective instincts. He sighed. All men except her uncle. And here was this Jew, as observant as a brand inspector.

"I hope to relieve her burden," he said, his voice no louder than before. With the saying, he knew he had crossed into territory that made him vulnerable to women again, as he had not been vulnerable since Felicia's death. "She is taking a perilous journey to return that dog to me. I doubt she knows how perilous."

His fears returned when the Jew shook his head. "I could only give her a handful of coins." The man looked away. "It was so little, but it was business. If I overpaid everyone, how could I feed my own wife and hopeful children?"

"I understand," Marco replied. "I am a businessman, too."

The man seemed to choose his words with care. "She kissed the comb before she handed it to me. I think it meant a great deal to her."

"It did. I believe it was her only remaining possession from her mother."

The Jew smiled at him, and it was a man-to-man smile, not the smile of Jew always careful among Christians. "Then you must mean a great deal to her."

Do such things happen so fast? Marco asked himself in wonder. "I believe she is scrupulous about returning the dog," he said, even as he felt his face flame. *Dios*, he had not blushed in years, not since he first saw Felicia after their wedding, standing before him in only her shift.

The Jew shrugged. "As for how perilous the journey will be, she knows, Señor. She asked me, 'Señor Jew, where is Valle del Sol?' " He shook his head, suddenly a father with daughters of his own. "I told her it was too dangerous, so close to Comanchería, which turned her pale. I also assured her it was too far for the handful of coins I had given her, but she smiled anyway and left my shop."

He reached under his counter then and pulled out the tortoise shell comb, "Please, Señor, give this back to her when you find her."

Marco pulled out his money bag. "How much do I owe you?"

The Jew named an inconsequential sum that made Marco wince. That would get her no closer to del Sol than Española, if she was a lucky woman, and he thought she was not. He paid the sum and pocketed the comb.

"Thank you for your information," he said politely.

He was in a hurry to retrace his steps toward San Pedro and his wicked teamsters, but he paused before the glass-topped case. He knew he would find what he wanted, but he wouldn't know what he wanted until he saw it. Ah. He pointed.

The Jew removed the ring from the case and laid it in the palm of his hand. A row of tiny, blue-enameled flowers were etched on the surface of the ring.

"What flower is that?" Marco asked.

The man chided him with a gentle smile. "Señor, you know that we Jews may not own land here. I have no ground to plant such a flower, or any flower, for that matter. I do believe, though, that you might call it a forget-me-not, *No me olvides*."

"I'll take it."

They dickered a moment out of politeness, but Marco knew he would have settled for any sum the Jew asked, and he sensed the Jew knew it, too. He paid the sum named and waited while the Jew wrapped the ring in a small twist of paper.

Outside the shop, he had a moment of indecision, which resolved itself quickly, because he knew he would not return to Santa Fe until spring, and Spanish wheels of government revolved slowly. He hurried to the governor's palace, past the *Indios* sitting there with trade goods for barter, and up to the clerk at the high desk. A few words, and one of his favorite functionaries hurried toward him, which gratified Marco for no more reason than it was nice that the Mondragón name meant something in Santa Fe.

Again, he had no time for preliminaries. "Señor Obregon, would you pass on a request to your district's *juez de campo*?"

"Anything within my power," Señor Obregon said, his hand to his chest.

"I have reason to think that Don Felix Moreno, *fiscal*, might have some questionable cattle." *Maybe he does, maybe he doesn't*, Marco thought to himself. *I would like someone to investigate him, harass him and cost him money.* "I might be wrong. I also have a suspicion there might be cattle somewhere in the name of Paloma Vega, who used to live on a ranch near El Paso. Her family died in a Comanche raid seven or eight years ago"—he crossed himself—"and the cattle and land seem to have vanished. Poof!"

Señor Obregon pulled a government face that meant he was thinking. "This Paloma—"

"Vega. I do not know her other names."

"Vega was the survivor?"

"Yes. She is the niece of Felix Moreno."

The two men looked at each other. Señor Obregon put away his government face for a small moment and produced his disgusted face. Only a small moment. In another second he was official again. Marco suspected that someone unaccustomed to business in Santa Fe never would have noticed a thing.

"She alone survived." *And now I have to find her dog.* Marco touched the little ring in his doublet. *And see how far I get.* He shrugged. "It might mean contacting the *juez* in the El Paso district. Maybe a winter project, if life is boring for your *juez de campo*."

"Perhaps." The functionary bowed to indicate he was through. "God keep you safe from the Comanche. And may He go with you to Valle del Sol, Señor."

"And with you."

And with you, Paloma Vega, *wherever you are*, Marco thought.

Chapter Ten

In Which Paloma Vega Discovers Adventure

CABBAGE HAD NEVER been her favorite vegetable, but Paloma Vega decided she liked it well enough, especially when the non-existent side of beef did nothing to keep hunger away. Peeled off, a leaf at a time, the cabbage filled her belly. She offered a leaf to Trece, but he just sniffed, whined, and curled up closer to her.

"Adventurers can't be choosers," she reminded him, then fingered the coins in her apron pocket. "If *el viejo* stops anywhere for food, I'll find something. If Valle del Sol is far away, you may have to learn to hunt."

If Valle del Sol is far away, I'll find out how resourceful I am, and maybe how brave, she thought, as the wagon rumbled on. Since she was cold, and the cabbage wasn't settling too well in her stomach, Paloma had the leisure to consider what she had done. For a few years, she had mourned the shocking loss of her parents. She had gradually folded their dear images away in her heart as she struggled to make sense of her life in Santa Fe. After a while, she had resigned herself to hard work with no thanks.

She watched other children taken into the Moreno household as servants, seeing them go through the same pattern she went through, learning to serve with no thought of gratitude. The injustice of her treatment, when she should have been a cherished niece, became another thing to tuck away.

She sighed. The biggest loss had been her mother's tortoise shell comb; the biggest gain, the pair of sandals. And here was her beloved Trece, returned to her to give away again, once she found his new owner. She would be truly on her own then, but as the hours passed in the slowly moving cart, the reality seemed less terrifying. She could cook and clean, read and write. Surely someone needed her skills. Maybe there would be other tortoise shell combs some day, or maybe not. The memory of her mother would remain.

The wagoner stopped briefly at some nameless pueblo, not bothering with an inn, which did not surprise her. Anyone with nothing more than a cart full of cabbage probably couldn't command much beyond an inn yard, a little food for his donkeys, and a dry spot underneath the cart, once the donkeys were unhitched and tethered to graze nearby.

To her amusement, he knocked on the side of the cart. "*Hija*, I have cold water to share, and what do you know, I have found a scrap of a blanket that I don't need. Now that the rain has stopped, it really isn't that cold."

Shivering, she pulled back the tarpaulin and saw his breath in the frosty air. "Oh, father, you need the scrap," she chided gently. "I have a dog, remember?"

"A small one, Señorita," he argued back. He pounded his cloak, and she coughed from the cloud of dust. "See my warm cloak? Don't argue with an old man."

She nodded and accepted the scrap of blanket, which was warm and soft and no scrap. In a few minutes she was asleep again, lulled by cabbage.

She woke to the sound of the wagoner hitching his donkeys to the cart after the sun rose. Paloma peeled back the tarp, quickly noticing much more snow on the mountains, after a night of valley rain. It seemed to be inching closer, which made her shiver.

She cajoled some meat scraps—more fat than meat—from the vendor at a food stand beside the road. The chocolate made her mouth water, but that was nothing new; in the Moreno household, chocolate was the sole prerogative of Tio Felix and Tia Luisa. She shook her head over a tortilla, thinking how long her cache of coins had to last.

The vendor looked down his long nose at her and held out a tortilla that had been torn and scorched. "I could never sell this one, *chiquita*," he told her.

She took it, smiling her thanks and dropping him a small curtsy, reserved for those older than she was, that her mother had taught her. There hadn't been much reason to use the truly elegant curtsy that she had learned, the one reserved for bishops, viceroys, *capitán generales* and perhaps a husband, upon first meeting. She remembered asking Mama if a husband required that all the time, and Mama just laughed. "Husbands are only allowed one, *mija*," she had said.

Even the small curtsy startled the vendor. "You're no ordinary beggar," he said, not unkind.

"I am not a beggar at all," she told him quietly, putting the tortilla back on the counter. Cabbage would do just as well, she decided, turning away. She kept the scraps for Trece.

She rode beside the wagoner, Trece in her lap, on the slow journey to Española. They arrived in early afternoon, when the sun seemed to accelerate its descent, casting long shadows. The old man spoke to his donkeys, then turned to her.

"This is my stop, Señorita," he said, and Paloma heard the regret in his voice. "I would take you farther, but …" He shrugged his shoulders, saying no more.

"Thank you, old man, for taking me this far," Paloma told him. "Your cabbage was delicious, and look, the side of beef for the King of Spain is still untouched."

She climbed down and held out her arms for Trece. Then she retrieved her small bundle from the back of the cart and smoothed her dress.

"See the walking stick back there," the old man said. "Take it. Your dog hasn't grown into his bark yet, and you might need it."

"Do I just keep on the road ahead?" she asked, setting down her dog.

"Yes. In about two leagues, the Chama will join our constant friend, the Rio Bravo. A little farther on, you will see San Pedro, a monastery. Stop there. Perhaps someone will be traveling north and east and you can ask to go along." The old man gathered his reins again. "Go with God, *chiquita*."

Paloma continued her journey, Trece walking beside her. The afternoon was warm enough, the air filled with the heaviness of late summer weeds and grasses. The friendly lowing of cattle kept her company as she walked.

She was not alone on the road, not yet. As she walked through Española, she outpaced an old couple carrying a bag of grain between them, a mother with three stair-step children straggling behind, and a man with a cartload of apples. As she walked, unwilling to slow down, she haggled carefully for one apple and parted with another coin. For some reason, the vendor added two more apples, declaring he could never sell them because of worms. She bit into one and found only firm flesh. It seemed strange to her that the apple man didn't know his produce, but she decided not to argue with generosity.

Gradually, her traveling companions dwindled. She watched a man—a long time on the road because of his wrinkled cape—arrive at his house, call out, and scoop two children into his arms. From the shade of a tree with golden leaves across the road, Paloma watched until he went inside, his wife on his arm now and his children skipping ahead carrying his leather satchel between them and arguing about it.

You're wasting time, she reminded herself and whistled to Trece, who was nosing out a trail of one small animal or other—she hoped nothing larger than a rabbit. He was finding the road north a rich broth of scents more complex than those sniffed on a Santa Fe street.

As she strode through the waning afternoon, the dirt road belonged to her and Trece, still nosing along in front of her but slowing down. He flushed out the occasional bird, but had lost the energy to chase it. Paloma knew she would be carrying him soon.

She came to the confluence of the Chama with the Bravo and stood there a long moment, enjoying the sight even as she began to doubt. Beyond the fork of the Chama there were more mountains, all snow-covered and taller than the mountains around Santa Fe. She looked east to more mountains. Somewhere there was a pass and then God forbid, the threat of Comanches.

"You could turn back, Paloma," she told herself out loud. Trece looked up at her and cocked his head, interested. "You could retrace your steps to Santa Fe, give your uncle that deep curtsy and enough apologies to satisfy his pride. He would probably storm and rage, but he would let you back into his house." She looked south one last time.

"I will not turn back," she said in a firm voice. "Adventures are not meant to be comfortable."

She whistled to Trece again and followed the Chama.

PALOMA HAD TRAVELED nearly another hour when she heard a galloping horse behind her. She looked back, pleased, thinking it might be Don Marco Mondragón, but it was only a post rider, wearing the tunic with the red and yellow colors of the crown. *Are you going to Valle del Sol?* Paloma wondered, as she stepped to the edge of the road, picking up Trece so he would not find himself underfoot and trampled.

The rider checked his horse when he noticed her, and she drew farther into the shadows, not wanting to frighten his animal. To her surprise, he looked closely at her and then stopped. Paloma tightened her grip on her walking stick.

"You there!" he called as she tried to disappear into the fringe of wood behind her. "Is that your dog?"

She said nothing. She raised her walking stick and eyed him.

He laughed and pulled one leg from the stirrup and rested it across his saddle in that relaxed way of good riders.

"Don't be afraid of me," he said. "I have a wife and family near Velarde. I will be there tonight, if I push on. That *is* your dog?"

Paloma nodded, less wary, but not relinquishing her grip on the walking stick.

"Answers to the name Trece?"

"Yes, he does," she said, the words surprised out of her. She came closer. "How do you know his name?"

"I carried that very dog with me from the monastery just over the hill. I carried him all the way to Santa Fe a few days ago and set him outside the house of one Felix Moreno, *fiscal*. How did you come by him, Miss?"

"Someone gave you Trece to take to Santa Fe?" she asked, dumbfounded. "Who?"

"Father Damiano," he said promptly. "He told me to be sure the dog reached Santa Fe, because he didn't have long enough legs to get himself there." He laughed, which caused Trece to prick up his ears. "See? He knows me. Come here, boy."

He dismounted and Trece promptly trotted across the road to him. "Good dog." He gestured to Paloma. "I won't bite, Miss."

She came to the road, stooping to pet Trece, too.

"How is it that you have him?" the post rider asked. "Father Damiano didn't give me any reason, but I gathered he didn't want the dog to get lost. Is he your dog?"

"Not really," she replied, mystified. "I used to work for Señor Moreno. I am on my way to Valle del Sol to return Trece to Don Marco Mondragón."

"Valle del Sol?" The post rider removed his helmet and scratched his head. "I saw the *juez* pounding south like a madman as I headed north yesterday. What's going on?"

"I haven't the slightest idea," she said. "You say San Pedro is just over the hill?"

"It is. I am riding there to change horses and continue to Velarde." He put on his helmet and slid his boot into the stirrup. But then he stepped down and indicated that she come closer.

"I reckon you weigh very little. How about you ride in front of me and carry your dog? It's not far to San Pedro, but it will be dark soon and you shouldn't be on the road by yourself."

Paloma considered all the reasons why she should not, then nodded. She let the post rider help her into the saddle and took Trece from him when he handed up the yellow dog. He swung onto the saddle behind her.

"A tight fit, but a short journey," he said, his arms around her. "I ride this way with my children, now and then. Go ahead and lean back, Miss. I'm the king's messenger and I don't bite."

Paloma did as he said, aware how tired she was, and even more, how hungry. She had already discovered one problem with impromptu adventures: they did not involve much food. No wonder people generally stayed put.

"I think Señor Mondragón will be disappointed not to find his yellow dog in Santa Fe," he said as they rode along. "Will he be angry?"

"I have no idea," Paloma said. "I doubt he is happy. The señor paid one *peso* for this wandering dog."

The teamster whistled. "So much for a … what kind of dog is he?"

"He is a rare dog from the interior of China," Paloma replied, perjuring her soul without a qualm, because, for some reason, it mattered to her that Marco Mondragón not be thought a fool. "He is worth far more than a *peso*," she added, reasoning that if one lie was for a good cause, then tacking on another hardly mattered. She could sort out the finer points at confession.

She felt a twinge of guilt when the post rider nodded. "I can see that. Señor Mondragón raises sheep and cattle. A man with as much livestock as he possesses would want the best."

She said nothing more, figuring she was already deep enough in probable chastisement in the confession booth, where she had to tack on the sin of stealing a few coins from her miserable uncle, and whatever else the Lord might think unseemly about her behavior of the past few days. Besides, the cabbage of the last day and a half still sat like Cain's unwelcome offering in her stomach.

Paloma wasn't sure what she expected of San Pedro, but it was probably not a high wall, with the church's spire peeking over. The gate was still open, but several men in the habit of Franciscans stood there to close it. They had stopped when they heard the post rider.

"It looks like a fortress."

The post rider gave a low laugh. "Señorita, you are now officially on the frontier."

Chapter Eleven

In which Paloma Hears Father Damiano's Confession and Suffers Delusions from Cabbage

BLUSHING FURIOUSLY, ONE of the Franciscan fathers helped Palmona from the saddle. Women had no place in his ecclesiastical world. The post rider dismounted and headed immediately to a short priest with spectacles, a rare sight in New Mexico. The rider did most of the talking, while the priest nodded, then glanced at Paloma. All the while, Trece dashed between her and the post rider, circling around the patient horse, then dashing off again.

Paloma pressed her hand against her middle, longing for a necessary room and regretting each cabbage leaf of the last two days.

I will never eat cabbage again, she told herself.

With a wave, the post rider walked his horse through the gates and out of her sight. The little priest with the spectacles came toward her, a smile on his face.

"I am Father Damiano. And you are—"

"Paloma Vega, Father," she said. She looked down at the yellow dog. "And this is Trece, but I think you already know that."

He nodded, that smile playing around his lips. Paloma knew she had never met a less repentant releaser of someone else's dog.

"My child, I do believe you are an answer to my prayer."

"How would that be, Father Damiano?" she couldn't help asking, even as her stomach rumbled and threatened. "Apparently I have brought back a dog that *you* set free. Now I need to find Don Marco Mondragón and return Trece. Is he here, or has be already left for Valle del Sol?"

"He's in Santa Fe, looking for Trece."

Paloma sighed and turned away, resolved to be through with adventures. She turned back and took a deep breath, which was a mistake, because the lump of cabbage trapped and gurgling somewhere in her insides gave a fearful groan. Plain speaking was required, she decided.

"Father, I have been eating nothing but cabbage for two days and if I don't find a necessary soon, it will be ..."

Without another moment wasted, he took her arm, walked her inside the fortress monastery and pointed to a small door. "For the ladies."

Her face on fire, she hurried through the door.

Relief was a long time coming. "I can't possibly go back and face that priest," she said out loud, after some of the crisis had finally passed. Her stomach still writhed like it was struggling to escape.

Because her only other choice was to remain where she was for the rest of her life, she opened the door and went into the courtyard. To her relief, the courtyard was deserted, except for that one priest, the massive door secured against darkness and raiders. Trece—now on his back, being scratched by that priest—wasn't going anywhere.

Traitor dog. Trece, you could have told me this was some great deception, I, who raised you, she thought, without much rancor because she did understand dogs, and her stomach still hurt.

"Better, my dear?" the priest asked, standing up and trying to reclaim his dignity, even though she had discerned his secret: that he knew where disloyal pups liked to be scratched.

She nodded, too shy to look at him.

"Drink this, little one," he told her. "It will eventually dislodge the residue. Two days of cabbage, eh? I am not that brave." Still not looking at him, Paloma took the small glass he handed her. She sniffed it, and her eyes watered. She would have handed it back, but he was a priest, after all, and she had been raised to obey the men in black and brown. She shuddered, drank and shuddered some more.

"It's not bravery, father, it's hunger," she said bluntly. "Since I am going to Valle del Sol to return a dog and have only a few coins to do it, I have to be frugal. I may be two or three days in getting to such a place as Valle del Sol." She frowned. "But now you tell me he is in Santa Fe? How can I return a dog that *you* released?"

It was the priest's turn to look away, even though Paloma, suspicious now, thought he was merely hiding a grin that threatened to split his face in two. The moment passed and he regarded her with a kindly eye.

"My child, it is at least two weeks to Valle del Sol—a dangerous trip to attempt alone. Señor Mondragón will return from Santa Fe soon, I am certain. At that time, *you* can discuss del Sol with him."

People in adventures do not cry, she reminded herself, as tears began to spill down her cheeks. She turned away and sat herself on the lip of a fountain, much as Marco Mondragón had done in her uncle's courtyard. Just thinking of him made her sob out loud.

In a moment the priest sat beside her. Paloma thought she could swallow the rest of her tears, and she would have, if Father Damiano hadn't put such a comforting arm around her.

"I've left a horrible home to return a dog set free on purpose, and I am sick of cabbage."

He let her cry stormy tears, then, when she'd finished, handed her a handkerchief.

"Don Marco is only in Santa Fe, my dear," he repeated. "He has to return to San Pedro to retrieve his sinful teamsters." He chuckled again. "Now I must confess to *you*. Yes, I let that dog go on purpose with the post rider. I knew Trece would go right to you. My original plan was that Don Marco find you, as well."

"Why, Father?" she asked. She blew her nose hard.

He shrugged. "For those purposes that a man will follow a charming young lady. I may be a priest but I am not dead." He peered at her face. "And he was right about your eyes. They are so blue."

Startled, Paloma opened her mouth to speak then closed it. Better to say nothing. Then she blurted out, "Father, I am only here to return a dog and one thing more." She paused again, because it was brazen. *Go ahead, Paloma*, she told herself. *You will never say it again*. "I … I wanted to see Señor Mondragón's light brown eyes one more time. You know, before he returns to del Sol." She turned away, disappointed. "I suppose my adventure is over."

"My child, I believe your adventure is only beginning. Light brown eyes?" the father asked.

"Surely you've noticed them," she said quickly.

"I have not, my child," Father Damiano replied. "I leave that to a young lady." He gave her a little shake. "But now, do you think you could manage a soup of hominy and pork?"

"Meat?" she asked in surprise.

Maybe she shouldn't have said that. The priest looked away, as though collecting himself.

"A tortilla will do," she amended in haste. "And scraps for Trece, if you please. I really need to lie down after that, but I can wash dishes in the morning."

"I think not," he said gently. "You are a guest within our walls."

The priest stood up and gestured for her to accompany him. In a few minutes she was seated in the kitchen behind a bowl of soup. She waited while

Father Damiano blessed it, then devoted herself to a single-minded effort to empty that bowl of hominy and luscious pork. When the cook, an old servant slow on his feet, added a tortilla, Paloma sighed with pleasure. Trece, at her feet, was eating his own dinner and her stomach was full.

Finally, she pushed the bowl away, eyeing the portion she could not finish with regret. Father Damiano watched her with satisfaction on his own face. "I daren't finish that, since what I just ate is still sitting on top of cabbage." She folded her hands. "Father, I can work in your kitchen."

"You're our guest," he repeated.

"I *must* work. I can't return to Santa Fe. I took some coins from my uncle." Paloma felt her face grow warm. "I should confess that."

"I am inclined to call those coins wages."

She glanced at the priest shyly, waiting for him to speak.

He did finally, after he looked at the cook, who inclined his head and shuffled from the room. "My daughter, do you know what happened to Don Marco's family?"

"Not really."

"He loved Felicia and the twins—two fine sons. He left the hacienda one morning in a hot summer to inspect brands farther to the north. He returned two weeks later to find them dead and buried."

"Poor man," she said simply. "How does a man recover from that?"

The priest stood up and fingered the cross at his belt. "Some men drink, some men whore, and some men disappear inside themselves, which is what Marco Mondragón did. He applied himself to his duties, continued to take care of his cattle, sheep and servants."

"Why has he not remarried? I hear it is a comfortable state for men."

Father Damiano was silent for a long time, walking the length of the kitchen and back, as though trying to rationalize in his mind what he wanted to tell her. She understood his reluctance finally, and cleared her throat.

"Father, this is obviously a matter of the confessional. I should not have asked that question," she said, her voice low.

"Just think about it," he said. "You have a good mind, a shrewd one, if I may."

She did think, running her hands over Trece's warmth, seeing in her mind those light brown eyes and imagining them filled with tears. Her breath went out of her. "Does he think that if he left another wife while he went about his duties, he would return to find her dead? Oh, Father Damiano!"

He said nothing because she knew he couldn't.

"That is unreasonable," she said. "Such a thing might never happen again." She crossed herself. "Or it could. Who of us knows the mind of God?"

"No one."

She thought of her own life, not a long one yet, but a life with joy cut short at the sound of Comanches, an enemy who still rode through her dreams. "I have my own sorrows," she began, and haltingly told the priest who sat beside her about the horrible day when her parents died and she was left in a burning hacienda. She told him of her life in the household of Felix Moreno and her own fears that her life there would never change, making her bitter.

She chose her words carefully. "I do not understand what has happened. I think I just want to return Trece to his new owner. Adventures are not very enjoyable, are they?"

"Perhaps they could be, if shared," the priest said.

Paloma smiled. "Do you know something, Father? I like Señor Mondragón's light brown eyes very well, especially the way they seem to sparkle when he mentions Valle del Sol."

"I hadn't noticed."

"They do. I think that valley must be a wonderful place. I wanted to see it for myself." She frowned then, and set Trece back at her feet. "It is probably just another valley, but I couldn't stay in Santa Fe any longer and not know." She sat up straighter. "I want to find out what life has in store for me, Paloma Vega. Father, what will make Marco Mondragón realize that he can ride away and return to a wife and children?"

"Only the doing of it, and that takes enormous courage."

"I wish him well and hope he learns such a lesson, because he is a brave man. Otherwise," she said softly, "I suppose we must leave the matter in God's hands." She laughed then. "And *not* in the hands of a meddling priest, for that is what you are! Shame on you, Father Damiano."

She had never spoken so plainly before, but she knew she was right. She saw it in the way he threw back his head and laughed.

He sobered immediately, but there was nothing penitent about what he said next. "My dear Paloma Vega, *you* are brave enough for two. I predict that your adventure has only started."

She sat there in silence, feeling the war start up in her stomach between the cabbage and the pork. She pressed her middle. "That's all well enough, Father, but I should never have eaten so much. Excuse me, please."

Paloma hurried back to the women's necessary, staying there an uncomfortable time, red-faced from straining and even more from embarrassment. This was no way to carry out an adventure.

She must have looked shaken when she came into the courtyard again. Father Damiano waited for her with another glass of that vile concoction. She drank it without a word, then gasped, "This must be the worst cure in the world."

"Or the most useless. I haven't decided," he replied. "In the middle of the night, it may require a dash for the necessary. Let me show you a shortcut from your room. Child, I can promise that you will feel better tomorrow, either way."

Trece at their heels, the priest showed her the shortcut, which involved a path through the chapel, empty now, but soon to be full, because the bell was tolling.

"Let me show you to your room," Father Damiano said, leading her down a long hall almost to the end. He opened the door on a cell much the size of her tiny room at her uncle's house, with bed and crucifix. There was a bowl, pitcher and towel in one corner, but she paid the most attention to the brazier warming the room with *piñon* reduced to fragrant coals.

"So nice," she murmured. "Thank you, Father. From the bottom of my heart, thank you."

"Leave your dress outside the door. I believe we can make some improvements."

Paloma nodded, deciding there was no point in being embarrassed. Hadn't he seen her make two scrambles to the necessary? She noticed her small bundle containing her other dress. "I have something to wear tomorrow," she told him. "I left my sandals in the kitchen, but they don't fit anyway."

"I noticed. Sit down, Paloma."

She did as he said, and was moved when he took a cloth from the basin, knelt and wiped her feet. "Blisters. I have a salve for that," was all he said.

"As long as I don't have to drink it," she said, which made him smile.

When he finished, he left the room silently, followed by Trece. "Traitor dog," Paloma said mildly, then yawned. She unbuttoned her dress and stepped out of it. She shed her ragged chemise, too, washing it in the basin and draping it over a stool by the brazier. It would have been immodest to set that outside the door.

She crawled into bed, ready to be cold without Trece, but pleased to find a cloth-covered stone. She stretched out and sighed with pleasure. Maybe that was the strange thing about adventures: one turn and things were horrible, another turn and she had a warm rock at her feet. No telling what tomorrow would bring.

"I *MUST* SEE her for myself, Father."

Paloma opened her eyes. The room was still dark, but she heard voices outside her door. She raised up on one elbow, careful to keep her blanket about her bare shoulders. She rubbed her stomach and winced, still suffering, but not enough to make a dash for the necessary. Besides, there were those voices. It didn't sound like an argument, not really, just one determined voice.

In a few moments, all was silence outside her door, except for receding footsteps. Paloma turned over and made herself comfortable, then sat up again, blinking her eyes in surprise, as the door opened.

"Who … who … who?"

"You sound like an owl, Paloma Vega. Are you all right?"

What a relief. Señor Mondragón stood outlined in the dim candlelight from the hall.

"My stomach aches, but I am well enough," she said, shy and acutely aware that her chemise was drying by the brazier. "You probably shouldn't come any closer, because I am bare."

Foolish girl, she should have known such an admission wasn't calculated to stop a man, even one as honorable as del Sol's brand inspector. He came closer, Trece at his heels now, and sat down on her bed. Unconsciously, she shifted her legs to accommodate him.

"There's blood on those sandals you wore," he whispered. "I saw them in the kitchen."

"They don't fit," she whispered back, wondering why he should concern himself with her footwear. "Father Damiano said he has a salve for me."

What he did next did not surprise her, considering the late hour and his level of concern, which touched her even more than Father Damiano washing her blistered feet. He put his arms around her, his hands warm against her bare back. There wasn't any place on the narrow bed for her arms to go except around him.

His lips were close to her ear. "I hear you are having a trial over cabbages."

She chuckled, reassured now that he meant her no ill. A man intent on asking her about her digestion wasn't planning mischief as a second course.

Or was he? After he left, she thought about what he said, his arms still around her: "If it's any consolation, Paloma Vega, terrible things happen when I eat cooked onions. You'll serve them at your peril."

She wondered at that statement, which assumed so much, but his lips were in her hair then and she found it difficult to process information. She didn't think he kissed her, but her mind was muddled and her stomach was starting to gurgle again.

And then he was gone. When she woke up in the morning, she put it down to a cabbage dream. As she put on her dry chemise and reached for her other dress, Paloma vowed never to touch cabbage again, except in times of famine.

Chapter Twelve

In Which Marco Must Defeat Tradition

THE NEXT MORNING Marco was fingering Paloma Vega's sandals in the monastery kitchen when he heard someone clear her throat. He looked up, a smile on his face. Paloma held out her hand for her sandal. Ah, there it was, that shy glance before the second, unwavering look, almost as though she had to make sure of him before she went farther.

I hope you like what you saw at first glance, he thought. *I'm not a man a woman looks twice at.* Except that Felicia once had; nothing else mattered. Without rising, he held out the sandal, making her come closer.

"I could fix the strap, Paloma. Make it tighter," he said as he handed her both sandals.

"Would you? I've been barefoot for months."

She sat beside him on the bench now, wearing her second dress, which he recognized from her cousin's wedding. She handed back the sandals and sat there with her hands folded in her lap, reminding him forcefully again of his mother, born in Spain, whose parents paid an enormous dowry to his father. She looked at him, her glance shy then straight on, and he realized why. He doubted she spoke to men often.

"I will never eat cabbage again, because I had a strange dream last night."

"Oh?"

"I dreamed you came into my room and embraced me."

"I did. No dream, Paloma. I just wanted to make sure you really were there."

Her face turned rosy at that, and she smiled down at her folded hands.

"I still won't eat cabbage again, unless I'm desperate." She looked at him, her voice more animated. "See here, Señor, you can trust a priest if he tells you a person is present."

He didn't want to come up short in her eyes. "It's a habit of my profession as brand inspector: I have to see with my own eyes. You'd be amazed how many *rancheros* think I believe them when they tell me they have so many cows with a particular brand. They know better now."

"*I* might believe them, if I saw honesty in their eyes," she told him.

"You can tell an honest man by looking in his eyes?" he teased, wondering where this was headed, but enjoying her mild repartee.

"I saw it in yours when you captured Trece for me that first time," she said softly.

She took his breath away. "Thank you," was all he could say.

The kitchen was so quiet. Marco looked around in surprise, wondering where the old cook and his assistant had vanished. He thought they had been in the room when Paloma walked in so quietly on her bare feet. He looked down at her feet, saw the blisters, and remembered himself.

"Father Damiano left a jar of salve here." He picked it up. "Let me put some on your feet."

She could have said no; he was half expecting her to. Instead, she extended one foot and pulled up her dress slightly. He knelt beside her and dabbed on the salve, admiring the trimness of her ankle. She put out the other foot, and he did the same, application and admiration. He sat back on his haunches and looked up at her.

She wore a look he had not seen in years, an expression of quiet certainty that said she actually thought he knew what he was doing. How many times had Felicia given him that same look, even when he was at his blundering worst? She seemed to know he could be better and was willing to wait until he was. That look touched his heart with little healing fingers. He sat on the bench again, more than slightly amazed.

"Tell me something, Paloma. How far did you think Valle del Sol was when you started out from Santa Fe with Trece?"

"A day or two." She stared at her hands again.

"When did you find out how far it was?"

"The cabbage man told me. He said I would be weeks and weeks traveling and that snow was coming soon to the high valleys." She hesitated and then he heard real fear in her voice. "He also mentioned Comanchería."

"Were you not tempted to turn back?" He had to know, because he suspected he was in the company of a woman far braver than any he had ever known.

She gave him another familiar look, the one Felicia used when she wondered if his wits had gone wandering. Maybe all women—amend that to *wives*—had that look in their arsenal, the better to manage stupid men—amend that to *husbands*.

"Turn back? Never! I had your dog that you had bought for an outrageous sum. Don Marco, what on *earth* were you thinking? Besides …" She stopped and frowned at her hands.

"Besides what, Paloma? Better tell me."

"I wanted to see your light brown eyes one more time," she said in a rush. "They're such an interesting color."

And here he thought he knew women. He had been married to a fine one, but he was surprisingly ignorant. This shy girl, so ill-used by those who should have cherished her, was going to give him lessons, every day of his life that remained. He didn't begin to deserve her, but he wanted to try.

"Paloma."

He couldn't think of anything more to say. They sat there silent and he remembered how it had been with Felicia. They had grown up on neighboring haciendas and he had always known she would be his wife. When he was eighteen and a man, he and his father had formally ridden to Hacienda Robles and made an offer for her hand. He didn't even remember asking Felicia if that was what she wanted, because he had always known it was.

Here was Paloma Vega. He wanted her, but this time he knew he had to ask. Or maybe she had already given him his answer by blurting out that she wanted to see his eyes—his honest eyes, according to her. At thirty-one years old, he was floundering for the first time over a woman.

Marco did what any confused man would do: he avoided the issue. Earlier in the kitchen he had overheard Father Damiano tell the cook to prepare eggs and *chorizo* for Paloma Vega. In desperation he glanced at the fireplace, where a small pot hung. He went to it, sighing with relief to see the promised eggs and *chorizo*. Hominy porridge warmed nearby in another iron pot.

"Eggs or hominy?" he asked, grateful that his words didn't emerge in an adolescent squeak.

"Both," she said firmly. "Let me help."

Then she was beside him, her face still red with embarrassment, looking into the pot. She had picked up a plate and bowl from somewhere, and he found a ladle.

"Stop me when you have enough," he said, spooning hominy porridge into the bowl.

"That's enough." She held out the plate and he portioned out eggs and *chorizo*.

She took them to the table and he found tortillas basking under a cloth, moist and fragrant. He took some for her and a few for himself, even though he had eaten earlier with Father Damiano and the abbot. He joined her at the table, sitting next to her.

Paloma crossed herself, prayed and began to eat. She ate steadily and gratefully, which spoke worlds about her lack of regular meals, if ever he had any doubt. Grateful, because she was half smiling as she ate. He thought it was an unconscious gesture, but her hand had curved a little around the plate. Someday, maybe in a year or two, if she still did that, he would have to yank the plate away and see what happened. He chuckled. Probably she would conk him with a spoon.

There was a question in her eyes. He shook his head and kept smiling. "I feel good, Paloma," he said. "That's all."

When she finished, she puffed her cheeks out in a sigh that told him how full she was. "If I keep this up, I won't even fit my one dress."

Good! He wanted to shout. *I know a good dressmaker in del Sol; she's a madwoman, but she can sew. Honestly, I'd rather not be able to span your waist with my hands. You're too thin, Paloma Vega.*

He didn't know what to say, where to begin, and then he remembered her mother's tortoise shell comb. He took it from his doublet and handed it to her, watching her eyes as they softened. She didn't have to say thank you; her eyes said it for her.

Taking a deep breath of his own, he took it back from her and anchored it in her mass of hair. "There now. It's back where it belongs. The Jew told me he was sorry he could not pay you more."

"I could tell it bothered him."

"You looked in his eyes, too?"

She nodded. "I tell you I know how an honest man looks. Even a Jew."

"I saw the same thing, Paloma."

She cocked her head. "Then you lied to me earlier, when you said you told Father Damiano you had to see me asleep. You know *he* is honest. You can look in a *ranchero*'s eyes and know if he is trustworthy. Maybe I should be a *juez de campo*, too."

Paloma was teasing him. He was so delighted, he could have wriggled like a puppy.

"You caught me," he told her. "It's an instinct, isn't it?"

They sat in silence, close together. He took a deep breath. "Paloma Vega, please marry me."

If he had held his breath as long as it took her to answer, he would have dropped dead on the floor. The longer her silence stretched out, the more his heart sank. She looked down at her hands, glanced at him, then returned her gaze to her fingers, that he saw were twisted white.

"I wish I could, Señor Mondragón," she said finally. "Oh, I do."

"Then why not?" he asked, keeping his voice quiet, not wanting her to bolt.

"I have absolutely no dowry. Nothing at all." She looked at him, then away again, addressing the oven across the room. "My … my pride has taken a beating for years, but Señor, I cannot bend that far. I would break. Every good, honest man deserves a dowry, no matter how tiny. And you are better and more honest than most."

Breathe, Marco, breathe, he told himself. *In and out*. "Um, you could give me your mother's comb."

"Señor, you just gave it to *me*."

"What about Trece?"

"He belongs to you."

"He might, but why do I think that if you remain here and Trece goes with me, that he will break loose at the first opportunity and head right back to you?" *I would*, he thought. *Oh, please, Paloma.*

"That is your problem. I have nothing, and I will not shame so fine a gentleman as you with my poverty."

He leaned his back against the table, happy at least that she had not inched away from him. Their shoulders were nearly touching. He moved a fraction closer until they touched, and she did not pull away.

I have to think of something, he told himself. *Before God and all the saints, there must be something.*

He stood up then, thoughtful now where he had been in agony only seconds before. "I need to think about this matter, Paloma," he told her as he headed toward the outside door into the courtyard. He picked up her shoes from the floor. "I'll fix your sandals while I think."

He didn't wait for a reply. She had bowed her head over her hands and her slim shoulders were starting to shake.

Sandals in hand, he put his hands behind his back and walked the length of the porch. He turned a corner, where he came upon Father Damiano and Father Bartolomeo, gazing at him with eager eyes. He shook his head and walked on.

"Stop right there," the abbot ordered. He complied.

"She won't have me, abbot," Marco said. "She had no dowry and she won't shame me. *Dios mio*, why are women so *stubborn*?"

It was probably the question of the ages, and he should have known better than to ask it of two celibate priests. Father Damiano and Father Bartolomeo looked at each other, puzzled. He sighed and continued his circuit of the courtyard. He paused as he passed the kitchen window, glancing in to see Paloma still sitting there, her face in her hands. *Stubborn, stubborn woman*, he thought, and continued his circuit. Felicia was not this stubborn; she did whatever he asked, without question.

He stopped and raised his face to the sky, knowing that if there was any point to this, he had to tuck his beloved wife into his heart and ask her kindly to stay there. It had taken him eight years—eight years!—but today he knew there was room for two wives in his generous heart. He continued his circuit.

Father Damiano and Father Bartolomeo were no longer in sight. He hoped they had retired to the chapel to pray for him and Paloma. He smiled to see Trece come into the courtyard. He whined first at the door to the kitchen, where his mistress sobbed, then came to him, tail between his legs. Marco squatted to rub his ears. "I guess you know a poor second choice when you sniff one, eh, Trece?" he murmured.

He picked up Paloma's sandals and continued, Trece trailing along behind now. Marco halted, his heart in his mouth, when the kitchen door opened. Her face pale, Paloma came toward him, pausing first to pet her dog, who whined and yipped around her, much as Marco, just as miserable, wanted to do.

She came to him next, her hands folded in front of her. "Señor Mondragón, I could cut my hair and sell it. Would that be enough for a dowry?"

He sighed with relief, praising the Lord in his heart. She would never have made such an offer if she hadn't wanted this marriage to happen. But no, he couldn't have her do that, not and be honest with himself. He shook his head.

"No, Paloma. I like your beautiful hair on your head. I noticed late last night that it's even more impressive down around your shoulders. Please don't cut it. Where would you put your mother's comb, if your hair was gone?"

"It will grow," she said, emphasizing each word. "You are stubborn, too." She turned on her heel and left him.

He smiled at her retreating figure, assessing the womanly sway of her hips and finding it entirely to his liking. With enough eggs, *chorizo*, hominy, pork, turkey, venison, beef, mutton, tortillas, and flan on Sundays, he would like that sway even more. He knew that he was close to winning, even though he had not yet solved the problem. She still needed a dowry, something she could give him that was uniquely hers. Something she could point to with pride in the years to come, and know that no other woman could have given her husband what she brought to their marriage. He put her sandals behind his back and walked to the fountain.

He examined her sandals, frowning over the dark brown splotches on the foot bed and the thongs he could tighten easily enough. He could wash off the blood and make them serviceable for a few more leagues. Too bad he knew he would find no women's shoes in a monastery. Staring at Paloma Vega's sandals, taken from a poor box in San Miguel, he could have slapped his head at his own idiocy. He felt the tears start in his eyes again, but not in frustration this time, because he suddenly knew he had won.

He knocked on the door of the kitchen. He thought he heard a mumbled "Enter," but he was coming in anyway. Best to be formal now, because he knew what he wanted. "Señorita Vega, since there is no papa and no go-between, you will have to hear this from me. Kindly give me all your attention."

She looked at him, startled, her eyes wary now, but not so hopeless. She nodded.

He held out her sandals. "I am claiming your sandals as your dowry."

"You have moths in your head."

He was an experienced husband. Her comment was most unloverlike, to be sure, but it was already wifely.

"Not one moth, Paloma, my heart." He glanced at her, gleeful to see the tears start in her eyes at his endearment. Oh, he could do this. "Your sandals. I intend to hang them in my—our—*sala* in Valle del Sol, certainly a little lower than the crucifix, but not much lower, because they mean almost as much to me."

She didn't say anything this time. Her honest eyes were boring into his, seeking for that same honesty he knew was there, but which could only grow more obvious, the longer he was husband to this wife. "Explain yourself, Señor," she said, giving him permission to continue.

"You were willing to walk and walk on bloody feet to return a foolish dog to me to keep my feet warm. You had no idea where del Sol was when you started out, except that it was near Comanchería, a place that terrifies you."

She nodded, her eyes ever so serious.

"You can see the snow coming lower and lower down the mountains, same as me. You had a few coins in your apron and you were going to walk until you dropped, to the most dangerous place in the colony, if you had to, to return a runt."

He sank to his knees then, not because it seemed like a good idea when wooing a stubborn woman, but because his legs would not hold him. "I'm going to look at those sandals every day if I have to, and do my best to be the husband, father, rancher, and *juez* that someone as wonderful, brave and stubborn as you are deserves. Your sandals, Paloma. Give them to me. I never met such a brave woman as you."

She stood up, went to him, took the sandals from his outstretched hand and gave them back to him. "Done, my lord," she said. He staggered to his feet, reaching for her, but she backed away, her hand raised imperiously to hold him off.

As he watched, his mouth open, she lowered herself into the most impressive curtsy he had ever seen, her forehead nearly touching the floor. He had never even imagined such a graceful gesture. It was fit for the king of

Spain, but he was no king of Spain. This magnificent, regal display of humility was for him alone, Marco Mondragón, her promised husband.

She rose out of the curtsy as gracefully as she went into it, holding out her hand to him then throwing herself into his open arms, clutching as much of him as she could gather. He didn't waste time trying to kiss her; he just held her.

Paloma Vega kept him at arm's length then, looking into his eyes, then pulled him close, rose up, and whispered into his ear.

"Mama said I would only have to do that once."

He laughed so hard that she put her hand over his mouth to hush him.

Chapter Thirteen

In Which Marco and Paloma Obey and Sinful Teamsters Are Released from Bondage

PALOMA STAYED IN the kitchen while Marco went in search of Father Damiano and Father Bartolomeo, who by chance—they would never spy—were standing just outside the door. Or perhaps she was overly suspicious; life in the Moreno household could do that to a person.

Quite possibly we have been managed by masters, my dearest, she thought, as Marco, his face a delight to look at, returned so soon.

As she knelt with Marco there in the kitchen to receive a raft of impulsive blessings, she knew there was no calculation in the joy writ large on Father Damiano's face, in particular. And hers obviously. When he helped her to her feet, Marco whispered. "If you smile that big all the time, you might crack your face, my love."

And then it was brass tacks at the kitchen table, where she suspected all important matters would be covered, once she reached Marco's hacienda.

"We want to marry tomorrow morning," Marco said, holding her hand. "Fathers, you know we cannot wait or there will be too much snow and we won't reach del Sol this season. There is no time for banns."

I would wish for a dress, Paloma thought, but knew she would never ask, since there seemed to be a more important matter.

"How old are you?" Marco asked her.

Well, he had to know sometime. "I am just turned eighteen," she said with regret, wincing at how old she knew that sounded.

Her advanced years seemed to shock him not at all. "I am thirty-one," he told her with a shrug. "Paloma, eighteen is *young*."

"Not here," she reminded him, but he wasn't listening. He had turned his attention back to the priest, even as he took her hand under the table and rested it rather high up on his thigh. She pinched him and he moved it lower, but only slightly.

She wasn't listening, either.

"Paloma, Paloma, where's your mind?" Father Bartolomeo was asking gently. "The first obstacle is your status. You are an orphan?"

"It's not the first obstacle, Father," she replied, her voice just as soft. She increased the pressure on Marco's leg. "It's only the last one. I am grateful you cannot imagine my life before …" She glanced at Marco's dear face. "Yes, I am an orphan from El Paso del Rio del Norte."

"Your father?"

She took a deep breath. This would probably startle her almost-husband, but what could she do? It was the truth. "He was the *capitán general* of El Paso."

"*Dios mio*," Marco said under his breath. "Even more shame should be heaped upon your uncle."

"I recall the circumstances," Father Bartolomeo said, after a moment in thought. "The raid in 1772. Not only your hacienda but several others were put to the torch by Comanches." He frowned. "How is it that none of your father's wealth of cattle and land came to you? I doubt the Comanches took all the livestock. Even if they did, the land remains."

"You would have to ask my uncle," she said. "I was eleven. What did I know about land and cattle? Mama …" She faltered, but for the first time she was not alone in terrible memories, not if Marco's pressure on her hand was any indication. She swallowed. "Mama shoved me deep under a bed and I stayed there while … while … everyone died and the hacienda burned." She leaned against his shoulder. "I waited two days under the bed. I was alone when I came out and I walked to El Paso." She looked down at her feet. "I was barefoot then, too." She looked up at the abbot. "Yes, I am an orphan."

Father Bartolomeo nodded, the concern evident in his eyes, and also a sort of lurking humor that warmed Paloma. "I am going to declare you my ward in chancery. I will so attest in a document that will be sent to Santa Fe, where it will make its ponderous way to Mexico City. Maybe in nine months or a year, it will arrive there." He chuckled, glancing at Father Damiano. "Give it at least three months, where the archbishop will countersign and return the document to Santa Fe, another nine months. Depending on the season, it may be a month or two before it arrives back on my desk. Permission granted to marry."

Paloma felt her heart drop to her bare toes. "So long?"

"We're not waiting three years to marry."

She looked at Marco, surprised at his clipped words and decidedly militant tone. *I am now in such good hands*, she thought in relief.

Father Bartolomeo put his hand to his heart. "Señor Mondragón, I would never suggest a three-year wait." He smiled at them both, then wagged his finger at the *juez de campo*. "Marco, Marco, are you forgetting how we do things upriver? Paloma, you have become a distraction to one of my favorite men, if you have made him forget how business is done here. Paloma, are you so certain you want to hitch your wagon to such a *fulano*?"

"I do," she replied, smiling in the *fulano's* direction. "But please: *I* do not understand how business is done here."

She heard the breath go out of her almost-husband. His chuckle was self-deprecating. "I am not a fool, *gracias a dios*." He turned toward her. "Here is what this abbot will do: he will send that document testifying you are his ward in chancery. He will ask permission for you to be married to a handsome fellow from Valle del Sol, who has cattle and sheep and a responsible position on the frontier. That would be me. Widower, landowner, handsome fellow with light brown eyes"—Paloma felt her face flame at that—"and taxpayer."

"And long-winded *fulano*," she teased.

Marco gestured to the conspirator-priests. "Fathers, she already talks to me as though we were married."

Father Bartolomeo picked up the narrative. "Either I or Father Damiano here, an unabashed romantic, will marry you tomorrow morning. When the document allowing permission finally arrives, I daresay you will have a baby or two." He laughed. "Father Damiano, they can both blush—even our widower, landowner and taxpayer. When this outdated document giving permission arrives, I will hold it over my head and say, *Obedezco pero no cumplo*—I obey but I cannot comply ..."

"Because you have already married us years before," Paloma concluded. "That is how business is done here?"

"And has been since 1610, my love," Marco said. "I do the *obedezco*, too, when I get permission regarding some issue of brand inspection that I have already solved and settled years before. If we waited for permission to do anything here on the upper river, there would probably be one lonely bachelor and a cow or two. Maybe a chicken."

Paloma laughed and leaned against Marco again. "This will be a legal wedding?"

"In the eyes of Spain and Holy Church," the abbot told her, "three years from now. In the eyes of God, tomorrow morning, my dear one, and His all-seeing eyes count more."

"*Obedezco*," she said softly. "I obey."

SHE SHOULDN'T HAVE worried about a dress. Once Marco came back from signing a document to send on its way to the archbishop in Mexico City, he took her hand and walked her outside the open gates to the nearby pueblo, where three woman sat sewing.

"After I left your room last night, I picked up that dress you left outside the door," he explained. "Father Damiano told me where to take it this morning. These women have taken it apart and are making you two more dresses. They'll be plain, but they'll be warm. Oh, a cloak, too. Maybe a skirt, if there is time."

"You're good to me," she said simply.

He smiled at her solemn face. "That's how it's done. Didn't your Mama tell you? Once your family—you—paid the dowry, it was my part to furnish clothing."

"Did you do that for Felicia?" she asked, wondering how he would feel about mentioning his dead wife.

The smile he gave her was her answer. It was the relieved smile of someone given permission to bring up a subject dear to him. "I certainly did—dresses, scarves, shoes, cloaks." He stopped. "Do you mind if I mention her now and then?"

Paloma shook her head. "She was your wife and you loved her. I am just happy that you waited all those years for ..." she gave him a smile of her own, "for a yellow dog to warm your feet."

"There will be more dresses and shoes that fit, once we reach del Sol," he told her. "For now, this is the best I can do." He turned his attention to the seamstresses. "Ladies, this is my wife—or she will be, tomorrow."

She blushed. Marco squatted by the women for a moment, speaking to them in a language she did not know. Rising to his feet, he took her arm again. "They'll be done by evening." He leaned closer. "I asked them to make you a chemise or two, as well. Is there anything else you wish, of a personal nature?"

"Shoes," she said. "But that would be impossible on short notice."

"Alas, it is," he agreed, "but I have a solution, if you don't mind wearing moccasins. I'll loan you a pair of socks, as well. You'll be in the wagon for most of the journey, unless you want to share my saddle with me."

"I might like that," she told him shyly.

"I might like that, too," he said, equally shy. "My horse is strong and you don't weigh much."

Paloma thought a moment as they strolled toward the monastery again. "You gave the women of the pueblo my dress this morning, before I had even agreed to anything?"

He nodded, looked away and smiled into some distance she couldn't see. "I did. Should I do my own *obedezco* over that?"

"No. You were right."

IN THE AFTERNOON, Marco went to the fields with Father Damiano to watch his sinful teamsters finish burning the stubble there and preparing the land for a long winter's sleep. Paloma watched him from the rampart of the monastery, amused to see him pitching in to help after a few minutes. His laughter and that of his men drifted toward her on the wind, along with the smell of the burn. She liked what it told her of how he worked with his servants, and it suggested how he would want her to work with his house servants.

"I can do that," she said into the same breeze that blew from the fields. "I will treat no one the way I was treated. Never."

The afternoon before Paloma's wedding provided the first hours of leisure she had known since arriving in her uncle's house years ago. Now it was heaven on earth to kneel and pray in the chapel, and then just sit there on one of the few chairs by the door, contemplating the mystery within. *All those prayers of relief, until I was beginning to think they would never be answered*, she thought. *The Lord's ways are mysterious.*

Marco joined her later in the afternoon, kneeling to pray as she had done. She remained quietly where she was, admiring the set of his capable shoulders. So many burdens had been placed on them. She vowed she would not be another. She went to the front of the chapel and knelt beside him to add her prayers to his. When he finished, he covered her clasped hands with his, and her heart was full.

Dinner was simple fare again. Because she was a woman, she waited until the priests, novices and other men had finished their meal in the refectory. She would have eaten then—heaven knows she was hungry—but she found it pleasant to help the cooks, obviously kin to the women of the pueblo so diligently sewing for her. Even though she did not speak their tongue, in a few minutes they were laughing together as they slapped tortillas and cooked them on the familiar griddle. By the time Marco and Father Damiano joined them in the kitchen, there was a warm pile of tortillas ready.

Marco sat beside her at the table. As she ate wonderful *posole*, thick, red and meaty, and dipped tortillas, Paloma caught him watching her.

"I probably shouldn't eat so much, but it is so good," she told him.

"You should eat more," was his reply as he handed her another tortilla and took one for himself, adding a line of honey and rolling it tight. "I will do my best for you on this journey, but it will be mostly dried meat." He nudged her shoulder. "No cabbage."

She nudged him back. "And no cooked onions for you, eh?"

She finished the *posole*, smiling to see the cook tip a little of it into a bowl for Trece, who kept moving from her feet to Marco's and back again.

Marco cleared his throat and she gave him her attention. "Before I left Santa Fe to find you—"

"Trece?" she asked, interrupting.

"No, to find *you*. I will admit that now," he replied. "Before I left, I went to a favorite official of mine in the governor's palace and asked him to ask his *juez de campo* to discreetly look into your uncle's cattle and land doings." He shrugged. "I don't know if anything will come of it, but I fear you have been greatly wronged and cheated. Whether anyone can prove it remains the question."

Paloma nodded. "Until that time, my sandals will have to suffice for a dowry."

"Any land and cattle of yours can never take the place of what you gave me this morning," he said, his voice firm. "Paloma, I already have land and cattle. What I didn't have was a potent reminder of your kind of courage."

"But you are already a brave man."

"I can be braver," he said simply.

There was nothing she could add to that.

"All I want to achieve with any possible investigation of your uncle is vindication for you." Their shoulders were touching, so she felt his chuckle more than heard it. "And I wouldn't mind shaking him up a little. Such a bad man."

She would have been content to sit beside him all evening, but he had to see to his teamsters, making sure all the panniers were ready for his mules in the morning, and other necessities for the journey prepared. Paloma went down the narrow hall to her room, pleased that Trece had followed her almost-husband to the corral. *Where you will probably be underfoot*, she thought with a smile.

The smile left her face and tears filled her eyes as she opened the door and saw the pile of clothing on her cot. Scarcely believing her good fortune, she went closer, holding up a dark green dress of wool, warm and substantial, and then another in black—the color worn by matrons, which is what she would become tomorrow. She fingered two large aprons of the kind that covered the whole dress, an actual petticoat—she couldn't even remember her last one—and two chemises, delicate and soft.

On the floor was a pair of moccasins and two pairs of black wool socks.

"Those are my socks," Marco said.

She turned around to see him standing in the doorway.

"I can spare them," he told her, in answer to her inquiring look. It appeared he could already read her mind. "I always keep back a lot of spun yarn each year. When we're home, you can knit yourself some socks that fit."

She looked at the moccasins. She sat down on the bed, her legs unable to hold her. “Marco, of all that happened on the day my family died, this one detail I remember most vividly. I hid under that bed and watched moccasins walking back and forth through the room. It seemed like hours. Could I just wear the socks and not the moccasins?”

“They’re Tewa moccasins, my heart, not Comanche. There’s a difference. I want you to wear them because the days are growing colder. When we reach del Sol, I’ll take you to my cobbler.”

“I will wear them, if you will lace them for me,” she said finally.

“Every morning, without fail,” he told her.

He hesitated then. Even in the low light of the room, she saw his uncertainty and gave him room to speak.

“Paloma, ours is a strange sort of union, I think,” he said at last.

She gave him her full attention, thinking back through the years to those moments she watched her mother listen to her father, her hands clasped in front of her. Paloma did the same thing. He must have noticed the gesture because he smiled. Was it familiar to him from his life with Felicia?

“Perhaps we need to get to know each other better. It’s going to be two weeks and more of travel with no privacy. I won’t make any demands on you, such as will be my right, after tomorrow morning. And you have rights, too.”

“I thought I did. Thank you.” She said it with dignity, then changed the moment with a small laugh. “You should know something, though; it’s your right to know, even if it was part of my confession to Father Eusebio in San Miguel.”

“I would never ask to know of anything between you and a priest,” he said quickly but with firmness. “That will never be my right.”

“This might merely interest you then.” She took her own deep breath. “For the first time, I confessed lustful thoughts to him. When I … when you came back to my uncle’s house so drunk, I gave you that cloth and really enjoyed touching the back of your neck.”

Marco smiled. Though he tried to keep his voice serious, he failed utterly, in her opinion. “These are weighty admissions, Paloma. I have my own confession: I made more than a few glances at your ankles. They’re quite fine.”

“No privacy on this journey to del Sol?”

“None whatever. Goodnight, Paloma and God’s blessings on you, even if you are a rascal.”

“So are you.”

He nodded, agreeable to that, closing her door and leaving her free to just sit there and marvel at how her luck had turned after a drought of so many years.

Chapter Fourteen

In Which Travelers Keep Their Feet Warm

As THE TEAMSTERS loaded the mules early next morning, Father Damiano married Paloma Maria Cecilia Vega Moreno, daughter of the former *capitán general* of El Paso del Norte and his Spanish-born wife, to Marco Mondragón Sanchez, rancher, brand inspector and occasional *fulano*. Trece whined outside the chapel door, but even Father Damiano had his limits.

Paloma wore her new green wool dress, and a breathtakingly beautiful white lace mantilla that usually formed part of the religious clothing reserved for Santa Maria herself, who presided in statue form from her special niche in the Lady Chapel. Four times a year, and for special feast days the Mother of the Christ Child received a change of clothing. The abbot thought *Nuestra Señora* would have no problems sharing her mantilla with a pretty bride who possessed nothing much except extraordinary courage, determination and grit, much like Our Lady Herself.

The Tewa women who had made her clothing so quickly insisted upon arranging Paloma's brown hair. When they finished, her hair was woven in an attractive Pueblo pattern, with her mother's tortoise shell comb in place. Our Lady's mantilla finished Paloma's bridal attire, giving her impressive height.

Paloma knew there was little point in searching for a mirror in a monastery, the training ground for future priests and monks. There weren't even any windows with glass in them, so far north. One glance at her almost-husband's face told her everything she needed to know, and it was as good as a mirror.

"I wish your mother could see you," he said, as he held out his arm for her and they walked into the chapel together.

Perhaps she can, if God is merciful, Paloma thought, as they knelt. *I believe He is.*

Intent on this amazing and wholly unexpected thing that was happening to her, Paloma probably would have remained dry-eyed if Marco had not presented her with a ring decorated with tiny blue flowers. As she had waited in his store for the Jew to price her mother's comb, she had admired that very ring. He couldn't have known.

"Forget-me-nots," he whispered, his lips close to her ear, as he slid it onto her finger. The ring was only a little too large. "I'll wrap it with yarn from Mondragón wool, so it will fit better."

While Marco was supervising the final loading of the mules, Paloma changed into the snug bodice made of linen, and the brown wool skirt. She folded the white mantilla carefully, making a sign of the cross with each fold, then carried it back to the Lady Chapel, where she put it in the inlaid chest. She stayed a moment on her knees in the chapel, hands clasped together, grateful.

When she returned to the main hall, Father Damiano was waiting, a dark brown cloak over his arm. He handed it to her. "The ladies of the pueblo finished this last night," he said. "They have another gift, too." He laid a small woven blanket in bright colors across the cloak on her arm. "This is for your first child."

Paloma felt her face grow warm as she caressed the little blanket. "Will you tell them thank you for me?" she asked. "I trust my … my husband has been generous with them."

"And then some," the priest said. He gestured for her to walk beside him.

He was silent for the length of the hall, which gave Paloma time to summon enough courage to look at him.

"Father, what is it you wish to tell me? I know there is something more."

"Only this, my child, and it may prove to be your greatest challenge, as the new wife of Señor Mondragón. He is a brave man and you could not have found a better provider if you had tripped over him in the marketplace."

Paloma smiled at that, already feeling a certain dignity to be the wife of a man who overpaid Tewa Indian women, spent a fortune for the small dog walking beside her now, and worked with his servants.

"I know that already, Father. What else?"

It seemed to her ears that Father Damiano chose his words with unusual care. "You already know his greatest fear."

Paloma nodded. "Poor man. Thank God he found the courage to marry me."

"It took him eight years," Father Damiano told her. "I suspect he did it because he loves you more than he fears death."

She mused over his words as they walked along in silence.

"Father, it may be that I will have to accompany him on his duties, at least until he can assure himself that I am going to live."

"That is what concerns me. It may take time."

"It may. I have the time, if he does," she said, her voice soft.

There was nothing more to say. Priest and bride walked into the courtyard. The late morning sun was warm on her back. She probably would not need her new cloak today. Clouds gathered to the west, but for now, it was enough to enjoy the sun on her face. "Life is made up of small things, Father," she said, closing her eyes and lifting her face to the sun. "I promise you I will take life little by little and encourage the *juez* to do likewise."

"I believe you will, my child," the priest told her. "Kneel and I will bless you, and then you and I had better go to the corral."

Her heart was full as he made a small sign of the cross on her forehead and blessed her to be fruitful and multiply, urging her to fill her husband's heart and life with the joy that had been missing for too long. He blessed her with dignity beyond her years, and added something else that made her smile: "Paloma, may God make you as useful to the *juez de campo* as to your husband and lord."

When he finished, Father Damiano helped her to her feet and kissed her brow. To her further surprise, he pressed his forehead against hers for a brief moment, which brought sudden tears to her eyes. Her own father had done that on the last morning he rode out to the cattle with his sons.

At the sound of firm footsteps she already recognized as her husband's, Paloma looked around. "Tell me something, father, because I suspect a conspiracy. Did the abbot sentence Marco's teamsters to hard labor just to keep them here and give him time?" She leaned close. "They are not such bad men."

"You have a certain instinct," Father Damiano said, impressed, and her heart warmed to the praise. "I believe Marco would do well to rely on your services as a *juez*."

They laughed together, because the idea was fanciful.

Paloma grew serious quickly. "You have always had his best interests at heart, haven't you?"

He nodded. "You are kind not to call us busybodies," he whispered in turn. "Perhaps you are already as wise as your own brand inspector."

"I will be, if he needs me to ride with him until he is easy in his heart," she said simply, then turned her face toward her husband, who stood at the open gate.

Father Damiano took her by the hand and led her to Marco. He placed her hand in her husband's, much as her own father would have done, had he survived the Comanches.

"Take your sweet wife to Valle del Sol, Señor Mondragón," he said most formally. "Bring her back now and then, so we can see with our own eyes that you are treating our daughter well."

Marco inclined his head toward the priest, understanding at once the role Father Damiano had assumed. "I will, most gracious father-in-law," he said. "I will treat your daughter well." He gave her such a protective glance then. "I will keep her safe."

TEAMSTERS, HORSES, MULES and wagons, the caravan of Marco Mondragón traveled into an autumn afternoon still warm in that teasing way of changeable weather. As he rode beside the wagon where Paloma sat, he admired her arms bare from the elbow down, visible in the half sleeve of her linen basque. He thought of the milk cows on his ranch and the cream and butter. He would make a pact with his cook that they begin a campaign to put more flesh on those handsome bones.

The idea made him warm in that area of his body that had seldom been exercised of late. He touched spurs to his horse and rode toward the head of the procession, turning his thoughts to more mundane topics than his wife's handsome bones. Hadn't he so much as promised her that he would not expect any marital exertions until they knew each other better? *Marco, sometimes you are a fool,* he thought mildly. *She did say she lusted after you, and then you had to get so righteous. Meh.*

He smiled to hear her laughter down the line. He had asked his *mayordomo* to sit with Paloma on the wide wagon seat, mainly because the old man who had served his own father so well would answer any questions she had about the ranch. Also, from the way he was stumping around this morning, Andrés' rheumatism was signaling a change in the weather, and the wagon would be more comfortable

Marco glanced back at his new wife, who smiled at him before returning her attention to Andrés, talkative old fellow. It pleased him to know that his wife would be easy with the house servants and work alongside them, much as he did with his field servants.

He stopped the caravan an hour later at a copse of *piñon* pine and underbrush. It was a good place to relieve themselves. He helped Paloma from the wagon and whispered to her to go into the brush for her private needs. The teamsters, eyes to the front, went to the other side of the wagons to do their business. He wished he could have given Paloma more privacy, but that was the journey.

He knew she would never say anything, but Marco thought she might be hungry. When she returned, brushing down her dress, he handed her two apples from the food wagon. She accepted with no hesitation.

"Just tell me when you are hungry," he said.

Her face clouded over. "I am always hungry. Sometimes I wonder if I will ever be full," she told him.

"Then you should say something, my heart."

She shook her head. "I am not used to asking for things."

He picked her up and lifted her into the wagon, holding her close for a moment to whisper in her ear, "Ask for whatever you want from now on, wife."

She surprised him by kissing his cheek quickly before she grasped the wagon seat and pulled herself onto it.

Pleased, he went back to the wagon for a strip of *carne seca*. "Chew on this, too, then," he told her, touched at the light in her eyes.

The clouds finally reached them as they rode steadily into the afternoon, bringing cooler, and then chilly air. "Autumn is here," he said out loud to himself, looking back at his wife, who was rubbing her arms. He rode back to her wagon, gesturing to the young driver sitting next to Andrés to stop.

"Better get your cloak, Paloma," he told her. "It's going to blow soon, and maybe snow."

She did as he said, crawling nimbly inside the wagon, now that it was stopped. With as few possessions as she owned, it took no time to find her new cloak.

It was snowing in earnest when they stopped for the night. Paloma had hunched herself into a compact figure, hood up, arms tucked inside her cloak now, her face serious, maybe because her jaw was clenched against the chill.

Despite the snow, his servants built a fire. Paloma stood before it a long time, careful not to get too close, but her face reflected her enjoyment of the warmth. His journey cook, another old retainer of his father's, produced a pot of beans from the other wagon and a stack of monastery-made tortillas. After a short while, the beans bubbled and the tortillas regained their moist warmth. More *carne seca* completed the meal, rounded off with apples.

Sitting next to his wife, Marco watched her eat. He enjoyed the gusto with which she sopped up all the bean juice in her earthenware bowl and chased each black bean around until the bowl was empty.

"More?" he asked.

She nodded, still shy about food. "Just another tortilla."

"With honey?"

She nodded again, leaning against his shoulder as she watched him dribble honey onto two tortillas and roll them tight, handing her one and eating the other himself. Her sigh of satisfaction went right to his heart. Still she leaned against him, shivering until he put his arm around her and then his cloak, too. In a few minutes she relaxed. He thought she slept, shivering now and then.

"Andrés, do you think we will be able to continue our journey in the morning?" he asked, keeping his voice low so Paloma would not hear.

"If God is merciful," the Indian said, smiling at Paloma in the way he probably smiled at his grandchildren. "This one does not complain."

"I doubt she ever will."

"Then you are a lucky man."

I am lucky, he thought later, as he helped Paloma, half asleep, into the tight space in the wagon between the apple keg, cornmeal and rough wooden box containing her precious clothes. He tucked a pillow under her head and covered her with a blanket. When they had stopped for the noon meal that day, he had been amused to see her inside the wagon with the box open, just looking at the clothes he had paid the Tewa women to sew, touching the fabric.

"You'll be warm enough here," he told her. The snow was falling heavier now, the wet snow of autumn that sometimes broke the branches of trees that had not yet discarded all their leaves. It would be followed in the weeks ahead by dry snow that squeaked underfoot in the deep cold.

"Will you … is there room for you?" she asked.

"I'll sleep under the wagon," he told her. "May I keep Trece tonight for my feet?"

"Certainly you may. I could move some boxes in here—"

"No need, Paloma."

He could tell she was not happy with him. Her face was close to his, so close he wanted mightily to kiss her. Why had he said he would not rush things? Could a man be too nice?

"Your men will think there is something wrong if you are not in the wagon with me," she whispered, her breath tickling his ear and sending shivers of a different kind down his spine.

"I never worry about what my men think," he assured her. "Let's allow ourselves time. Good night, Paloma."

She sighed and lay down, tugging the blanket high on her shoulders.

Marco walked around the diminishing fire, throwing on more scraps of wood. He saw that his men had made brush shelters, where they slept, two and three close together, absorbing one another's warmth. He lay down under the wagon, his blanket doubled and Trece at his feet, just as he had hoped would happen when he bought the yellow runt in Santa Fe. After a few minutes of feeling sorry for himself, he closed his eyes and slept. He was used to cold and hard ground and snow.

He was sleeping soundly, wrapped tight against the cold, when Paloma shook his shoulder. He sat up, alert, his head just brushing the underside of the wagon. He knew it was her without seeing her, because her hand went to his shoulder in such a gentle way.

"Are you all right?"

She shook with cold. "I've never been so cold in my life," she whispered, looking around to make sure no one else was awake. "How do you stand it?"

Maybe he *was* a fool. Paloma Vega had so little body fat that it was no wonder she shivered and shook. *Well, that's it*, he thought, crawling out from under the wagon and shaking out a startled Trece. He took Trece to the nearest brush shelter. "Here, Andrés," he whispered. "Have a dog tonight." He heard his *mayordomo's* low laugh.

Wrapping his blanket around him, Marco helped Paloma back into the wagon and followed after. He shifted the kegs and boxes until he had created space just large enough for two.

"Lie down, Paloma," he whispered. "I'll spread both blankets on top of us."

Her hair was long and soft and smelled of *piñon* pine, a favorite odor, part of his life since birth. But it was more than the fragrance of *piñon*. He breathed deep of her woman's odor, so much more pleasant than a man's smell. She shivered as he put both arms around her and pulled her close. Still she shivered, which began to worry him. He had seen men shiver like that until they died of cold. He pulled her tight against his chest and gradually he felt her relax as his warmth penetrated the core of her body.

Marco slept for several hours, waking up as the night sky seemed to lighten because of the falling snow. All was silent in the clearing as the snow piled deeper. It was the kind of night that always filled him with contentment when he was sitting in his *sala* by his own fire, his feet up. Strangely, he felt some of that same contentment. Maybe it was the fact that someone needed him again. Whatever it was, he enjoyed the feeling.

As he watched Paloma, she woke up. She looked at him, saying nothing for a long moment.

"How strange this is, but I am too warm now," she told him, her eyes on his. "I will take off my dress."

She removed it quickly, raising up and letting in the cold air, then covering herself again and moving back into his arms.

He was warm, too. It was a moment's work to remove his doublet, linen shirt and his leather pants, then pull the blankets over them again.

"There now," he said. "Go to sleep, Paloma."

Her skin was soft and he had trouble relaxing, until the gentle rise and fall of her shoulders let him know she was asleep again.

It didn't last long. "I am even warmer," she whispered. She removed her chemise and cuddled close, naked.

No fool, he kissed her. Her arms went around his neck and she returned his kiss. She was no expert, but neither was he, not after eight years on a fallow field. The rest of his clothes came off, Paloma helping.

"We weren't going to do this so soon," he whispered in her ear as his hands roamed over her body. They lingered a moment on her ribs, then moved to her hips, with their better padding.

"That was your idea. I want you," was her answer as she began her own tentative exploration of what, besides whiskers and a deep voice, made him different from her. She had a delicate touch and took her time as his breath came faster.

He concentrated on the soft hair between her legs finally, pleased as she began to murmur and move a little. She was warm all over, no longer the shivering woman who had requested his presence in the wagon to take away the midnight chill.

A tentative exploration of his own assured him that his wife was quite ready and decidedly willing. It may not have been the marriage bed of any bride's dreams, but he already knew Paloma Vega was a woman who expected little. Only think how pleased she would be in a few weeks to keep herself warm—and him, too—in his bed at the Double Cross, with its mattress of clean wool and its soft sheets and Indian blankets.

As he entered her to no complaint beyond a slight hesitation followed by a soft exhalation of breath, the last callus seemed to fall away from his heart. His wife's legs wrapped tightly around him, Marco took his pleasure as the snow fell on the canvas top of the wagon and the stars and planets continued their own movements across the night sky.

In the course of the universe, nothing had changed, Marco thought a few minutes later, as Paloma, truly his wife now, lay relaxed beside him. God was good to him again.

Paloma said nothing, but Marco felt her eyelids moving against his bare arm, so he knew she did not sleep yet. He smiled in the dark at the fluttering sensation.

"Wife, could you train that expensive dog I bought to sleep on a pallet beside our bed?" he asked, tracing the contour of her breast.

"I can," she replied, and he heard the humor in her voice. "Trece was no bargain, was he, if he does not warm your feet."

"I never made a better purchase, Paloma Vega," he assured her.

His eyes were closing when Paloma cleared her throat.

"Hmm?"

"I have seen your brand on … on—"

"Buciro, my horse?"

"Yes. Two crosses and an M?"

He nodded. "The M is for Mondragón, of course. One cross is for my grandfather, and one for my father."

"Will you add another someday to represent you?"

"I might, but two is enough. Everyone in Valle calls my hacienda The Double Cross, so I do, too. Is two enough?"

Silence. He smiled.

Chapter Fifteen

In Which Paloma Is Worn Out by Adventure Again

"YOU TOLD ME only yesterday that I could ask for whatever I wanted," Paloma whispered in her husband's ear at that time of early morning when the sun was gearing itself for another day. "I want you again."

Without a word, Marco obliged her. Now that she had some idea what was going on, Paloma gave herself to the sensation with more pleasure, enjoying the rhythm of love. When her husband moaned and pressed his face into her bare shoulder to silence himself, she kissed his sweaty hair. She wanted him to continue, but she was too shy to ask. It would keep. Obviously lovemaking was something Marco Mondragón was inclined to want from her, so the future looked rosy, since she found it pleasant, too.

"I'm heavy," he whispered finally, rolling off of her. "And look, it is light now."

"The better to see you with," Paloma whispered back as he sat up, naked and peaceful, leaning against the apple keg in the crowded space. She admired the beauty of his body, well-muscled and strong, the body of a man who worked hard.

Only weeks before the Comanches had come, Paloma sat in the middle of the little apple orchard, daydreaming. Her mother assured her there would be a husband for her, someone noble and kind and capable, much like her father. She had dreamed about such a husband then. Fourteen was the age of marriage in New Mexico, and she was just three years away from that. After the Comanches destroyed her family, she tucked that memory away in her heart, knowing she should probably never seek it out again.

Her eyes filled with tears, looking at her sudden husband, sitting there naked, his long legs propped up in the tight space, a smile on his face that she could only call satisfied. Her wounded heart began to heal as she realized she had put that smile there.

"Why tears, my heart?" he asked simply.

She told him about the apple tree and her dreams she had lost, only to find them again. "Mama said I would find a capable man," she said after a long struggle. "I will love you all my days, Señor."

She could tell she had touched him. "Of that I have no doubt," he said, after his own struggle. He reached for her again. "Come here."

She did as he asked, pulling one of the blankets with her to sit in his lap. Shivering, she wrapped the blanket around them. Paloma listened as the beating of his generous heart returned to normal and closed her eyes, content. "I intend to be a credit to you, Señor," she told him.

"Marco," he reminded her, kissing her own sweaty hair. "Let us not be formal, what with us bare, goose bumps on my rump and me leaning against an apple keg. Probably getting splinters."

She giggled. "We don't even need a yellow dog."

They laughed together—a quiet, personal laugh reminding her of her own parents. They had often laughed like that over something she had no part in. It had puzzled her at the time, but now she recognized it as the intimate laughter of lovers. She told Marco, who just nodded, a slight smile on his face.

"It's been a while for me," he told her simply.

She burrowed closer and kissed him. Her eyes closed and she slept again.

She woke soon enough as he heard him sigh, "Paloma, that rump of mine is really cold. Let's get up."

She stifled her laughter because she smelled a cooking fire now. The others were up and moving about. She shifted enough to peer through a small gap in the canvas, which gave that husband with the cold rump a good excuse to take a delicate nibble of her own posterior. Startled, Paloma gasped aloud, which made him laugh. The teamsters looked in the direction of their wagon and she felt her face flame.

With as much dignity as she could muster, she wrapped the blanket around herself. "You are disgraceful," she whispered, looking into his merry eyes. "Now I will never be able to leave this wagon."

He dressed quickly, his breath leaving little puffs in the air. "Too bad for you, Paloma. It's a long way to my valley. I doubt a whole barrel of nothing but apples will be much better than a wagon of cabbage."

Marco left the wagon. In a few minutes, she peered through the canvas gap again, smiling to herself as he stood with his men, warming his hands around a silver cup that suddenly looked so inviting.

Oh well, oh well, she thought as she dressed.

She climbed out of the wagon with what she hoped was at least a shred of dignity. After dealing with personal business, she joined the circle and accepted the earthenware cup the cook handed to her, his eyes lively.

Might as well leap into it. "Why on earth do you work for this disgraceful, rude rancher?" she asked no one in particular, then took a sip.

It pleased her to no end when Marco, in the act of drinking, suddenly spit out the hot liquid. Eyes merry, he wiped his mouth while his teamsters laughed. The cook stirred the beans, singing a little song. And there was traitorous Trece, going first to her husband for a pat before coming to her.

"Paloma, you'll do," Marco said. He went to his own mount, leaving her standing by the fire with Andrés.

The *mayordomo* picked up Trece. "He can stay with me at night," Andrés said. He gave Paloma a slight nod, which had in it deference and something more. "Señora, you cannot know how long it has been since any of us have heard the master laugh that way. We love him, too."

He said it simply and she understood. Paloma, freed from embarrassment, chose her words carefully. "I will be welcome in his hacienda?"

"You already are, Señora."

WITHOUT ASKING, PALOMA took her turn gathering twigs and tending the fire at each of their camps on the long journey from middle desert floor to breathtaking mountain passes. She brought water to the horses without being asked and took over the bean pot on those days when the old cook was too crippled by the cold and snow to do more than lie in the food wagon and groan. Soon she was slapping out her own tortillas, which truly were better than his. When Andrés shot a deer, she took her turn with the cleaning, then did amazing things with a roast, apples, onions and sage found along the trail. She especially reveled in the admiration in the teamsters' eyes as they ate. They were hard workers, too, and obviously not immune to what began to resemble cuisine on a journey that probably hadn't ever featured such a concept before. She began to wish for chocolate to make a memorable *mole*, but there was none.

"It may be that you will have to come on *all* my brand inspection trips," her husband told her one evening as they all huddled close to the campfire, shoulder to shoulder, and ate. "We are coming home better fed than usual."

"You know I am not a woman to stand idly by," she reminded him. "I will be happy to come on all your inspections."

She absorbed the relief in his eyes, mindful of what Father Damino had told her. "However long you might need me to do that," she said for his ears alone.

He swallowed several times at her soft words, and she found sagebrush across the road suddenly fascinating. So fascinating, in fact, that she left the fire and gathered sage into her apron. When she returned to the fire, her husband was himself again.

Paloma refused to be embarrassed when Marco shifted things around in her wagon, moving the apples into another, and the bigger boxes elsewhere, too, to make room for them both. In their nest of blankets they were almost comfortable, especially when she found herself more and more in a warm embrace.

She was hard put to maintain her own silence on the night when she was practiced enough in lovemaking to understand what pleasure really meant. Her husband's sigh of satisfaction was ample reward.

"Now you know, wife," he said, pulling her into what had become her favorite place, nestled close with her head resting on his chest and one leg thrown over him.

She nodded, pleased with her body, but, womanlike, not totally. "I wish I weren't so thin."

"That will change, when we reach my hacienda," he said, his lips on her hair. "Do you like pork or beef better? What about eggs and cream?"

"Oh, stop!" she whispered, poking him in an area she already knew was sensitive. "I like it all. You'll turn me into a fat woman."

"There are no fat women in my valley," he replied. "We all work too hard for that. You'll just turn into a woman with curves here and there, and I'll have to watch my back when my neighbors become envious."

They chuckled together over that, Paloma because she knew he was crazy, and her husband—maybe because he knew he was, too. How would she be sure? She hadn't met his neighbors yet.

Whenever they were both sufficiently awake, Paloma relished the moments when Marco talked to her of his hacienda, his servants, the church, and the wide valley, approached through narrow canyons. He spoke with such love for his home that she knew she would love it, too, even if for no more reason than he loved it.

"You call it 'your valley.' Why is that?" she asked one night.

"It is my valley," he said simply. "After the Reconquista in 1692, the Mondragóns started moving north and east, always on the frontier, but not through the mountain passes yet. My great grandfather was given a land grant to claim that land on the edge of Comanchería for Spain."

"The valley is a buffer between the Comanches and the rest of New Mexico?" she asked, her eyes closing in marital satisfaction.

"We are." He kissed her breast. "Not a place for the timid."

He told her of José, the rag picker, who carried himself like a *hidalgo*—a nobleman's son—and Erlinda Grande, who was the valley matchmaker. "I have seen enough of her," he whispered one night. "She might be disappointed in you, at first, because you weren't part of her plan for me. It won't last long, if you fix her a stew like the one tonight."

"They will know I am poor," she said another night, before they slept.

"There was nothing about you in Santa Fe that ever said *poor* to me," he told her. "The way you comport yourself, your hands clasped in front of you, your head high. You never were poor, my heart, only a little down on your luck for a while." He kissed her. "Your luck has changed."

After more days of travel, slower now, through the cold and increasing snow, she wondered about her luck, only until Marco woke and smiled at her. Or perhaps it was the day he picked her up to put her behind him as she tried to cross in front to the fire. His "Be more careful, *chiquita*," was a caress more than a warning.

His kindhearted regard gave her confidence to ask one night, after lovemaking, "Tell me about the Indians."

Her husband must have understood the offhand way she tried to ask. He gripped her shoulder tighter and spoke softly in her ear, as though soothing a child with bad dreams. "Let me tell you about them." He put his leg over her this time. Maybe it was an unconscious gesture of protection. Whatever it was, it eased her heart. "Not too heavy? No? It is this way, Paloma, my own dove: there are Comanches, and I fear them. So much that I am extremely careful." He caressed her shoulder. "There was one *ranchero*, a friend of my father, who declared that he feared not even the Comanches. He no longer lives in our valley, or any valley, for that matter." He kissed her shoulder. "You already know what Comanches can do."

She nodded. He ran his hand along her hip next. "There are also Navajo. Some say they are Apache, too, and their language has its similarities. I am wary around them, but I have known some fine ones. My orchard man is part Navajo, and we argue about peaches." He chuckled and kissed her hair. "He brings me good ones. And there are Ute Indians to the north. I know their language, and I think I know them, for the most part. We exist together."

"That's a lot of Indians," Paloma the dove said. "More?"

"Of course. All of my servants except my sheepherder are some part Tewa or other Pueblo." His voice took on a softer tone. "Felicia was part Tewa, which is why I speak that language well enough to joke and argue in it. I trust them with everything I have."

Including your heart, she thought. *It must be a generous heart, because I think—I know—there is room for me, too.*

"It's like this, Paloma: let me tell you a little *dicho*. There was once a man who built a rope bridge across a high gorge. His neighbors thought he was crazy. It was a small gorge, as gorges go, but he took several years, twining the best rope made from the strongest hemp. He took the time to make friends with a Ute ropemaker, and learned everything he could. One of his soldiers had worked for the royal engineers of Spain, and he was put in charge of the bridge. When it was done, the man tested it for a month and longer, gradually adding weight." He chuckled. "He still uses that bridge today. Some say it is dangerous, and I say yes, it is. But there is this: everyone who uses that route—I, among them—is very, very careful."

"I do understand."

"I rather thought you would."

"Sometimes a healthy fear makes a dangerous road safe."

"It does. And so I maintain a healthy fear around Indians. And so should you."

"Will I know who to trust?" she asked, her eyes closed now.

"You already do. You have a discerning heart."

ON ANOTHER NIGHT, when the wind howled and the snow blew sideways, Paloma shivered in the wagon until her husband arrived, snow-covered and cold, himself.

"We've pulled the wagons close together and put the animals inside," he told her. "We may be here a few days, so the men have built more substantial shelters of branches and brush." He peered close at her in the failing light. "You are not to worry! There is food enough and we will be warm."

"Trece?" she asked, her teeth chattering.

He laughed and touched the frown between her eyes. "He's already at the bottom of Andrés' blanket roll." He pulled out an earthenware bowl wrapped in a scrap of blanket. "And here are beans, tortillas and the rest of the venison. We'll be careful of our food to make it last."

Paloma ate quickly, wishing it were more. He must have seen the longing for more food in her eyes, because there was a sudden shadow on his own face. "It will be better soon, *chiquita*," he said. "One more mountain pass will see us to the valley and my sister's hacienda."

"I don't mean to complain—" she began.

"And you haven't," he finished. He put his cloak around her as she shook. "We may have lost four days in San Pedro, but you and I needed those days, and we can't overlook my sinful teamsters." He kissed her ear. "Besides, I can guarantee that those two busybodies in San Pedro are praying for our safe journey."

Paloma smiled because she knew he wanted her to, and it was easier, as his warmth became her warmth. Her eyes closed and she yawned. "I learned a long time ago that if I go to sleep, then I'm not hungry."

It was a casual reality to her, so she was sorry to see such dismay in his eyes. "Oh, please! I didn't mean to upset you," she said in real distress.

He set his lips in a firm line and hugged her closer. After a few silent minutes, she felt his chuckle. "Poor Paloma. You sit in a cold mountain pass because you listened to a smooth-talking man in a monastery kitchen—"

"Father Damiano or Father Bartolomeo?" she asked, because his chuckle was contagious.

He shouted with laughter then, which brought a chorus of groans from his teamsters in their crude shelters and only made him laugh harder. "They envy me," he whispered to her.

"No. They think your wits have gone wandering," she said. "I am sorry to have to break the bad news to you."

THEY WERE TWO days in the last pass to Valle del Sol, waiting out another storm. Paloma gathered sticks whenever the wind uncovered them. She kept her eyes on the high mountains around them in the narrow pass, impressed with their cold beauty. Inside her Tewa moccasins, she wore two pairs of Marco's stockings. Even then, the cold seeped through and she spent most of her time in the wagon, happy enough to listen to stories about Luisa Maria Mondragón Gutierrez, her sister-in-law, and about Marco's childhood on the hacienda in a beautiful valley three-sided by mountains, with a long view of the rising sun to the eastern plains.

Clasped in her husband's arms, she closed her eyes as he described his hacienda, his servants, his animals, and his duties as *juez de campo*. She dozed more than she listened, because the cold was working on her thin body in ways that pained her husband almost more than it pained her—she was used to privation. She couldn't get warm and she found herself unable to stay awake.

Embarrassed, she protested when he called Andrés into the wagon one particularly cold night to sleep with them, sandwiching her between both men. Trece came, too, whimpering and licking her cold face. As much as she cried with shame, Paloma gradually warmed until her continuous shivers stopped. She slept more peacefully then, no longer plagued by the cold.

When she woke the third morning, the snow had stopped, along with the wind that had laid much of the pass bare.

"Early snows are like that," Marco said, as he rubbed her legs with warm hands and handed her a cup of soup. The meat was unfamiliar. "One of my men trapped a rabbit, so here you are."

"I doubt you pay him enough," she murmured, pleased to see the way her harmless banter made his light brown eyes brighten because she felt restored enough to tease.

"I doubt it, too. Listen to the melting today, *chiquita*. Tomorrow the wind will blow warm again from the south and we will be on our way. That is how it is, on the eastern slope of the Sangre de Cristos. Real winter hasn't even arrived yet."

He watched her drink the soup and handed her a knife to spear the meat. "And when winter does arrive, you will be warm and well-fed in my hacienda. As simple as that."

In the morning, the snow had melted enough to allow a narrow passage one horse wide. Marco helped her put on both of her dresses and the brown wool skirt, and wrapped her in her cloak. He mounted his horse and Andrés handed her up to him.

"We'll ride ahead with four riflemen," he told her.

"The wagons? The others?" she asked, looking around, worried.

"Two more days will see the pass open wide, and they will follow," he told her as he spoke to his horse and they started up the trail. "I want you at my sister's hacienda tonight."

"I'm trouble for you," she exclaimed, dismayed.

"I hadn't noticed."

BY RIDING STEADILY, they arrived at Hacienda Gutierrez in late afternoon. The higher they climbed, the colder the weather, even though the sun was out now and the sky the blue of the Virgin's cloak. She bore what she could, then tried to sleep away the afternoon. To her irritation—she told him what she thought—her husband made every effort to keep her awake and talking. As it was, she was half dozing when Marco spoke to his horse and they stopped as gates opened and then closed behind them.

In a few minutes, and after whispered words that she couldn't quite make out, she found herself in a warm room. She sniffed and sighed with satisfaction—a *piñon* fire. Maybe they had returned to San Pedro, but that couldn't be.

There were more whispered words, first from her husband, his voice so familiar now, followed by a gasp, more words and then the low, companionable laughter of two who knew each other well. She struggled to open her eyes, then gave up.

Chapter Sixteen

In Which Paloma Meets Kinder Relatives

WHEN PALOMA OPENED her eyes again it was early evening. She looked first at Marco, sitting on her bed, then his sister in the chair beside him. She looked back and forth again and smiled, which relieved Marco's mind. "You both have light brown eyes."

"We do, indeed," his sister said. "My dear, are you warm enough?"

"Not quite," Paloma said, her eyes on Marco again. "I will be, when your brother comes to bed."

It was simply said, and it warmed his heart. He ran his hand down her arm, enjoying the feel of her almost as much as if he had never done that to another woman. "Paloma, this is my sister, Luisa Maria, the widow Gutierrez."

Paloma reached out to the woman seated so close to the bed, no words spoken. Luisa leaned closer and took the proffered hand.

Funny that he should want his sister's approval of his rash act. She was three years older than he, and her opinion still mattered to him, even after all these years. It touched his heart when Paloma raised herself up on one elbow, leaned closer, and kissed Luisa's hand in the manner of a dutiful child.

The gesture was as perfect as Paloma's beautiful curtsy to him in the kitchen at San Pedro. His heart softened even more as Paloma rested her cheek against Luisa's hand and closed her eyes. The exhaustion on her face told him volumes about the limit to her strength, she who had been starved in Santa Fe for years, then dragged through cold mountain passes. His heart beat a little faster to think what would have happened to her, if she had truly tried to walk from Santa Fe to Valle del Sol. And he knew she would have tried.

Until his vision cleared, he had to focus on the wooden figure of San Isidro, patron saint of farmers, watching these proceedings from his corner niche.

"Are you hungry?" Luisa asked, her voice softer and more tender than Marco had heard in years, considering that she and her sons ran a *rancho* almost the size of his own and had no more time for frills than he did. That she was still a woman, he had no doubt. Too bad that Ramon Gutierrez had blundered just once with Comanches. All it took was once.

"I am hungry," Paloma replied. She closed her eyes again.

Luisa smoothed the blanket on Paloma's shoulder. "I will remedy that." His sister looked at him. "Don't be a blockhead, Marco. Get in bed with her. She's cold."

He chuckled as she left the room. "I never get any respect from my sister," he told his wife, as he took off his boots. His doublet and trousers came next. Paloma held up the covers and he slid in beside her, happy to hold her in his arms and know that she did not have to spend another night outdoors, shivering.

She came into his arms so naturally, pillowing her head on his arm, that he felt she had been there beside him forever. Testing his luck, he sang a Tewa lullaby to her that he remembered from Felicia. It made her smile and nestle closer. Funny how a song he had not even dared to think of in years could finally close a yawning chasm in his heart.

He was nearly asleep, too, when Luisa returned with lamb stew and bread so fresh that he salivated. The kitchen odors must have roused Paloma, because she stirred in his arms.

"Eat, you two," Luisa said, setting the tray by the bed. "Make yourself useful, brother. Paloma, when you're done, would you like a bath?"

"Oh, I would," his wife said, as she sat up beside him. "Just show me where the buckets are and I'll haul the water."

"Not in my house," Luisa said with some of that starchy firmness more familiar to Marco than her softer side. "You are a guest here and the wife of my favorite brother."

"Her only brother," he pointed out, just before the door closed, so he heard Luisa's laugh. After a blessing on the food—the perfunctory kind because he trusted the Almighty understood that his wife was hungry—he handed Paloma a bowl and a spoon.

She ate with her already familiar economy, not wasting a drop. "*Oh, dios*," was all she said, leaning against his arm while she ate in bed. He divided his hunk of bread and she took it without a word.

As they were finishing, he heard a knock.

"Come," he said.

The door opened on two servants with a tin tub, which they set in front of the fireplace without a word. Back and forth they went, and others, too, until the tub was full. Luisa followed with towels and soap, which she placed beside the tub.

"I will leave you to it," she said. She laid a nightgown across the foot of the bed, put her fingers to her lips, kissed them and blew the kiss to Paloma, which made her sigh.

He took off his wife's clothes and helped her into the tub. The water was just right and she sat down with another sigh. He washed her hair, then her body, until she took the cloth from him for her intimate parts.

As much as the exercise aroused him, it also saddened him to feel and see her ribs. There were even scars on her back he had not noticed in the half-light of the wagon. Some looked recent. His heart hardened against the Morenos.

"How did you get these, my heart?" he asked.

"Tia Moreno doesn't—didn't—have a lot of patience when I brushed her hair," she said simply. "And you remember how my cousin was so unsatisfied with all of us, right before the wedding."

She gave him such a look then—pride and humor, mingled with love. "Thank God you cannot tack these scars next to my sandals in your—"

"Our—"

"*Sala*."

He helped her dry off. Felicia had never let him help her that way, even though he had wanted to, but Paloma didn't seem to mind. After she pulled on the nightgown Luisa had left—too large and leaving one bare shoulder exposed—she sat on the end of the bed and handed him the comb.

Felicia had always taken care of her own hair. He was new at this, and it humbled him how generously Paloma turned herself over to him. Her surrender did not make her weak in his eyes, because he already knew her mettle. He began tentatively to comb out her tangles, then, after a few minutes of silence, found himself humming. By the time her brown hair was straight and tangle-free, he was as mellow as a man could be. How did Paloma know such a simple thing would relax him, too?

As if reading his mind once again, she said, "I remember my father doing this for my mother and for me." Her voice was dreamy, content.

"My heart, I wonder if he enjoyed it as much as I do," he told his wife, his lips close to her ear.

She laughed, a soft sound meant to go no farther than the two of them, just as his words were intended only for her ears. How was it that a young woman cut loose as a child from her own parents and turned over to wolves could be so wise?

"How do you know to do these wifely things?" he asked. "You certainly did not learn them from the Morenos."

Her intimate laugh was becoming almost as potent as the sight of her body. "My mama used to call me her most observant child. 'You watch me all the time,' she used to say. She was right; I did. I watched both of them." She sighed. "They were so happy. I want to be as happy as they were."

"I believe you will be," he murmured back. "Her most observant child? There were others, then."

She nodded. "I had two older brothers, Claudio and Rafael. They rode with my father that … that day. And Mama … she was expecting another. *O dios,* what the Comanches did to her …"

He just held her then, his arms light around her. In a few minutes her head sagged against him and she slept. He lowered her gently to the bed, arranging a towel under her head because her hair was still damp. He left her to take his own bath.

He was seated in her bathwater, cooler now. He didn't fit as well, but the water was a comfort. He closed his eyes in exhaustion and opened them a few minutes later to find Paloma beside the tub, washing *him* this time, her nightgown off.

"I don't want to get it wet," she told him, practical, as she lathered soap in his hair, her fingers strong in his scalp and so soothing.

"You're supposed to sleep," he protested, but not very much, and certainly not with the intention of being obeyed.

"You washed me," she observed. She went closer to the fireplace where the servants had set two more brass cans of water, warm now, and just right to pour over him. When she scrubbed his back, he could have whimpered like a puppy with the pleasure of it all. *Dios mio*, eight years without this, and now someone to wash his back again. Why on earth had he ever thought that a yellow dog would be enough?

"To think all I wanted was a yellow dog," he whispered to her, and she just smiled at him. Here she had been a wife for not much beyond three weeks, and she knew him that well. Amazing. "I'm astounded you married someone as stupid as I am."

"Marco, you are by no means stupid," she scolded gently. Her scrubbing had turned into a caress. He closed his eyes when he felt her lips on his back. "As for Trece, well, you know a good dog when you see one. I just came along."

He kissed her, and then they didn't bother with whether he was dry or not; the bed was close, the sheets absorbent. When she slept again, he tucked the blankets tight around her, dressed and went in search of his sister.

He found her in the kitchen, talking quietly to her cook. Luisa turned around to observe him, a half smile on her face. What was it about sisters? He knew that expression and it made him blush—*him*, Marco the landowner and brand inspector and officer of the crown.

With no comment beyond a widening of her smile, she handed him an earthenware cup of hot chocolate. He warmed his hands on it until she sat down with her own cup and a plate of *biscoches*.

"Smartest thing I have done in years," he said finally, not meeting her eyes at first. *Ah, you know me too well*, he thought, and looked at her.

She nodded, serious now. "I thought you might do something of that nature in Santa Fe."

"You knew more than I," he replied.

"You've been more restless lately, little brother. Santa Maria's matchmaker will be disappointed, but probably no one else. Tell me about her. How did this happen?"

For the next hour, Luisa listened as he told their story. She laughed at his description of the Holy Church's meddling priests, and wiped her eyes, along with him, as he told of his wife's courage to return a dog.

"She was prepared to walk to Valle del Sol, even after she understood how far it was. And now you know her great fear of Comanches, or as much as she has told me."

A shadow crossed his dear sister's face. "We have all suffered."

"Andrés will be here tomorrow with the teamsters and wagons," he concluded, happy to move along from a subject so painful. "You can see Trece for yourself then, that ball of fluff I paid one *peso* for." He touched Luisa's cheek, running his finger down the track of her tears. "How will my servants react to their new mistress? Especially those servants who came with Felicia."

"She will have to prove herself," Luisa said after much thought.

"She will," he said simply. "Paloma loves me. They'll see it."

PALOMA WOKE UP when her husband finally came to bed. Her eyes half open, she heard his clothes drop beside the bed and then let him draw her close, her warm sleepiness infusing him until he could sleep, too. She roused him before morning, her lips on his back, and he obliged her.

Afterwards he held her, silent, until she returned to sleep. When she woke up later, he was gone. Paloma sat up, seeing daylight through the closed and barred shutters. She scrambled out of bed, unsure of herself, certain it was late and knowing she should be up and doing. There was warm water in a brass can by the washstand, so she used it before she dressed in her own clothes, which had been freshly laundered.

Since Marco had done such a fine job on her hair, she only needed to comb it quickly and tie it back with the same leather strip she had been using since San Pedro. Barefoot, she padded quietly toward the kitchen odors.

There they were, brother and sister, talking at the kitchen table. When she hesitated in the doorway, Marco held out his hand to her. She came closer and let herself be absorbed into his generous orbit. In another moment, she was seated at his side and eating *chorizo*, followed by eggs and tortillas. And drinking milk, a luxury she could not even remember.

"The sun is up and it is time for us to continue our journey," he told her.

Paloma couldn't help her small sigh, and her husband interpreted it correctly. "It's but a short way now, Paloma," he assured her. "We'll be home soon."

Will they like me? she wanted to ask.

With a kiss on the top of her head and a nod to his sister, Marco left the kitchen. Paloma half-rose to follow, then sat down again, shy in the presence of the silent woman who was watching her so closely. The scrutiny made Paloma shiver a little; whenever Tia Moreno had given her such a look, the back of her hand usually followed.

She chose her words carefully, but did not mince them; after all, she was a wife now, whatever her new sister-in-law thought of the matter. "I will take very good care of your brother, Señora Gutierrez," Paloma said. "He will have all my obedience. Please don't think he has made a mistake in me."

"You *are* a surprise," Luisa Maria admitted, "and yet …" She shrugged. "Time will tell, my dear." She tentatively covered Paloma's hand with her own. "It is probably a good thing that you are used to hard times." She tightened her grip around Paloma's wrist, not strong enough to hurt, but firm. "Just don't ever break his heart."

You don't know me, Paloma thought. She turned her hand over suddenly and grasped Luisa Maria's. "I don't have it in me to break your brother's heart, Señora, but only time will reassure you."

"Then that is where we will leave it."

Chapter Seventeen

In Which the Mondragóns Avoid Other Relatives

ONE OF THE doors from the kitchen opened onto the family garden, fallow now and dried up. Whatever had remained in bloom before last week's cold and snow drooped and withered. Someone had cleaned and brushed her moccasins and left them by the back door. Paloma laced them tight and continued down the garden path, which she thought would lead eventually to the stable.

And there he was, talking so casually to his sister's horse servants, which told her much about his ties to Hacienda Gutierrez. She came no closer than the door, because there were two other young men with him. She drew back a little farther when one of them turned around. When he regarded her with that same measuring stare as Señora Gutierrez, Paloma knew this must be one of her sister-in-law's sons. Was everyone so protective of Don Marco Mondragón that they saw her as a threat?

Marco turned, too, and gestured her closer. "My dear, here are Juan and Antonio Gutierrez, my nephews, and now yours, too."

They bowed to her. She curtsied.

She returned to the house, hand in hand with her husband, to collect her few belongings and bundle up in a warm, knitted sacque that Luisa Maria insisted she take. With her cloak on, she was ready to ride.

"I promise to provide your own horse for you, when we get home," Marco said after he waved goodbye to his sister as the gates opened.

"I like this," she whispered to him. Her husband answered by pulling down her hood, kissing the top of her head, and putting it back up, his arms tight around her as they rode into the brilliant blue of a Valle del Sol morning.

WITH THEIR GUARD of riflemen from the wagon train, they soon came to Santa Maria, a town with buildings as well-fortified as the hacienda they had just left. People walked in the square with a purposeful air, the cold making them intent upon business. The small square featured a fortress of a church that faced what Marco called a presidio. She heard the scorn in his voice.

"A presidio means protection, husband," she reminded him.

"Hardly," he said. "Ten drunkards and one corporal afraid of the dark." He tightened his grip on her. "And there is rumor that even these worthless men will be withdrawn next year."

"Why?"

"Spain is poor. I heard in Santa Fe that our king is contemplating an alliance with the American colonies in revolt, so far to the east of us. He may decide to pull all his troops to La Florida, as a buffer against England." He kissed her ear. "We are small tortillas in Valle del Sol."

"But the Comanches …" she began, trying to sound offhand, unconcerned and probably failing. He already knew her too well.

He chuckled. "They keep us on our toes. I'll tell you more about them tonight."

The cold had either begun to loosen its grip on Valle del Sol or Paloma had good reason to be grateful for Luisa's loan of the wool sacque. Or it may have been Marco's warmth. In another mile, Paloma pulled back the hood and looked around with interest. Mountains soared around them to the west, those passes through which they had traveled, but they also curved protectively around Valle del Sol. She had lived a long time in Santa Fe, but as she looked at her new home, this Valle, she remembered the vast meadows around El Paso, drier than this and not nearly as prosperous.

"What is this river we follow?" she asked.

"The Santa Maria, named by my grandfather," Marco replied. "It comes from the mountains and is never dry." He crossed himself. "In summer you will see more cattle and sheep than now." He rose up slightly in the saddle, alert and measuring the land in that way of ranchers. "This land belongs to Alonso Castellano and now your cousin, Maria Teresa, too, or at least, her dowry. Alonso should have moved his livestock closer to his home place by now. Well, it is not my concern, at least until his cattle go missing and he comes crying to me to help him check brands. *O dios mio*, we have company."

Please don't let it be Comanches, Paloma thought in panic as she closed her eyes and tried to burrow inside her husband's chest.

"No, no, Paloma. Don't be afraid," he said, his free hand across her chest now and pulling her tight to him. "It's Don Alonso himself. I know from

Father Damiano that they came through San Pedro a few days before you."

Marco spoke to his men, who waited at a discreet distance as his neighbor approached. "Alonso rides like a sack of meal," Marco whispered in her ear. "Do I sound too proud?"

"You know you do," she said crisply.

"All shame on me for my sins," he replied, unrepentant. "Don Alonso, may I introduce my wife, Paloma?"

Alonso stared, his mouth open, and then he began to laugh, as though he did not believe his eyes. Humiliated, Paloma looked down at her hands.

"You really did it," Alonso said, moving closer. "We heard rumors."

With no visible command, Marco backed up his horse. Or perhaps Buciro wanted more distance of his own volition. Who could tell about horses?

"I really did it," Marco said, and Paloma heard the frost in his words. "Mark you, Alonso, I am content. Good day to you, neighbor."

Paloma raised her eyes to Alonso's face, suddenly afraid for her husband and wondering what rumors about her the Castellanos had already started. What she saw moved her more to pity. The man's face was troubled now, as though Marco had scored a real hit.

"But I have a dowry," Alonso said. Even in her humiliation, Paloma heard the disappointment. She also heard something else, the pout of a little boy unhappy with the way matters had turned out, but bragging all the same. "Gold, cattle!"

"So do I have a dowry, neighbor," Marco said. "One far better than gold or cattle. And now good day again."

A word to his men and the barest dig of his spurs, and they moved past Don Alonso. "I hope he and I do not have trouble sharing this valley now," Marco said to her. "Could you hear his disappointment, or am I imagining it?"

"I heard it, too, husband," she said quietly. "I know my cousin. Poor man."

"But he is rich now! Didn't you hear him? Paloma, you're a generous soul," he told her. "All the same, let us give them a wide berth for a while."

"We can give them a wide berth forever," Paloma said fervently.

"No, no. We don't do that in the valley."

"I could."

"No, you can't, not as the *juez de campo's* wife. Your cousin might actually need you some day. Or you might need her." He kissed her head, as she sat, remarkably stiff now, in front of him on the saddle. "Trust me here." He peered around at her face. "Paloma, trust me. Let's go home now."

She nodded, daring only to glance in Alonso's direction and look away. He still sat where the road from his hacienda met the highway, looking a little forlorn, almost as if he had wanted Marco to invite him to dinner, to spare him from Maria Teresa.

Maybe her heart was kinder now, because Marco was right: she did feel sorry for Alonso Castellano. Still, it would take a miracle for her to ever love her cousin, and up to now, her life had been remarkably lacking in miracles.

Another hour's ride and they had crossed the broad valley, moving toward the foothills. "My land—our land—is all around you now," Marco said, correctly interpreting the way she looked from side to side. "And you are wondering where on earth we live. Like moles in the ground? Birds in the trees?"

Her stomach growled, which made him chuckle. "As long as it has a kitchen, eh, wife?"

"And a bed for you, husband?" she shot back, wondering if she was being too forward.

"Not you? Paloma, I must have been interpreting your little sighs and moans the wrong way then. My apology."

"Hush," she whispered, her face fiery now. She kept looking. "Where have you hidden your hacienda?"

"You're precisely right, and I can take no credit, since it was my grandfather's doing. He took the crown's land grant to settle in the most dangerous place in the whole colony, because he was hungry for lots of land. Here we are."

Paloma gazed at the sheer cliff in the near distance, with a grove of trees still clinging to their leaves in this sheltered area. She looked back at her husband, a question in her eyes. There was a *rancho* to find, and she couldn't.

"Let me give you a clue, lovely wife. Francisco Mondragón was a humble stone mason in Spain, and a shrewd man—Valle's first *juez de campo*, and a smarter man than I. Look again, *really* look."

She looked again, seeing a grove of trees and a stream or an *acequia* flowing close by. Then she saw it, a hacienda unlike any in the valley they had crossed, with its *rancho*s made of the red adobe of New Mexico.

"Clever man," she murmured, taking in the wall built of the same stone as the nearby cliffs, a fortress. She leaned forward, making out a stout gate that had weathered to a gray that matched the stone. She could see no signs of life, at first, but she looked closer and saw the guards on top of the wall, watching them, dressed in gray cloaks. "It would not be easy to sneak up on the Double Cross," she murmured.

"I never think that, and you shouldn't, either, because it makes a person complacent," he said promptly, raising his arm and getting an answering salute from the guards. "I live here, always aware that someone could do just that."

She leaned back, suddenly content, as she remembered his little *dicho* about the man with the rope bridge. "It is so dangerous that it is safe," she said softly, more to herself than her husband. "Thank you."

"For what?"

"For being Marco Mondragón, I suppose," she said softly.

They rode forward to the grove of trees, pausing in a small clearing which she saw was highly visible from all points of the stone masterpiece before her. In a few minutes she heard the scrape of wood as a bar was probably lifted from its iron cradle inside. The door opened on surprisingly silent hinges.

"My clever grandfather," Marco said in her ear. "The gate only swings out. If some force tried to swing it in, there is a terrible racket. Sounds like cats mating."

Marco kneed his horse forward and they rode through the open gates into the world of the Double Cross. Paloma looked around in delight at the activity so hidden from the outside. The compound was high-walled, stone and impervious to fire. Marco pointed to the long, one-story building with a deep porch and hanging baskets that probably held flowers in the summer. "My home is now your home. Welcome, Paloma Vega de Mondragón. May you prosper and be fruitful here."

He said it so formally that his words touched her heart. As Father Damiano has taken the role of her father at San Pedro when he told her brand-new husband to cherish and protect her, now her only slightly used husband assumed his own father's role, inviting her into the Double Cross to become a Mondragón.

She had not been old enough to learn the ritual, but her heart told her what to do. Without a word, she slid her bare hands under his gloved hands on the reins and turned them palm up, placing herself in his care.

Chapter Eighteen

In which Marco Gets New Slippers

"MAY I NEVER add to your burden, but only subtract from it," she whispered, equally formal.

Marco started to kiss her, but looked around and touched his forehead to hers instead. A group of his retainers had gathered to gape at the strange woman who shared his horse. He gestured, and an older Indian stepped forward, nodding his head and smiling. Marco handed her down to him then dismounted, taking her hand.

"Emilio, this is my wife, Paloma Vega, come from Santa Fe to make me a happier man," he said simply. He turned to her. "Paloma, Emilio is my steward. He first served my father, and has probably forgotten more about the Double Cross than I will ever know."

Paloma nodded to the steward, who was some combination of *Indio* and Spaniard, as were so many in the colony. The satisfied look in his eyes told her she had an ally. "I am pleased to meet you, Emilio," she said, properly deferential to a man who was a valued servant, and enough advanced in years to deserve her respect. "If there is anything you would wish me to know or do, please tell me, and I will do it."

She must have said the right thing, because both men looked at each other and smiled.

"It was time, wasn't it?" her husband asked his steward, who put his hand to his heart. "Emilio, would you bring me a hammer and a nail? And my saddlebags?"

Marco kept her hand in his, holding her close to his side. She wanted to explore the stone compound, but a glance took in the tidy buildings, the guards pacing a wooden catwalk along the stone wall, and the grass and trees inside the enclosure. An *acequia* flowed through it, and there was a well, too. Even if some enemy managed to stop the irrigation ditch, there would always be water on the Double Cross.

My husband has thought of everything, she told herself, proud to be part of this careful man's life.

"I didn't notice any ranch as well-protected as yours in this valley," she said.

"I said that to my father once. He laughed and told me that *his* father used to be teased about that, until the Comanches came and everyone gathered here to stay alive. I see no reason to change." Marco kissed her hand. "Paloma, I can keep you safe from everything except … except disease."

There it was. Paloma had wondered how much pain he had endured on each return to his own property, since the death of his family. Now she knew.

They walked toward the hacienda, a building made of the same gray-flecked stone of the walls, with barred windows, shuttered now from the inside against the cold. Willow baskets hung at intervals from the ceiling of the porch that spanned the front of her new home. They were empty now, but she already imagined spring flowers.

As Paloma looked toward the entrance, the double door opened and a woman stood there. Her simple dress and apron were impeccable, and she wore a bunch of keys at her waist.

"Is she the housekeeper?" Paloma whispered to Marco, not taking her eyes from the woman standing so composed in the doorway. Even from a distance, Paloma noted the surprise on her face.

"She is Sancha, my housekeeper, who came with Felicia all those years ago," he whispered back.

"I hope I can measure up."

"I have no doubt that you will."

Paloma could not help noticing the slight hesitancy of the woman as they approached the doorway where she stood. She stood, blocking the way one second too long, before stepping back and holding out her hand to usher them inside. Paloma glanced at her husband, who looked so suddenly serious. He must have noticed, too.

"Sancha, may I introduce my wife, Paloma Vega?" he said. "She will be your mistress now."

Beyond a frown so fleeting that Paloma could have imagined it, the servant's face betrayed no emotion as she began to unfasten the cord that held her household keys in place. Paloma put out her hand to stop her, and Sancha looked up, surprised.

"Not yet, please," Paloma said, her voice quiet. "You know far more than I do, and I will learn from you. When you think I am ready, then I would like the household keys. I am pleased to meet you, Sancha."

Sancha's deep curtsy was all that courtesy required. Paloma glanced again at Marco, noting the slight smile she interpreted as approval. She knew her horrible aunt would never have behaved in such a passive way to a servant, but Paloma had learned in Santa Fe to use Tia Moreno as a bad example.

"I would very much like to see the kitchen first, husband," Paloma said to Marco. "Say what you will, it is the most important room in the house."

"I defer to you," Marco said. "Lead on, Sancha."

As she stood in the kitchen doorway, Paloma made no effort to hide her sigh of admiration. Working all those years in her aunt's dingy kitchen, she had imagined a place like this. Her daydreams had never gone beyond working in a room that was light, airy, clean and purposeful. Her hands to her mouth, Paloma looked around in delight at the whitewashed walls, the heavy red tile underfoot, and handsome oak table and benches and the blue and white Dutch tiles lining the outside of the fireplace, serving no purpose beyond pleasing the eyes of those who worked there. In a corner by the fireplace, a small Indian boy sat on a stool, turning a spit where a turkey roasted, its juices hissing on the coals below and releasing a most fragrant aroma.

The other servants stood at a higher work table, cutting and chopping vegetables and eyeing her shyly. Paloma smiled at them, then turned to Sancha.

"What can I say? Your mistress knew what to do with a kitchen. I will enjoy working here."

"You don't have to work in here," the housekeeper protested, but Paloma heard the pride.

"Of course I do," Paloma replied simply. "I welcome the opportunity." She pointed to the closed door. "The pantry?"

"Yes, mistress," Sancha said, opening the door, her gesturing hand spontaneous now, with no hesitation.

Paloma looked inside, feeling her own heart expand as she admired how beautifully its contents were ordered, so soothing to her after so much disorder. She saw kegs, barrels, vegetables drying overhead, bins full of what she knew would be flour, cornmeal and beans. She breathed deep of the spices hanging there, recognizing the fragrance of basil, rosemary, thyme, and lemon grass.

"You can eat your way through it," Marco teased, standing next to her now, his hand on her shoulder.

She jostled him in the ribs, which made him laugh. "I intend to," she told him, which made him move his hand to her neck in a caress.

The other door opened onto what she knew was the kitchen garden. She opened that door and stood a long moment, taking in neat rows fallow now, but ready for distant spring. She heard the gurgle of the *acequia* and imagined herself on her hands and knees, weeding the rows and coaxing the tender plants next spring. She wanted to hug herself, wondering how it was that God's grace finally extended to her, too. As Father Eusebio would have said, "It ith one of lifeth mythterieth."

Sancha remained in the kitchen as Marco led her past the dining room—"I can't even remember when we last used it," he told her—and into the *sala*. Emilio met him with a hammer and nail, and Marco's saddle bag. He lingered for a moment, obviously interested, then left.

Without a word, Marco took her sandals with the blood dried on them from his saddlebag. He tapped in a nail by the corner fireplace, a little lower than the crucifix, as he had said he would, then hung her sandals from the nail.

"Now the room is complete," he told her, and she heard the struggle in his voice. "Before, it was just a *sala*. Come here, Paloma."

She came into his arms and they embraced wordlessly, his lips pressed to her hair, her cheek against his chest, as she relished the beating of his generous heart.

"What do you think of our *sala*?" he asked finally.

Through blurred vision, she admired the benches bright with Indian blankets, the buffalo robe on the floor, the table with an ornate candelabra that must have come from Spain, and the two high-backed chairs by the fireplace. The walls were plastered a rich blue, which contrasted with the red tiles on the floor and the little border of more blue and white Dutch tiles midway up from the floor.

"Even in my father's day, we never used this room for more than formal interviews and chastisement," he said. "Let's find a better use for it, eh?"

She nodded. "I still wish I could have given you land and cattle."

"Do I need land and cattle?" he asked, both arms around her now. "But I think it matters to you."

She nodded again, and he walked her from the *sala*. The hall was cool and dark. He opened the doors to show empty bedchambers, then paused before a closed door. He put his hand on the latch, but he did not raise it. When he shut his eyes and rested his forehead against the door, she suddenly knew whose room it was. Paloma doubted he had opened that door in all the years since his twins had died. She put her hand over his.

"I don't need to see it now, my love," she whispered. It was her turn to take his hand and lead him to the last room, which was larger than the others. "Ah," she said, hoping to make him smile. "And this is where you plan to keep me warm and covered every night, if you can."

He laughed at that, a relieved, full-throated sound. "That is my intention. Some afternoons, too. This one comes to mind."

"Well then, close the door," she told her husband, her hands already on her buttons, willing to make his pain go away in the best way she knew, now that she had been his wife for three weeks.

He shook his head. "Not yet. I've been listening to your stomach growl since the kitchen." He looked around. "I like what Felicia did in my house, but this room was too dark after she died. I had our—my—bedchamber whitewashed, but you can do what you want."

Paloma shook her head. "I like bright rooms. The better to see you with, maybe."

He gave her such a look that she thought he had changed his mind about the kitchen, except that her stomach began to growl. He smiled and took her hand, leading her toward the kitchen again.

When they passed the family chapel, he hesitated. "We pray in here each night." He went to the altar, genuflected and reached for a candle snuffer hanging from the knotted rope around Saint Francisco's habit. As Paloma watched, curious, Marco pulled back the woven rug in front of the closest bench, exposing the wood floor underneath. He pressed the snuffer into a corner of one plank, and raised it enough to reveal an iron ring. With a quick tug, he raised the four attached planks and motioned her closer.

"There's a ladder. The room is small. A path from it leads to the grove of trees closest to the cliff face. If there is ever trouble, this is where you go, and you don't ask questions." He lowered the planks, replaced the rug and gave the snuffer back to Saint Francis.

"Have you ever—"

"When I was a child. There was a summer when the Comanche Moon seemed never to set. We slept down there nearly every night."

In silence, they walked back to the kitchen, where Sancha had set two bowls and a platter containing slices of turkey covered with beans and chilies on the table. Paloma's mouth watered as the housekeeper put a basket of hot bread by the turkey then stepped back, her eyes proud.

Aware of being observed, Paloma ate only a little, even though she wanted more. Marco understood. A few words, and the kitchen emptied of servants. He sliced off more turkey for her and increased the depth of her bowl of beans and chilies.

"More bread?"

"Maybe later," she said. "We have some business elsewhere."

He gave a low laugh, then turned his attention to Emilio, who had come into the kitchen with business. As the men talked, she wandered into the empty hall. Since no one was about, she opened the door her husband could not open and stood a moment, gazing at two cribs, hand-carved toys, and two adult chairs close together. Quietly she closed the door on all that grief. "I pledge to you that we will use this room again, husband," she whispered.

When Marco came to their room, she was already in bed, even though the sun was scarcely past its meridian. He locked the door behind him.

"Emilio has work to occupy him for several hours," he told her as he unbuttoned his shirt. "That's the side of the bed you want? How is it women know these things?"

They made quiet love in the bright room, quiet because she was used to that, after three weeks in a wagon, with teamsters sleeping close by. Marco was less quiet. It pleased her that as skinny as she was, she could satisfy such a man and make him groan.

"The walls are thick," he assured her, well-aware that she was still not completely satisfied. He obliged her, slower now as she came again with a sigh. She shifted his weight, but stopped him when he tried to move away.

"More?" he asked, his lips close to her damp hair.

"Not now. I just want you," she told him. "Am I some freak of nature?"

He shook his head. "I've been told I have considerable prowess by one, and only one, very honest source," he teased, which made her chuckle.

After he was lying beside her, Paloma pulled back the sheet and admired him, seeing his body in brightness for the first time. She touched a scar on his thigh that looked newer than the one on his chest. She brushed her hand against his lower hair, then ran her hand down his legs. She kissed the scar on his thigh, which made him utter something close to words but not quite and fondle her hip.

"A Comanche lance?" she asked, when she was at his side again, his arm around her. She pillowed her head on his chest. His heartbeat was only beginning to slow down.

"Yes. Last fall, some five hundred of us ranchers and soldiers and three hundred Indian allies, mostly Utes, rode north with Governor de Anza after Cuerno Verde, a Kwahadi Comanche. We put his village to the torch, killing people and horses—they hate that—and taking prisoners."

"I remember when the governor returned to Santa Fe," Paloma said. "There was a great Te Deum in San Francisco and all the Morenos went. We celebrated more modestly in San Miguel." She moved closer. "I remember ears tacked to the walls of the governor's palace, and other things I should not mention."

"Did it bother you?" he asked, his hand on her leg.

"Maybe not as much as it should have," she said, after long thought. "I remember what other Comanches did to my mother."

His arm tightened around her. "We found Cuerno Verde and his men returning from an attack on Taos and fought a three-day running battle." He touched his thigh. "I got this on the second day, which meant I missed out on the final kill."

"How far from here?"

"About fifty leagues, near the Rio San Carlos. The Kwahadi have not troubled us since, but I will never trust them."

"Were you happy?" she asked, hoping her question did not startle him.

He didn't rush his answer, which made her think no one had asked such a question. "It's hard to say. I was glad Cuerno Verde was dead, but I did not enjoy wading through bodies and cutting and slashing. Too bad there is not a better way. After all, it is a big country."

Paloma closed her eyes.

HOW DID I feel? Marco asked himself as Paloma slept beside him. Funny how this woman he now called his own had asked a question no one ever dared to ask. In truth he had felt hollow. He was no soldier. All he wanted was to raise his cattle and sheep in peace. Still, de Anza had commended his efforts, and Marco knew he could fight.

He could have slept, too, and then wakened his wife after he was able again, but he got up instead. He washed himself with warm water that practical Paloma must have brought from the kitchen, probably under the scrutiny of Sancha. He wasn't sure he would have been so daring, considering that no one usually needed warm water in the middle of the afternoon, except a man and woman newly married. *You're braver than I am*, he thought, thankful that he was master of his house and his servants would not dare give him knowing glances.

He dressed quietly and unlocked the door, then tiptoed down the hall to the outside door, thankfully seeing no one. He stood on the porch as he always did, looking at the order around him, then went to his office by the horse barn. In a few minutes he was deep in the latest documents he had brought from Santa Fe, chafing at new regulations he would probably have to ignore, because the government of Spain hadn't a clue what he needed on the frontier.

Shadows were lengthening across his desk and he was thinking about lighting a lamp when the door opened and Paloma came in. Her hair was neatly twisted into a bun low on her head, a far cry from the tangle on his pillow only a few hours earlier. She wasn't a tall woman, but he knew how long her legs were and how good they felt around his body.

She looked at him, her expression quizzical. "What are you thinking?" she asked.

"I am thinking I should have remarried years ago, then I am grateful I didn't, because where would you and I be then?"

Paloma crossed herself, and he knew she felt the same way. He smiled and returned his attention to the last of the recent *cédulas*, laws three years old at least, while she looked around his office. She pulled out a brand book, one of three volumes in the bookcase close by. She looked around, then naturally sat in the chair beside his desk where Felicia used to sit.

"If I am not interrupting you …"

He folded the useless law and gave her his attention.

"What is your jurisdiction?"

"North and south of us, then west nearly to Taos. No one is farther east than we are."

"Are you often gone?"

"Not in winter. You'll have to put up with me, Paloma. That's all there is to say."

She eyed him so long that he wondered if he could move everything off his desk and accommodate such a glance. She looked at the book again, and closed it.

"I have only a fleeting memory of my father's brand," she said, folding her hands on his brand book.

"Could you draw it?"

"If I thought about it long enough, perhaps. It's been many years."

She turned away, her face troubled, and reshelved the book. She looked down and must have noticed Felicias's knitting. He had never had the heart to remove it from its place beside the chair she sat in when he worked late and she kept him company. He could tell from Paloma's expression that she understood.

As he watched, practically holding his breath at the sweetness of what he saw, she took out Felicia's last project, a pair of slippers for him, half finished. He swallowed as his new wife tenderly ran her hand over Felicia's work. She took a deep breath and pulled the knitting needles from the ball of yarn that was probably dusty now. In a moment, she was knitting where Felicia had left off. He closed his eyes at the sound of clicking needles and knew how good God was to him.

Chapter Nineteen

In Which Old Joaquin Muñoz Cries Foul

HUNGRY, BUT UNWILLING to interrupt the sweetness of his wife knitting, Marco continued farther into the mound of paperwork on his desk. No one else on the Double Cross except Paloma could read and write, but he had always encouraged his neighbors to send him notes or drop by, if they needed his services. Many of them could not read, so he was familiar with the handwriting of Father Francisco, who had become Santa Maria's scribe.

Because he had been gone from early September and it was almost November, there were many little scraps of paper, most from Father Francisco, with messages short and nearly cryptic; paper was scarce. It was the usual list: missing cattle, found cattle, neighbors angry about whose hay was whose, irrigation cheats, silver table knives that walked away. He knew that most of the problems had probably been solved weeks ago during his absence, much in the manner of *obedezco per no cumplo*—"I obey but I do not comply." Still, he was their brand inspector, and petty complaints warranted a visit to each plaintiff. It would be a good opportunity for Paloma to meet her neighbors.

Chin in hand, he watched as she continued knitting the slippers Felicia had begun so many years ago. He smiled when she started to hum, and reminded himself to visit with Sancha and Perlita *la cocinera* this evening, to see what they could do to increase Paloma's intake of food in order to round her shape. *Flan tomorrow,* he thought. *That's a good start, and I like it, too. Why should flan be just for special occasions?*

He dragged his attention back to the task in front of him and arranged the pile of complaints into those distant and those nearer. He almost overlooked the scrap on the bottom of the pile, the first note. He reached for it and the scrap fluttered into Paloma's lap. She handed it to him, after a glance at it that made her frown. "I *thought* I could read," she murmured. "What horrible handwriting."

He didn't bother to suppress his groan. "I get the strangest complaints from this man." He turned the scrap this way and that, and then read aloud, " 'My boots are gone, stolen by Indians. Joaquin.' "

"*O dios*," he griped. "Have you ever had someone who follows you around, plaguing your life, even though you confess often—generally telling the truth—go to Mass and live a clean life, as much as a sinner can?"

"Remember my relatives?" his sweet wife chided.

"Only too well. Such a man is Joaquin Muñoz. He proses on and on when he corners you at Mass, or maybe a market fair. I've seen people leap behind trees to avoid him."

"But you would *never* do that," Paloma said.

"I'm as guilty as my neighbors," he told her cheerfully. He put the scrap on the top of the pile. "We'll visit him tomorrow morning, because he's nearby. Get the worst over first, I always say." He reached across the desk and touched her hair. "You'll want to try out the mare and the sidesaddle waiting for you."

Her expression changed into something so tender, almost as if she understood his great fear of leaving a wife behind. Even now, just thinking about his return eight years ago to find his family dead made him breathe a little faster. Surely she couldn't be aware of that, but he already knew how kind she was. He couldn't say he was surprised when she put down her knitting and came to him, cradling his head against her breasts as his arms went around her.

HE MUST HAVE finished shifting paperwork later than he realized, or possibly that little walk along the *acequia* with his lovely wife took longer than he thought, because supper was over in his kitchen by the time they arrived there. Marco had told his servants years ago not to wait for him for meals, so he was not surprised. Perhaps Sancha wanted him to have a little more time alone with Paloma.

Supper was green chili stew made with turkey, and more hunks of bread for dipping. Maybe *la cocinera* had taken her own look at his slim wife and decided on flan without his urging. It came to the table rich with rum sauce and quivering. Paloma looked at it for the longest time, maybe trying to remember when she had last eaten a sweet of any kind. The expression on her face after the first bite did not go unnoticed by the cook, who nodded, satisfied, and left them alone.

"I could eat this all day," she said, after silently finishing her bowl of flan.

The look in her eyes made him cup his arm protectively around his dessert, to ward her off.

She laughed and leaned closer. "Tell me about Joaquin Muñoz."

"He's really old, nearly sixty, I think, and a widower. It seems to me that he spends his life complaining about something or other."

"He lives alone?"

"With a few slaves—Indians taken in raids by Comanches and sold to him. He also has Comanche slaves from de Anza's raid. I prefer servants to slaves."

"Comanches like to trade?" she asked. He heard the disbelief in her voice.

"Hardly anyone is better at it. When they're not pissed and bothered about something, they are surprisingly human. I still never trust them, but some do. Open up." Marco took a spoonful of flan and gave it to Paloma. "Señor Muñoz has a daughter in Santa Maria, the widow of a blacksmith." He ate the next spoonful as Paloma watched. "Wait your turn! Pepita has had her eye on me, even though I am somewhat younger."

"Maybe word has gotten out about your prowess," Paloma teased.

"There was never anyone but Felicia and you, so who would know?" he said simply. "Paloma, I love you."

IT WAS PALOMA'S turn to confess her feelings later, after prayers in the chapel with the servants. While he chatted a few minutes with Sancha and the cook, then walked outside with Emilio, she went to their bedchamber. She stood in the doorway and watched the two men, heads together, saunter across the compound to the stable.

After taking a deep breath of the *piñon*-scented evening air, cold now, she closed the outside door and prepared for bed, kneeling a moment at the *reclinatorio*, thanking God for His goodness. Sancha must have directed a servant to bring in a brass can with warm water. Paloma washed herself and went to bed, relishing her full stomach. She woke when Marco came to bed and gladly made love to him.

Her husband rose before dawn. He put a hand on her hip, whispering to her that she did not have to get up so early. One thing led to another and neither of them got up so early.

Funny how sweet conversation could be, after love. "What can I do to nudge Sancha into becoming an ally?"

He thought a moment. "I have an idea. I happen to know that for some reason, Sancha does not care to gather eggs. I supposed she could have delegated it to another, since she is my housekeeper now, but when she came here with Felicia, she was just a servant. Felicia started gathering eggs for her. I'll show you where the henhouse is."

Hand in hand, they tiptoed from the still-dark hacienda like children bent on mischief. He gave Paloma a basket and pointed to the henhouse. "Make Sancha happy," he said and kissed her cheek.

It's funny what people do not care for, Paloma thought as she gathered eggs, getting pecked for her pains. *Maybe that jab of the hen's beak bothered Sancha. I think of flan and eggs with green salsa and eggs with chorizo, and eggs with eggs. So easy to like eggs. I just think of what they will become, and overlook the chickens.*

Even though it was cold, she mulled around that idea, thinking of Sancha and her understandable reserve. "I want Sancha to like me almost as much as her darling Felicia," she said out loud, but softly. "She will become my ally. I am not certain how yet, but it will happen."

She looked around. No one had heard her. *Maybe it is as simple as liking eggs. I will like Sancha starting now*, she told herself.

She took another bucket and dipped water from the *acequia*, shivering as she washed off each egg. Dawn was shaking off a cold night when she came into the kitchen with a bucket of clean eggs. Sancha was just unlocking the door to the pantry. She looked up in surprise as Paloma came in through the kitchen garden door. She nodded her approval, which made Paloma smile.

"Good morning, Sancha," she said. "Thank you for getting warm water for us last night."

It sounded simple, almost stupid. She thought of all the times Sancha must have done just that for the mistress of the house who had taken her along when she married Marco Mondragón. Better than most, Paloma knew that servants were there to serve. No one in the odious Moreno household had ever complimented her. As she smiled at the housekeeper and went back to her room to finish dressing, she glanced back to see Sancha admiring the clean eggs, a look of pleasure on her face.

Breakfast was eggs and sausage with green chilies, tortillas and baked apples drenched in cream. Declaring he was not over fond of cream, Marco shared his portion with her after she had finished her own. He also shook his head at finishing his milk, and pushed it toward Paloma. As Paloma drank it, she glanced at the cook, who was nodding to her husband.

"Hmm. You are in a conspiracy to fatten me," she commented later, as he helped her into the sidesaddle after morning prayers.

"No one gets fat in Valle del Sol," he assured her as he mounted. "Let's just call it smoothing the fabric over your bones."

"You may call it whatever you like," Paloma said generously.

The sun had topped the mountains when Paloma, Marco and their four outriders paralleled the cliff face south on a more obscure road than the one followed yesterday to the Double Cross. Marco had slung his own bow and quiver of arrows over his shoulder.

"Do you have a firing piece, husband?" she asked, curious.

"I seldom use it. The bow is faster and I am better with it."

Smoke billowed up from the chimney at Hacienda Muñoz, adding its feathery plume to other cooking fires Paloma saw all over the valley, greeting another day with cornmeal mush, eggs and sausage. The hacienda was located on a bench overlooking Santa Maria, where the view of the Texas plains far to the east stretched on and on.

"He chose a high place," Paloma said. "What a fine view he has."

"Joaquin's grandfather came into Valle del Sol with my grandfather and probably had more land, too. Lately, though …" His voice trailed off. "Well, let me say that Señor Muñoz just might be too old to manage it. Or so his daughter Pepita tells me." He sighed. "And tells me. *She* is the managing sort."

They waited a long time on horseback in front of Hacienda Muñoz before someone swung wide the gates. "I wonder if Joaquin has a retainer any younger than he is," Marco whispered to her as they rode inside into the courtyard.

Although the hacienda had been built as a fortress, there were obvious signs that Señor Muñoz had relaxed his guard—the few watchmen on the parapet, the general air of shabbiness, the weeds growing tall beside the *acequia*. She let Marco help her from the saddle and executed what she hoped was the proper depth to her curtsy to the old man who had limped from his hacienda and now regarded her suspiciously from under bushy eyebrows.

Silent, standing close to Marco, Paloma listened as her husband went through the proper ritual of greeting. Everything was as it should be, but without any obvious warmth.

Señor Muñoz led them into his kitchen, where she knew all business took place in Valle del Sol. With its dirt floor and walls in need of whitewash, this kitchen was a pale cousin to the one at the Double Cross. She sniffed, noting the absence of good kitchen fragrances. This kitchen was sour and smelly.

She sat, hands folded politely in her lap, as her husband held out the small scrap of paper with its cryptic message about boots.

"You have probably found these by now," Marco said, when Muñoz just stared at the scrap, as though trying to decipher the message, too.

"My best pair of boots," he said finally, and glared at Paloma's husband. "I have wondered when you would get around to me. My best boots!"

"I was in Santa Fe and some time on the trail," Marco explained. "Don't you remember?"

"Of course I remember!" Muñoz snapped.

Silence. Paloma glanced at Marco, who was trying to remain calm, as a *juez* should.

"Señor, have you found them?" Marco asked at last.

"I have not! Do you think I would misplace my own best boots?"

Marco shrugged, and the old man just glared.

"Excuse me, Señor Muñoz, but were they stolen?" Paloma asked, since the men were engaged in a staring match.

It was as if she had reminded him. Muñoz slapped the table. "They were. And by Toshua, my slave."

"The boots disappeared and then Toshua, as well, so you assume it was him?" Marco asked, teasing out bits of information like a doctor would tease out a splinter.

"*Fulano*! I chained him to a post in one of my outbuildings but he refuses to confess," the old man replied. "It is your job to make him confess."

"I'm *not* the Inquisition," Marco protested. "I can talk to him. Where is he?"

Paloma glanced at Señor Muñoz, disquieted now as he seemed to be wondering that very thing. As the silence lengthened, she spoke in a low voice meant to be soothing. "Señor, will you take us to him?"

"I haven't seen him in a while," he said, reluctance evident in every syllable, as though he was a small child expecting a huge scold.

"Surely someone is feeding him," Marco said.

Muñoz shrugged, and Paloma felt goose bumps march up and down her arms.

"I remember a loaf of bread," he said finally. "Back when there were leaves on the trees. I must have told someone to feed him."

Marco leaped to his feet. "We have to find him," he said. "Take us to him right now. I insist."

Remaining seated, Muñoz just gestured to the wider world. His expression fierce now, Marco took Paloma by the hand and ran outside, looking around. There were numerous outbuildings, some of them poor dwellings for his slaves and servants. Marco pointed to a shed. "Start this way, Paloma. I'll go that way."

She did as he said, an archer following her. Frightened, she worked the latch on the structure, barely more than a shed. The door was warped. Without a word, the archer shouldered it open. Nothing but a rotting harness met their eyes. The archer looked around in disgust. "You would never see such a mess on the Double Cross," he muttered.

They went to another shed, and another. Nothing. Marco was out of sight now, on his own search. *How do you misplace a man you have chained?* Paloma asked herself.

Nothing. She looked around, discouraged. All that was left was a henhouse, at least she assumed that's what it was, because it reminded her of a similar building on her father's hacienda. No chickens were about, but there was no mistaking a flat pan for grain, quite empty, and a low door next to a closed hatch with a pulley system—the rope rotted away—where at some point in the past generation or two, chickens had entered and exited.

She and the archer looked at each other. He shook his head and started toward Marco, but Paloma went to the small door, which opened easily. The odor that assaulted her nostrils made her step back in horror, trip over her skirt and sit down with a plop.

"Get Marco," she called over her shoulder as she stood up, covered her nose with the hem of her skirt, and crouched down to look inside.

She heard nothing. There was only a sharp smell of human urine and feces. She swallowed down breakfast again, and crouched there as her eyes became accustomed to the gloom. Gradually she discerned the outline of nesting boxes, and then the sight of a naked man chained to pole in the far corner.

In disbelief, she looked at him, some instinct telling her that he was a Comanche. She hesitated, afraid to go closer. There were enough links on the chain to allow him to lie down. The area around him had been cleared of the rank straw that littered the rest of the henhouse, almost as though he had scoured it for any bits of grain, feathers, or egg shells to eat. He had defecated in one area, maybe back when he thought he might be taken from this hole. Now he sat, head down, in his own filth, his efforts to remain clean too much. As his strength had waned, he had lost all hope. His knees were drawn up to his chest and his forehead rested on them. He sat still and she could not hear him breathing.

One loaf of bread since the leaves had been green. "*Dios mio*," she murmured. Señor Muñoz had starved his slave to death over a pair of missing boots. "*Pobrecito*," she said, her voice a little louder. Not in her worst moments in the Moreno household had she been treated as poorly as this Comanche.

She took a deep breath and regretted it, because the stench made her eyes water. It couldn't have been tears at the man's plight. This was a Comanche. "*Pobrecito*," she said anyway, ready to scramble away from the entrance and look for Marco.

She heard a small sound. It could have been a mouse in the straw, but even a mouse wouldn't pass through such a foul hole on his way to some place better.

The chained slave had raised his head. Paloma held her breath as he stared at her, unblinking—eyes like a hawk, wary and alert despite his obvious distress. She knew she would not move one step closer, not ever. Comanches like this had gutted her mother and then peeled back her scalp while she was still alive and trying to hold the slippery unborn baby slit from her womb.

As Paloma watched him, almost too afraid to move now, he slowly held out his hand to her.

Never, she thought. *Never*.

She could have kept her resolve without a qualm, if she hadn't looked into his eyes again. This time she saw something human. She knew what it was to be hungry. She knew what it was to never bathe, because that was a luxury for others. She knew what Father Eusebio would do, and Father Damiano.

They are priests, she reminded herself, *sworn to help the wounded. I am not and this man is my enemy*. She started to back out, then remembered her own bloody sandals Marco had tacked to the wall in his *sala*. "Are you brave or not, Paloma?" she murmured, and decided she was not.

If she hadn't looked into his eyes one more time, she could have closed the door, lied to her husband, and left the man to die. But she looked, and saw the honest man. It chafed her, but she could not deny the look.

She inched closer, still terrified. Out of the corner of her eye, she noticed an egg in a nesting box he could not reach. She knew he could see it from where he sat, and she wondered how many days the sight of food had tortured him. She put her hand around the egg, certain it must be rotten.

Gently, she rolled the egg toward the Comanche, and watched, tears in her eyes, as he crammed it, shell and all, into his mouth.

"I have been hungry, too," she whispered, as the odor of rotten egg rose to compete with the stench of the filthy man. She went to the door and walked into the sunlight, breathing deep, as the Comanche called after her.

To her relief, Marco was running toward her. She wanted to grab him and never let him go, but someone else needed her more.

Chapter Twenty

In Which Paloma Is Braver Than She Knows

"YOU FOUND HIM," Marco said, taking her arm. He felt her tremble and caught her as her knees gave out.

"I need to get some water," she told him. "A bucket. A cloth."

He pointed her toward the weed-choked *acequia*. Concerned, he watched her stagger toward the water, as if she had seen too much in the henhouse. He ducked inside, gasped, and wondered why she hadn't fainted at the sight.

The Comanche, eyes wide open, stared at him as he crunched through an egg shell and chewed doggedly. Marco turned his head and took shallow breaths, determined not to vomit and disgrace the Mondragóns.

"Do you speak Spanish?" he asked.

The Comanche swallowed, retched, and nodded.

"We will get you out of here," Marco said, sitting back on his heels "If you make a move to harm me or my wife, I will kill you without a qualm. Understand?"

The Comanche nodded. He closed his eyes, after fixing Marco with a look of resignation, something he never thought to see on a Comanche's face. As his eyes accustomed themselves to the gloom of the henhouse, Marco saw the running sores on the man's legs and around his neck, where the iron collar bound him.

"All this for a pair of boots," Marco said, more to himself than the captive.

The Comanche shook his head slowly, as if to move more would jog his head loose from his neck. "I did not," he whispered.

Everyone says that, Marco thought. He looked back to the open door, wishing he could knock down the flimsy wall and let in fresh air and sunlight. And then his wife stood in the doorway, a bucket in both hands. She hesitated, and he did not blame her.

"Come closer," he said. "He will not hurt you. He speaks our tongue."

Still she hung back. He watched as she looked at him for reassurance. It was the same patient look, as if he knew more than he did. When Felicia did that, he had wanted to tell her, "I'm just feeling my way through life, same as you."

Paloma came closer and set down the bucket next to him. Even in his extremity, the Comanche lunged on the chain toward the water. Paloma gasped and tried to burrow into Marco's side, but she did not run from the henhouse.

"He's just thirsty, my love," she said, maybe to bolster herself.

She still crowded close to him. He held his breath as she sat up straight then, hesitated, then came close. She cupped her hands, dipped them in the bucket, and held her hands close to the Comanche's mouth. Little ripples formed on the water, because her hands shook, but she did not back down.

I'm not that brave, he thought, as the Indian lapped from her hands.

When he finished, she dipped her hands again and he drank again. And again. When he finished the third time, she shook her head. "Too much would not be good for you. Let me wipe your face. I know I always feel better when someone does that."

Marco nearly laughed at the puny effort, considering that the Comanche was covered in filth, but he could not deny her sincerity. Calmly she ripped a section from her petticoat, dipped it in the water, then wiped the man's dirty, rancid face.

"You have been eating terrible things," she murmured as she wiped around his mouth. "I will make you some cornmeal mush to start out with." She rocked back on her heels and looked at Marco. "We have to remove this iron collar. Where is that wretched Señor Muñoz?"

"I do not know that he will let us do anything," Marco said. He stared, unprepared for the look his wife gave him.

"He had better!" she said, her eyes narrow, lips tight. She ripped off another length of her petticoat and dipped it in the water, then dabbed at the Indian's ruined neck. "This will help until we get the collar off. I'm going to find Señor Muñoz."

Marco watched the Indian's eyes as she left, both of them wincing to hear her vomit, once outside of the chicken coop. He had not a doubt that she would return with the key to the iron collar.

"Tough woman. Married long?"

Marco looked at the Comanche in surprise. "Three weeks."

"I had a woman like that once. She scared me, sometimes."

Marco couldn't help but chuckle, amazed at humor from such an unexpected source. He had grown used to the stench, so he sat back on his heels. "Would you like more water?"

The Comanche's few comments must have worn him out. He nodded, his eyes closed.

Marco dipped more water from the *acequia*. He had an unused handkerchief, which he put in the water, then handed to the Comanche to suck on.

"What's your name?" he asked, after he had dipped the handkerchief two more times.

The Comanche said something incomprehensible, then, "Toshua. I am Kwahadi. You are the Mondragón who lives behind stone walls."

"I am, and I'm here to discuss the theft of Señor Muñoz's boots."

Toshua shook his head again and closed his eyes. At the sound of his gentle wife's voice—not so gentle this time—Marco went to the door of the chicken coop. He grinned to see her shaking her fist at Señor Muñoz and saying things to him that she must have heard from his sinful teamsters. "Impressive," he murmured. "Paloma, you'll give him a heart attack."

He knew he could have helped her, but she didn't need any help. He watched her going at the old *ranchero* like a wren taking on a chicken hawk, demanding the key. Muñoz grabbed the keys from his belt and held them as though to slash her with them, but his wife was quicker. She sidestepped the keys when he threw them at her. Paloma picked up the keys, glaring at Muñoz. Marco smiled.

"He wasn't going to do a thing!" she fumed, when she came to him, the fire in her eyes increasing his appreciation of the woman prepared to walk to Valle del Sol to return a yellow dog. "What are you grinning at?"

"Hey, hey, calm yourself, Paloma, my little dove," he teased, grasping her by her shoulders. He kissed her forehead, and gave her a gentle push. "Get that collar off the Comanche. I'm right behind you."

She stopped in the doorway. "I can't. You do it."

"No, Paloma."

"You're the *juez de campo*," she whispered, backing up again him.

"You will be tending him."

"And why is that?" she snapped, and he heard all the fear in her voice.

"*You* gave him water from your hands. *I* wasn't even that brave. Look you there, he is sucking on my handkerchief."

She looked. He knew she would help Toshua when she sighed.

"We can't leave him here." She walked slowly toward the Comanche lying on the filthy ground. She stopped when he opened his eyes, and held out the ring of keys. "I might hurt you, because I don't know which key it is," she whispered as she sank to her knees beside the prisoner. "I don't mean to hurt you."

Toshua grunted. Gently she took the handkerchief from his mouth, dipped it in the water bucket, and tucked it under the keyhole on the iron collar. He couldn't help his groan when she pressed the collar against his ravaged neck, trying to work the key in the disgusting lock.

"I'm so sorry," she said. "Let me try another key."

She tried four times. The fifth key turned the lock and snapped open the collar, which made Toshua sob in pain. Marco steadied the Indian's head while she gently worked the collar off his neck. When his neck was free, she stared at the collar and threw it across the chicken coop with a sob of her own.

"Marco, do you think he has been here for as long as you were gone?" she asked.

"I fear so." He looked around. "He has eaten everything he could reach, and probably drunk his own piss." He eyed the pile of feces. "And maybe more. He wants to live, Paloma."

She nodded.

"It's hard to imagine a master so cruel," Marco said, as he carefully unwound the length of Paloma's petticoat from Toshua's neck and soaked it in the water bucket. He handed it to Paloma, who applied it to the man's neck again.

"Do you have any powers to remove a slave from his master?" she asked, as she ripped another hunk off her petticoat, dipped it in water and wiped his chest. "Can you invent some?"

"Paloma, I am *juez* because I am an honest man," he reminded her.

"I mean it, Marco. This man is coming with us, if I have to thrash that dreadful old man myself."

It was quietly said, but he knew his wife well enough now to know she was not leaving without the Indian whose tribe she feared above all others. He took his knife from its scabbard and handed it to her.

"Sit over here. If he makes a move, kill him," he told her, wrapping her fingers around the knife handle. "I'll deal with Señor Muñoz, and I'll find a cart."

The old man was sitting in his kitchen, staring at the cold fireplace. It was such a far cry from Marcos' own kitchen that he felt a twinge of pity. *I wonder if I would have become Joaquin Muñoz eventually, if I had not needed a yellow dog*, he thought. *It can be so easy not to care anymore.*

"Señor Muñoz, Toshua is coming with me, the better to interrogate him and find your boots."

It sounded logical to Marco, and the old man must have thought so, too.

With a dismissive flick of his hand, he rose from the table and stalked into the hallway. He just stood there. Marco bowed and left.

He found a handful of Señor Muñoz's thoroughly cowed slaves, biting back the urge to demand from them why they had done nothing to at least feed the Comanche, a slave like they were slaves. Obviously they were more terrified of the old man. A few terse orders and they scurried to hitch a cart to a bullock that looked as ancient as they did. They could not move fast enough to suit him. All he wanted to be away from Hacienda Muñoz with his wife and what was likely a dying Comanche.

Gagging and retching, his men carried the Indian from the henhouse and set him none too gently in the cart, atop a dusty rug Marco had snatched from the hacienda. After so long in the darkened chicken coop, Toshua had to cover his eyes with his hands to shield them from the sunlight. Marco hated to do it, but as carefully as he could, he tied a cord around the man's wrist and bound him to the cart. Paloma stood beside him, and Marco's arm went naturally around her shoulders. He kissed the top of her head, even though she smelled nearly as bad as the Indian now.

"I'll get you another bucket of water and you can sit with him."

She nodded and he helped her into the cart. It touched him to see her arrange her skirt so carefully around her ankles. *Ladies will always be ladies*, he thought. She had by now sacrificed the rest of her petticoat to the Comanche, part of it around his neck, where the wounds had begun to bleed and weep, and the rest modestly covering his private parts. With her last remaining scrap, she dabbed at the lesions on his arms then sat back and looked at Marco.

"I don't even know where to begin," she said.

THEY WERE TWO hours getting back to the Double Cross. Clouds had gathered and spit snow and sleet now. He rode by the cart, distressed to see the Comanche shiver. Paloma had pulled what she could of the kitchen rug around his body, but it was a puny effort. Breaking his own rule of never traveling with less than four guards, he sent one man ahead to alert Emilio and Sancha what was coming and have a bath and some lamb ointment ready.

"Where will we put him?" Paloma asked. She had inched closer and closer to the Indian until her arm was under his head.

"There is a smaller storeroom off the kitchen. Sancha can empty it and find a pallet. I want a door we can lock, but he needs to be warm, too."

"Do you think Sancha will help me with him?"

"Everyone will, Paloma," he told her, wanting to shout it to the distant mountains. "Do you think anyone wants to admit less bravery than La Señora Mondragón?"

His reward was a faint smile. "I don't feel very brave," she said simply. "Not at all."

"The Señora Mondragón I heard raking over Señor Muñoz was braver than lions."

She gestured for him to come closer. Balancing herself in the slow-moving cart, she stood by the railing. "Marco, the strangest thing happened when I went into the hacienda to find him."

"Say on, my love," he encouraged, as his horse kept pace with the cart.

"He was just standing there in the hall, almost as though he did not know where he was." She looked away, and he saw her embarrassment. "I know that is absurd, but that was what I saw."

Marco nodded. "Absurd? Hard to say. Didn't he misplace a slave for two months?"

"We know Señor Muñoz is a hard master," Paloma countered. "*Ay de mi.*"

PALOMA SIGHED WITH relief when the cart lumbered into the courtyard of the Double Cross. Snow fell in earnest now, and she had not heard even a groan out of the Indian for the last mile. Part of her tired brain thanked God that the Comanche was dead, and now there was one fewer Indian to plague the colony. The other part of her brain resented that Toshua would die, after she had tried so hard to keep him alive. *Where is the justice in all this?* she fumed to herself.

For the last mile, she had wanted to put her head on his chest and see if Toshua still breathed. Absently, she brushed the snow off the Indian's body. She would let them take the corpse to the wagon shed, where he could wait out the storm. No need to clean him up. While it was true that the Holy Father himself had decreed centuries ago that Indians had souls, she did not think His Holiness knew how unlikely that was for Comanches.

Suddenly the Indian grabbed her wrist. She gasped, then heard the sound of Marco's knife coming out of its sheath.

"No. Wait," she said as Toshua relaxed his grip. "He lives, but not much longer, if we do not hurry."

Their faces averted from the awful sight that even the snow and cold could not hide, the guards took a corner of the rug and hauled the Comanche into Sancha's clean kitchen. The housekeeper stared in disbelief and crossed herself once, and then again, as if she needed more proof against a Comanche.

"We will never get this one clean," she said to Marco, her apron covering her nose.

"Yes, we will, Sancha," Paloma said, rolling up her sleeves. She looked at the guards, no more willing than Sancha. "Put him in the tub and stand ready."

They did as she said, while Marco watched. The water was warm and

Toshua struggled for only a moment before the possibility of his survival must have taken root somewhere inside his starved brain, or maybe his dusty heart. How would Paloma know where a savage's emotions lingered, if he had any?

Marco spoke a few words and the guards left. He seated himself at the table, where he could guard as Paloma and Sancha bathed the Comanche. After Toshua started to cry—the women worked as gently as they could around his lesions—Marco helped.

Two hours and many changes of water later, the Indian was as clean as he was going to get that night. His long hair lay in an evil-smelling pile. He had set up a fearful wail when Sancha whacked it off, not comforted until Paloma put her lips close to his almost-clean ear and whispered, "It will grow again. Your hair is full of filth and lice."

"I am no man without my hair," Toshua had whispered back.

"Yes, you are. Don't be a *fulano*."

"A ... *fulano*?"

"Just don't argue," Paloma said gently.

He was silent, his lips in a tight line, not resigned, which she decided was a good thing for a Comanche. Maybe he really would survive this ordeal by water called cleanliness. *You had better live, you evil man*, she thought. *I'd hate to think I did this for nothing.*

When they finished, Marco called in more servants to hold Toshua upright while Paloma dried him. She sent Marco to their bedchamber for a night shirt, which Toshua refused to wear. Paloma just shrugged.

"I can't convince my husband to wear it, either," she said, which made Sancha turn away and laugh. "I won't have you there nude while we feed you. What do you want?"

Unable to stand upright by himself, the Comanche pointed to the towel and gestured that they wrap it around him. Paloma did, then sat him down on the bench by the table. She took a bowl of corn mush from Sancha and a spoon. "Open your mouth."

"I do not trust you."

Paloma ate the spoonful of mush and another. She had eaten nothing since breakfast and she wanted to eat it all. "I don't trust you, either, but I know what it feels like to be hungry. It's not poisoned. Shall we try again? That's better. You can eat this and no more, and drink some milk."

"I never had milk."

"I hadn't either, before I came here."

He ate in silence then, his eyes half closed. By the time she held the cup of milk to his lips, he was leaning heavily on the table, unable to sit upright. When he finished, Paloma wiped his lips.

"In the morning, you will have more mush and two eggs."

He surprised her with a slight smile. "I ate eggs in Señor Muñoz's chicken house."

"Ours are better. I promise." She winked back tears and looked at her husband. "Help me get him to bed."

Sancha held a lantern high and opened the door to the small storage room so close to the fireplace. The room was warm. Sancha had moved everything out of the room and the servants had found a cot. They sat Toshua down on the cot, Marco swinging up his legs and covering him with a blanket. Paloma put a thick cloth behind his head then knelt beside the cot, applying the lamb ointment that Emilio had left on the kitchen table. Toshua tried to lick it off her fingers.

"No, no," she told him gently. "This is to heal the sores on your neck. I promise there will be more food in the morning. I promise."

She stayed there on her knees, Marco's hand on her shoulder, until the Comanche closed his eyes and slept.

"This was a strange day's business," she said, as he helped her to her feet. "Is this the way things are for a brand inspector?"

"I never know from day to day, Paloma." He locked the door, and kept his hand on her shoulder as they walked down the corridor.

He helped her into the tub in their bedchamber, sitting beside her as she washed herself and cried. When she was dry, he took his turn, and then crawled into bed beside her. He was silent a long time, and she thought he slept.

"Where do you suppose those damned boots are, Paloma?" His voice was drowsy.

She kissed his cheek. "Personally, I doubt they are missing. I don't think Señor Muñoz knows where anything is. Since you put me in charge of a wretched Comanche, the boots are my problem. A *juez de campo* can deal with more pressing issues than missing boots. Go to sleep, husband."

Chapter Twenty-one

In Which the Mondragóns Discover the Dubious Pleasure of Relatives

MORNING CAME TOO soon, except that Marco had been lying awake for the better part of an hour, wanting his wife but too wise to trouble a woman who still looked exhausted. He lay next to her, comparing her slim shape, tucked close to him for warmth, to that of the more robust Felicia. He decided that each would do equally well. Half Tewa, Felicia had been a pleasing caramel color. Paloma was white, with freckles on her shoulders. Somewhere in his own ancestry was an Indian or two, so he was darker than Paloma and lighter than Felicia, as were many people in New Mexico.

"What?" came his wife's sleepy voice.

He kissed her shoulder. "You have eyes in the back of your head? I was admiring your freckles."

She muttered something then sat up. "Toshua. Should we—"

"See if he is still alive?" he finished. Paloma got up quickly.

He was alive. When Marco opened the storeroom door later, knife drawn back and ready to throw, he saw the Comanche lying there watching him, eyes alert. Marco decided that a Comanche with a shaved head was hardly the warrior with long, flowing hair, paint and a buffalo-horn headdress. All the same, he opened the door cautiously and stood there, returning stare for stare.

He thought of a hundred things to say, but discarded them all and merely asked, "Are you hungry?"

Toshua nodded. He tried to rise in that dignified way of Indians that Marco always admired and never could imitate. He ended up on his hands and knees, head lolling, looking anything but warlike. Marco sheathed his knife and helped the man to his feet. Toshua staggered. For one moment, Marco feared the slave was going to reach for his knife. All Toshua did was steady himself, his hand on Marco's arm. The look he gave Marco was one of shame, which made him wonder if shame made Toshua more dangerous or less so.

But he knew Toshua was hungry. After insisting that Toshua wrap that towel around his waist, Marco led him into the kitchen. He fastened the Comanche to an iron ring by the fireplace, after making sure there was nothing nearby that could possibly be turned into a weapon. Toshua merely looked at him, then leaned his head against his arm, tired still.

A gust of cold air meant Paloma had returned with the eggs. Her cheeks ruddy with cold, she smiled at Marco and gave the Comanche a wide berth.

"You let him drink from your hands yesterday," Marco reminded her. "And now you're afraid?"

"I'm not certain what I was thinking yesterday," she admitted.

You were thinking only of saving a life, Marco thought, willing to let her be as frightened as she wanted today, if that meant she would always be cautious.

By the time Sancha came into the kitchen, followed by Perla *la cocinera*, Paloma had cracked four eggs into a bowl and whipped them to a froth. Well-schooled in Sancha's moods, after all these years, Marco knew how displeased his housekeeper was to see a Comanche chained to her fireplace. He could understand; all he had ever made her contend with before were bum lambs.

Ah, her hands to her hips. He knew all the signs. "Señor, how long will this savage remain in my kitchen?" she asked.

"I don't know," he said honestly. He knew better than to lie to his housekeeper. When he lied, there was always an automatic slowdown in kitchen efficiency, and he could count on cold water for shaving. "I will assign one of my guards here, too."

"So we will be stumbling over two useless men, one who would gut us and drink our blood, if we let down our guard?"

"I don't think it will come to that," he replied, amused. "You have my permission to club him with your biggest pot, if he so much as looks at you cross-eyed."

He glanced at his wife, hesitant but eager to help, if Sancha would only ask, and had a brilliant idea. Heaving a sigh worthy of an actor, he hoped that Paloma didn't know him so well yet that she could pick out a sham. So far, so good. "*Ay de mi*, Sancha, only the cold weather and the extremity of the savage's condition made me dare subject you and Paloma to this savage."

He waited a moment, hoping he knew Sancha as well as he thought he did. He did, to his delight. The housekeeper put her arm around Paloma, a sudden ally against such a man as a *juez de campo* who brought his work home and tied it to the fireplace.

"Come, Paloma. Let us cook those eggs and make some porridge."

Paloma nodded, fully aware of what he had done, if the veiled look she gave him was any indication. *Dios*, but he had married a smart woman. He even thought he saw tears glistening in her blue eyes at such treatment by her lord and master, when she looked at Sancha. Ah, yes. Sancha had noticed the tears, too, and tightened her grip on Paloma.

"Shoo, now! Paloma and I will manage in spite of you," Sancha said.

Marco went to the kitchen garden door. He glanced at Toshua, who was regarding him with something close to a lurking smile. *And the Indian is smart, too,* he thought. *I may actually have to explain myself to him.* "I'll be back for breakfast."

Proud of himself, he beat a hasty retreat.

MY HUSBAND THINKS he is so smart, Paloma told herself. She enjoyed the moment, standing in the protection of Sancha's arm, then laughed softly.

"Sancha, he so wants you and me to get along," she said, deciding that Felicia's dear servant and housekeeper wasn't one so easily duped by a man. "He resorts to the barest subterfuge, hoping to make us allies. I wish it, too, though, with all my heart." She put her hand in Sancha's. "I want to be a good mistress, as I know Felicia must have been. That is all."

Her honesty must have caught the housekeeper off guard. Sancha sat down, her expression less stolid, or so Paloma wanted to imagine. She sat down beside Sancha, aware of the interesting tableau they were furnishing for the Comanche. She waited for Sancha to speak.

"You cannot imagine how difficult life was here, after Felicia and the twins died," Sancha said at last, the words wrenched from her.

"I have a bare idea," Paloma told her. "When Marco showed me the hacienda the other day, he couldn't even open the door to the twins' room. Such loss!"

They sat together in silence, shoulders touching.

"We have all known loss," Paloma said finally. Silence. She glanced at the Indian, seeing something in his face, as well. *And so have you,* she thought, surprising herself. She thought again of the disgusting henhouse where Toshua had been locked away to starve, and wondered how a Comanche warrior could become a slave, himself.

"Eggs now," Paloma said to Sancha. "This man is so hungry." She laughed again, softly. "And truth to tell, so am I. Sancha, will I ever be full?"

"You will," the housekeeper said. She looked around, decisive again. "Now where is *la cocinera*?"

"She ran into the hall when my husband brought Toshua in here."

Sancha glared at the Comanche, blaming him for the sins of the world. "All of Perla's family died in a Comanche raid."

"I know how that feels," Paloma said, "but he is still hungry and my husband has put him in my care. Go find the cook. Please tell Perla that if I must be brave, she must be, too."

Easy to say, Paloma decided, as Sancha went after the cook and she was left alone with the Comanche. Without a word, she poured the frothed eggs into an iron pan and swung it toward the fireplace, stirring and adding salt and chilies until her mouth watered. When she finished, she put the eggs in an earthenware bowl and found a wooden spoon.

"Here you are," she said, setting the bowl in the Comanche's toweled lap. She gave him the spoon.

He handed it back to her. "You are hungry, too," he told her, his voice low but gruff in a way that suddenly reminded her of her brother, Claudio. It was such an old memory that she wasn't certain. Claudio had never liked to admit to a soft side, wanting to imitate his father instead, but he used to feed her from his own dish, when Mama wasn't watching. Funny that she should think of Claudio, killed by Comanches. It startled her.

"I *am* hungry," she agreed. "I spent a lot of years with little to eat, but *you* are the one who was eating a rotten egg only yesterday and … probably other things."

Toshua shrugged and held the bowl out to her with a shaking hand. She sighed at his weakness, and wondered if there was enough food at the Double Cross to bring him back to full health. Paloma sat down again at the table, eating three mouthfuls until the edge was off her own hunger. She put the bowl back in Toshua's lap, and gave him the spoon again. He ate this time, balancing the bowl and eating carefully, because his other hand was tied to the iron ring.

While he ate, Paloma mixed cornmeal and milk and added more eggs for good measure. By the time it was ready to swing over the fire, Perla had inched into the room again, her eyes wide and terrified, but prodded from behind by Sancha.

"He's just hungry, Perla," Sancha said. "The *juez de campo* expects us to take care of him."

Marco returned to the kitchen when Toshua was finishing his cornmeal porridge. "I think it will snow today," he said, as he sat down and nodded his thanks to Perla for the plate of eggs and sausage. He crossed himself and ate, his eyes on Paloma.

She sat beside him. Under the cover of the table, she put her hand on his leg. With a half smile, he moved her hand up his thigh.

"Señora. Tired."

Paloma patted Marco and went to the Comanche, who drooped visibly, leaning against the rope that bound him to the iron ring. She sat just out of his reach, wanting to clean his wounds again, now that he was fed, but uncertain. She looked back at Marco.

He was beside her in a moment. He took a jar from his doublet. "I mixed up some udder cream my father devised years ago for his ewes. It will be better than yesterday's lamb medication." He handed her the jar. "I'll sit close while you apply it."

You are determined I will care for this Comanche, she thought. "I won't hurt you," she told Toshua as she inched closer.

He seemed barely aware as she dabbed the cream on his neck sores. She flinched along with Toshua, even as she tried to be gentle, but he said nothing. His eyes closed. If he had not been roped to the iron ring, Paloma knew he would have collapsed on the floor.

"I wish we did not have to put him back in the dark room, but I suppose we do not dare leave a light in there for him," Paloma said.

"We either have to trust him or think of a secure place to keep him, where there is light."

"I do not trust him," she said quietly.

"Nor should you." Marco went to the kitchen door and motioned with his hand. Two of yesterday's guards came into the kitchen, helping the slave to his feet as Marco untied the rope. They half-carried him back into the storeroom.

"That will do, men," Marco said after they lowered Toshua to the pallet and just stood there. "Paloma?"

The archers went no farther than the door, alert to any movement, which gave her courage. Paloma knelt beside the Indian, applying another layer of udder cream. When she finished, she tugged the blanket higher on his shoulder. She had started to rise, but Toshua put his hand on her arm. She heard Marco's knife leave its scabbard and the archers step into the room.

"No, wait," she told them. Toshua's touch was light. Again she was reminded of her brother. She suddenly knew he meant her no harm. "Yes?"

"I did not take his boots."

Toshua's voice was faint but she heard the intensity behind his statement.

"Then we need to find them," she said. "Rest now."

Paloma stood in the doorway by the kitchen window, watching her husband cross the courtyard to his office by the horse barn. He stopped at the sound of the gates opening, his hand by habit going to the knife at his belt. She looked toward the gate to see a troop of riders pass through, surrounding a carriage pulled by two horses. By Santa Fe standards, it was not much of a conveyance, but it was painted a lively blue and yellow.

She glanced back at Marco, who was sidling along the wall of his office, trying to make himself invisible. She frowned at his odd behavior, and glanced at the cart again. It had come to a stop, and two of the outriders dismounted. One of them opened the door to the carriage as the other let down two steps and a lady descended.

Startled, Paloma glanced at her husband just as he opened the door to his office and hurried inside, closing it behind him. To her amusement, he stood by the window peering out like a wary child.

She knew who this must be: Pepita Camargo, the fearsome daughter of Señor Muñoz, the woman that her cowardly husband, the man of her dreams, had said other men in Santa Maria avoided. "Apparently you do, too, Marco," Paloma murmured. "And here I thought I had married a brave man, *un caballero muy fuerte*. I will show you how this is done, my lord and master."

Squaring her shoulders, Paloma crossed the yard to the wagon. Marco had told her that Pepita was the widow of a blacksmith, a man of some importance in Santa Maria—if the funny little carriage and numerous outriders were any indication.

The lady teetering toward her on improbable high heels was no taller than her little father, but with a comb of some altitude in her hair. Her face was lined, but her hair was the bright red achieved by henna. Fascinated, Paloma stared at her bouncing sausage curls as the woman minced along.

"My goodness," Paloma murmured to herself. She considered the matter, and curtsied just low enough to acknowledge deference to age.

"Pepita Camargo," the woman said, wasting not a word. "I have come from my father's hacienda and he demands his slave."

"Toshua is not fit to travel."

"My father is missing him and pining and carrying on and that wretched slave is my father's property!"

So this is how you work, Paloma thought. *You stand practically on top of your victims and breathe on them. No wonder the men run.*

Her heart pounding, Paloma stood there in silence until the woman backed away slightly. She felt small and young until she thought of her sandals nailed to the wall in the *sala*.

"Your father forgot where he put Toshua, so I cannot feel that he missed him at all," she said quietly. "We found him nearly dead yesterday."

Paloma clasped her hands tight in front of her as Pepita Camargo shook with anger and began a lengthy diatribe. In a voice that trembled with righteous indignation, she expressed her opinion of the district's *juez de campo*, demanded justice, implored half a dozen saints, wheedled and cajoled and ended with another appeal to the saints.

Paloma didn't have to look around to know that everyone, including

Pepita Camargo's outriders, had disappeared. It was just the two of them in the courtyard. She stood her ground, curious to know if Pepita even wondered who it was she was addressing.

Finally the woman looked at her and frowned. She took in Paloma's simple clothing in a glance that would have withered someone less resolute than the wife of the brand inspector. Pepita ran her fingers through the elaborate and wholly unnecessary fringe on the shawl she wore, as though seeking comfort from her obvious prosperity.

"Are *you* the sudden wife of our district's *juez*?" she demanded, her voice filled with equal parts of disdain and amazement. "Word has gotten around."

Sudden wife. Paloma thought about that. "I suppose I am," she replied, startled at the speed news could travel in such an isolated place.

"What was he thinking?"

"You will have to ask Don Marco," Paloma told her, letting that one roll off because she had a strong and unexpected urge to protect a Comanche. She began her own quiet attack. "Tell me, Señora Camargo: is your father in the habit of misplacing boots *and* people?"

She knew this would begin another lengthy gust of indignation, because she was familiar with women like this from her years in Santa Fe at the mercy of her relatives. She looked for it, and there it was—just the smallest hesitation on the face of Pepita Camargo, daughter of a fuddled man who misplaced boots and people. It was only a second's worth of worry, but Paloma saw it.

She listened in silence to the noisy complaints that followed, choosing instead to hear a daughter worried about her father but unwilling to admit anything to a "sudden wife." Paloma put up her hand finally, just a small gesture, a test of her own quiet power, since Marco Mondragón thought she was so brave. To her surprise, Pepita Camargo stopped talking.

"We will return Toshua to Señor Muñoz when he is healthy again and we have solved this little mystery of the missing boots, but not one second before. Señora, I have work to do."

She turned on her heel and went into Marco's office, where her husband smiled at her from his sheltered spot by the window.

"You are as cowardly as the men in this district," she said, amused. "I think she will leave now, because her audience is gone."

Pepita Camargo did. The gates had scarcely opened and closed on all that indignation when they opened again, this time to admit Don Alonso Castellano and his bride, Maria Teresa Moreno, Paloma's own cousin.

"*Dios mio*," Paloma said under her breath. It was her turn to stand well back from the window.

"Now who's the coward?" Marco teased. He took her hand, kissed it with a loud smack, and towed her toward the door. "Don't you just love relatives?"

Chapter Twenty-two

In Which the Mondragóns Discover a Wedding Present

"I DON'T LOVE these relatives," Marco's wife said under her breath. She tugged back on Marco's hand. "*I* dealt with Pepita Camargo. *You* can handle these."

"Could we face them together?" he asked.

"Oh? The way we faced Pepita Camargo together?" his observant wife teased.

Father Damiano had advised him to do what Paloma wished. "I'll do better," he promised, hoping his handsome good looks and prowess between the sheets would ease him through this next crisis, a mere five minutes after the prior one. He suspected that was the last resort of many a husband. As he recalled, it hadn't worked any better with Felicia. He blamed himself for marrying intelligent women.

"I'll give you another chance," Paloma said. "Probably one of thousands in the decades to come."

He kissed her hand. "You are wise beyond your years," he murmured, which made her laugh, even as she crowded closer to him when he opened the door.

The Castellanos had come on horseback—not Maria Teresa's favorite mode of transportation, Marco decided quickly, judging from the sour expression on her face. He wondered how long it would be before she teased and pouted her way to a carriage as silly as Pepita Camargo's.

He had to admit to a pang of envy as he saw the beautiful cape of fox furs that covered Maria Teresa's angularity. Paloma would have looked much better in it. He resolved to speak to the town's crazy dressmaker, the next time he went to Santa Maria. He could trap the foxes this winter, when winter pelts were at their peak.

"Welcome to the Double Cross," Marco said formally. "Would you care to..."

Apparently they would not. Maria Teresa ignored him, her small eyes fixed on her cousin's face, which had gone a shade of pale not found in New Mexico too often. Marco knew *he* could never look that pale. Marco eased his arm around Paloma's waist, dismayed to feel her trembling, where she had stood up to Pepita Camargo so bravely.

"Come into my kitchen," Marco said.

They dismounted and stalked into the kitchen. Maria Teresa looked around, displeasure written large on her face. "*We* do business in the *sala*," she said pointedly.

We do not, Marco thought. "Would you care for some..."

Maria Teresa dismissed him with a gesture, which made Alonso gasp. She turned to Paloma and her eyes narrowed.

"I told Alonso it could not possibly be true, but here you are, cousin," Maria said, with no preamble. "My father—your loving uncle!—said you stole from him and ran away."

"Really, Maria," Alonso murmured, his face red. "We don't know—"

"I believe you are referring to the change from the egg money that my wife used to see her on her way north to return a dog—the dog for which her loving uncle overcharged me," Marco replied, keeping his voice level because now his wife's arm was around his waist.

"Is that what Paloma told you?" Maria's voice seemed to rise an octave. "And you believed her?"

"Maria! This is our district's *juez*," Alonso hissed at his wife. "We might need him someday!"

Maria just sniffed. "Do your business, Alonso, and don't bumble this time."

By now, Don Alonso's face was an alarming shade of red. Marco looked at this friend from his childhood, dismayed because the man would not meet his gaze. He felt a sudden rush of pity at Alonso's bleak prospect of a lifetime with Maria Teresa Moreno.

"What is your business with me today?" Marco asked, amazed at his own calm, when he wanted to throw them out of his kitchen and turn them over to Señor Muñoz and his henhouse. He would have to congratulate Paloma on her forbearance in remaining in the Moreno household as long as she did.

"Th-this is a Moreno b-b-b-brand that you should register under my brand," Alonso stammered, holding out a much-creased document. "It came with her dowry."

Marco took it, not bothering to open the document. "Very well." He knew he should be polite, but the reason why escaped him. He tried again, because, after all, he did belong to a polite race. "If you would care for some hot chocolate…"

Alonso opened his mouth, but Maria was already heading toward the door.

"Perhaps some other time, Alonso," he said. *When you are alone, or better yet, a widower,* he wanted to mutter under his breath.

Alonso nodded, and ran after his wife, who was already out the door and shouting for an outrider to help her mount. The gates opened, and before they closed again, Marco heard the argument begin. He looked at his wife. "Paloma, I can't even believe that you are related to that *hechizera*."

"Think of all the tales she will spread around Santa Maria," Paloma said, her voice sounding so bleak. She turned her face into his sleeve.

"Once anyone spends any time at all with her, they will not believe them."

He took her hand and started her in the direction of his office, but stopped when the gates opened again. "We're busier than a Santa Fe marketplace today," he muttered, not in the mood for any more business beyond sitting Paloma on his lap and kissing the tears he saw glistening in her eyes.

He turned back to see his sinful teamsters, Andrés at their head, arriving with his wagons and goods from Santa Fe. Trece sat on Andrés' lap. He practically quivered with the delight of seeing Paloma again. "This is more like it, my heart," he told Paloma. "Our expensive dog is through traveling."

Andrés beckoned his wife closer and held out Trece to her. She took the little yellow dog and buried her face in his fur, hugging the creature, who wriggled and tried to lick her everywhere at once. Andrés looked behind him and shook his head.

"Poor Alonso," Andrés said, as he dismounted with a groan. "She was slapping him with the reins." He came closer to Marco. "*You* did much better at the same house in Santa Fe. Perhaps it was a miracle." Andrés crossed himself.

Marco nodded. He walked with his wife to the kitchen door. "Will you tend to Toshua? He is probably hungry."

Paloma nodded, not looking at him. He put his hands on her shoulders and gently brought her around to face him. He laughed when Trece licked him, too. "Paloma, don't waste another minute's thought on your cousin."

"I do not want shame to come to you, husband, because of my family," she said simply.

"How could it?" he asked, just as quiet. He looked around at his sinful teamsters, Andrés, and others of his household who had fled when Pepita Camargo set up the initial racket. "Are you aware—oh, I can tell you are not—

just how many defenders you already have at the Double Cross?"

One look into her fine eyes told him that she was not convinced. He did something he had never done before, not even with Felicia, because he was from a reticent race, those of Spain. He took her in his arms and held her close, then kissed her on the mouth, right there in front of everyone who worked for him. "Go help Toshua now," he whispered, when his lips had barely taken their leave of hers. "I'll send in an archer."

PALOMA STARTED TOWARD the kitchen, but stopped when Trece began to squirm in her arms. She set him down, and the little yellow dog raced back to Andrés, who chuckled and picked him up.

"So that is how the wind blows now?" she chided, amused. "Trece, you are faithless. Take good care of him, Andrés. Your master doesn't particularly need him now." She couldn't help smiling as Marco blushed.

She went into the kitchen. Sancha had been standing by the kitchen window, lips tight, arms crossed, disapproval etched on every plane. Paloma sighed. *I will never measure up now*, she thought. Whatever favor she had gained by gathering eggs for that prickly woman had been undone by her cousin Maria Teresa.

Or not. "Some of my relatives are horrid, too," Sancha said. She picked up a slice of bread with steam rising from it, still warm from the *horno*. She slathered butter on it and handed it to Paloma. "Here. You deserve a sweet, but I do not have any right now."

Her voice was gruff, but that was Sancha, Paloma decided. She took the bread, her mouth watering. "*Dios mio*, this is so good." She sat down and ate, licking at the butter as it started down her chin. She savored the texture. "Do you add cornmeal to your bread? I like the little crunch."

Sancha nodded, her eyes bright, even as she tried to be offhand and casual with Paloma's compliment. "It's nothing fancy."

"It's just right," Paloma assured her. "Do you think … would you butter another slice for Toshua?"

The stubborn look returned, but not with any serious conviction, to Paloma's relief. "I hate to cast pearls before swine," the housekeeper said, even as she buttered another slice, the bread not too thick and the butter not so plentiful.

"Sit a moment, Sancha," Paloma said, patting the bench beside her. As the housekeeper listened, she told Sancha of the henhouse, the odor, the rotten eggs, and the Comanche starving and desperate for even one of those old eggs. "He ate the whole rotten thing, shell and all," Paloma concluded. "We can give him bread and mush and eggs."

She left Sancha there, looking thoughtful, and went to the storeroom. She took the only key on the leather tie around her waist and fit it into the lock. *I should wait for the archer*, she thought, but opened the door anyway.

When her eyes accustomed themselves to the gloom, she knew she should not have opened the door. The Comanche's pallet was empty. Heart beating faster, she listened until she heard someone breathing right beside her. Flattened against the wall, the Comanche stood nearly touching her shoulder. With one shove, she knew he could be out the door and into the kitchen, where Perla had an array of knives gleaming on the table.

She couldn't think of anything to say. She knew screaming would make it worse. She waited.

"You should be more careful," the Comanche said. "I heard Pepita Camargo's voice, even in here. If you had been Pepita, you would be dead now."

"Would you hurt *me*?" she asked, when she thought she could speak without all the terror in the world showing in her voice.

"You saved my life yesterday," he replied, not answering her, but maybe telling her everything she ever needed to know about Toshua the Comanche. "I am hungry."

He was leaning on her shoulder now, still too weak to stand upright. Probably even Pepita Camargo could have thrashed him. Paloma let him lean against her. He clutched the towel around his middle. Without a word, she knotted the towel to the side.

"There now. Just lean on me and I will help you into the kitchen, where Sancha has hot bread and butter."

He offered no objections when she draped his arm around her shoulder to support him. They walked slowly into the kitchen, to Sancha's astonishment. Perla *la cocinera* grabbed a knife and backed herself into a corner. The archer coming through the door pulled out his knife, ready to throw it.

Without thinking, Paloma stepped in front of the Comanche, shielding him from the guard's knife. She helped Toshua sit down. "He's hungry. Here now. When you finish this, there is more."

He ate silently, economically, not wasting a bite and taking everything she offered him. After a long moment, Perla put down the knife and returned her attention to the bubbling *posole*. The guard hurried from the kitchen. Paloma was aware of Perla's little glances, and so was Toshua. He whispered, "What would she do if I got up suddenly?"

"Probably clang you with a pot."

She thought he smiled. Her attention went to the door then, because Marco stood there, the guard right behind him.

"You should have waited for my guard," Marco said, his words clipped, the lines around his mouth more pronounced. He sat down across from her, his eyes only on the Comanche.

"I know." She smiled her thanks to Sancha, who handed her a bowl of *posole*. She set it in front of Toshua. "I was foolish."

Marco's silence told her she had angered him. Paloma reached across the table and touched his hand. He ignored her touch and looked at the Comanche, studying him.

"I don't like keeping you in a storeroom with no windows, but I do not trust you with a fire for either light or warmth," he said finally. "Is there a word of honor among your people?"

Toshua shook his head.

"I can never trust you then?"

"Why would a Spaniard trust me?" Toshua returned Marco's stare, then must have felt he had made his point. He turned his attention to the *posole*.

"Maybe this Spaniard agrees with his wife, that you did not steal your master's boots."

Marco's glance had not wavered from the Comanche. Now Paloma saw a measuring look in his eyes, the eyes of a *juez* and not just a husband.

Toshua ate a few more spoonfuls of Perla's meaty *posole*, then put down his spoon. "I did not steal the boots. I would never."

"And you say you have no honor?"

"I say I have no use for boots, Señor."

It was said with a degree of conviction and a hint of lurking humor. Paloma heard it, and she knew Marco did, too, because he was not slow.

"You realize that if we find the culprit, I must return you to Señor Muñoz, because you are his property."

"You can try, Señor."

Marco smiled at that. "I suppose I can." He leaned forward, his whole attention on the Comanche. "Let me do this: until we solve this little riddle, you may roam free at the Double Cross and—"

Perla gasped and dropped a glass to the tile floor, where it died immediately.

Marco glanced around. "And abide by one rule: you will be my wife's protector, when I am not here. Swear to me."

Paloma stared at her husband, who would not look at her, then at Toshua, whose whole attention was focused on Marco. As she looked from one to the other, the knot in her stomach grew smaller.

Toshua shook his head slowly. "There is no need to swear to you. She has saved my life twice now, from the henhouse and from your guard and his knife. There is no word for honor or oath among my people; we do not need it."

Marco nodded. "I am trusting you with what is most dear to me."

"I know." Toshua returned his attention to the food, but looked at Marco again. "Your wife stepped between me and the guard with the knife. Do you realize what a prize she is?"

"I do."

"If I had thought to harm you earlier, I could have, but not after she stepped in front of me."

"That's good to know." Marco got up from the table. He patted Paloma's shoulder. "Bring him to my office when he is through." He looked closer at her. "You eat something, too."

She took his hand. "I'm sorry I worried you."

He kissed her cheek and left the kitchen.

Toshua sat still while she applied more udder cream to his ravaged neck, flinching when he flinched. When she finished, she beckoned Sancha closer.

"Do we have something he can wear?"

"Ask him what he wore at Señor Muñoz's hacienda," the housekeeper said, her eyes on Toshua, who regarded her calmly.

"I understand what you are saying, so speak to *me*," he said patiently. "I just had a breechcloth. I was always cold."

"Sancha, see if you can find some trousers and a shirt."

The housekeeper looked doubtful. "No one on the Double Cross is that thin."

"Then find a belt, too."

Sancha did, setting the clothes on the kitchen table. Toshua promptly rose to his feet and dropped the towel, which made Sancha gasp, and Perla turn away with a chuckle.

Trousers in his hand, Toshua frowned at them. "They haven't seen a man's strength before?" he asked Paloma.

"Probably not in the kitchen," she replied, her own face rosy. "Turn around and put on the trousers, Toshua."

He shrugged, as though the whole matter mystified him, but did as she asked. Paloma showed him how to attach the belt, and then buttoned the shirt, when he seemed not to know what to do with buttons. After she finished, he unbuttoned two of the wooden fasteners and rebuttoned them, nodding his approval.

Paloma put a poncho around his shoulders. "I don't have any shoes or moccasins for you," she said.

"I ate my moccasins in the henhouse," he told her. "Never mind."

Putting on her own cloak, she walked him to Marco's office through the lightly falling snow, mindful that everyone in the courtyard was watching them—the archers with arrows nocked against their bows, the guards by the gate with their hands on their swords. She glanced at Toshua, who seemed amused.

"Señora, my father once told me never to come near this hacienda," he said. "Everyone is armed and watchful,' he said. 'Find easier turkeys to pluck.' And I did."

Turkeys to pluck, Paloma thought. *My own family*. She gave herself a mental shake and opened the door to Marco's office.

Her husband looked up from the desk. He pointed to a stool by the fireplace, and then to the Comanche, who sat down. Paloma sat in Felicia's chair by his desk and picked up her knitting again. She had finished Felicia's slippers for their husband and was knitting a shawl for herself. The homely task soothed her almost as much as the palpable presence of her husband.

"Where will we keep this Comanche?" she asked.

"We'll think of something."

She nodded and returned to her knitting. She glanced now and then at Toshua, who was leaning against the fireplace, his eyes closed, exhausted.

"He would be dead now, if you had not found him," Marco said, following the direction of her gaze.

"If we cannot find the boots, we will have done him no favor," she said.

He frowned and turned his attention against to the scraps of parchment on his desk. "More places to visit, more complaints to resolve," he said, speaking largely to himself. "If it snows hard enough tonight, I'll be able to put off those visits and just stay in bed with you."

Paloma laughed softly, hopeful that Toshua really was asleep, and not listening. "Rascal!"

He gave her such a look. "Aren't you interested, too?"

Her face flamed hot, and he just smiled. "Very well, then! Let us hope for snow." He picked up a folded document and opened it. "And here we have a brand from your lovely cousin. Did you know the *fiscal* dealt in cattle?"

"I would have thought the closest he ever came to cattle was stepping on a cow flop after herders drove their livestock through the square." She chuckled. "He did that once, and I got my ears boxed because I laughed."

Marco held up the parchment, turning it this way and that. "I've never seen a brand quite like this one. Here is a star, and is this a V? Take a look."

Curious, Paloma put down her knitting and stood beside him, looking at the parchment, her hand on his shoulder. Her eyes widened and she gasped, clutching him tighter. Toshua looked up, alert.

She couldn't help herself. She started to drop to her knees, but Marco grabbed her and pulled her onto his lap.

"*Dios*, Paloma! What?"

She turned her face into his shirt. "That is my father and mother's brand! How can it be Maria Teresa's now?"

Chapter Twenty-three

In Which Marco Fails at Least One Constituent

MARCO HELD HIS wife tighter, his lips in her hair as she sobbed. He looked at the brand again, the star and the V.

"Estrella," he whispered. "Your mother's name?"

Paloma nodded. "Estrella Maria Jesusa."

He gave her his handkerchief. "Is the V for Vega, your father's family?"

She shook her head, saying nothing until her tears subsided. She blew her nose vigorously, and tried to sit up, but he gently put his hand against her head and kept her where she was. With a sigh, she settled in.

"Mama's name was Estrella Moreno, sister to my horrid uncle. Their father owned much land and many cattle near El Paso del Norte. There were other brands, but I don't remember them too well."

"And your father? What about his brands?"

She gave a sigh that ended on a ragged note, telling him all he needed to know about his wife's attachment to her father.

"Papa had no brands. He came from Spain, somewhere near Cadiz, I believe. He had been appointed capitán-general of the district. He married into land and cattle, and what do you know, he even loved my mother. It wasn't arranged." She gestured to the parchment. "This was Mama's brand, and Vega means meadows, as you know. It had nothing to do with Papa." She managed a smile. "The brand was hers before Paper was hers. It's just a coincidence."

She blew her nose again. "They used to sit close together at breakfast and laugh about this and that." Her eyes had a faraway look. "If I had been ever so good, Papa would put me in front of him on his horse and we would go to the *vegas* to oversee the cattle. Our land had lovely meadows." Her expression turned stormy. "And now my cousin has been given their brand! There are cattle somewhere, aren't there?"

"Most likely, my love, and land doesn't vanish," he told her. He leaned forward. "Before I left Santa Fe, I asked the *juez* in that district if he might have time to check some brands that could belong to your uncle." He kissed her. "But I have to tell you, there is only your word against your uncle's, and which one will people believe?"

"His, of course," she said calmly, "especially if he is spreading stories that I robbed him before I ran away."

She settled herself against him. "Mama always told me the star and V were branded on me forever. I had a necklace with the Star and V when I came to Santa Fe. It disappeared one day, so I suppose that it no longer true." She patted his chest, then rested her hand inside his shirt against his skin. "So *who* is the thief in the Moreno household?"

"It could still be you, because you have stolen my heart," he whispered, not willing for Toshua to overhear everything, even if he did look like he slept. He kissed her, and Paloma had no objections.

Paloma seemed disinclined to leave his office and he was content to catch up on paperwork in his office while she knitted. So much red tape found its way to the poor colony of New Mexico, almost as if the place would amount to something someday. He thought of the few soldiers in Santa Maria, wondering how soon they would be withdrawn to shore up other parts of the colony. There was no mistaking the feeling that the officials in Santa Fe were trying to find ways to pull in their troops. The governor had said as much, but de Anza was an honest man and knew better than to try to fool his brand inspector closest to Comanchería.

Soon we will be on our own in this hard place, he thought, watching Paloma knit so peacefully. He hoped there would be babies with this tenacious, lovely person, but then they would be even more vulnerable with little ones to worry about, as the sun slowly set on the Spanish Empire in this distant part of the world. Still, what could a man do but live his life?

"Why the noisy sigh, my husband?" Paloma asked him, when he had thought he was keeping his worries to himself.

He could lie, but he already knew she would see right through that. "I fear the sun is setting on the colony of New Mexico, Paloma," he told her, as he stacked more papers together.

He saw no fear in her eyes. Marco just knew that if Alonso had said those words to *his* new bride, he would see an eruption of hysteria. Paloma merely frowned, finished the row, and looked at him, her eyes merry.

"If this is true, we can wet down all the government paper and red tape in this office alone, add some ox-hoof glue, and make a barricade that could probably hold off the entire Comanche nation," his observant wife told him. "I will believe you when a year or more passes without any new government documents from Santa Fe."

"Wise of you," he murmured, feeling surprisingly cheered. He looked at the Indian, now stretched out in front of the fireplace. "What do we do with him? I think he will be your protector, but I do not *know* that for certain. I must admit I have more confidence in him than I do in Alonso Castellano and his horrible bride. Did you see how she sawed on her horse's bridle? I would not care to be a Castellano horse. They probably have sore mouths."

Paloma nodded, her eyes on the Comanche, too. "You are right about Toshua. Let us confine him to the storeroom at nights, and let him roam free during the day. I will keep him in my sight."

He agreed reluctantly, deciding finally that if his wife, who had good cause to dread and loathe Comanches, could be so charitable, he could, too.

AFTER A FEW days, Marco had to wonder who was watching whom. He noticed that with few exceptions—himself, and Sancha and the *cocinera*—Toshua invariably kept himself between Paloma and all others on the Double Cross and any visitors. One virtue of that was that Pepita Camargo's next visit was much shorter than the irritating woman probably intended.

It did not surprise him that Pepita did not recognize Toshua as the slave from her father's hacienda. Apparently it didn't surprise Toshua, either. After the Comanche kept himself between Pepita and all her attempts to scold and lecture Paloma for harboring a slave who did not belong on the Double Cross, Toshua said as much. As the blacksmith's wife flounced back to her ridiculous carriage, Toshua stood there, his hands on his hips, shaking his head.

"Do we all look alike to them?" he asked Marco, after Paloma went inside the hacienda. "She doesn't recognize me as her father's slave."

This is the first sentence you have addressed to me, without being addressed first, Marco thought, gratified. "No, she doesn't," he said.

THE NEXT WEEK passed safely enough as Marco settled into a pleasant routine with his wife and preparations for the coming winter. Barely a night passed when they did not make love. For the first time in eight years, he found it difficult to get out of bed in the mornings. She was warm and comfortable, and he began to notice a softness to her, as the effect of sufficient nourishment made itself known.

While he was discovering what meat and bread were doing for his wife's body, he couldn't help noticing that Toshua was regaining his strength. The gaunt look left his face, and he no longer sat huddled close to the fireplace, shivering even when he wore rough cotton trousers and a poncho similar to those of Marco's laborers. His servant who cobbled shoes grudgingly gave Toshua a deerskin and let him make his own moccasins.

Marco felt a lift to his heart the evening he returned with Paloma from checking a neighbor's brands to find a smaller pair of moccasins on his desk. "*Mira*, Paloma, your faithful Comanche has made moccasins for you as well." He picked them up and handed them to her. "Do they fit?"

Her hand on his arm, Paloma steadied herself, tried on the moccasins and nodded. "I never thought I would wear Comanche moccasins," she told him. She tightened her grip. "I also never thought I would ever escape my uncle's house." They walked to the hacienda together, holding hands in the twilight. "After all those years, I was beginning to settle into the routine of hard work and no future, because it was my fate. This probably sounds silly to you."

She said it quietly. Marco knew exactly what she meant, and so he told her. As he had dragged himself through the months and then years without Felicia, he had been in danger of turning into one of those statues of the saints, wooden and expressionless. Lately, though, some saint was blessing his life, since Paloma was in it now. He was too much a son of the church to credit a yellow dog.

Trece, that faithless dog, had definitely changed his allegiance to Andrés, who still appeared faintly embarrassed by so much devotion from what was, for all intents, a useless dog. Trece minced after his *mayordomo*, acting like a dog four times his size. Andrés had taken to carrying the ball of yellow fluff around. No one had the nerve to laugh at the hard-bitten old retainer and his worthless pet.

"It's a relief to me," Paloma had told Marco one night as he brushed her long brown hair in the privacy of their bedroom. "Trece would expect attention from me, and I would rather give my attention to you."

AS TIME PASSED, Pepita Camargo tempered her approach to solving the mystery of her father's missing boots. Because arguing with him or Paloma brought no results beyond intense scrutiny from an upstart Indian, she changed her tune. She became reasonable, for the first time Marco could remember.

She came to the Double Cross in the middle of November, respectfully asking for an audience with the brand inspector, rather than barging onto his property and making demands. Marco considered it a good start.

"Is my father's slave still alive?" she asked, over diluted wine and *biscoches*, Paloma's idea of the perfect afternoon treat. His office had never been so elegant.

Marco nodded. "Toshua has been regaining his strength. As nearly as we can understand, your father tied him in the henhouse and forgot about him."

Pepita said nothing for a long moment. He knew she wasn't one to apologize for her own behavior, and certainly not her father's. Maybe the lengthy pause was all he could expect.

"He swears he did not steal your father's boots," Marco added.

Pepita clicked the cup decisively into the saucer. "You believe him?"

"I do, actually."

He waited for a storm of protest from this volatile woman he had known since childhood, but she was silent. He mentally apologized to himself for not thinking long and hard about the missing boots. They seemed so unimportant, especially since he had started going through the brand book to update it, and other neighbors had visited regularly with new concerns for the *juez*. And if he was honest, he had been spending more time with Paloma than working in his office or on his own cattle range. As he watched Pepita's face, he thought about the boots and Joaquin Muñoz's other slaves and felt an unexpected ripple down his back. "Are any of his other servants missing? Perhaps someone else …"

Pepita shook her head immediately, her face a hard mask now, the face of someone unwilling to even consider such a catastrophe. Watching her expression, he felt a growing disquiet. He knew she would never tell him anything.

"Tell me, Señora, do you know if your father has accused someone else of stealing his boots?"

She started to shake her head again, but she stopped. "He did mention a kitchen worker, one of the Comanche children captured in Governor de Anza's raid …" Her voice trailed off. She stood up suddenly. "I must leave. It looks like snow."

He stood up, alarmed now. "Have you seen this kitchen worker recently?"

She did not answer him. He let her go, wondering if they had not searched hard enough after Paloma found Toshua in the henhouse. When Paloma had sent an archer to summon him to the henhouse, he had turned away from other outbuildings on the Muñoz hacienda. What if Toshua wasn't the first one accused? Or the last?

"*Dios mio*," he murmured. He grabbed his cape and ran to the horse barn, calling to Andrés.

For the first time in his cautious life, he didn't wait for outriders. His big gelding ate up the two leagues between his hacienda and Hacienda Muñoz. He passed Pepita's carriage, wiping snow from his face, mingled with tears of anger now at his carelessness. In his heart, he knew he should have kept looking.

"Careless man, careless man," he muttered as he raced his horse through the wide-open gates at Hacienda Muñoz. But who was more careless? Joaquin Muñoz, to leave the gates swinging wide, or the *juez de campo* to not complete his search two weeks ago?

He threw himself off Buciro and pounded on the door to the ranch house, demanding entry in the name of the crown. Her eyes huge, a frightened slave opened the door. He grabbed her by the shoulders, terrifying her so badly she sank to her knees and pressed her forehead against the tiles.

"God forgive me," he muttered. "Where is your master?"

Wordless, she pointed down the hall toward the kitchen. He ran down the hall and stared in the kitchen to see Joaquin Muñoz sitting there with a blank expression. He had a spoon in his hand, halfway to his lips. He was staring at the spoon, as though wondering what to do with it.

Marco put down the spoon and took Muñoz's chin in his hand, shaking him. "In the name of the crown, I am going to search your outbuildings."

Apparently he said it with enough force to rouse the old man. "Marco Mondragón!" Muñoz shouted in turn. "Where are your manners, little boy? I will tell your father!"

"He's been dead for ten years, *viejo*," Marco snapped. "Don't hinder me."

Marco ran out the kitchen door, looking around at the ranch outbuildings, rendered more unfamiliar by the falling snow. Where had he left off two weeks ago, when the archer summoned him? Why was it *ranchero*s had so many outbuildings? He made a mental note to inventory his own property and burn down what he did not need.

With dread in every step he took, Marco checked an empty grain bin smelling of nothing worse than mouse turds, then another. A third outbuilding had no back wall, and the fourth one made him sink to his knees in sorrow.

She was only a little girl, tied like Toshua had been, but with the iron lock around her ankle, and fastened to a center pole in the shed. She lay face down on the dirt floor, the chain too short for her to do anything except scrabble at the dirt with her fingers. Her chained ankle was rubbed to the bone, so desperate she must have been to free herself. He looked away, his heart heavy.

He came closer, turning her slightly. She had stuffed dirt in her mouth, desperate for nourishment, and died that way, her eyes open and staring. Rather, they would have been her eyes, but small animals had been at work. He hoped she had died of the cold, because people told him it was a peaceful sort of death, like drifting to sleep.

He sat down heavily by the little body, staring at the ruin of a pretty Indian child. She was frozen solid now, which must have discouraged the mice and rats. He sat beside her and remembered de Anza's expedition against the Comanche, and his own part in that signal victory over a people who had preyed for years on his own kin and friends. He remembered the wine he had drunk and the pleasure he had taken in watching other men more vengeful than he take their own scalps and violate little ones not much older than this slave-child beside him. He had watched, so he was no better than they.

He could leave her there, and send his own men tomorrow to bury the body somewhere on Muñoz land, except that suddenly seemed so wrong. After a long moment steeling himself—he who had seen so much in his life—Marco took off his cloak and wrapped the child securely. It was only a moment's work to batter down the center pole and lift the chain off. He sobbed when it came away so easily, wishing the little one had possessed the presence of mind to do what he had just done. He picked up the child and carried her from the shed, facing into the storm, wanting to punish himself for being so stupid.

Eyes ahead, Marco crossed the yard and came face to face with Joaquin Muñoz, who must have roused himself from his stupor.

"Stop there! Even if you are the *juez*, you cannot take my property," the old man declared.

"I can and will, in the name of Carlos, King of Spain. Move aside, old man."

Muñoz did. As Marco passed, the old man lifted the cloak and stared at the dead girl. A curious light came into his eyes. He looked at Marco.

"I wondered where she was," he murmured. "She usually brings me hot water for shaving in the morning." He shook his head. "But she stole my boots."

"For all I know, your boots are under your bed," Marco snapped, moving away because he did not want that poor excuse for a master to touch the body. "I will see you hanged for this."

Joaquin merely shrugged. "No, you will not. She was just a Comanche slave. Ho there, where are you taking *my* property?"

"I intend to bury her on better land than yours," Marco replied, sick to his heart.

He tied the little one on his horse behind the saddle—Buciro stepping around at the whiff of death—then mounted, feeling older than the old man who watched him by the gate now. Once away from the hacienda, he cried. He hoped never to visit again, ever.

All he wanted to see, as he rode through the snow, was Paloma coming toward him. How had one woman become so indispensable in such a short time? God's mystery. He stared again. It was no wish. There she was, riding toward him through the snow.

Chapter Twenty-four

In Which Marco Frets and Toshua Leaves

PALOMA DID NOT think her husband would be angry when she followed him, but Toshua exploded when she had the guards lock him in the storeroom.

"I am your protector!" he stormed, from the other side of the stout door.

"I know you are. I will take along archers. I promise." *Mostly I do not want you to see what I fear my husband will find*, Paloma thought. When he rode from the Double Cross, Marco had shouted to her something about storerooms he hadn't checked.

They were barely a league from the old man's hacienda when Marco came toward them through the falling snow, almost an apparition. He rode slowly—not on the alert or looking to the right and left, as he had on much of their journey toward Valle del Sol. Anyone could have surprised him.

Paloma wanted to scold him for leaving by himself and being so careless, but when he raised his eyes to hers, she saw such despair that she was silent. She did nothing more than lean toward him and cover his gloved hands with hers.

Tears had frozen to his face. She looked away to collect herself, then squeezed his hand. Noticing the small bundle behind his saddle, she tightened her grip.

"Who was it, my love?" she asked finally.

"A little slave, probably from the de Anza expedition." He sobbed out loud. "Paloma, she tried so hard to free her foot! And what does Joaquin Muñoz do but look at me and dare me to do anything about it!" His chin sank back to his chest. "He has me, because there is nothing I can do, beyond burying her on my own land." The look he gave her was fierce and made her start. "I will *not* put her in his earth."

Back on the Double Cross, he insisted on burying her himself, in the family graveyard. She saw the penitential gesture for what it was, and shook her head when the guards asked her if they could help. At his side, she walked with her husband to the family plot, carrying the shovel while he cradled the child so tenderly in his arms. Her own heart broke, knowing how devastating it must be for him to walk to that cemetery and see his whole family laid out in a neat row. *Please, Father Eternal and all the saints, let me give him a child someday,* she prayed silently, as he dug the grave in the snowstorm.

The grave was far deeper than it needed to be, which brought home forcefully the enormity of the double guilt he felt, the impotence of a *juez de campo* and the grief of a bereft father.

When the grave was finished to Marco's satisfaction, he put the child in it, his cloak still wrapped around the broken body. Paloma shivered as he filled in the hole, then knelt beside him and recited the Rosary many times until he finally rocked back on his heels and stood up. He gave her a hand up, and they walked slowly back to the hacienda, with its welcome lights and fragrant plume of *piñon* smoke rising. His hand was heavy on her shoulder as she grasped him around the waist.

"We cannot keep this from Toshua," she said, after Marco seated himself at the kitchen table and took a cup of hot chocolate from Perla.

"I'm afraid to tell him." Marco sipped the hot brew, then just sat there with his hands around the earthenware cup, warming his fingers. "We've started to give him free rein around the hacienda. It would be easy for him to give us the slip and kill that wretched man." He shook his head. "But it would be worse to keep him locked up in the storeroom. Let's let him out." He gave her a crooked smile. "Maybe I almost wish he would slit Joaquin's throat."

He walked with her to the storeroom and waited while she unlocked the door.

"Toshua?" she asked, speaking into the dark room. "Please come out now. And … and do forgive me."

Again, the Comanche was standing beside the door. He took her hand, but it was a gentle gesture. She tugged on his fingers and he followed her into the kitchen.

Toshua looked from her to Marco. "Who was it this time?"

"A little girl. We do not know her name."

Toshua's head went back in surprise. He clasped his hands in front of him, holding them so tight together that they turned white. "I know her name but I cannot speak it, now that she wanders with restless spirits." He looked at Paloma. "You would probably translate it as *linda*, or pretty." He sighed. "There are no other young Indian children at the hacienda of that evil man. Not now, anyway. All gone."

Paloma nodded, her eyes on Toshua's face. Marco shifted slightly, as though even the mention of the child brought him great discomfort.

"Señor Muñoz said she brought him shaving water," he said.

"And he accused her, too?"

Marco nodded. "He must have. I should have kept looking, after you were found. I should have searched and—"

"Don't, Marco," Paloma pleaded. "How could you know?"

He said nothing, keeping his lips tightly shut. She kissed his cheek, which brought a slight smile to his face, if not his eyes. He shook his head when *la cocinera* tried to put *posole* in front of him. Perla set another bowl in front of Toshua. Paloma took Marco's bowl from Perla and set it in front of her husband. She put a spoon in it, and he was wise enough to eat. Toshua had no trouble eating his bowl clean, even lifting it to get the last drop.

When the Comanche finished, he pushed the bowl away and planted his elbows on the table. "I could kill him for you," he told Marco.

"You could. I have considered that," Marco replied, sounding not even slightly surprised at the Indian's generous offer. "If we did that, we would not be following the process of the law."

"That is so important out here, nearly in what you call Comanchería, when there is no governor to stick his long nose in your business?" Toshua asked, obviously puzzled.

"It is to me."

"I do not understand you."

"I wouldn't expect you to."

"Did you … did you know this little one?" Paloma asked. She nodded to the cook when Perla set *posole* in front of her.

"The old man paid only one *medio* for her at the Taos slave auction," Toshua said, not disguising his bitterness. "I know that because he boasted about the bargain. She was afraid, so we spent time together, just sitting mostly, sometimes talking Nurmurnah, even though the old man flogged us both when we did that."

It was the most Toshua had said at one time. Paloma put down her spoon. "How is it that your Spanish is so good?" she asked him.

He gave Marco a wry look, as if wondering what a *juez* would think. "One of my three wives was a *ranchero*'s wife I captured in a raid on La Isleta."

Surprised, Paloma glanced at Marco, too. He only sighed and looked at them both. "We punish and you punish, do we not? How is it that you are a slave, Toshua? Did men like me swoop down on your settlement and somehow carry you away?"

The Comanche smiled at Marco's skepticism. "Nothing that worthy of a warrior happened to me." He turned a little to face Marco, as if trying to exclude Paloma from the conversation. "You Spanish have only one wife at a time."

"That's enough," Marco told him. He put his hand on Paloma's leg.

"Not for the Nurmurnah. We have hides to scrape and tan and we need more women." He scratched his head. "I suppose you hear stories about my people respecting the … uh … older among them."

"Certainly."

"Don't believe them. Maybe that is true of Utes, or even the Shoshone, our ancestor-race." He paused, and Paloma saw the shame on his face. She forgot herself for a moment and touched Toshua's arm.

"My wives found a younger man and threw me out," he said at last, the words dragged from his throat. "They told lies about how I treated them, and the tribe cut me loose to wander." He glanced at Marco. "I thought my position was so secure in my tribe, but I was wrong. And that is why you should not trust the Castellanos, Señor."

"You couldn't have heard those conversations," Marco said.

"I sit here in your kitchen and people talk," Toshua said, with a shrug. "I cannot turn off that place where I think."

Marco took Paloma's hand. "The Castellanos must be spreading lies about the few *cuartillos* of the egg money Felix Moreno gave you."

"I doubt it is *cuartillos*," she said, squeezing his hand. "By now, I have probably walked away with all the money lying around loose in my uncle's house, and broken into the governor's strongbox, too." She regarded both men, one so dear to her, and the other whom she did not trust. "We have a more important matter, and that is what to do about Joaquin Muñoz. What *is* the matter with him?"

They sat in silence for a lengthy time. Marco spoke first, hesitant. "When I went there today, I found him in the kitchen. This will sound stupid. He was holding a spoonful of food to his mouth, as if wondering what to do with it." He looked around. "You're not laughing."

"No. I am thinking of the look on his face when I saw him standing in his hall, as if wondering where he was," Paloma said. "Toshua, has he killed other slaves?"

The Comanche looked at the two of them and propped his elbows on the table, imitating them. "I do not know. Once I saw him stare at his daughter when she came for a visit in that silly carriage. It was as though he did not recognize her."

"Then it is entirely possible that he really forgot where he put you and that poor child," Marco said. "When I pounded on the table, demanding his attention, Joaquin seemed to recall himself." He looked around the table. "Who knows how long he had been staring at that mouthful of food?"

"What should we do, my husband?" Paloma asked at last, when the silence stretched on.

"We find the boots," he told her, decisive now, which relieved Paloma's heart.

He said something next that did not relieve her heart. "Toshua, I will not lock you up tonight. I want you to make a pallet and sleep near my bedroom door. If you are to be the protector of that which I hold most dear, how can you do your duty behind a locked door?"

Paloma cried out. Marco took her hand. "Where do you sleep in my bed?" he asked gently. "Where?"

"Next to the wall," she said, tears in her eyes. "How can you do this to me?"

"He will have to go through me first to get to you, and he cannot," Marco replied.

"I know that," Toshua said and turned his attention to the *posole*. Paloma got up and left the kitchen, standing silent in the hall a moment before walking to the chapel, where she knelt on the floor until her knees ached, saying no prayer. After an hour Marco joined her, separate at first, then holding her tight in his arms.

The grip turned into a caress, unmindful of the Indian-carved saints around them and the benign look of the Virgin Herself. "Paloma, I have been thinking about this place and Spain so far away. I am convinced that we must learn from the Indians around us."

"Do you trust Toshua?"

"I must ... we must ... learn to trust him. You saved his life twice—he told me how you stepped in front of him when my guard was ready to throw his knife. I doubt he can harm you now. To live here in the coming years, we must forge new ties. Spain is slowly withdrawing, and I will *not* leave my home and the graves of my loved ones, and retreat to Santa Fe," he told her.

"Maybe I should not have worked so hard to get a yellow dog to you," she countered, even as she held out her hand for him to help her up. "It appears I have gone from the cooking pot into the fire."

"You have, Paloma," he said in all seriousness. "Soon we Spaniards will be left alone here in Valle del Sol." He held her off from him for a moment, his eyes troubled.

After watching his expression change from hard to tender, she put her hands on his face.

He kissed her hands, then pulled her close, speaking into her hair. "I was going to be noble and offer to let you return to Santa Fe where life is safer. I would buy a house for you, and visit you there once or twice a year," he murmured.

"Save your breath. I would never leave you," she told him, raising up to kiss him.

Easy to say, until a few hours later when family prayers were over and Toshua made ready to bed down on his newly arranged pallet close to the door of their room.

"I won't give you a weapon," Marco said.

"No need. I already have a knife from the kitchen," Toshua said. He pulled out Perla's favorite butcher knife from under his pallet.

Paloma's eyes widened, and the air seemed suddenly colder in the hall. "She keeps those locked up."

Toshua shrugged. "Maybe not well enough. I can pick your puny locks, landowner, and lift your latches. Want me to show you how?"

Marco shook his head. He squatted by the pallet, where Toshua had laid down, his eyes heavy with exhaustion. In spite of her misgivings, Paloma could not help her sudden swell of pity for a man still recovering from two months of incarceration and starvation. She went into the dark kitchen, where only hot coals still glowed, and took half a dozen tortillas from the food safe. She put them on the floor by Toshua's pallet.

"There were times in Santa Fe when I wanted a little cache of food. This is yours," she said. She laughed softly. "Of course, you have probably already figured out how to get into the food safe."

In answer, Toshua pulled back the pallet even farther and showed her more tortillas.

"You're a quick study," Marco said, more to himself than the Comanche. Paloma heard the respect in his voice. "Consider this: tomorrow my woman and I are going back to Hacienda Muñoz to search for those damned boots. It could be that I want you to create a diversion outside while we search inside."

"I could divert *all* of us and kill the old fool," Toshua said.

"I have told you why that will not do," Marco reminded the Indian patiently. "Just be ready to ride with us in the morning, after it is light."

The Comanche did not agree or disagree. He yawned and closed his eyes. Marco stood up and took Paloma's hand, tugging her after him into their bedroom.

He stood beside the closed door, his hand on the latch, indecisive, then put his hand down, leaving the string out. "I do not want him to think we do not trust him," he whispered to Paloma.

I don't trust him, she thought.

Marco was turning toward the wash stand, his hands on his doublet, when

Toshua knocked on the door and spoke. "Señor, do not try to impress me with your faith in this Comanche by leaving the latch out."

Paloma put her hand to her mouth, so Marco would not hear her laugh.

Marco went back to the door. "You are certain?"

"Of course. If intruders get past me, I do not want them to have an open invitation into your bedroom, where your greatest treasure sleeps. Don't make my task so hard."

Marco laughed and pulled in the latchstring. Shaking his head, he stripped, washed and got into bed. Paloma took her time, wondering about men. She left on her shift and tried to crawl over her husband to that safe side of the bed. He grabbed her around the waist when she straddled him and tickled her. Paloma shrieked, then covered her mouth with her hand, as she tickled Marco back with the other.

"I am not so certain I like someone lying just outside our door," she said much later, when she patted around the bed, trying to find her disappearing shift.

"He's not there," Marco said drowsily. "I doubt he has been there since he told me to pull in the string."

She stopped. "What are you saying?"

"I am saying he is gone."

Paloma pulled on her shift and padded to the door, listening for a moment. She opened the door.

Marco was right.

Chapter Twenty-five

In Which Paloma Makes a Discovery

SINCE PALOMA SOLACED him twice during the night, Marco had no qualms about letting her sleep late. He stood for a long and pleasant moment just looking down at her as she slept. When he got up, she had moved into his warm spot, stretched like a puppy and muttered something incoherent before returning to sleep.

He reminded himself how strange were the workings of fate, considering that he had set out for Santa Fe with nothing more on his mind than finding a small dog and selling his wool clip to the Jews. Toshua was right; Paloma was his greatest treasure.

He dressed quietly and opened the door to see Toshua lying there asleep, or at least pretending to sleep. The Indian opened his eyes.

"Are you surprised to see me?"

No, he was not surprised. "I thought you would be here. Now tell me what you have done to Joaquin Muñoz."

Toshua rose in that singularly graceful way of Indians and rolled up the pallet. "I did nothing to him. I stole a horse from the Double Cross and spent the evening watching my *master*." The word *master* came out like bitter fruit.

"How could you steal one of my horses? I have excellent guards." *Better to know this now*, Marco thought, with some chagrin.

"They are excellent guards. The best in the valley. I am better," Toshua said with a shrug, as if inviting Marco to accept the plain fact.

Marco decided he would. "Continue."

"I spent part of the night in Señor Muñoz's kitchen, just standing still in one dark corner and watching him."

"You have a nerve," Marco said, not even trying to disguise his admiration.

Toshua shrugged again, but there was a half-smile on his face. "I could have killed him. He spent a good part of the night just staring at his hands, as if he wondered who they belonged to. What is the matter with him, Señor?"

"I wish I knew." Marco appraised the Comanche for a long moment, even though he knew such scrutiny was considered bad manners by Spaniard and *Indio* alike. "He did not see you at all?"

"No. Would it surprise you to know that when I snatched my Spanish wife—number three, and only the gods knew what I was thinking—her *ranchero* husband did not even know I had taken her from his own bed without a peep?"

"Nothing would surprise me," Marco said frankly. He thought of his own woman sleeping so peacefully on the other side of the stout door and wondered if he should just kill Toshua right now and get it over with. Trouble was, he didn't know if Toshua would kill him first.

It was as if the Comanche read his mind. "I will never bother your wife," he said, lowering his voice as if Paloma stood with her ear pressed against the door. "She saved my life two times." He gave a short laugh utterly devoid of humor. "If Pepita Camargo had come into the chicken house, I think she would have left me there. Not your woman, even though she fears me."

Marco nodded. He gestured toward the kitchen and Toshua followed. Or he started to follow him as a slave would, except that after a few steps, they walked side by side. Only Emilio, his steward, did that. Marco thought he might dislike it, but he didn't.

Perla was already stirring the pot of mush over the recently roused cooking fire. Marco noticed that she regarded Toshua calmly, with none of the fear of recent days. *What magic has this slave worked on all of us?* he asked himself as he sat down and gestured for Toshua to do likewise.

"What else did you do at Hacienda Muñoz?" Marco asked after Perla brought them each a bowl of mush and chilies and he made the sign of the cross over it.

"I set all his outbuildings on fire," Toshua said calmly, after his first bite.

"You did *what*?" Marco exclaimed.

Toshua merely shrugged again. "You wanted a diversion, Señor. It's going to burn for quite a while."

MARCO HAD NO trouble waking Paloma. She came awake as she always did, like a flower unfolding. She smiled at him, put her hands behind her head, and moved over, in case he felt like returning to her side. When he explained what had happened, she was suddenly all business, searching for her shift, lost during last night's dealings, then dressing quickly.

"Ride with me. I'll keep the old man outside, and you can search his hacienda," he said as she hurried into the kitchen with him. He stopped long enough for Perla to slap together a bread and cheese sandwich for his wife. Breakfast in hand, she ran after him to the stable and they were in the saddle before she finished the last bite.

As they rode, he told her what Toshua had done. She merely nodded, not any more surprised than he had been.

Smoke rolled into the sky, providing more interest than usual to a bitter cold Valle del Sol dawn. "He really did it," Paloma murmured, "and on a horse stolen from the Double Cross?"

Marco reined in beside her, and they sat, knee to knee. "I'd rather not spread that about, but yes. And here I think I am so clever and careful."

"You are," his kind wife reassured him. "It's just that Toshua is unusual. Do you think he is following us now?"

They both swiveled around, and Marco laughed, even as he shook his head to see a distant figure on horseback. "Paloma, I am embarrassed to think how many times he could have killed us."

She reached over to touch his arm. "No, husband. He is protecting us."

"*You*, anyway," he said, willing to have her assuage him further, because it felt so good.

"*Both* of us, my love," she said, so kindly. "I do not know how much I trust him, though. It is a hard thing he is asking of me. And you."

IT WAS. AS she watched her husband ride toward the small, hunched figure who stood, hands on hips, with his back to them and watched his property burn, Paloma dismounted by the hacienda. She stood in the shadow of the portal, thinking of Toshua. She asked herself how long she had nourished her ill-use by the Moreno family in the rich soil of her distrust of Comanches, after the shocking deaths of her parents and brothers. There was never one without the other.

She knew it would be easy to continue her distrust. The raid on her father's hacienda had set in motion all the abuse she had suffered since that morning the Comanche rode their masked and painted horses into their courtyard. She did not want Toshua to protect her; she had a husband for that now. She wanted the Indian to melt away into the mountains, or east across the plains, and never trouble her again.

You are under no obligation to me, Indian, she thought, as she entered the Muñoz hacienda. *Anyone would have saved you from further torture in that henhouse. Pray do not single me out for protection. I wish you gone.*

Paloma forced her mind back to the business at hand—finding a pair of old boots. Marco had described the boots in question, made of fine-grained Spanish leather and passed down from the old man's father and his father's father. They were thigh-high boots in the style of the last century, with a diamond design embossed down the side.

Marco had told her not to worry about any servants she might encounter. "They are a cowed lot," he had said. She knew what that felt like, and could assure them in all sincerity that she meant them no harm.

The three female servants she did see—wispy creatures, almost ghost-like in their thin frames—backed away and scurried down the dim and foul-smelling corridor. Their wails and moans sent prickles down her back. She did not have to wonder how Señor Muñoz had abused them.

Hurrying quickly, she searched the rooms. The skin prickled on the back of her neck when she whirled around as the dismal creatures eyed her from the open doors then ran away screaming when she looked at them. "Marco, Marco, I need you *here*," she murmured, hoping she would not see the hollow-eyed servants in nightmares.

Most of the rooms had nothing in them except mouse nests and trash that pack rats must have tucked away. She started shivering halfway down the hall, either from cold or fear or both.

The chapel unnerved her. She was used to crosses with the dying Christ on them, suffering for the sins of the world in general and the sins of New Mexico Colony in particular. Or so it seemed to her, who knew something of suffering. But the Christ in Señor Muñoz's chapel seemed to bear the special burden of misery peculiar to Hacienda Muñoz. His staring eyes had the stark pain she remembered too well from her first glimpse of Toshua, barely alive in the henhouse. Señor Muñoz's Christ was as angular and thin as the Comanche chained by his neck, looking at her, pleading for something she could never supply.

She went through the chapel quickly and left it with a huge sigh of relief, gasping as the terrified women continued to run away from her. She thought of Pepita Camargo, the daughter and only child of this hidalgo, who had stooped to marry a blacksmith, dead now. Marco had told her how the people of Santa Maria gossiped about Pepita's descent into a lower class with that marriage. Standing in the Muñoz hacienda, Paloma understood completely why a woman would be so desperate to leave this ghastly place that she would take any respectable offer, no matter how far below her own sphere.

The kitchen yielded nothing except a woefully ill-stocked pantry and storeroom, which contrasted bizarrely with a cupboard of tarnished silver plates, cups and bowls—a testament to better times. She left the kitchen, after bracing herself to see the flighty servants, bolder now and darting close to her like swallows swooping and diving around their nests.

"Go away," she said crossly. "I mean you no harm, but go away!" Goose bumps marched down her back in ranks.

There was only one room left—Joaquin Muñoz's chamber. Indecisive, she stood outside the door, her hand on the latch. She opened the door and stepped back at the stench within, covering her nose with the hem of her skirt.

She doubted anyone had made the bed in years; certainly no one had changed the sheets, which were stained and brown. A mound of clothes filled one corner. Her heart nearly stopped when the pile rustled and mice ran out, bumping into each other in their fright. The source of the dreadful stench was all around. Señor Muñoz much have eaten all his meals in here and then left bits of food to rot. She stared in disgust at all the filth, wondering what the impeccable Sancha would make of this.

Breathing as shallowly as she could, Paloma opened the massive wardrobe, the handsomest piece of furniture in the entire hacienda. Several dresses hung there, clothes from an earlier era, evidence that a woman lived here at one time. Marco said Dolores Muñoz had died years ago.

She lifted clothes and opened drawers but found no boots. She turned next to the carved chest at the foot of the bed, ignoring the three women who stood in the doorway, eyes wide, pointing at her and jabbering to each other in an unfamiliar dialect. She shivered to see them, wishing Marco were next to her. Cautious, she opened the chest, glimpsed a grinning face, shrieked and slammed it shut. The women in the hall screamed, too, and fled, bumping into each other like the mice.

"Oh, dear God," she murmured, wishing herself anywhere but there.

She stood there, suddenly remembering the vegetable man and the cart of cabbages, and Trece and the adventure she had begun on the other side of the mountains. "You wanted adventure, Paloma," she said grimly, and opened the chest again.

The face still stared up at her, but it was a kachina mask, white and leering at her through empty eye holes. Paloma let out the breath she had been holding, ashamed of her foolishness. With hands that shook, she lifted out the mask. Underneath were neatly folded small shirts and breeches, carefully layered with sage and other sweet herbs.

"And what is this, Señor?" she asked. Marco had told her that Pepita was the only fruit of the old man's stingy loins. Maybe he was wrong. Someone had preserved these childhood treasures—a sinew-wrapped ball, a handful of glass marbles, a wooden cart and carved oxen to pull it.

How little we know of other's lives, she thought, staring down at the chest's contents until her heart began to beat in regular rhythm. Hard to imagine the old man had once had a wife and children, but the evidence was all around her. Now there was no one to care for him, or about him, except the silly

Pepita Camargo. *How close are any of us from this kind of sad ruin?* she asked herself. She fingered the child's clothing, wondering how many more months or years confined in her uncle's home it would have taken to render her bitter or demented.

Staring at someone's sad treasures was getting her no closer to the boots. Paloma looked around the room. It took all her courage to yank clothes away from the stinking mound in the corner, but she did it, shrieking every time a mouse darted out. Nothing. She looked around and decided on the last place.

She knelt beside the rancid bed, pulling back the drooping bedcovers to peer into the gloom and dust. Her eyes filled with tears as she saw two lumps far back near the wall. She couldn't reach them, so she took a Comanche lance beside the fireplace and poked about, pushing the objects forward.

Green leather boots with an embossed diamond pattern—the kind of boots Marco's grandfather probably wore as he came into Valle del Sol many years ago. Thigh-high boots of a conquistador, boots that had cost a young child her life and nearly killed a Comanche warrior. Boots carelessly shoved under a bed, forgotten. Hadn't Marco predicted in jest that they would find the boots there?

Still carrying the lance to ward off the three harpies, she picked up the boots so distasteful to her and ran out of the hacienda, never wanting to enter it again. Lightheaded, she stalked to the two men who stared at the now-smoldering ruins. She called Señor Muñoz's name and threw the boots at his feet when he turned around, first to glare at her, then to look down, dumbfounded.

"They were under your bed, old man," she snapped, then skewered Marco with a glance, daring him to say something about her rudeness to a *ranchero.*

"For this, a child has died, and a Comanche slave nearly starved to death," Marco said. As he spoke, he seemed to turn into a brand inspector and not her lovely husband. "In the name of the king of Spain, I declare you should be arrested and confined."

Señor Muñoz looked him up and down as though trying to reduce him to the child who probably used to ride with his father to visit Hacienda Muñoz, the second-best land grant in Valle del Sol. "Should be? *Should be?* Where will you confine me? And who, in all of this colony, will care that I killed a Comanche slave, even if it is against the law?"

"Toshua cares very much," Paloma muttered under her breath, and her husband said, much louder, "I care."

"There is no jail. You cannot confine me," Joaquin began.

Marco stopped him with one upraised hand, command written all over his face. "I cannot confine you, this is true. But by God and all the saints, if you and I are still alive in the coming spring, I will take you to the governor himself in Santa Fe."

Joaquin regarded him silently and turned away. He picked up the boots and started for the hacienda, then stopped, turning around to shoot his last arrow. "You will return Toshua to me. He is *my* slave."

"He is *my* witness," Marco replied, his voice matching the old landowner's for menacing calm. "He will ride with us to Santa Fe in the spring. Until then, he is mine."

The two men stared at each other. "What's more, Paloma and I are riding to Santa Maria to insist that your daughter take you into her household," Marco said, firing *his* last arrow.

The arrow struck home. Joaquin dropped the boots, bowed his head and cried, "Señor Mondragón, how will I call myself a man then?"

Paloma could not help her sharp intake of breath. That was it. Señor Muñoz was well aware of what was happening to him. Until this ugly business with the missing boots, he must have been staving off his daughter, who wanted to do precisely that. He was an old, fuddled man in a country that did not see many old men. His daughter was ready to manage his life, and he was not prepared for that step, beyond which was the grave.

I think I understand you, Paloma thought.

The two men stared at each other like two roosters at a cock fight. She came between them and took her husband's hand, which was knotted into a fist. "I have an idea. Let us go into Señor Muñoz's house and I will fix breakfast."

Chapter Twenty-six

In Which Paloma Finds a Solution and Marco Measures Her Waist

"I WOULD RATHER breakfast with Attila the Hun," Marco whispered to his wife as they walked together across the courtyard.

"So would I, husband," she said, tugging him along. "Don't you see what is the matter?"

"He's a man going mad. He *must* be with his daughter!"

"That is what Pepita wants, but he is a proud man," she whispered to him. "I can see it now: She goes to his hacienda and badgers him and he feels so much less than a man. Should he stay with her? Of course. He is a menace. But I feel sorry for him."

I thought I understood women, Marco said to himself as he let her lead him toward the hacienda. "Don't feel sorry for him. This is a horrible man, Paloma."

"I know all about horrible men, my love," she said, surprisingly serene, for someone who had stomped outside with a pair of green boots only minutes ago. She took his hand. "When I went in his room—so smelly, so dreadful—I opened a chest, and there were clothes that must have belonged to a little boy once."

"I never knew he had a son."

"Joaquin Muñoz has suffered, as we all have."

"He has still done terrible things, my love," Marco told her, but he knew his argument sounded weaker.

"I suspect that none of us is wholly bad or wholly good." Paloma kissed his cheek. "Maybe even my *juez* has his moments. Deny that you just outran all your official powers to say he could not have his slave back."

"I do not have that power," he admitted, but softly, and only into her ear. "I am trusting he does not know."

"It is this way: You already suspect that the Castellanos are spreading lies about me around the valley. All of you are proud men, I suspect."

"Well, I …"

She stopped him with a look. "I am as Spanish as you are, Señor Mondragón. Maybe even more, because I have no *Indio* blood and I think you do."

"Guilty as charged," he said, trying not to smile now. He knew where this was going. "Yes, I am proud."

"If you come down hard on Señor Muñoz, even though he richly deserves it, my wretched cousin will have even more ammunition to level against me. She will say I am influencing you. I can tell you my cousin does not care about slaves. She will only see this as your weakness, especially since you married me. Her husband is probably spineless enough to go along with whatever she dreams up."

"Most certainly."

They were at the door to the hacienda now. Joaquin was already inside, shouting for his servants.

"We clean up these Augean stables and keep an eye on the man, so he does no more damage?" Again he saw the ruin of that little girl, her mouth full of dirt, trying to eat something, trying to free herself, trying to stay alive for one more day, because that was what people did.

She seemed to know what he was thinking. "We cannot bring her back," she whispered and kissed his ear. "If Señor Muñoz is still alive in the spring, you can take him to Santa Fe—"

"Where the governor—a good man, but a realist—will do nothing. All we will have bought from this is time."

"Perhaps good will, too," his wife said.

"What about Toshua?"

"I am counting on him to melt away into the Staked Plains, where others of his band live."

Marco shook his head. "I told you he has sworn to protect you."

"So did you, when you married me. I don't need two protectors," she replied quietly. "Help me now. *El Viejo's* servants are frightful and I need a firm housekeeper here. I need Sancha."

"I will lay you a fire, and when Señor Muñoz is eating, you and I will try to think of some way to convince Sancha that she is needed here. Can we do it?"

"I expect we can," his wife said, still serene in the face of such an obstacle.

He laid a quick-burning fire that would settle into day-long warmth, with proper attention, and kept his eye on the three miserable servants, who looked almost as demented as their master. Joaquin sat silent at the table, shaking his head now and then, as though to clear it.

Paloma found cornmeal and chilies, and soon *posole* bubbled like lava in the iron pot. Somehow, his wife convinced one woman to make tortillas. The soft slap of the maize between her hands seemed to relax the old man. On more instructions, another servant found honeycomb. The third woman lugged in a kettle of water to swing over the fireplace. The servants seemed calmer now. Trust Paloma to find something for everyone to do.

It took all Marco's discipline to eat a meal with the old reprobate, the child killer. Paloma knew how hard it was. She sat close to him, their thighs touching. She kept up a calming conversation with Joaquin, who stared at his spoon for a long time, then fed himself.

"There was an old priest like this at San Miguel," Paloma whispered to Marco. "He seemed not to know where he was. Father Eusebio was so kind. I think this is a special kind of madness, husband."

"If you had seen that little girl …" he started, then put down his spoon and left the table, unable to eat another bite. He stood outside in the cold for a long moment, wishing that he was the man his wife thought he was.

He looked around the courtyard and decided that the walls were still strong, even though so few men patrolled them. True, it was winter, and he knew—hoped—the Comanche were far away. Perhaps if he augmented the guard, Sancha would be safe enough, provided Paloma could convince her to tend this old fool. But hadn't Sancha taken care of him for years after Felicia died, when he was worthless and maybe a fool himself?

He walked to the open gate and down the road, with its little rise toward his own property. There sat Toshua on his Double Cross horse. Trust a Comanche to steal a good one! He gestured and Toshua rode closer.

"My wife thinks that now you have a horse and a bit of freedom, you will bolt to the Llano Estacado."

Toshua shook his head. "There is nothing for me in the Staked Plain. I have no hair so I am no man. My women have thrown me out and I am not even a warrior in my band's eyes."

Marco agreed silently, grateful for only one wife at a time. "When he occasionally thinks clearly, *el viejo* demands that I return you. I have told him you are my witness and will remain with me until spring, when I will take the old man to justice in Santa Fe."

"There is no justice for Indians," Toshua said gently, as if reminding him.

"I know. Paloma is going to convince my housekeeper Sancha that she should come here and straighten out this wretched man's affairs. Does that surprise you?"

Marco could see the Comanche's answer in his smile. "Not at all, Señor.

Señora Mondragón is a kind woman and probably better than you are."

"I think so, too." Marco patted his stolen horse. "You picked my second-best horse and no one saw you?"

"No one."

"Very well. He is yours, then. I won't ask you to swear me an oath because you will not. I would ask you to help me keep my housekeeper and my woman safe, if they are here helping this foul, demented fellow."

Toshua regarded him in silence for a long moment. Marco returned him stare for stare. Toshua was thin and he shivered in the cold wind. The Comanche was right: he did look like half a man, with his hair shorn. There was nothing in his eyes of particular friendship or kindness. He was a Comanche, quite capable of wheeling on his fine horse and doing exactly what Paloma hoped he would do. And just maybe, he was also an honorable man.

"I will do this thing," Toshua said. "Where Paloma is, there I will be, whether she knows it or not."

Marco nodded and turned his back on a man fully capable of killing him in seconds. *Spain is fading*, he told himself as he walked back to the hacienda. *If I am to stay here on my land, things must change.* When he reached the open gate and looked back, Toshua was gone, or at least out of sight.

Inside, he watched as his wife took a warm cloth and wiped Joaquin Muñoz's face, all the while scolding him for letting his hacienda turn into a pigsty. Probably at her order, the three servants were sweeping and washing plates caked with old food. The odors in the kitchen made him blink and wish himself elsewhere, but there was Paloma, probably doing what she had seen Father Eusebio do, tending to someone worse off than she. This was the woman he wanted to introduce to the people of Santa Maria. No telling what lies Maria Teresa Castellano had already circulated.

He stood there awkwardly until she patted the bench beside her. He didn't want to sit next to someone as foul-smelling as Joaquin Muñoz, but there she was, doing her best to make the old rip comfortable.

"How will you convince Sancha to move in here for a while, until we settle this matter?" he asked.

"Sancha likes to be in charge. Let us see if she trusts me enough to manage the Double Cross. And you."

He wondered if Paloma had any idea how much she had already changed. Her cheeks were starting to fill out, but she was still thin, reminding him of Toshua. Maybe they had even more in common—the woman and the Indian had a certain resolute air. Someday she might see it, if Toshua remained at the Double Cross, and they all lived long enough.

AMAZING THAT THE day had gone so fast. They left Hacienda Muñoz after Paloma had tucked the old man into his bed and ordered his servants to make sure he stayed there, on pain of some fearsome punishment she must have communicated in a telepathic way to his ancient, confused staff. Shadows stretched across the road home, speaking of ever-shortening days and longer nights. He knew how the cold would clamp down on the valley. Marco glanced at Paloma as they rode into the Double Cross. And now Andrés had the yellow dog to warm his feet. Marco had no need of such a pet now. He knew his feet would be warm tonight.

But could Paloma convince Sancha to take on such an onerous project as Joaquin Muñoz? Sancha was a formidable woman. He admitted to himself he had been half-afraid of her for years.

"You could enlist Sancha's sympathy by telling her I ordered you to tell her to go to Hacienda Muñoz. Paint me as the villain. I don't mind," he said, proud of his generosity.

Paloma just laughed. "Oh, you mean paint us *both* as victims, as you tried to do earlier?"

This woman of mine, Marco thought, amused more than embarrassed. "Yes, that's what I meant. Paloma, why did you marry a fool?"

"Because I love him," she said promptly. "I'm going to invite Sancha into the *sala* for a chat. I'll put the matter to her honestly."

Fair enough, he thought, giving her a little bow after they dismounted. He took her horse's reins and led the animals to the horse barn while she blew him a kiss and went into the hacienda. After he finished currying both horses and appointed five of his herders and guards to prepare for an extended stay at Hacienda Muñoz, Marco went to his office. Better to give Paloma free rein to approach the prickly Sancha. If she failed, Paloma could come to him for comfort in the office. If he were there, she would not have to face the scrutiny of critical servants in the house.

He stared for a long time at the star and Vega brand that Alonso Castellano had left with him to register in the brand book. He should have done that and returned it a week ago, even if it had come to Alonso in an illegal manner. He could not prove any wrongdoing, so he had better register it, no matter how his heart rebelled against this affront to Paloma. He copied the brand in his official book, stamping his seal in warm wax, making it official for Alonso's use, even if it really belonged to Paloma Vega.

He must have dozed then. When he opened his eyes, there stood his wife, looking at him with some sympathy. She wore the housekeeper's keys at her waist.

"How did you do it, Paloma?" he asked. "What trick?"

She sat beside him in Felicia's old chair and picked up her knitting. "No trick," she told him, casting on. "She already knew what had happened to

Toshua. I told her about the little child, and that Señor Muñoz was not right in the head or the heart. That his hacienda was a mound of rotting garbage, the servants were cowed, half-mad creatures, and this assignment would take every ounce of her skill as a housekeeper. Oh, and that she would have to watch her back because Señor Muñoz was a sly fellow."

"You made the task remarkably appealing," he teased. "How could she resist?"

Paloma put down the knitting and fixed him with that clear-eyed gaze he was coming to relish. "She leaped at the chance. Marco, she told me how bored she has been, of late, with everything running so well on the Double Cross."

"I thought she liked all the calm and order," Marco said, disappointed he had not recognized Sancha's restlessness—he, who prided himself on his kindness as a master.

"She needs a change. She gave me the household keys almost before I had finished making my appeal. Then she bullied me out of three of your best house servants. I agreed, of course." She stood up and came around the desk to kiss his cheek. "How could I say no to that? I'm a little afraid of her, too."

"And you think I ..." He stopped and pulled her onto his lap. "Why do I try to fool you?"

"Because you are a man and in charge of a dangerous place," she said, getting off his lap. "There is a turkey roasting, a small boy turning it, and I am hungry."

He put his hands on her waist, and noticed something even more important to him than the bunch of keys hanging on her apron.

"*Mira*, Paloma. My hands do not come so close together around your waist!"

She laughed as he touched the front of her dress, where the buttons were starting to strain a bit across what was still a slim bosom, but more rounded now. He put his finger through the gap and she giggled. When his touch turned to a caress, she sighed.

"Is it the flan twice a week?"

"Probably, and all that cream you think I need," she said, undoing those straining buttons. "Is that better?"

Of course it was. As much as he wanted to do more, Paloma had said there was turkey and she was hungry. He patted her tender flesh, enjoying the greater heft, then buttoned her shirtwaist. "I recommend a visit to Carmen Saltero, the dressmaker," he suggested, standing up and closing his brand book.

"In Santa Maria?"

Marco nodded, taking note of her sudden apprehension. “Don’t be afraid of what the Castellanos might be saying, Paloma.” He caressed her cheek. “Just words. Ultimately, it is deeds that count in Valle del Sol.”

Chapter Twenty-seven

In Which Good Christians Tell Tales

PALOMA WAS A wife after an official's heart, Marco decided. She was ready before he was on Sunday, something Felicia had never been so good at. With Felicia, there was always one more scarf or necklace to try on or reject. Maybe when Paloma had as many dresses and scarves as Felicia, she would take more time, but he doubted it. He had never met a more practical woman.

Although it was early, Marco knew there would be lanterns lit in the kitchen at Hacienda Muñoz, now that Sancha had been working there since Tuesday. He only had to indicate with a nod of his head that they should stop there on the way to church. Paloma nodded and followed him without hesitation, even though she had been to Señor Muñoz's hacienda several times since Sancha was installed.

He was the last person through the gate to the hacienda. He looked back to see Toshua in the distance, and gave a little wave. He knew the Comanche would remain there, watching over Sancha, since the Mondragóns were on the way to Santa Maria with sufficient guards. And when they returned, he would follow them back to the Double Cross, unseen and silent.

In a moment of rare candor, Toshua had assured Marco that the extra guards who now took their turn watching Hacienda Muñoz were capable and didn't need the Comanche's invisible presence. "I would never have tried to steal your—*my*—horse, if *those* particular guards had been watching your stables," Toshua had told him. That offhand remark made Marco spend the better part of a day reminding his men of their duties, something Toshua didn't need to know.

Sancha met them at the door, taking Paloma's hand and pulling her inside, and giving Marco the half-curtsy, friendly nod that their master-servant relationship had settled into, after all these years. He looked around appreciatively, sniffing the pleasant odor of sage, with none of last week's reeking garbage and old-man smells.

"Joaquin?" he asked, knowing he should have been over sooner, but grateful to have left that to Paloma.

"Señor Muñoz still sleeps," Sancha told them as they walked toward the kitchen. "He has those moments where he is perfectly clear and others …" She shook her head.

"Did … did he tell you about the little boy's clothing I found in the chest?" Paloma asked.

Sancha nodded, her eyes troubled. "Their first child. Carried off by Comanches when he was not more than three years old."

"He could be alive somewhere," Paloma said. "Is it any wonder he has such hatred of the Comanche?"

"You would never be so cruel as to tie up a little Comanche girl by the foot and let her starve," Marco pointed out, unable to forget. "And there is Toshua."

"Don't think me better than I am, husband," she replied. "I spent a long moment in that henhouse, wondering what to do." She looked at Sancha. "Does the old man feel any remorse over the boots stuffed under his bed?"

"Now and then. He is starting to demand that Toshua be returned to him," Sancha told Marco.

"I explained to him why I am keeping the slave."

"You would have to explain it every day, because he does not remember." Sancha gestured them into the kitchen, clean as never before. "I even mentioned Pepita Camargo yesterday, and he stared at me, as if wondering who I was talking about." She held out both hands. "This is a peculiar madness."

"Do you feel in danger?" Marco asked. "We can end this arrangement today."

"No, no. He is a sad old man who knows he is losing his dignity."

She looked at Marco and he knew what she was thinking, as sure as if she said it out loud. *As I might have become, without Paloma in my life*, he thought. *After too long, a man just doesn't care.*

In the kitchen, Sancha supervised breakfast preparations. The three nervous servants had settled into the purpose and serenity that comes from careful management.

"Sancha works magic," Paloma whispered to him as she watched the servants move efficiently at their tasks.

"No magic, Señora," Sancha said, overhearing, but obviously pleased. "All servants need is someone to direct them in a kind manner." She looked closer at Paloma, and Marco held his breath with the loveliness of her expression. "You probably wished for that, before you decided to return a yellow dog."

"I did," Paloma said. She groped behind her for Marco's hand, and he obliged her. She smiled, almost to herself. "Perhaps it is just as well that my particular keepers were not as kind as you, Sancha, else I might never have wanted to … return that expensive yellow dog to a man who paid too much."

"Perhaps Don Marco was a countryman—a *paisano*—so awed by Santa Fe that he did not understand how to bargain."

In all the years Marco had known her, it was the closest Sancha had ever come to a joke, and she said it with that lurking smile he had not seen since Felicia's death. The kindliness of the whole exchange pleased him; they were two women chiding their master at his expense, and he loved it.

"I am certain that was it, Sancha," Paloma replied.

"Or just maybe I saw something in you that I wanted," she told Marco later, after they left the hacienda. "You would not think me forward if I admitted it now?" She blushed and looked away.

Her obvious reticence, even though they knew each other quite well now, touched Marco's heart. "May you always see something in me," he told her, equally shy, which earned him another glance and a smile.

It was her last smile of the morning. As they rode into Santa Maria, Marco watched his friends and neighbors appraise his new wife and turn away, not from shyness, but from suspicion—if their sour expressions and over-the-shoulder glances were any indication. Startled, he glanced at Paloma, hoping she had not noticed, but her usually expressive face grew more solemn. Soon she was looking down at her hands as they rode slowly through the single street toward the church. When her shoulders began to droop, he knew the Castellanos had been hard at work, spreading lies.

"What has happened here?" he murmured, loud enough for her to hear, so she would not think for one second that she was alone in this new misery.

"I warned you about my cousin," Paloma whispered, after he helped her from the saddle on a side street by the church. "She has a sharp tongue. That is probably why my uncle had to cast a wide net to find her a husband."

He suddenly felt too angry and sick at heart to walk inside the church. He hung back in misery. "What story can she possibly spread?" he asked, ready to get back on his horse. In fact, he turned to unwrap the reins from the hitching post.

"Most certainly the main story is that I am a thief," Paloma told him, her hand on the reins to stop him. "Those few *cuartillos* have probably grown into his entire treasure chest and one-half his property by now."

Her matter-of-fact words stung his heart, but gave him the courage to leave his horse tied to the post and take her hand. "What else could she be spreading?"

Paloma shrugged. "Whatever she can think of."

"Why?"

She shrugged again. "Some people are small of heart and soul." She leaned closer to him and touched his arm to pull herself closer. He obliged by leaning down a little.

"It is this, my love: I know she is disappointed that of the two men who arrived in Santa Fe, her future husband turned out to be Alonso. You are much more handsome and capable-looking. She is jealous and that makes her even more petty than usual." She looked around quickly and kissed his cheek. "I am ever so much more fortunate."

"But if she has told everyone you are a thief—"

"Probably worse," Paloma said. "She always has a lie."

An honorable man, he put his hand on his horse's reins again. "We don't have to stay here for such tales."

Again she touched his arm, giving him a little shake this time. "There is one thing else you need to know about Maria Teresa Moreno: she always muddies her nest. Give her time, and she will be her own worst enemy."

She looked around at the people giving them sidelong glances as they went into the church. "Good Christians love to tell tales. Do you think people confess even half of what they do and feel?"

"I know I don't," Marco said. "Do you?"

"Most generally," she told him. "After all, I confessed to Father Eusebio that I had lustful thoughts about you, and that was after only two days."

He laughed out loud, which caused the good Christians to gape and then to whisper among themselves, darting more glances their way.

She shushed him, blushing. "At least I do not have to confess anything about what we do now."

"Even in my office?" he teased in turn.

"Especially in your office!"

IT WAS EASY to tease, but harder to bear the glances and whispers as they went into the church after which the town was named. The church was almost as plain as her beloved San Miguel, which gave Paloma a pang, thinking of the dear fathers who had sustained her through trying years. *Chin up, Paloma*, she told herself. *These people will think you do not want to be here.* They would never understand that she did not wish to be anywhere except at the side of her husband.

Still, she could not deny the hurt, no matter how brave a face she had put on the matter, for Marco's sake. She knew he was not a man used to being the butt of rumor. He was the brand inspector, after all, and so much more. She tried to see herself as the townspeople saw her, a young woman in plain clothes, thin, unfamiliar. Without a doubt, everyone knew the *juez* had left the Double Cross two months ago for his visit to Santa Fe, to take his cattle, his wool clip, and that year's documents detailing district brand inspections and cattle sales. He did it every year. They knew he was a man eight years without a woman. Maybe they thought he had acted hastily in finding a woman to replace someone Paloma already knew was well-liked in Santa Maria. Maybe they thought he had settled on the first female he saw. Or maybe they thought she had used witchcraft to trick him into marriage.

You do not know me, she thought, keeping her eyes down and her hands folded in front of her, as her mother, that lady of Spain, had always taught her. *And if Maria Teresa has been spreading lies, I will have to prove myself.* It seemed a daunting task.

But here they were, shoulders touching, kneeling together in church. She did not have to face this alone, as she had faced so much alone since her mother had shoved her under the bed and the Comanches came. She took heart and prayed for simple things—that Marco's farrier would recover from a crippling bout of rheumatism, that Perla *la cocinera* would have relief from her aching back, that Marco would suffer less remorse over the dead Comanche child.

She seldom asked the Lord for much, but this time she had a special wish. It had been several years since her last monthly flow, quenched—Father Eusebio had blushed to give his opinion—by too little food and too much work. She didn't entirely understand the association of monthlies with babies, but she wanted, of all things, to give Marco Mondragón more children. If restoring her flow would help, she knew she could overlook the inconvenience of it. Such a simple wish. In this time after the harvest and before the celebration of the birth of Our Lord, if the Virgin was not too preoccupied with more important matters, perhaps she would incline her ear toward a nobody with a simple request, teetering on the edge of the Spanish empire.

Halfway through the Mass, Paloma overcame enough shyness to look around. Closer to the front in all her finery was her cousin, restlessly shifting from knee to knee, and not so close to her husband. She made a great show of rattling her rosary, while Paloma used her fingers to count imaginary beads. Maybe she should ask Marco for a rosary. She had brought a lovely one with her from her ruined home, but it had disappeared, along with her star and vega necklace, almost as soon as she arrived in Santa Fe. Poor Alonso, to be saddled with such a wife. Paloma could have told him that nothing he did would ever be enough.

She glanced at Pepita Camargo, sitting close to the front as well, which seemed to be the choice spot to see and be seen, and possibly worship. She wondered only briefly why her own *juez de campo* had stayed well back. One look at the man so close beside her—his eyes closed, his lips moving—gave her the answer her dusty heart craved. He was here to worship, perhaps also to make some small amends for the death of that child. She knew that he felt the whole weight of the valley on his shoulders. It was a good thing those shoulders were strong and used to burdens, and not slim and sloping like Alonso's. She closed her eyes then and concentrated on what she owed the Lord for her amazing change of fortune.

When the Mass ended, Marco helped her to her feet. Paloma couldn't help but notice Alonso Castellano had left Maria Teresa to struggle upright on her own.

Marco whispered in her ear. "Father Francisco has been giving me the high sign. I never ignore him."

Dutifully, she followed him down the narrow hall to the area not even dignified enough to call an office. She curtsied and knelt when Marco introduced her, content to feel the small sign of the cross on her forehead, Father Francisco's own welcome to Valle del Sol. There were only two chairs in the room; Father Francisco sat in one and her husband in the other. With a smile, Marco gestured to her and she sat on his lap, which made Paloma blush and the priest tug at his chin, his eyes merry.

Father Francisco wasted no time with preliminaries. He leaned forward. "My son, you should know that the Castellanos are spreading all kinds of rumors about this sudden wife here on your lap."

"I assumed as much," Marco said. "Let me guess. She stole money from Señora Castellano's father. Paloma, tell him what really happened."

She did, telling her story quickly, because she knew he was a busy man. She took it as far as her marriage, and Marco finished.

The priest nodded. "I thought as much. Some people believe her, and others ..." He shrugged. "They know the *juez* and have faith in him, as I do. We will wait it out, like good Spaniards, eh?"

"You will also hear tales from Pepita Camargo, who is certain I am withholding a Comanche slave from her father and have established my own people at Hacienda Muñoz. She will likely tell you I am determined to cut her out of her inheritance, once I have murdered her dear father."

Father Francisco didn't even blink. "Ah, yes, that bit of nastiness has reared its ugly head, too. Do you know she is circulating a petition to have you recalled as *juez de campo* for the Comanchería District?"

She felt Marco's flinch and heard his sigh. "Who would want such a thankless job?" he murmured. He told Father Francisco everything that had happened at Hacienda Muñoz. "Sancha, other servants and some of my own guards are there now, trying to help the old man. I fully intend to take him with me to Santa Fe in the spring, to answer for his deeds. It will probably come to nothing, but that is my duty to *all* of the crown's people, including its Indians."

"Bravo, Señor Mondragón," Father Francisco said. "I will remember you in my prayers. Come to Santa Maria for Mass as often as you can this winter." He looked at Paloma. "Señora Mondragón, what would you wish from me?"

Bless me to be fertile, she thought, too shy to speak what was in her heart. *Oh, please.* "I can wish for nothing more than I already have, Father," she whispered. "I think I am the most fortunate woman in the valley, and that is enough."

The priest nodded. As they watched, he rummaged in the drawer on his desk. "I have only one drawer. Why is everything so jumbled?" he muttered. "Ah, here we are. For you, Paloma Mondragón. I noticed you were using your fingers during Mass."

He handed her a rosary, worn from much use. "It belonged to an old, old woman. Señora Elisabeta Roybal, Marco. You remember her."

"I do. She was your most faithful parishioner." Marco rested his hand on Paloma's shoulder. "If I misbehaved during Mass, she always thumped me." He gave her shoulder a little shake. "Now if I fall asleep and start to snore, you can thump me. Felicia used to."

"Señora Roybal, God rest her soul, died while you were gone," Father Francisco said, and crossed himself. "On her deathbed, she told me to give her rosary to a young person, because it had fifty years of prayers and petitions rubbed into the wood. For you, my daughter. Go with God."

"Father, one moment. Bless me, please, if you will," Marco said. "I sometimes find it onerous to be *juez de campo*." He glanced at Paloma. "Lately, I'd rather just be a rancher and a husband."

"Kneel, my son, and let us get to it," the priest said.

Paloma knelt beside her husband, taking his hand, as Father Francisco wished him all success in a long, long list of duties. Perhaps she had not been aware before how much the district depended on her husband. Just listening to his obligations due to the distant crown made her resolve to work harder to provide the comforts that would make his life easier.

When the priest finished, he put his hands on Paloma's head, something she had not expected, and murmured, "And may the Lord bless you with those silent wishes of your heart, dear child."

How does he know? she thought, grateful.

Chapter Twenty-eight

In Which Toshua Listens Too Well

MARCO TOOK PALOMA'S hand as they left the church. "Now who do you think will be waiting to shake a fist at us outside?" he asked. "I put my wager on Pepita Camargo."

"No, no. It will be my cousin," Paloma said. "I think Pepita is not someone to stay away from her Sunday dinner a second longer than necessary."

"If I win, you will scrub my back tonight," Marco told her. "And if you win, I will scrub yours."

Men, Paloma thought, amused. "You think you are so shrewd. Whichever of us wins, the end result will be the same."

He laughed, kissed her hand, and opened the door. He shook his head. "You win, Paloma."

Suddenly it was too much. Tears welled in her eyes. "All I want is to be left alone," she whispered.

"I'll take care of this," he told her, squeezing her hand then releasing it. "Don Alonso, what is it you demand of me?" He bowed, a gesture bordering on insolent. "As your *juez,* you need only ask."

"You are a useless *juez de campo*," Maria Teresa said, moving in for her attack even as Alonso stood there, silent. "*Why* have you not returned my brand to my husband, with the mark of registration on it? You have had it for weeks and weeks now."

"Two weeks, Señora," he said. "That is all. I will ride your way some day this week with your documents."

"You will bring it tomorrow!" she insisted, as Alonso paled.

"I will bring it when I am ready," Marco replied, not raising his voice. He gave Alonso a look of such pity that the other man winced. "I have wondered about its legality. Do you have cattle right now bearing this brand?"

Maris Teresa's nose went up. "Of course we do! How dare you question anything? My father has a ranch near El Paso!"

Paloma could not help her sudden intake of breath. Maria Teresa threw a triumphant look her way.

"Papa tells me it is a very fine ranch," she said.

"Yes, it was," Paloma said, the words wrung out of her, angry at herself for showing her wretched cousin for even one moment that it mattered to her. "A beautiful ranch, indeed."

Maria Teresa stared at her. "Cousin, how is it that you have seen this ranch?"

Because it is my ranch, Paloma wanted to say. *Your father has stolen it and I have no proof. I have been double-crossed by my own relatives.* "I used to live in that district," she replied softly, wanting nothing more now than to get away from her cousin and nurse that wound in private.

"Papa tells me it will be mine someday," Maria Teresa said. "We expect you tomorrow with our brand, *juez*."

Maria Teresa looped her arm through her husband's arm and towed him away. Alonso looked back once, his expression one of acutest misery. Marco stood there, his head down, sunk in his own misery. Paloma took his arm, but she did not tow him anywhere.

"We have no proof."

Paloma sighed to hear those words wrung out of him. She leaned her head against his shoulder. "Mama said it was branded on me. She was right, because I still remember how lovely the ranch looked in spring, when the orchard was in bloom. I have my memories. It is only land and cattle, husband."

"My specialty, courtesy of the crown," he told her, not disguising his bitterness. "How is it that I can protect and defend other people's brands, but I am powerless to help my own wife?"

"It doesn't matter." In all the years she worked for the Morenos and dreamed of her old home, she never thought she would say such a thing. Maybe some things were better gone forever. She wanted to tell him that, but she didn't think he would hear her. "Let's go home."

He stood another moment, then looked at her. "We have one other person to visit. It's only a short distance. Remember?"

They walked the two blocks in silence. When the wind picked up and blew cold, she shivered. There would be more snow soon.

"Here we are," Marco said, as they came to a small house set back slightly from the road. "I saw Carmen Saltero during Mass," he told her as he knocked.

The woman who opened the door holding a chicken leg was barely four feet high. Paloma glanced at her husband, curious.

"Carmen, here is my new wife, Paloma Vega. She has need of your particular talents."

"*Ay de mi*, you forget it is the Sabbath."

"Not I, but here we are, unlikely to return to Santa Maria until Christmas. Such a dilemma."

"Come in," the little woman said, gesturing as grandly as a person could, with a chicken leg.

Paloma followed her down a narrow hall and into a larger room, where she stopped in surprise, staring at an unexpected assembly of women. Her first thought was to turn around and apologize to Carmen Saltero for interrupting such a large gathering. She looked again. "*Dios mio*. I thought …"

Carmen laughed. "Everyone does, the first time. Did my ladies startle you?"

"A little."

Paloma let go of Marco's hand and walked from mannequin to mannequin. They were of different shapes and heights, made of cloth stiffened inside some way, some wearing nothing more than a shift. One was dressed in blue wool, with handsome bone buttons. Paloma looked down. The skirt with its knee-deep flounce had not been hemmed yet. Another dressmaker's dummy wore a bodice and part of one sleeve, somehow managing to look demure in her shift. Attached to the back of each mannequin was a name. There were two Bacas—first names different—a Borrego, several Roybals (Anna Maria, Cristina Maria, Diana Maria, Paca), a Lucero, an Archuleta, a Garduño, a Marquez.

There were other figures against the walls, dressed in simple black cotton, their heads shrouded. *These must be the ones who no longer need your services*, Paloma thought in amazement. She walked by them more carefully, as though in a graveyard. More Roybals. A Sandoval. An Alaniz.

She stopped before a short mannequin with a figure much fuller than her own. As Paloma fingered the black cotton, her eyes filled with tears. A Mondragón. "Felicia," she whispered. "I am taking good care of him."

She glanced back at her husband, who was talking to the little dressmaker with such morbid taste in dinner guests. Maybe Carmen Saltero had never married. Maybe these ladies were her family. Whatever the reason she had made a mannequin for each customer, her talents with a needle were abundantly evident.

Paloma almost did not want to turn her back on the ladies who clustered around, because it seemed impolite. Maybe it was more than that. As she returned to her husband's side, she felt a little ripple of fear, as though if she turned around, the dressmaker's dummies would have all advanced a step or two in her direction. This was not a house where she would ever leave her bedroom after dark.

Marco smiled at her. Surely he knew she had just visited Felicia. "Alas, my love, Carmen reminds me that it is Sunday and she does not do business on the Sabbath. Not even measurements. I have pointed out to her that you are a small woman, but measurements are measurements, even those for small women who wouldn't take much time."

"We can return later," Paloma said. She looked at the dressmaker. "You do such lovely work. Maybe someday, when it is not the Sabbath—"

"How is this?" the older woman asked, staring at the table and her half-eaten dinner. "It must be a miracle, but here is twine."

She set down her chicken bone and picked up a ball of twine on the dining table. Such a strange place. Paloma had never put twine on a dining table.

"Since it is here, the Lord intends me to add to my guests," Carmen said, unrolling the twine quickly. "I will work so fast that the devil will never know. You say the Ave, Señor Mondragón, to distract El Diablo." She picked up a piece of charcoal. "And look here! Charcoal!"

With barely a quiver in his voice—Paloma knew better than to look at him—Marco did as she asked, saying "*Ave Maria, gratia plena …*" in a loud voice. Expertly, the seamstress looped twine around Paloma's waist, then made a charcoal mark. Another mark on the twine from her waist to the floor. Another from neck to wrist. Paloma barely felt the twine around her breasts and hips, but she heard Carmen's low, "Tsk. He does not feed you enough," which made her smile. The neck to waist measurement ended Carmen's rapid tour of Paloma's slender frame. The woman crossed herself when Marco finished the last *Ave*, then laughed. "You have fooled the devil, Señor."

"Good! May I suggest that you add an inch to Paloma's waist, breasts and hips? I am doing my best to see that she has more to eat."

"I will, Señor, but I will also make two dresses in the size she is right now. No woman wants to be untidy, eh?" Carmen touched Paloma's cheek. "Simple garments, so you can make other alterations yourself, child, as you put on weight." She laid the marked twine on the table and wound the ball again. "I will snip tomorrow, if the marks are still there," she assured Paloma in a low voice. "I think they will be, because your husband has a loud voice and the devil is not so smart."

Marco nodded. "She'll need a warmer cloak, too. What do you think, Paloma? Five or six dresses for everyday and two nicer ones for Sundays?"

Paloma nodded, dazed with so much generosity. Better not to prick the devil's ears with too many details, since it *was* Sunday. She dared a glance back at the ladies behind her, relieved to see them just standing there. As she looked, she noticed they were grouped in small cliques, perhaps as they would stand in real life, with their friends. She would have to ask Marco later.

Carmen gestured for Marco to bend down, and she whispered in his ear. He nodded, then kissed her cheek.

"Paloma, we had better ride."

Paloma curtsied to the dressmaker and her silent company. As she followed her husband back down the hall, she heard a clink of coins as he dropped the leather pouch she had noticed around his waist. She couldn't help her low laugh. Carmen would find the coins in the morning when the Sabbath was over, the devil none the wiser.

Arms linked, they strolled back to their horses so patiently waiting. He helped her into the saddle, mounted his own horse and they left Santa Maria behind.

She did not have to wait long for him to explain the strange scene in Carmen Saltero's house.

"She went mad twenty years ago when the Comanche last raided through Santa Maria and killed her husband and five children. My father was *juez* at the time, and my mother a wise woman," he said. "Mama told me later that up until then, Carmen Saltero had only one dressmaker's dummy, the kind with the expandable waist and hips. Perhaps your mother had one of those."

"She did."

"When Carmen finally gathered herself together and began to sew again, she started making those individual figures. The good people of Santa Maria tried to have her burned at the stake for a witch, but the *juez* said no. He sent Mama to her for measurements. I suppose the others reasoned that if my father and mother had confidence in the mad dressmaker of Santa Maria, there was nothing to fear. She made beautiful dresses for my mother, God rest her soul."

Paloma nodded, then shivered in spite of herself. "I don't mind admitting that the ladies gave me a start."

"I thought they might. And there was Felicia, in the company of angels."

Paloma nodded. Maybe land and cattle really were nothing. "I get the feeling, husband, that registering brands is just a small part of your duties as *juez de campo*."

"You've found me out! I watched my own *juez*, my father, consider even the smallest matters seriously. He told me, 'If they are bringing a problem to you, my son, then it matters a great deal to them. Never laugh.' "

MARCO WAS HAPPY enough that Paloma chose to keep her own counsel on the ride home. He couldn't help smarting over Maria Teresa's rudeness to him, and how she was changing a lifelong friend—granted, a tedious one at times—into a spineless stranger.

He finally spoke as they passed Hacienda Muñoz, looking back to notice Toshua behind them now at a distance. "Paloma, do you sometimes feel that we Spaniards are too touchy about honor? Your cousin wounded mine, and I've been feeling sorry for myself. Are we too proud?"

She didn't say anything for a long time, glancing back as he had glanced back to see Toshua trailing them. He could tell she was uneasy about the Comanche, and he wondered if he should be more uneasy, too. Maybe he shouldn't trust the Indian. Funny how that unsettling visit to Santa Maria had upset him, he who had starved before, and fought Comanches, and survived wounds. The Castellanos had only words as weapons, but they hurt.

"When I came to the Morenos from El Paso, I left my pride behind," his wife said finally. "I knew that for certain the evening I scrabbled around among the plates returned to the kitchen after dinner, trying to find something more to eat among the bones and seeds."

He looked away, wondering at his own shallowness, in the face of his wife's articulate honesty.

"Are you too proud? That is something you have to decide for yourself, husband," she said, then withdrew into her own thoughts again.

Unwilling to think of his many shortcomings just then, Marco gestured Toshua forward until the Indian was riding beside him. *Maybe if I remain silent long enough, he will speak to me first*, he thought.

When Toshua spoke, it was for Marco's ears only. "Why does your woman cry?"

Startled, Marco glanced at Paloma. Silent tears turned her loveliness into such vulnerability that it shook him. He reached over and touched her hand. She managed a smile, then looked away.

"I think she is ashamed of her horrible cousin," he whispered to the Comanche. "I'll tell you later."

He did, after they arrived at the Double Cross. While Toshua led the three mounts to the horse barn, Marco put his hand on his wife's shoulder and walked her through the garden, to the warmth of the kitchen. "Such a long day, Paloma," he said to her. "If you just sit here at the table, Perla will serve you. You're the mistress here, and you've ridden a long way today."

She nodded, head down, a servant again. He silently cursed Maria Teresa Moreno de Castellano for her rudeness.

"Do you think I will always be at the mercy of my relatives?" she asked.

The words were wrung out of her. *Por dios, say the right thing*, he told himself. "At their mercy? Unlikely, my love. Only this morning, you told me that Maria Teresa always muddies her nest. Remember that *dicho*—'Patience, and shuffle the cards.' "

He went to the horse barn, shaking his head at his puny effort to comfort one so dear. Toshua had curried and grained his mount, and started on Paloma's tidy little mare. As he curried his own horse, Marco told the Comanche what had happened in Santa Maria, releasing his own anger by discussing it. Toward the end of his narrative, he stopped, acutely aware that he should have said nothing to the man who burned down Joaquin Muñoz's vacant outbuildings.

"It's a Spanish matter," he said hastily, trying to gather up hot words already spoken. "You are to do no harm to the Castellanos. I spoke out of turn."

"No, you spoke out of your heart," the Comanche corrected him. "Show me this brand."

They finished in silence. Marco stooped to pet Trece, who had flounced up in all his furry majesty to rub against his legs. He laughed as Trece darted back to Andrés, sitting on an overturned bucket and smoking.

"We eat dogs that size," was the Comanche's only comment as they left the horse barn.

Marco lit the candle on his desk and looked through his dwindling stack of correspondence for the brand registration. Toshua stood as still as a post while Marco looked at it for a long time, then handed it over. "It is a star and a V for *vega*, a meadow. Paloma said she came to Santa Fe after the Comanche raid, wearing a necklace of the brand."

"Where is it now?" Toshua asked, handing back the document.

Marco shrugged. "It disappeared in Santa Fe. I suspect her uncle stole it, and I think he appropriated the land and cattle rightfully Paloma's."

"Kill them," Toshua said simply.

If life were only that simple, Marco thought, with his own measure of rue. "I have no proof to support my suspicions. Paloma was a child at the time, and she has no documents. The Comanches set fire to her hacienda, but she stayed under the bed, as her mother had commanded her. She said the flames came close, but she did not run."

"Your woman is a brave one," Toshua said. "The People were probably waiting and watching for them to run."

"She said that she heard several servants who did just that, dying at the hands of the Comanches."

Toshua outlined the brand with his finger. "She has stared death in the face and not flinched. She is a better woman than my three wives. See that you treat her well."

Marco nodded, wondering if he had just been threatened. He remembered Felicia's father saying much the same thing to him on the morning of his wedding. He shook his head. It was a crazy thought, a wild Comanche sounding so much like his father-in-law. Maybe he was tired, too.

He closed his brand book. "Do nothing to harm the Castellanos. I spoke out of turn and—"

"You spoke from your heart," the Comanche insisted again.

"No harm to the Castellanos," Marco repeated. "Sleep here tonight, if you wish. It's warm. Are you hungry?"

Toshua shook his head, smiling. "I can fool your guards, but not Sancha. When I thought I was hiding near Señor Muñoz's hacienda, she saw me, waved me in, and invited me to dinner. I have already eaten."

Marco laughed. "It appears that you and I have underestimated women in our lifetimes."

Toshua nodded, serious again. "Let us not underestimate Señora Castellano."

Chapter Twenty-nine

In Which the Brand Inspector Investigates and Disappoints Himself

MARCO SPENT A restless night, fearful he had said too much to Toshua. Careful not to waken Paloma, who liked to curl up so close to him, he got up twice, both times to throw the bolt on the kitchen door, open it slightly, and just stand there until his eyes adjusted to the gloom and he could see his office next to the horse barn. He prayed Toshua had not left the Double Cross, and wondered if there was a saint somewhere in the vast pantheon of heaven who protected blabbermouths.

There must be. After a night of half-dozing, half-sleeping, all-worrying, Marco woke up to a day cold and bright with sunlight, and Toshua heading toward the kitchen with gathered eggs. Marco let out the breath he must have been holding all night, admiring a man who could carry a bucket of eggs and still look formidable.

After another sleepless night spent worrying, and another, Marco decided Toshua had no plans to ruin the Castellanos, even though they richly deserved it. He slept well finally, then went about the business of winter in Valle del Sol, which this year, after so many fallow seasons, included his new wife.

His greatest pleasure was watching Paloma adjust with real grace to her new role as mistress of the Double Cross. She wore the keys of her domestic office around her slim waist, supervising the work of the servants Sancha had trained so well, rather than just pitching in and doing the work herself. He began to notice subtle changes in the kitchen, as Paloma made it even more efficient. She had a knack for organization, which made him suggest to her one night in bed that she take a look at his untidy office and work her magic there, too. His answer was a blinding smile and a kiss.

She went with him willingly every other day to Hacienda Muñoz, where Sancha had worked her own magic. The house was clean and tidy, and so was Joaquin Muñoz.

"He does not object so much to my presence now," Sancha told them over hot chocolate in the kitchen, while Joaquin dozed in his *sala*, cleansed now of years of clutter, dust and mouse turds. "I sometimes think he gets lost in his own house," she said.

"I noticed the same thing about him," Paloma assured her. She told the housekeeper about the old priest at San Miguel who used to forget where the refectory was. "Maybe this is something that happens to older people; not all, but some."

"How many older people do we see, to know for certain?" Marco asked. "There are so few in New Mexico."

The three of them contemplated the matter in silence until the hot chocolate was cool enough to drink.

Pepita Camargo dropped by once while they visited her father, tight-lipped disapproval stamped all over her face. "Don't think for a moment that I am not aware of your attempt to steal this *rancho* and my inheritance," she declared.

Marco could only repeat again and again that he had no such designs. He pointed out to Joaquin's irate daughter that one badly run *rancho* in Valle only invited Indians to prey upon all. "Pepita, you have my blessing to run this place yourself, with your own servants," he had told her. Each time, she shook her head, content to rail and complain and let others do her duty.

NOVEMBER LITERALLY SLID into December this year, as more and more snow fell, melted, froze and iced them into their winter confinement in the valley. Carmen the dressmaker managed to send a pasteboard box of Paloma's new wardrobe with the royal courier, who arrived at the Double Cross with the last of the season's mail from Santa Fe for the *juez*.

The courier thawed out in the kitchen, smiling gratefully at Paloma's hospitality and offer of a bed for the night. Food and drink warmed him enough to allow him to point to his dispatch bag, make a sour face, and admit that it contained Pepita Camargo's threatened petition.

"There are a few signatures, but I would not worry, Señor Mondragón," he said, as he mounted the next morning and prepared to ride toward Taos, provided he could find a pass still open. "All dither and bluster." He winked and gathered the reins. "We know Governor de Anza is too wise to take it seriously." He laughed then. "Besides that, we know it must wind its way to Mexico City and probably Spain." Again a pause, as if he gauged Marco's sense of humor. "And even beyond that, who would ever want to be brand inspector on the border of Comanchería?"

I would, Marco thought, even though he knew the courier wanted him to laugh at the absurdity of it all. So he laughed, but was happy enough to send the man on his way—rested, warmed and fed and full of enough local gossip now to entertain the next destination on his lonely round.

When the man was gone and the house their own again, Paloma tried on her new dresses. As Carmen promised, two of them fit. The others were still a trifle large. She made her own face, not as sour as the courier's, but enough to register chagrin. "Marco, I know you mean well, but I really don't like to drink so much cream," she told him, as he unbuttoned her dress and eased his hands around her bare waist.

He put his hands on her breasts, hefting them, until she laughed, and said maybe half cream and half milk would satisfy him. "Maybe I am just naturally slim," she said later in his ear as they lay close together.

"There are very few fat people in Valle del Sol," he agreed, comfortable and inclined to sleep, even though it was barely mid-morning. "I cannot see your ribs anymore, but I can still feel them."

Paloma nodded, drowsy herself. "Cream, then," she agreed. She sat up on one elbow to look at him, then looked away, shy. He waited. He could tell she had something to tell him, and he thought he knew what it was.

"If I weighed more, then perhaps …" She paused and rested her head on his chest, so she did not have to look at him.

His hand went automatically to her hair; he could help her through a private subject. "Paloma, when did you last have a monthly?"

Her voice was small, sad. "Several years ago. For all that I worked in the kitchen, there was never much to eat, not with Tia Moreno watching every move we made. I … I mentioned the matter to Father Eusebio once in the confessional. I think it made him angry, so I must have embarrassed him."

He kissed her head. "He wasn't angry at you, love, but at the people who should have taken better care of you. Patience, Paloma."

"Is that your remedy for everything in Valle del Sol?" she asked, sounding piqued enough to make him smile.

"Pretty much. Time moves slowly here."

She sighed and nestled closer. "Above all things, I want to give you a child. I don't know much, but I do believe the matter of monthlies has some bearing on the matter."

"It does. Again, patience."

She nodded this time. He felt her eyes close, and then there was a damp spot on his chest. “There are too many empty bedchambers at the Double Cross.”

He couldn’t have agreed more.

BY THE END of the next week, Marco knew it was past time to ignore returning the brand document and the district transfer to the Castellanos. Since their return from Santa Maria, Paloma had ridden without complaint with him to the various *ranchos* in the valley, where he had government business. He didn’t have the heart to compel her to ride with him to Hacienda Castellano; neither did he wish to leave his wife behind. He assuaged his own worries by sending a messenger ahead, stating his business. There would be no wasted time away from the Double Cross.

That morning over eggs and *chorizo*, when he mentioned his destination, she agreed reluctantly to ride with him, even as her face went pale. *Don’t be irrational, Marco,* he scolded himself. *She will be here when you return.*

“You needn’t ride with me this time,” he told her, even as he wished with all his heart she would disagree and insist upon accompanying him.

To his dismay, she did not. In fact, her sigh of relief told him worlds about her feelings toward her horrid cousin. “Thank you,” she said, and kissed him. “I will have a very good dinner for you when you return this evening.”

“Toshua will be watching here, as always,” he reminded her.

“I suppose,” she said, her voice taking on that neutral tone that he hoped she would never use on him.

“We must trust him, Paloma.”

“Why?”

Toshua was in his office when he went there to gather up the documents. After Marco had suggested it, he had taken up his residence in the office, which meant little more than a blanket on the floor by the fireplace. He rolled it and tucked it away behind the map chest, leaving no other indication of his presence, because he had no possessions.

At least Toshua was dressed warmly now, in the style of Marco’s servants: homespun shirt, wool pants, moccasins, with a poncho wrapped around his shoulders. His hair was finally starting to grow again. He looked up from his contemplation of the cold hearth when Marco entered.

“Do you need me to accompany you?”

“No. Stay behind. I am leaving Paloma here this time.”

“I could keep you company.”

Marco regarded the Indian, seeing something close to sympathy in his usually stoic expression. He knew he had never told anyone why he feared to leave his wife behind. How did everyone seem to know?

“I am going to the Castellano hacienda, to return the brand document and provide a transfer seal." He couldn't help his sour face. "Yes, I have put it off! Did you never put off some unpleasant duty?"

"We all do," Toshua replied, amused. "We are not so different, you and I."

Marco nodded, struck by the honesty of the Comanche's words. He was still thinking about them when he rode out of the Double Cross with his usual four guards.

It was his first visit to his old friend's hacienda since they had all returned to Valle del Sol, and there were changes. The servant who opened the door on his knock, an older woman he had known for years, had a preoccupied, unhappy expression on her face, a far remove from her usual good cheer. It was almost the expression he remembered on Paloma's face, the first time he saw her in Santa Fe.

Instead of leading him to the kitchen—where all business among friends was conducted in the colony—she directed him to the *sala,* which, despite new rugs and wall hangings, looked even colder than usual. He took off his gloves and pushed his hand into the small of his back, massaging it, knowing there wouldn't be any hot chocolate for him during this visit. There wasn't even a log burning in the fireplace.

"Well?"

He turned around, startled, still not accustomed to the rudeness which now seemed to be part of Alonso Castellano, because he had married it. "Señora Castellano," he said, and nodded to Alonso. "And you, my friend."

"Hand it over." Maria Teresa held out her hand.

Alonso glanced at Marco, shame on his face. "Marco, I—" he began, but his wife cut him off.

"I trust you have found no illegality in this brand," she said. "What could be wrong with it?"

He took out the document, looked at the star and *vega* one more time, and put it in Alonso's hand, even though Maria Teresa stretched out her hand, too.

"It's *my* brand!" she declared.

"And Alonso is your lord," he replied. He spoke to his friend, who seemed to wilt from the shame of such a wife. "I recorded the transfer seal, of course. Do you have any cattle so marked yet?"

"Not yet. In the spring."

There was no welcome, no invitation to sit down, no offer of food, no suggestion that he grain his horse. As Marco nodded to them, both standing like statues unfamiliar with each other and their own *sala*, he couldn't help thinking of his own house, and the sweetness of the welcome there for three generations, and with any luck for more generations. His anger turned to sorrow for his friend.

"Good day, then. Perhaps we will see you in Santa Maria for Christ's Mass."

No one showed him out. He was halfway across the yard and ready to whistle for his mount when Alonso called to him. He turned around.

"Marco, will you ride with me?"

He nodded. With a glance back at the house, as though he expected his wife to come storming out, Alonso motioned for the stable boy to provide some hay for Marco's horse while another servant saddled his own. In a short time, they were on the road toward the Double Cross.

Out of sight of the hacienda, Alonso pointed toward a nearby canyon, stark and snowy. Marco turned to ride beside him, waiting for an explanation.

"I don't want Maria to worry," he said, when they topped a small rise and were some way from the hacienda. He whispered, as though she could hear him from that distance.

"Why would she worry?" Marco asked, eager to get home, because the cold was settling in and the afternoon shadows were already turning the mountains purple.

"For the past two weeks, I have been steadily losing cattle."

Dios mio, Toshua has found a way, Marco thought, appalled. "Many?" he asked, hoping he sounded more noncommittal than he felt. Did his voice rise and squeak? Pray God Alonso was too preoccupied to notice.

"A few at first, then more and more. There must be close to thirty gone now." He looked around, as if the creosote bushes had ears. "I haven't said anything to Maria."

And what would she do? Shout at you? Beat you? Marco asked himself. He made some appropriate gesture. "It would be rare for anyone to rustle your cattle now. I have heard no rumors of savages in the vicinity." *Except the Comanche in my keeping, the man I told all about Paloma's lost brand*, he thought remorsefully. "I should be returning home. I can come back tomorrow." Suddenly he was desperate to get away, desperate to see Paloma alive and whole.

"Come with me now," Alonso said, gesturing to his own outriders, who were moving slowly behind them and chatting with Marco's guards. "One of my herders noticed tracks this morning. With your men added to mine, I would not be afraid to follow them."

"Alonso, there was a time when you and I weren't afraid to follow *any* tracks," he murmured under his breath, as he fell back on the narrow trail that climbed into a canyon. His own sense of caution made him unlimber the bow slung over his shoulder and reach for an arrow.

Single-file, they climbed higher and farther into the slot canyon, one of many such canyons on Rancho Castellano that made Alonso's land less valuable. As they rode, he noticed more than one or two hoof marks and cow flops. He also noticed horseshoe prints that looked familiar to him. Pray God Alonso didn't notice.

"My herder turned back at this point," Alonso said. "Should we go on?"

Marco kneed his horse and took over Alonso's point. He looked back as they climbed to see Alonso falling farther and farther back. *Coward,* he thought. *These are your cattle.*

The hair on the back of his neck rose higher, but he rode steadily into the canyon. He knew it would narrow soon, and then widen into a decent meadow. When his father was failing, he had told Marco to get to know the land around him. "You never know, son," he had said, and those had turned out to be his last words. Marco took those words as his motto and his caution, if he planned to ever be an old man in the valley.

Inexplicably, his own outriders had fallen back. He rode on alone, into a silent world. Some unknown thing had spooked his men, and it made him pause, too, until he realized what it was. No birds sang. Granted, many of the summer birds that peeped and sang through glorious warm days had fled south, but the winter birds had their own good cheer that usually rang so clear in cold air. Nothing. "You never know, Father," he muttered to himself, as he completed the gradual twist that would open up the small meadow before him.

He thought he knew what he would find. Even then, the sight startled him into an exclamation that made his horse's ears prick up.

The small *vega*, white with winter, bloomed brown and red from Alonso Castellano's slaughtered cattle.

"*Mea culpa, mea maxima culpa*," he murmured, as the weight of his complicity clamped down like the cold. He had said too much and loosed a dog of war on his neighbor. "All my fault."

Chapter Thirty

In Which Maria Teresa Knows Fear

MARCO RODE THROUGH the valley of death, counting cattle. Forty cattle lay dead, their throats slit. Stunned at such waste, Marco sat in silence until his legs began to tingle with cold. "You could just have easily have killed the Castellanos," he murmured finally, and wheeled his horse around. He turned back for another look, remembering his duties. The cattle did not appear to have been dead more than a day or two, but Alonso had said they were missing over several weeks.

He sat a moment longer, trying to calm himself, doubting that Toshua would actually kill the cattle. He knew how Comanches relished a good trade. He shook his head, wondering, disturbed at such wickedness.

Shock on their faces, his outriders clustered close together at the mouth the little *vega*, a meadow so pretty in summer, so deadly now.

"*Indios*?" one of them called, but came no closer.

"Just one Indian," he said softly, so they could not hear, then raised his voice. "Who else would do this, but Indians?"

He rode toward them through the carnage, keeping his nervous horse controlled as he wondered what he could possibly say to Alonso. Maybe Pepita Camargo was right to circulate a petition. Maybe he was unfit to be *juez de campo*. In telling the Comanche about the double-crossing Maria Teresa and Paloma's uncle, he had committed a sin so gross he flinched to think of the confessional.

For my sins, he thought. He forced himself to review his puny arsenal of facts that started to shrink as he catalogued them. For all he knew, Paloma's father had willed the land and the brand to his wife's brother, in the event of his death. Paloma had been a child; all she knew was what had happened on that bloody day when the Comanches rode onto her family's land.

He shook his head to clear it. Paloma's father would never have deeded property to his brother-in-law, because he had older sons, the ones who had died with their father that day. Still, what did he—Marco Mondagón, brilliant brand inspector—know of the circumstances? Knowing less than nothing, pained that his pride had been punctured by a woman who would have been thoroughly unpleasant to anyone, he had complained to a savage. The Indian, doing what Indians do, had avenged the wrongs committed against Paloma, who had saved his life in a madman's henhouse. The chain of events was diabolical, and his part shamed him.

In silence, he rode the short distance back to Alonso and grabbed his horse's bridle, leading his friend forward to see the death in the meadow. Alonso went pale and even swayed in the saddle, his eyes wide, his mouth open. "What will I tell Maria Teresa?" he asked plaintively, as though Marco could supply him with something glib to gloss over all that blood and bone.

"The truth. What else is there?" Marco snapped. "We live in a hard place." *That I just made harder*, he thought.

Alonso put his hand on Marco's arm, even as he turned away. "You don't understand. She already is badgering me to sell out and move to Santa Fe."

Marco stared at his friend. "You don't just walk away from a land grant."

Miserable, Alonso wouldn't look at him. "I know that. She follows me from room to room, demanding this and demanding that …" He paused, embarrassed. "Does your wife do that?"

"Never. Paloma likes it here." Might as well say it. "Thanks to Maria and her aunt and uncle, Paloma had nothing to hope for in Santa Fe. And let me assure you, Alonso, she did not steal the family treasure. It was a *cuartillo* or two that she did not return, after buying eggs from a vendor."

Alonso sighed heavily. "I know. I do not understand why Maria is so bent on ruining her cousin." He looked away again. When he spoke, his words were tentative. "Marco, I am wondering—not certain, mind you—just wondering if maybe the Morenos had a good reason to look far afield for a husband for Maria Teresa."

"It seems unlikely," Marco lied, not willing to hurt his friend even more. He looked at the carcasses one last time, this time as a *juez de campo*. "Have your men harvest the hides, at least, and there is plenty of meat for your servants. Check the brands and bring me a list. I will enter the details in my log and take the information to Santa Fe next spring." *For all the good that will do*, he thought.

As they rode toward Hacienda Castellano, Alonso seemed to wilt inside himself in dread anticipation of his wife's reaction. Marco allowed himself the little luxury of imagining *his* return—Paloma's wide-open arms, her smile and probably even her gentle scolding if she touched his hands and found them too cold. There would be food and talk and probably a hot bath waiting for him. And here was his boyhood friend, who had nothing sweet to look forward to.

Maria surprised him. Stumbling over his words, Alonso managed to gasp out what had happened to their livestock. Maria's mouth opened in a silent scream, and she sagged against her husband. Embarrassed, Marco looked away when she made sudden water right there in the doorway.

"I must leave this terrible place!" she shrieked. "We will be dead before sunrise, meat for buzzards."

"No, you won't," Marco assured her, speaking loud to be heard over her lament. Damn him, Toshua had fulfilled Marco's demands to do no physical harm to the Castellanos. What he had done was worse; Toshua had left them vulnerable to every birdcall, every shadow, every creak of the floor, every tiny alteration from the generally boring routine of wintertime in Valle del Sol. Toshua had reduced them to walking, breathing terror—a Comanche specialty.

He doubted Toshua would do anything else on Castellano property; he didn't need to. From now on, Maria Teresa would never know a single day without fear.

He couldn't leave the hacienda fast enough, especially when it became evident that Maria's terror had caused her bowels to evacuate, too. So much for the fine lady in church in Santa Maria, so busy spreading malicious gossip about her cousin, Paloma. He would never say anything about this, of course, not even to Paloma; a gentleman didn't do that. He expected no such charity from the Castellanos' servants. Disgruntled already, they would tell this tale until it went beyond Valle and popped up next year at the great fair in Taos. Maria Teresa Moreno de Castellano was ruined; she just didn't know it yet.

Upon reflection—something he had time for on his silent ride home—Marco found himself grudgingly admiring Toshua. At the cost of a rancher's thirty cattle, the Comanche had changed matters for Paloma. Cutting through obedience to a distant law that meant nothing to a Comanche, Toshua had protected them both.

Still, there was no reason to celebrate, because Marco was a civilized man and intended to remain that way, even if Spain withdrew entirely from New Mexico's vast but unprofitable wilderness. He had to talk to Toshua. Tell him what, Marco had no idea, but he couldn't just go around terrorizing other citizens of the valley, even if they richly deserved it. *And I will have to watch my tongue*, Marco told himself.

And then his mind and heart focused entirely on Paloma. As the sky darkened, he began his own sunset journey gripped by fear sown by the deaths of other loved ones. He knew it was illogical to think for even one moment that Paloma would not be there, but he could not help himself. His horse's walk turned into a trot, then a canter and finally a gallop as his outriders raced to keep up with him and his own fright, one that Toshua could never help because Marco would never admit it.

If she is dead, I will die, too, he thought as the familiar gates of the Double Cross slowly opened to receive him. He raced his lathered horse inside, followed by his outriders. He threw himself from his mount and ran toward the hacienda, even as Paloma opened the door. She watched him a moment in surprise, then ran toward him as though she understood his fear.

She grabbed him and threw herself into his open arms, trying to hold as much of him as she could.

"You're here!" he gasped.

He nearly bowled her over in his relief, which made her laugh. "Marco, you're a great big silly," she whispered in his ear as he held her up. "Where else would I be?"

Only the greatest force of will kept him from sobbing out loud in relief. How was it she knew his need? Had Felicia come from the spirit world somehow to visit this second wife and tick off on her fingers all the ways to keep Marco Mondragón contented? He was stupid to think it, but he knew God's tender mercies had not abandoned him after all.

"Where is Toshua?" he asked.

"In the kitchen. We were eating," Paloma told him.

He kissed her head and said he would join them as soon as he finished currying his horse. He spent a long time brushing his lathered horse, tossing more flakes of hay his way and dumping in extra grain, performing his own penance for Buciro, a four-footed old friend who only did what he was asked.

Toshua had finished eating. He sat there at the table, his arms folded, frowning down at his empty bowl. Marco thought about taking this discussion into the *sala*, but dismissed the notion, not willing to turn into Maria Teresa and deliver a scold in a cold room. He also knew he did not want to chastise the Comanche; he liked his own cattle alive and grazing.

He shook his head when Paloma offered dinner. She sat down close to him again, obviously puzzled.

"I know my cousin did not offer you any food, Marco, and you have been gone all day," his wife hinted. "Some hot chocolate, at least?"

He nodded, not wanting it, but not eager to disappoint the mistress of the Double Cross. It did taste better than he thought it should, considering his own stupidity, and his willingness to suffer some sort of penance for the

Castellanos' pain, unleashed on them by his impulsive words to a Comanche.

He told them both what had happened to the cattle at Alonso's ranch, his eyes on Toshua. Blast and damn the Indian for showing not a flicker of remorse or surprise. When Marco told them of Maria Teresa's abject terror, he noticed something in Toshua's expression—the tiny uplift of one corner of his mouth. It was so slight a glimpse of satisfaction it might have been Marco's imagination, especially since Paloma's exclamation of distress was immediate.

"*Pobrecita*!" she said, and there were tears in her eyes.

Marco glanced at Toshua in time to see a puzzled expression wipe away his smirk.

"But she has done you wrong," Toshua said, clearly curious. "Why should you feel sorry for her?"

Marco glanced at his wife's face then, wondering the same thing, and, churl that he was, glad Toshua had beaten him to the question.

"You're right, Toshua. She has treated me poorly." Paloma picked up Marco's barely touched hot chocolate and sipped it, obviously trying to understand her involuntary reaction. "Still, it doesn't follow that I hate her."

Toshua flinched, as though she had pushed him. "I will never understand women," he said, which made Marco laugh.

"You see why we Spaniards only want one woman at a time?" Marco asked him.

Paloma glared at them both, and then her expression softened. "Maria Teresa has never known want, or trouble, or … or any unpleasantness. Now she is unhappy with the husband her father chose and a long way from home, alone and frightened. That is a lot of change for someone used to an easy life."

"I suppose it is," Marco agreed, dragging the words out of his mouth with pincers. He had no intention of forgiving Maria Teresa for her inexcusable, malicious rudeness to his wife. This was a grudge he intended to nourish.

Paloma twined her fingers through his, apparently going to love him anyway, even if he didn't understand women. "It's this way, Marco," she said, glancing at Toshua and then at him, where her gaze lingered. "To live here successfully in Valle del Sol, perhaps it is better to be acquainted with disaster. Maybe it helps to be an adventurer, too, which Maria is not."

He was silent, struck by her words. He thought of his own worries about Spain's almost-certain withdrawal from an isolated frontier no king or grandee in Madrid or Cádiz could even begin to understand. He was a first cousin to disaster, with no plans to ever leave this land he loved so well.

"Marco, all we can do is live as best we know how," she told him, increasing the pressure of her fingers in his. "The Lord God has showered many tender mercies on Maria Teresa. Now he is showering some on me." She gave the Comanche a long look, until he shifted restlessly on the bench. "Leave it alone, Toshua. I can forgive Maria Teresa."

She knows he killed those cattle, Marco thought, uneasy. Knowing this, it only followed that she knew her husband had been the blabbermouth.

"I do not understand 'forgive.' "

Marco glanced at Toshua. He could not explain forgiveness to the Comanche, when he himself did not feel it.

Both of them were looking at Paloma now, and she blushed under their combined scrutiny. "Oh, you two!" she exclaimed softly, affectionately even, then turned serious. "Until you told me this sad story of Maria Teresa, I wasn't so certain I could forgive her, either. Maybe I cannot. Time will tell."

She left the kitchen. He listened; soon, he heard the door to the chapel creak open. He observed Toshua, seated so quietly across from him. "I believe you meant well," he said, unsure how to pick his way through this bog he had created. "I should never have said to you what I did about the Castellanos and that cursed brand."

"They have cheated and double-crossed your woman," the Comanche reminded him.

"They have," Marco agreed. "I cannot prove it right now. Even if I could, what would Paloma think of me, if I exposed them? I doubt that Maria Castellano has any idea what evil her father has done." He managed a small laugh. "I do not understand women, either, but I am not willing to risk losing the affection of *this* one."

"That I do understand." Toshua stood up. "Go kneel with her and rattle those beads and pray to someone who might or might not be paying any attention to you here in *my* land."

"What will you do?" Marco asked.

"I will go to bed," Toshua said, his lurking humor evident. "And I will make you no promises."

As he walked down the hall toward the chapel, Marco knew that was all he could expect from a savage. He stopped outside the door and looked back, remembering the Comanches he had killed in his life, especially last year with Governor de Anza. *Were we any less savage than they?* he asked himself, struck by the thought. No one called *him* a savage, but there were times …

"Paloma, you are right," he murmured as he opened the door. "None of us is wholly bad or wholly good."

Chapter Thirty-one

In Which the Brand Inspector Knows Fear

PALOMA SIGHED WITH relief when the door to the chapel opened. In a moment, her husband knelt beside her. She smelled his weariness. He should really be in bed, asleep after his long day. She didn't want him to confess anything to her, but she knew him well enough now, and knew that he would.

She sat back on her heels, listening with her whole heart as Marco told her how he had complained to the Comanche about Maria Teresa's rudeness to her that had cut him to the quick. He admitted that his own pride had suffered, and that he had spoken out of turn to someone who could not possibly understand. *I am not your confessor*, she wanted to tell him, before she understood she was precisely that. As the wife of a good man who was sometimes not so good, it was her duty to listen and absolve. She listened and absolved, knowing that it might be her turn for confession someday, over some other matter. That was what husbands and wives did, or so she thought. She was still new at marriage.

"What's more, I cannot reprimand him. How would he understand me?" he said. "Did you notice how surprised he was when you said you felt sorry for that … that *hechizera*?"

"She is *not* a witch," Paloma said firmly. "Unpleasant maybe, but not a witch."

By now they were both sitting cross-legged on the hard tiles, facing each other, not paying particular attention to the deity.

"I probably disappointed Toshua," Paloma said and started to laugh. She stopped soon enough, because Marco only managed a weak smile. "Don't worry, my love." She thought about what Father Damiano had told her in such confidence at San Pedro and forged ahead, placing her hands gently on his knee. "Don't worry about me. I will always be here when you return." She leaned forward to kiss him. "What I really didn't like this evening was the panic in your eyes when you looked for me."

He made an inarticulate sound in his throat and held out his arms for her. She was in them in a moment, holding him close.

"Father Damiano did not tell me about your great fear; I guessed it. Marco, I will ride with you to the ends of the earth if you require it, but maybe you just need to have a little faith."

"It's hard," he said finally. "I thought I could do it today. I was only going to Alonso's. I almost could not breathe as I flogged my horse home. You married a weakling."

"I did not!" she declared emphatically. "I married a man who treasures women." She kissed him again. "Let us leave it at that for now, shall we?"

She knew he was not satisfied with himself, not a man like Marco, who took his duties seriously. There may have been a puny garrison of soldiers billeted in Santa Maria at an undersized *presidio*, but the real authority of the crown resided in the *juez de campo*, a solitary man in a big land.

"How long have you been *juez*?" she asked.

"Ten years, since my father died and I turned twenty-one."

She sighed. So much responsibility.

After she bullied him into smoked beef and chilies, she bullied him into the bathtub and scrubbed his back while she sang to him. Gradually, she felt the tense knots of his shoulder muscles relax. She poured in more hot water and left him to just sit there, his knees up in the tight space, his eyes closed. When she came back into their bedchamber with a dry towel warmed near the fireplace, he was nearly asleep. He offered no protest when she dried him off and pulled back the blankets so he could crawl into bed. He was asleep before she even started on her buttons.

HE MUST HAVE slept late, because the room was light when he woke up and looked around. He sniffed and smelled good things. Dressing quickly, he followed his nose, ready to apologize if it was really late, but more hopeful that Perla might be elsewhere, so he could fool around with the mistress of the household.

Alonso sat in his kitchen, shoveling in beans and cheese, and mopping it all up with Paloma's tortillas, every bit as good as Perla's. He looked up with a guilty expression to see Marco standing in the doorway. "I think I have eaten your breakfast," he apologized. His hunger spoke volumes about how Maria Teresa managed her own kitchen.

"No, no," Paloma scolded gently. "There is plenty more. My mother always had extra in her kitchen, in case someone stopped by."

Alonso must have understood what she was really saying. He paused, mid-sop, and his cheeks reddened. "But probably not your Tia Luisa Moreno, eh?" he said quietly.

"No. I had a better example than Maria Teresa did," Paloma replied, just as quiet. "Don't worry, Alonso. You are always welcome in this kitchen. Sit down, husband. I should be able to find a moldy tortilla for you, and maybe some half-cooked beans. I'll shake out any rocks."

Marco smiled at her, and accepted hot chocolate. "Alonso. You're early."

"It's nearly noon."

"Then I trust I have not kept you waiting long."

Reaching for his leather portfolio, his friend handed him a page that had been used for other writing and crossed through, paper being scarce. He pointed to the freshest ink, tapped it with his finger and waited.

Marco sipped his chocolate, then set down the cup and stared at the page. "What *is* this, Alonso?" he asked, in a voice he barely recognized as his own. "My cattle, too? And Jorge Maestas' and Pepe Calderón's?" he asked, recognizing the brands of two other nearby ranchers. "I knew I had lost one or two recently, but this is winter, when such things happen. What *does* this mean?"

Alonso's head went down in shame. "After you rode away, I spoke to my herders. Maybe I was more forceful than usual. Maybe they had already heard of Maria Teresa's … terror. Fernando Bustamante went to his knees, pleading for forgiveness."

"For *what*?" Marco demanded.

"He had been running off livestock, one at a time, and hiding the cattle in that box canyon." His expression hardened. "He thought he would build up his own herd at my expense! And my neighbors' as well. When you sent the messenger earlier, saying you were coming, he panicked and slit their throats, knowing *you* would find the cattle, where *I* probably would not. He wanted to make it look like Comanches. Marco, I am so ashamed. Here is my tally." With a shaking finger, he indicated the paper that Marco held. "Forty dead cattle—ten of mine and ten each from you and our neighbors." He sighed. "And I am still missing twenty more."

"It wasn't Indians?" Marco asked, as though he did not hear properly. He glanced at Paloma, who appeared equally astounded.

"It was only my servant," Alonso said, in all humility now. "I have had him flogged. You may mete out whatever additional justice he requires, even death." He looked away. "I am still missing twenty more beeves, but Fernando has sworn on his mother's grave that he had nothing to do with those."

"How badly did you flog the man?" Marco asked.

"He won't walk anytime soon."

Marco heard Paloma's little exclamation and watched her dart from the room, her hand to her mouth, probably feeling those stripes on her own back.

"Perhaps that is sufficient. Has he a wife and children?"

"He has. He cried and cried and said I do not pay him enough, so he had to steal from me," Alonso exclaimed, indignant. "I have already assured him his children will become my slaves, because he owes all of us a great debt in cattle."

"Perhaps you do not pay him enough," Marco said, wondering—and not for the first time—how any servants of Spanish ranchers survived. "Don't enslave his children, and that is an order. Go home, Alonso. I will inform Pepe and Jorge about their lost cattle. Just go home."

"I would rather stay here," his friend said simply. "My wife is in hysterics, barricaded in her room and vowing she will never come out until I have agreed to leave the valley." He looked around, his eyes wistful, and Marco felt a surge of pity replace his anger. "Your home is peaceful. Please may I stay awhile?"

"No, my friend. You must find a way to her heart. You are bound to her by vows." Marco spoke as gently as possible. His heart spilled over with gratitude for his own circumstances. His long drought was over; he feared his friend's was only beginning. Hadn't he just said *her* room, rather than *our* room?

Alonso nodded and left. Marco stared at the document in his hand, the brands so familiar to him. He had to quiz Toshua, because there must be more to this story. First he sought out Paloma.

The chapel was empty. He went into their bedroom to see her kneeling at their *reclinatorio*, her hands clasped in prayer. He did nothing more than rest his hand on her shoulder, which made her lean her cheek against his hand.

"Marco, do you ever want to gather up broken people and mend them?"

"Lately, all the time."

TOSHUA WAS IN Marco's office. The Comanche had made the office his particular province, keeping the fire stoked, and the ashes cleared. Marco sat down at his desk and leaned back in his chair. Toshua watched him, his gaze unwavering and disconcerting. *I will not look away first*, Marco thought.

"Toshua, Alonso Castellano came here to tell me that one of his herders confessed to stealing those cattle. When he feared discovery, he slit their throats, in order to blame Comanches." He leaned forward, his eyes still on the Indian's. "Where are the cattle *you* rustled?"

Toshua looked away. "The twenty I spirited away are deeper in the little canyon just to the north of the box canyon. They are alive. I took those the first week after your woman was made so unhappy by that weakling and his foolish wife." He smiled then. "I was going to steal more, but I watched that herder one night and left the rest of the thievery to him."

Marco let out an exasperated breath. "Can you return them just as quietly?"

"You know I can." He came closer, leaning his hip against the edge of the desk. "You knew I had not killed the cattle."

"Of course. Do you think *I* am a fool?" Marco asked. "I doubt there is a Comanche alive who would ever destroy such a trading opportunity. Tell me: were you planning to drive them into Comanchería and use them to get back in good odor with your own band?"

Toshua shrugged. "I thought I might try, until your soft-hearted woman grew such big tears in her eyes over that worthless woman of Don Alonso's. Those blue eyes must make it hard for you to rule her with any firmness."

"I don't rule her. I just love her," Marco said. "You will return Alonso's cattle?"

"It's not a thing I am proud of, because the People do not return cattle," Toshua retorted. "Kindly do not mention it again."

Toshua left the office in all dignity, which meant Marco could have a quiet laugh in private. He stared at Alonso's scrap of paper and transferred the information to two other sheets, one for Jorge and the other for Pepe. At least the Castellano's thieving herdsman had been no respecter of persons; each of them had lost ten beeves to his avarice.

He glanced outside the window when he finished, watching high clouds scud across the sky, heading toward Comanchería and out across the plains of Texas. If he left now, he could deliver the documents to the ranchers and be home before Paloma even missed him. Or more to the point, before he missed her. He would show her he was a brave man and a faithful one, trusting God to keep her safe in his absence.

In charge of her emotions again, Paloma nodded at his plans and made him two sandwiches of beef left over from last night. She kissed him and waved goodbye.

MARCO KNEW HIS neighbors. Jorge Maestas grumbled and glowered, calling down all manner of creative maledictions on the entire Castellano lineage, past, present and future. Pepe Calderón shrugged, called it the will of God, and urged Marco to spend the night, since the high clouds of afternoon had lowered ominously.

He shook his head and started home, watching the approaching storm over his shoulder. When the wind blew harder, he turned up his collar. When the snow pummeled him, he hunkered down in his saddle. When he could see nothing because of the swirling flakes that blew at him from all directions at once, Marco gave his horse his head and wondered how soundly Paloma would scold him for being an idiot.

He arrived home long after dark, his face sore from the hard bits of sleet that had flung themselves through the winter sky at men foolish enough to be out in a storm. He didn't expect Paloma to fling open the door this time and rush out to meet him, because she was smarter than that. He curried his horse, then glanced at the office as he passed by on his way to his house.

He stopped. There was no light in the office, no smoke curling upward. He hoped Toshua had not decided to return Alonso's missing cattle in the teeth of the storm.

When he opened the door to his home, no one ran to meet him. Panic rose in his chest like a partridge flushed from the brush. He took out his knife when he heard unearthly wailing from the kitchen.

He ran down the hall, calling Paloma's name, and hurled himself into the kitchen.

Sancha crouched there, sobbing and tugging at her hair. His knife clattered to the floor and she looked up, then redoubled her wails. He willed his heart to beat again as he lifted her bodily to her feet and shook her.

"Why are you not at Hacienda Muñoz? Where is my darling?" he shouted.

Sancha sobbed in his arms. Desperate for answers, he wanted to shake her until she spoke, but he resisted. His arms went around her, holding her up, much as she had done eight years ago, when he returned to the Double Cross to find only death.

When her wails and moans turned into hiccups, he snatched a napkin from the table and held it to her ravaged face. She blew her nose and collected herself.

"*Por favor*, Sancha, *por favor*."

She looked at him as though he was the ultimate final tribunal, the last stop before judgment and assignment to hell or heaven.

"Señor Muñoz ran away. I thought he was asleep, but the old man ran away," she said, her voice so low he had to lean forward to hear. "We looked everywhere around the hacienda. We rode here, the guards and I, and told Paloma." Sancha began to wail again.

"Stop it!"

She took a deep breath. "That savage said it wouldn't be hard to find him, so they saddled up. He said they didn't need guards, that he was enough." She sobbed again, then stopped at the sight of Marco's fierce glance. "The storm began an hour later, with snow blowing in all directions. What will we do?"

Tears in his eyes, Marco opened the door leading into the fallow kitchen garden. Snow crowded all the corners of the night sky, coming from everywhere and all points of the compass at the same time. He rested his forehead against the cold windowpane, remembering in an odd, disconnected way the stories of his grandfather husbanding those panes of glass through mountain passes to this valley. He calmly fought down all the despair in the universe and turned around.

"We will wait until the storm lifts, Sancha."

"Can we trust that savage?"

"Have we any choice?"

Chapter Thirty-two

In Which a Warrior Fights and There Is Blood

THE STORM BEGAN after Toshua dismounted to look at the ground, squatting there and staring at something Paloma could not see. He looked at the darkening sky in some annoyance, as though it was little more than an inconvenience, like mosquitoes.

The sky frightened her, growing darker and darker long before nightfall. Ice chips, cutting her skin, tumbled out of the sky before the snow, driven almost horizontal by the wind that made her shiver and wish for the warmer cloak that the crazy seamstress in Santa Maria had promised to sew for her. She wanted to tell Toshua to turn back. Maybe Señor Muñoz had decided to call on a neighbor and hadn't really wandered away, lost. She shook her head. He would never do that. She remembered his blank expression during a visit last week, when she mentioned the Roybals, and then the Obregons, his closest neighbors. "And who might *they* be?" he had snapped. "You chatter on about people I have never heard of."

As she considered the matter, she thought again of the old priest at San Miguel who wandered in his mind like Señor Muñoz. There was a spring day she had managed to sneak away from the Moreno household, just to enjoy the sun as gentle as lotion and the new buds on the apple trees. She had found Father Cristóforo in the mission courtyard, his face to the sun. When she joined him there, two sun worshippers after a long winter, he spoke to her of his days at the University of Salamanca, the lectures he was attending, and his landlady who served sour cabbage soup three times a day.

The longer she listened the more she realized he truly thought he was eighteen again, and ready for scholarship. Startled at first, she decided to join in Father Cristóforo's fluid memory because it was harmless and he seemed so happy. It touched her heart when he kissed her hand and declared undying love, in that way of callow scholars in a university town—or so Father Eusebio would have her believe, when she told him about her afternoon with the balmy old man.

"What about you, Señor Muñoz?" she murmured through teeth that chattered. "Are you a young man again, fighting savages in Valle del Sol? Could you not have picked a warmer day?"

At Toshua's suggestion, she dismounted and walked, too, looking for footprints rapidly filling with snow. The clouds lifted briefly, flooding the valley with weird light just long enough for her to see a scrap of material snagged on a creosote bush. She handed it to Toshua. "He has a dressing gown of this fabric."

The Comanche fingered it. "Then he is probably cold now."

He did something next that touched her heart. Standing beside her he nudged her shoulder with his own. "I missed that scrap, but you saw it."

She nodded, pleased all out of proportion at the compliment. Her brother Claudio had nudged her like that. Suddenly the storm didn't seem so frightening.

Kneeling again, Toshua ran his hand carefully along a row of bent twigs. "This way," he said with a gesture.

She followed him, stopping only long enough to snap off a fairly straight fallen branch to use as a walking stick. She walked beside him when she could, but as the snow deepened, he put her behind him so he could break the trail.

Later, when she thought about it, Paloma knew that the old cabbage man on the trail from Santa Fe would have called this an adventure. Perhaps her whole life was going to be an adventure now, and God knows she already had a glimpse of how uncomfortable that could be. *I want to go home to Marco*, she thought, the instant before she slipped on the icy chips coating the rocks, landed on her bottom and sailed a short distance down a dry wash like an otter at play.

She slipped and slid to the bottom, frightened at first and then embarrassed as she tugged down her dress and looked for her lost shoe. The Comanche stood above her on the path, his hands on his hips, probably irritated.

"I'm sorry! Just lean down and give me a hand."

As she reached up, she heard lumbering footsteps and then a shout as Joaquin Muñoz pushed her sideways and threw his knife at Toshua, bending down. With a soft grunt, the Comanche toppled into the dry wash, too, the knife sticking out of his thigh.

"No! No!" Paloma shrieked, grabbing for the old man as he drew his sword, the antique she recognized hanging on the wall in his *sala*. With a start, she realized he was wearing the old helmet, also from the *sala*, and that ridiculous dressing gown.

"Santiago!" he shouted, the old war cry of the *conquistadores*.

With a cry of her own, Paloma struggled to her feet and thrust her walking stick between his legs. The old fellow fell into a heap, tangled with the stick and the sword. As he tried to free himself, she grabbed the blade, wincing as it cut her fingers, but hanging on until he let go. She sank into the snow beside Toshua, who lay there, his bloody hand on the knife in his leg.

"Pull it out!" he told her. "Hurry!"

Paloma did as he demanded, unprepared for the gush of blood that followed. She kept one eye on Joaquin, who reeled from side to side on his hands and knees now. She looked at Toshua, his face suddenly more expressive than usual as he grasped his bleeding leg. She slid out of her petticoat, and stuffed it against the wound.

"Look out!" Toshua said, his voice strained with desperation she had not heard before, even in the henhouse. "Duck!"

She ducked, closing her eyes as the sword whistled over her head. She gave the old man another push as the flat of the blade landed on her back. With no hesitation now, she picked up her walking stick and clouted him with it. He groaned, moved his legs and lay still.

"*Dios mio*, I have killed him," she murmured, and turned her attention to the Comanche. With shaking hands, she unfastened the belt about her waist that held the keys she had forgotten to leave in the hacienda, in her rush to find Señor Muñoz. With a clatter, they disappeared in the snow. Using her belt, she tied her petticoat to Toshua's leg, pressing down hard on the wound until he groaned.

The light was going fast, but at least the arroyo offered some protection from the snow. Or so she told herself, since there wasn't much likelihood they were going to leave the dry wash before morning. She continued to press against the wound, wishing for the skills of Father Eusebio and just the sight of her husband, who would know what to do. She sat there in miserable silence until the Comanche touched her hand.

"I wish I knew what to do," she whispered.

"You're saving my life again. This is three times."

When Toshua told her to, Paloma gradually released the pressure on his wound, until she did not feel any more blood flowing. In the gathering dark, the blood looked black and waxy. She wrinkled her nose against the strong odor of iron.

"He thought he was at war," she whispered to the Comanche, desperate for him to talk to her so she would not feel so suddenly alone. She wanted him to open his eyes. "He shouted 'Santiago!' and look, he is wearing that old helmet."

As she watched Señor Muñoz, she saw his leg move. When he groaned, she closed her eyes in gratitude that she had not killed an old fellow reliving some youthful adventure. She knew it had to be an adventure more exalted than eating cabbage and trying to find the owner of a yellow dog, on a road she had never traveled before.

"I need to look at him," she told Toshua, who nodded, not opening his eyes.

She nodded and crawled to Joaquin Muñoz, after pushing the sword in Toshua's direction. The old helmet had twisted around, so she carefully gentled it from his head. With a fierce expression, he reached for the sword lying by Toshua.

"I must defend you, my lady," he gasped. "There are Comanches and Apaches everywhere! Don't you see them?"

She pushed the sword farther away with her foot, then put her hand on his chest. "Only one Comanche, and you wounded him. I suppose you think you are my hero, *mi caballero muy feroz*," she said. "We can leave it at that, if you wish. If you think I am safe, I am safe."

Her back ached, and it took her an endless amount of time to move Toshua farther down the wash and close to a cluster of desert bushes, puny protection. Joaquin was lighter, but no less a dead weight as she struggled with him. She knew Toshua had been wearing his poncho when they started out. After a long moment debating whether to leave the two enemies, she scrambled up the wash and found the blanket and her horse. She knew Toshua's mount was much smarter than her own. Her husband had complained about that at length one night in bed, grousing that the damned Comanche had chosen to appropriate the smartest horse in the stable, next to his own. Maybe the gelding was smart enough to head to the Double Cross. Too bad it could not speak and point the way; so much for Toshua's smart horse.

She tied her own horse to a tree, and removed the saddle. "I need your blanket more than you do," she whispered to her horse.

She slid back down the arroyo with the horse blanket and Toshua's poncho. She tucked a blanket around each man and sat between them, the sword in her lap, a warrior by default.

As she sat there, wrapped tight in her cloak, her back sore and her hand paining her, Paloma felt something she had not felt in several years. It was just the slightest trickle down her inner thigh, but she blinked back sudden tears of gratitude. "My goodness, these things happen at inconvenient times," she said out loud in wonder.

Since Toshua and Joaquin both slept, Paloma tore a small strip off the petticoat binding the Indian's leg and put it between her legs. With a sigh, she lay down between the savage she had saved for the third time, and the old man dreaming of his youth who thought he had saved her. The snow was letting up now, falling straight instead of sideways. They could probably keep each other warm until the sun rose. She had the sword and wasn't going to let go. That wasn't what warriors did.

MARCO PACED HIS house all night, chafing at the snow and cursing the tardiness of dawn. The snow had stopped after midnight. An hour later, Emilio banged on the door to tell him that Toshua's mount had returned to the horse barn. Marco spent the next hour in the chapel, praying to *el padre celestial* and all the saints that the horse had left tracks they could follow, if only the wind would not blow them away.

Everyone wanted to ride with him, but he took his six best men and extra horses and blankets. He was too prudent to leave the Double Cross unprotected. As soon as the sun rose across the plains to the east, they swung into their saddles and followed the faint trail. His head ached from lack of sleep and from listening to Andrés' babbling about all the people who had survived snowstorms. To blot out Andrés' relentless good cheer, Marco imagined what he would say to Pepita Camargo when he visited her in Santa Maria to give her the bad news about her father. He thought about the Jew in Santa Fe who had sold him the little ring, and Father Damiano, who had sent the letter on its way that would eventually make his marriage legal. He thought of the bloody sandals in his *sala* that he had claimed as Paloma's dowry. If everything was over now—that which had begun so recently—he did not know what he would do. He couldn't help the groan that rose in his throat, turning it into a cough when Andrés looked at him with sympathy. He had endured years of sympathy. Now he just wanted Paloma.

The sun was up and even warming his face when he saw them. He rose in his stirrups, alert, then relieved beyond measure. Resting an old sword on her shoulder, his wife walked in front of a horse bearing two men—the Comanche sitting behind, his arms tight around an old man wearing a conquistador's helmet and a dressing gown. He had never seen a stranger complement of travelers, or one more dear to his heart.

Paloma had no objection to sitting in front of him on his horse, although she refused to do so until she was certain Toshua and Señor Muñoz were taken care of, according to her liking. He watched her linger a moment at Toshua's side, and watched the Comanche touch her head, then give it a little shake.

"Señor Muñoz has been complaining for the last hour, demanding to know why Sancha let him wander away," she said, when she was resting comfortably against him, his cloak around them both, his lips on her tangled, dirty hair. "*Ay de mi*! Last night he was part of an expedition against the Comanches and Apaches. Poor old man, dreaming dreams. He is not well, but we cannot cure him."

She sighed and burrowed closer. "I don't mean to keep rescuing Toshua." She closed her eyes then and slept, worn out with adventures.

SANCHA CRIED AND scolded and took away his darling Paloma to clean her up and put her in bed. She slept most of the day, while his servant with the most medical talent sewed Toshua's leg and helped him limp to his pallet in the office, closer to the fireplace this time, because he still shivered. Marco and his riders took an irate old man to his daughter's house in Santa Maria. Acting in the name of the crown, he told the silly woman what had happened and ordered her to look after the father who needed her now, the man sometimes old and sometimes young, and mixed up in his head.

He probably exceeded his authority when he assured Pepita that her father would not go to Santa Fe for the murder of the little Comanche slave. In exchange for that bit of dubious leniency, he demanded that Joaquin Muñoz sign over his ownership of Toshua to Marco and Paloma Mondragón.

Pepita did as he asked, expressing her regret about the petition on its way to Santa Fe. He only nodded sagely, unwilling to tell the woman that Toshua had informed him, before he drifted to sleep, that he had stolen the courier's pouch not long after the man had left the Double Cross. The petition was probably fluttering across east Texas by now.

"I did not kill him," Toshua had insisted, before his eyes closed. "You are strange about things like that. It is a weakness."

Marco returned to the Double Cross late in the day, aware as he rode through the gate this time that he had not felt even a momentary panic that Paloma would not be there. Sure enough, she was awake and sitting with Toshua in his office. Sancha must have bandaged her hand. He sniffed the wintergreen that he assumed his old housekeeper had applied to the bruise on Paloma's back. Pleasantly tired, he yawned and sat back in his chair. He rummaged in his pouch for the document from Pepita and held it out to his wife. She read it, and her eyes narrowed with something close to suspicion.

"I cannot believe this is within your powers, Marco," she said.

"I am certain it is not, but that is how we do business here, so far away from Santa Fe, not to mention Madrid. What should we do with such a pernicious piece of paper? I don't want a slave."

"Nor do I. Let us free him."

"Do it," Marco said with a smile. "Or try to."

His lovely wife—the one with more heft to her breasts now, and smoothness to her hips—gave him another fishy stare, quite similar to one Felicia might have given him, if provoked. *I am home*, he thought in gratitude.

He watched as Paloma knelt by the pallet and told Toshua what she held in her hand. "I give you your freedom," she said.

"I won't go. You have saved my life three times."

Good luck, Paloma, Marco thought, amused.

Maybe she was still tired, because she did not argue with the Comanche. To Marco's surprise, she scolded him. "You're being wretched about this, I hope you know," she said.

Again the Comanche tousled her hair, much as Marco's older sister used to tousle his hair. "I think you would not leave now, even if I threw you out," Marco said softly.

He knew he spoke too softly for an ordinary man to hear, but he already knew Toshua was no ordinary man. His hand still on Paloma's hair, Toshua looked at him, just a small glance, but it was enough. In another moment, he slept.

Hand in hand, Marco and Paloma walked across the courtyard to their home, where business was done in the kitchen, and the sandals hung in the *sala*. He had reluctantly returned the sword and helmet to Pepita Camargo. They would have been fine additions to the décor, but he didn't think Paloma would agree.

He took off his clothes and left them in a dirty pile. Handing him his nightshirt, Paloma pulled back the covers so he could crawl between them, ready for a cuddle and a long sleep. She sat on the edge of their bed, making no move to join him, shy now, her face rosy, for some reason.

"I have news for you, husband," she said at last, her excitement almost palpable.

"Mmmm?"

"I … I started my monthly last night in that dry wash."

Delighted, he smiled at her shyness, and the pleasure reflected in her own eyes.

"Do you … do you have the supplies you need?" he asked gently, shy himself. This was not a subject he would ever be comfortable with.

"Sancha helped me. There is a little box in the storeroom that Felicia left. I didn't think you would mind."

"Certainly not. Paloma, this *is* good news."

She nodded, still reluctant to look at him. She turned her back to him and unbuttoned her shirtwaist, removed it, then slid off her skirt and both petticoats. He watched, interested, because he liked the shape of her and the more abundant curve of her hips. Wearing only her knee-length chemise, she was bending over to gather her clothing, when he noticed something he had never seen before. He looked closer, wondering why it had escaped his attention. *Dolt, you've never paid much attention to the back of her knee*, he thought.

"Paloma, come closer."

She turned around, her arms full of her clothing, a question in her eyes.

"Just … just set that down, come closer and turn around again."

He sat up in bed. She did as he said and turned away from him. He raised her shift a little and stared at the mark on her right thigh just above where her knee bent. "*Dios mio*," he whispered, running his finger over the small mark. "Closer. Lie down. Just stretch out on your stomach. Good. *Dios mio*."

She looked over her shoulder at him, craning her neck to see what he stared at. "I can't see anything."

"Feel it."

She knew right where to touch. "It's just my birthmark."

"No, it's not. It's a brand. A tiny star and a V."

Paloma gasped. She turned over and sat up, reaching for him, her eyes filled with tears. He held her close, murmuring to her.

"You told me once that your mother said you were branded. All of us are, I suppose, by our parents, our successes, our failures. With you, it is more. Do you have any recollection of this happening?"

Paloma shook her head. "I must have been so young. That is *my* brand," she exclaimed in wonder, and then her voice hardened. "It is not Maria Teresa's. What have the Morenos *done*?"

"Cheated you, double-crossed you. Foiled you at every turn."

She turned her face into his nightshirt. He expected her to cry, but she did not. He held her, knowing she was a woman to think things through. "I thought about their wickedness last night. It didn't hurt as much as it used to," she said at last. "Maria Teresa has the official brand, but I am the lucky one."

Flattered, he held her off a little to look at her before giving her a kiss.

"Would it … do you think it would stand up in a court of law?" she asked, when she could speak.

"Hard to say. It's so faint. A good *abogado* could raise all kinds of doubts, I suppose. Does it matter?"

She considered his question. "Maybe not. Besides, do I want to show my backside to complete strangers? Husband, I am tired. Let's go to sleep."

He settled lower in the bed again, his wife in his arms. He felt his eyes closing, too, after such a busy day and a previous night of no sleep. "Advent will be here soon, my love," he said, drowsy. "Let's ride into Santa Maria. You will want to meet Doña Graciela Chavez. She always sees that the Christ Child is wrapped in a warm blanket for the outdoor nativity scene. I'll tell you how it became the business of the *juez* on the way to town. Do you think other brand inspectors have to deal with such trivialities as I do in Valle del Sol? My feet are cold."

"Put them on my legs, husband. Your expensive yellow dog follows Andrés everywhere and I don't mind."

They slept as the moon rose.

Epilogue

WHEN THE LEAVES began to turn color, Father Damiano knew it was only a matter of time before Marco and Paloma Mondragón came to San Pedro by the Rio Chama, seeking shelter for the night. After all, a *juez de campo* had records to take to Santa Fe each year, where they would be stacked with reports from other districts and probably ignored. Such was the business of the crown. More than that, Father Damiano hoped the Mondragóns might tell him of their year on the frontier. He could decide for himself whether a marriage made in comparative haste had proved wise.

Hand in hand, they came into his office, kneeling for his blessing. He gave it with pleasure, delighted to watch them exchange glances that told him volumes about lovers, comrades and true partners.

Marco had sent Father Damiano a letter in early summer, explaining the mystery of old Joaquin Muñoz, a pair of boots and a Comanche. The brand inspector had asked the priest to keep his ear to the ground over any attempt to have him removed from his office of *juez de campo*. Father Damiano was pleased to assure the man that nothing of the sort had happened.

"What of Señor Muñoz?" Father Damiano asked. "Is he with you?"

"Alas, no," Marco replied with a shake of his head. "He died a month ago. Pepita vows he perished from a broken heart, since we had to remove him from his land."

"She may be right," Paloma chimed in, the sadness in her eyes unmistakable. "Still, we could not leave him on his hacienda."

"What of the Comanche?"

"As far as it is possible for a Comanche to promise anything, he promised me he would remain on the Double Cross during our visit to Santa Fe," Marco said. "It is safer for him."

"He remained unwillingly," Paloma said. "He thinks he is my protector." She leaned her head against Marco's arm. "I don't need two protectors. I still wish he would fade into the Texas plains, but who can reason with a Comanche?"

After Marco excused himself to help the teamsters stow the year's wool clip for the night, Paloma lingered behind. She was quiet still, but with an air of confidence about her now that touched the priest. He could not profess any great personal knowledge of women, but she had the demeanor of a wife well-loved, the mistress of a household, the other half of an officer of the crown.

They already knew of his own sorrow; Father Bartolomeo had gone the way of all flesh that winter. With an ache in his heart, Damiano wished he could have told his great old friend that their prayers for this well-matched couple had not been in vain.

Paloma had more to tell him, speaking quietly, her head down. She spoke of her yearning for a child, but such a gift seemed not to be part of God's plan. Damiano blessed her to be fruitful, promising Paloma he would remember her little petition in all his prayers.

"Marco tells me I am too impatient, but I know this is his desire," Paloma said. After hugging him, she went to the door and added, "There is so much land, and we need sons." Her expression grew wistful. "It's more than that. I just want a baby. Do I ask too much?"

"No, my child," Damiano assured her. "All in God's time. We know He likes to do things His way, not ours."

Officiating as the new abbot of San Pedro, Damiano blessed them again before they left for Santa Fe. They laughed when he confessed he was already looking forward to their return visit in a few weeks, when there might be more time to talk. In the unspoken part of his blessing, he included his own request from the beloved wife of Marco Mondragón. She did not ask too much; he knew she never would.

Father Damiano stood a long time at the open gates of San Pedro, watching the Mondragóns until they were out of sight. He chuckled to see Andrés bringing up the rear, a yellow dog carried in his own pouch that hung from the *mayordomo's* saddle.

When he turned to go through the gates, he caught a glimpse of a horseman, one staying well back from the trail in the cottonwoods and willows along the river. The man rode a spirited horse and he look like an *Indio*. Father Damiano was the first to admit that his eyes were weak, even with spectacles. How could he be certain?

Bryner Photography

A WELL-KNOWN VETERAN of the romance writing field, **Carla Kelly** is the author of twenty-nine novels and four non-fiction works, as well as numerous short stories and articles for various publications. She is the recipient of two RITA Awards from Romance Writers of America for Best Regency of the Year; two Spur Awards from Western Writers of America; a Whitney Award for Best Romance Fiction, 2011; and a Lifetime Achievement Award from Romantic Times.

Carla's interest in historical fiction is a byproduct of her lifelong interest in history. She has a BA in Latin American History from Brigham Young University and an MA in Indian Wars History from University of Louisiana-Monroe. She's held a variety of jobs, including public relations work for major hospitals and hospices, feature writer and columnist for a North Dakota daily newspaper, and ranger in the National Park Service (her favorite job) at Fort Laramie National Historic Site and Fort Union Trading Post National Historic Site. She has worked for the North Dakota Historical Society as a contract researcher. Interest in the Napoleonic Wars at sea led to a recent series of novels about the British Channel Fleet during that conflict.

Of late, Carla has written two novels set in southeast Wyoming in 1910 that focus on her Mormon background and her interest in ranching.

You can find Carla online at www.carlakellyauthor.com.

Made in the USA
Charleston, SC
02 November 2014